Raymond Kennedy's

LULU INCOGNITO

"The trouble with innocence," Mrs. Gansevoort went on, endeavoring to make a fine point, while reaching with her fingertips to
touch a prospective blossom, "is that it provides its own sole protection against the depredations of nature; and nature—God, for
that matter, the grand texts notwithstanding—has never shown
much liking for it. Nature favors the bright eye! the sharp tooth!
the cunning few! Nature is a tyrant queen. Make a mistake with
her, and she cuts off your head."

LuLu

INCOGNITO

RAYMOND KENNEDY

VINTAGE CONTEMPORARIES
Vintage Books

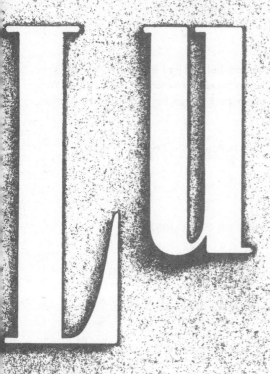

INCOGNITO

A DIVISION OF RANDOM HOUSE
NEW YORK

A VINTAGE CONTEMPORARIES ORIGINAL, MARCH 1988
First Edition

Copyright © 1988 by Raymond Kennedy

Library of Congress Cataloging-in-Publication Data
Kennedy, Raymond A.
Lulu incognito.
(Vintage contemporaries)
I. Title.
PS3561.E427L85 1988   813'.54   87–18873
ISBN 0–394–75641–X (pbk.)

BOOK DESIGN AND TYPOGRAPHY BY CHIP KIDD

Manufactured in the United States of America
10   9   8   7   6   5   4   3   2   1

To Branwynne, my daughter

LuLu

INCOGNITO

There was, after all, the mystery of Lulu. It was not a question
of what she had done, or even of what happened to her, but
of who she was. She was so little known. Lulu was one of that
vast multitude who strive all through life to avoid the attention
of others. In school, she showed no desire to distinguish herself
in her studies, while socially she selected her friends from among
the least of her classmates, girls like Betsy Padden and Yvette
Lamoureux, neither of whom was prepossessing in any way.
By the time she was twenty-one, Lulu was fading into the clay
of life.

She worked as a countergirl at the F. W. Woolworth store
in downtown Ireland Parish, an old factory town in Massachusetts, where she was little more than a statistic on the work
sheets. She was the face behind the candy counter, a polite,
hardworking soul, whom Mr. Ranger, the young floor manager,
once characterized as "a sort of bottled-up type." She rarely
used cosmetics, and never dressed up or fixed her hair in a way

designed to attract notice. In the end, had anyone asked about Lulu, about her life and days, it is not impossible that her truest witness on earth, the person with the fullest understanding of her heart, might very well have been a young man who was himself a stranger to her, an ingenuous eighteen-year-old base-ball player with the unlikely name of Soldier McNiff. He, Sol-dier, was an admirer from afar, however, so that his knowledge of Lulu would have been at best impressionable, something in the nature of a lover's divination.

Lulu lived in what was once called the French Quarter, a decaying tenement district that stretched along the Misquami-cutt River below the dam. She lived with her mother and grand-mother in a fifth-floor walk-up on South Summer Street. Their kitchen windows looked out onto vacant lots and a distant in-dustrial canal. At evening, the canal waters turned a murky red in the setting sun. The front of the apartment faced the street. Directly below lay a small triangular park, with a bench, a sickly tree, and a flashing yellow caution light. In the early morning, the shadow of the massive, smoke-blackened Precious Blood Church, which dominated the old Canadian-French neighborhood, reached all the way to Lulu's doorstep, and formed a shadowy cross on the cobbles and cement of the little park below.

Lulu slept in the front room, in the big mahogany bed that once belonged to her mother and father. On the wall behind the bed hung a big framed picture of a suffering Jesus, a painfully realistic portrayal that showed the actual penetration of the thorns and the beads of sweat on His temples. The vanity mirror opposite her bed held a collection of dry palm leaves from years past, while scapulars and tarnished medals could be found scattered among her things in her dresser drawers. The room was plain to the point of bleakness.

Here, every night before retiring, Lulu knelt on the floor beside her bed and acted out a custom which seemed to her as old as time itself. Although she realized that nightly prayer was not observed any longer by most people, she could not bring herself to suspend the ritual. In fact, on those few occasions when she had missed saying her prayers, the ache of remorse was such that she felt compelled to double her devotions the following night. Usually, Lulu prayed in English, but sometimes when the mood took her, she would recite the Act of Contrition in French, as she had first learned to recite it in Sunday school as a child. In most recent times, however, during the spring of that year, 1951, Lulu had fallen into the habit of remaining on her knees by her bed for quite a long spell, sometimes a quarter-hour or longer, speaking her prayers half aloud, and sometimes turning her head in such a way as to catch sight of her own face reflected in the mirror.

The face that looked back at her from the shallow depths of the looking glass was wan and spiritual, a pale oval glowing softly among the shadows of the darkened room. Lulu wondered if the face was beautiful. It was only weeks later, when she thought back upon these peculiar late-night communings with herself, that she suspected a connection between them and other changes in her daily life, for it was during these same spring weeks that she struck up a friendship with Agnes Rohan, the druggist's daughter.

Agnes was Lulu's senior by about three years but was far more worldly. Lulu was flattered by the older girl's attention, though Agnes was a blustery, outspoken sort of person. From the beginning, Agnes talked down to Lulu, teasing her and playing the part of the older woman, of one whose background and social connections were superior. Ironically, it was only because of Agnes Rohan's airs that Lulu was able to accommodate herself to her, assuming the role of younger sister. She went almost nightly to Rohan's drugstore at the corner of Cabot and Park, and sat at the end of the soda fountain, nursing a Coke and making small talk with Agnes. The only time Agnes actually upset Lulu with her brash tongue was the evening in April when Agnes said, as if making a confession of it, that her first impression of Lulu was that she might have been the sort of girl who preferred intimate friendships with other girls. Lulu colored in embarrassment.

Agnes further aggravated Lulu's discomfort. "Not that it would matter to me if you did. But you did come in an awful lot when I was working." She smiled from behind the soda fountain. "I noticed how you were looking at me."

"I never came in for that!" Lulu protested, flushing.

Agnes's eyes expanded with curiosity. She questioned Lulu softly. "What did you say?"

Lulu was visibly stunned. "I never came in to look at you."

Agnes made a face. "I didn't *say* you had. I said you used to come in a lot when I was on duty, and I *thought* you had. Past tense," she added.

Lulu felt the skin along her hairline grow hot and prickly, and for several minutes afterward she suffered that odd sensation she experienced when most upset, the feeling of being like two persons in one, two Lulus, with the inner shocked Lulu watching in helpless dismay as the outer Lulu struggled to appear calm.

Lulu was so upset by the redheaded young woman's observation that she did not return to the pharmacy for nearly a week. She tried several times to recall her original impressions of Agnes Rohan, the series of casual exchanges by which they'd gotten to know one another; but her reflections yielded almost nothing. If anything, she felt that it was Agnes, not she, who had initiated conversation. Still, there could be no denying that Lulu had in fact gone repeatedly to the Rohan pharmacy during the evenings of late winter and early spring, when they two had become increasingly familiar. Lulu also knew in her heart that, had their situations been reversed, Agnes Rohan would not have come back repeatedly: Agnes was not like that. Agnes did not court other people. She never once called Lulu on the telephone, although she regularly specified the day and hour Lulu was to call her. In any event, by the end of May, the two girls had begun to socialize outside the pharmacy. Sometimes they went to the movies on Saturday nights, not to the Bijou or Majestic, certainly, which were located in Lulu's own Canadian-French neighborhood, but to one of the uptown theaters.

Afterward, Agnes would often take Lulu out for a sandwich or cake and coffee at the Phoenix Luncheonette, and deliver herself of a lengthy critique on the motion picture they had just seen. Lulu listened with keen interest, for she had never thought of a movie as anything but a passing entertainment. She was surprised to be told that the quality of a motion picture depended not so much on the stars or story as it did upon the person who directed it. At the end of such evenings, when Agnes opened her bag to pay the waitress for their check, if Lulu intruded, and made a sincere effort to pay for her own food and drink, Agnes Rohan was capable of being firm on the point. "You do *not* pay," she would insist, with a benign flash of her eyes.

By that time, the start of June, Lulu and Agnes were going out regularly. Lulu had grown accustomed to following Agnes's lead. Agnes always made a point of opening the door for her, and helped Lulu on with her jacket or sweater, and was generally very solicitous of Lulu's comfort and well-being. If it was raining, Agnes held the umbrella protectively above Lulu. If Lulu sniffled, Agnes was quick to buy her a package of Kleenex or cough drops. Within a short space of time, Lulu had the distinct feeling of being safe in Agnes's presence. And if Agnes sometimes corrected or upbraided her, it was usually, Lulu knew, because she had disappointed her friend in some way.

Lulu was coming out of herself. She was not so foolish as not to realize it; something expansive was under way in her spirit. She knelt at night on the cool linoleum beside her bed, with the reflection of her face, a pale oval, hovering dimly in the shadows of her vanity mirror nearby, like the face of the Holy Maiden herself, whom she was taught to supplicate as a child, or even, perhaps, like the face of her own childish innocence, held up to her, as upon a dark page. She had a premonition, both holy and baleful, of something coming toward her in darkness. She even wondered on occasion if Agnes Rohan, the pharmacist's daughter, was not a precursor, a sign of things to come. Sometimes in the daytime Lulu wondered if she was not losing a grip on her mind.

One night in June, Agnes walked Lulu home from the drugstore, and she confessed, in soft tones, to having something on her breast she wished to make known. Agnes spoke quietly as they walked through the silent, deserted streets. She said that she had lied to Lulu the week before and wished to confess now that the previous Saturday she had not gone to Susan Teehan's bridal shower, as she had previously alleged, but had instead gone to the movies with someone else, someone other than Lulu, an old friend from up the hill named Marie Lenihan. Agnes appeared very contrite. She hoped very much, she said, that Lulu would understand, because she did not want a lie to be the death of their good friendship.

Touched by Agnes Rohan's admission, Lulu assured her friend that the incident was not important. But Agnes refused to be absolved of guilt so readily, and vowed then and there to make it up to Lulu. Agnes was so penitent-seeming that Lulu guessed she was playacting somewhat, but could not be sure. She enjoyed, however, seeing Agnes behave in an apparently helpless way. When they reached Lulu's doorstep, Agnes showed her a brave smile of repentance, and produced from the pocket of her oil slicker a small gift-wrapped parcel, which, with a show of solemnity, she pressed upon her friend. Lulu was left standing at her stoop as Agnes turned and walked back along South Summer toward the bus stop beyond the Precious Blood Church. She watched Agnes go, her slicker catching the sickly yellow glow of the blinking caution light. The package contained a Parker pen-and-pencil set, and a card simply inscribed, "Mea culpa. Love, Agnes."

From that evening on, Lulu was a little more assertive, not to the point of defying Agnes, or of ever having words with her, but in her general manner. She felt accepted by the red-headed young woman. She realized that Agnes's attraction to her was somehow unusual, but knew her friend's feelings were genuine. When Lulu came outdoors now in the evening, and walked up South Summer to the pharmacy on Cabot Street, she did so in the knowledge that Agnes was anticipating her arrival and would be disappointed if she failed to appear. Now and then, Agnes tried to make Lulu jealous, by bringing up again the subject of Marie Lenihan—who was "very intellectual," said Agnes, and with whom she had once been "as thick as thieves." But Lulu would not rise to the bait. Agnes was Lulu's admirer. That was an open fact.

Lulu, who had never been courted in any way, and never once gone out with anyone, now found herself in the position of one who is able, in subtle ways, to arouse and manipulate another's admiration. Sometimes while Agnes was talking, Lulu would swivel a quarter-turn on the fountain stool and pretend to take an interest in the display of perfumes nearby, but only to show Agnes the profile of her face and throat. If she looked back suddenly, she would often catch Agnes, frozen in space, staring at her. This gave Lulu a strange stirring sensation inside, an emotion she was always quick to mask behind a genial smile. Lulu never openly articulated the idea to herself, not even in her innermost musings, but Agnes, it was clear, was deeply infatuated with her.

There was only one occasion when Agnes found cause to be angry with Lulu, the evening her old friend Yvette Lamoureux came into the drugstore by chance and was delighted to discover Lulu there. They spoke animatedly for several minutes; and when Yvette departed, Agnes, rattling and banging utensils in the steel sink, showed her displeasure by imposing five minutes of silence upon Lulu. Finally, in the spirit of one who has been fulminating without letup for several minutes, Agnes exclaimed: "That you would have anything to do with a little pimple-faced, four-eyed Canuck nonentity like that, who can barely speak the language, and buys her clothes at the Franco-American shop, is a mystery to me!"

In her heart Lulu might have enjoyed her friend's jealous outburst, but she was not immune to feelings of fright over the spectacle of the redhead's flaring temper. Lulu's fingers trembled as she tried to separate a soda straw from its wrapper: she was relieved when the crisis passed. She was also, she discovered, secretly gratified that Agnes, in her anger, had cast Yvette Lamoureux in such a preposterous and contemptible light. Yvette was indeed beyond any hope of reclamation: a foolish, unimaginative young woman, squat and bespectacled, who chewed her fingernails and talked incessantly about her family and neighbors.

"I'll never speak to her again," Lulu said, surprisingly.

Agnes stopped what she was doing and regarded Lulu gravely. The anger was subsiding visibly in her eyes. "Do you mean that?" she asked, softly.

"Yes," Lulu insisted.

True to her word, the next time Lulu saw Yvette Lamoureux approaching, coming toward her carrying a bag of groceries at the corner of Cabot and Bridge, she turned her head away and crossed the street. Yvette was the first person on earth Lulu had ever openly ostracized. She was secretly flattered by Agnes's having elevated her above Yvette, and was resolved to honor her word. She would never speak to Yvette again, no matter how awkward it might be. It was part of her life with Agnes. When Lulu told Agnes that evening what she had done, Agnes made no reply but simply gazed at Lulu with a look of deep thankfulness in her eyes, which, while probably much affected, strove to speak volumes.

The following Sunday Lulu went for the first time to Agnes's house, a handsome Dutch colonial set back elegantly behind trees on Dartmouth Street. She was intimidated at once by its spacious rooms and plush furnishings. She felt horribly out of place as her eye took in the impressive array of gleaming expensive details all about her and caught occasional glimpses of the emerald green lawn stretching away luxuriously outside every window. She thought of her own home as shabby, and felt painfully awkward and shamefaced. When Agnes came to her then, and put her arms about her, and pressed herself snugly against Lulu, making Lulu feel profoundly her swelling bosom, and touched her hair, Lulu fought back tears. She closed her eyes and allowed Agnes to caress her. The two young women stood next to the spinet in the parlor, its burnished surface shining darkly in a bar of sunlight from the window. Lulu, with a sudden gasp, broke down and wept like a child.

●

If it had not been for Mr. Rafferty, whom Lulu, by a stroke of fortune, had met the very next week, she could not have guessed what might have happened to her. As it was, the memory of her afternoon with Agnes troubled her deeply. She tried to suppress the recollection of what had happened in Agnes's room, the alien sensation of Agnes's flesh, the look of ardor in her flushed face, her breath pulsing warmly against Lulu's naked shoulder and throat, and the passionate, unheard-of protestations. The thought of it left her dizzy. It struck Lulu as so improper, so immoral, that she trembled when she reflected on the condition of her soul. She even wondered if Agnes Rohan was not, in the true sense of the word, diabolical. At work, she thanked her stars Agnes never came to the store. As the days went by, she breathed easier. On the following Saturday, nearly a week since the lamentable episode with Agnes, Lulu met Mr. Rafferty, and after that, her conscience was somewhat appeased.

Later she could not remember whether it was she who sat down next to Mr. Rafferty during coffee break at the Woolworth luncheon counter, or he who sat down beside her; but she would never forget her first impression of him, a youthful but silver-haired gentleman dressed to perfection in a blue pin-cord suit with a dark blue shirt and striped necktie. Or his first remark: "You," he said, "must have a very wicked godmother."

The fact that Lulu was, as always, tongue-tied, did not appear to discourage him. He kept the conversation going for both of them.

"I know it isn't the cat that's got your tongue. Being mysterious is the damsel's prerogative in fairy tales. How long," he inquired, "have you been kept secret?"

When Lulu colored with a mixture of pleasure and embarrassment, unable to reply to his blandishments, Mr. Rafferty flashed a sudden, truly engaging smile.

"Never mind," he said. "Have your glazed donut and coffee, and I will rack my brain. How many guesses do I have? Three?"

Lulu at last managed a reply. "Yes, three."

"Very well, although it won't require three," he said, and showed her a playfully canny eye. "One guess will do it. You've been kept hiding for about fifteen years. Am I right?"

She swallowed, and responded quietly with a question of her own. "What happened fifteen years ago?"

"You're asking me?" he cried.

At that, Lulu laughed sharply, and looked at him. He was sitting back in an attitude of wonderment. "Only you could know that," he said. "At heart, we are all mysterious. God invests us all with a certain mysterious core. Everything, if you ask me, is mysterious. A *tree* is mysterious! There is simply no getting at the heart of anything. That's God's portion."

Lulu listened with interest. She had a natural taste for spiritual subjects, and found the man's way of expressing himself to be as engaging as that of Father Charpentier, the pastor of the Precious Blood.

"But you are another case altogether," he said. "With the wicked godmother and the stepsisters standing over you, and you down on the paving stones, a-scrubbing!" He gestured, happily. "How long *has* it been? Seventeen years? Twenty? You can thank your stars that's over. What's your name?"

"Lulu," she replied.

"Lulu! Now, that's more like it! Lulu is one of those names given in this country to dreary little bobbin girls who put up their hair in pincurls, but in Europe, it will please you to know, the name Lulu resonates with fabulous overtones. *Femme fatale* types! Creatures of the great salons who drive men of genius to distraction."

"You were in Europe?"

"I went with a gun," said Mr. Rafferty. "Today, you couldn't get into Europe with so much as a penknife in your pocket, but I disembarked with a sixteen-pound Browning automatic rifle and my face corked as black as that grill!" He signaled Millie, the countergirl, to refill his coffee cup. "Tell me," he encouraged Lulu, "in which department do you show off your expertise? Crockery?"

"No!" she responded.

"Millinery?" he exclaimed. "Hardware? Notions?"

Lulu was charmed by his bright talk. "I work on the candy counter."

"You do?" He sat back in a pretense of shock. "I'm going to cultivate a friendship with you, if it kills me. Spearmint leaves! Maple creams! Canada mints! I can't live without the stuff. Candy is my vice. Look." He took a bright, paper-wrapped cylinder from his suitcoat pocket. "Necco wafers."

"We carry everything you mentioned," said Lulu, trying to keep pace with the man's rapid-fire thinking.

"I am sure you do. And a great assortment of tempting confections besides. One thing I avoid," the man confessed, "is chocolate."

"I never eat chocolate," Lulu hastened to agree.

"I'm glad to hear you say that. But I could have guessed. I'll tell you how I know." He touched his cheek. "By your skin. Chocolate-eaters have buffalo skin. You have skin like a peony. You must bathe in rainwater. Don't laugh!" he cried. "I grew up on a farm in North Dakota. We had a rain barrel by the back door so that my three idiotic sisters could wash their hair with the stuff Saturdays. And they had dreamy hair. They were ugly as sin, all three of them, but had long glimmering manes that were the envy of the West. If we were judged only by the people standing behind us, my three sisters could have ruled the earth!"

Lulu loosed a peal of laughter that was most unlike her, for she rarely laughed aloud, but the picture of the man's three sisters, a trio of Rapunzels seen only from behind, struck her as humorous. The man also laughed. After Millie had poured him a second cup of coffee, he added quietly, "I hope you never become a fat cow like that."

Lulu winced at the gratuitous cruelty of the man's remark, and marveled more than ever at the sheer spontaneity of his speech. She was accustomed to small talk, harmless and congenial, in which the mere act of talking was more meaningful than the thing said.

She looked at the man sitting beside her as he stirred sugar into his coffee. He was young to be silver-haired, but old by Lulu's standards. He had been in the war—he said so—six or seven years ago—but was, she guessed, older than Al Ranger, the assistant manager, who was twenty-six, and had several times described in amusing detail how he had spent the evening of his nineteenth birthday digging a hole on the beach at Normandy.

Later, standing in back of the candy counter, tying on her apple green apron, Lulu saw the gentleman making his way down a distant aisle toward the street doors. He glanced neither left nor right, but strode briskly with a smart military bearing. She guessed that he must have been an officer, and concluded also that he was not a downtown Ireland Parish businessman. He was too bright and clever-seeming: that is, he had an out-of-town air, which, later on, caused him to return to Lulu's thoughts more like a character in a drama than a flesh-and-blood person. There was a touch of perfection about him, something timeless and incorruptible, in the way he dressed and comported himself, in his grooming, his hair, his manicured fingernails and crisp summer suit.

By noontime that day, it had begun to rain. Lulu ate lunch at the fountain on wet days. More than once, she looked about to see if the man might reappear. She could not begin to specify what the man had said or done to awaken certain thoughts about herself, but all that Saturday afternoon she was beset with feelings of remorse about herself and her past, of the beribboned schoolgirl she had once been, the breastless, tentative child who had steadily retreated over the years, quietly, without bugles or muffled drums to signal the withdrawal, but inch by inch, minute by minute, with her defeat no doubt etching itself in the very molding of her face; and she guessed, with a throb of concern, that it was something unfavorable about the man that aroused her self-pity—something dark, invidious, disobliging. Truth was, he frightened her a bit.

He did not come back to the Woolworth store that afternoon, but Lulu was certain he would return.

Even on sunshiny days, when the doors of the little glass orchid house in the garden behind the Wistariahurst Museum were thrown wide for air, Mr. Rafferty carried with him a slender umbrella tightly rolled. He was an elegant man, certainly in the eyes of Mrs. Claire Monaghan, as well as of Janice, her niece, the two ladies who operated the little public art museum on Pine Street in Ireland Parish. Claire called him "the living epitome of a New England gentleman," with his silver hair and ideal mannequin posture.

Twice weekly, Mr. Rafferty came to the museum, arriving inside the big front doors at the same hour precisely. There he would pause momentarily, the brass ferrule of his umbrella describing a slow glittery arc as he turned on his heel and accustomed his gaze to the relative gloom of the imposing marble-columned entrance hall before setting out briskly in the direction of the Music Room or garden doorway. Although the older woman would never confess as much, it was out of consideration for Mr. Rafferty in particular that she had initiated some months ago the custom that had come to be "the coffee hour."

Each afternoon at four, Janice, the niece, was required to boil up a quantity of water in the tall steel urn set up in a side vestibule, and set out teacups and saucers for any patron who might wish to enjoy a cup of coffee at an outside garden table. If Janice resented the extra work, she never said so. Her only complaint all around was centered upon Mr. Rafferty's habit of leaving her a ten-cent tip beside his drained cup. The sight each time of that tiny glittering coin peeping forth from the shadow of the saucer offended Janice in a way she could not readily explain. It was not that the tip was inadequate, although it was, nor that the dime was always juxtaposed to the drained teacup in exactly the same position on the table, nor, even, was it that Mr. Rafferty never gave a sign of recognizing Janice, however many times she might pour out his beverage. She couldn't put her finger on it. After all, Mr. Rafferty never made small talk with anyone, unless it was to ask a polite question or two of her Aunt Claire, and that always pertaining to the exhibits.

It was quite surprising, therefore, to the two Monaghan ladies, when, on a Sunday afternoon in June, Mr. Rafferty appeared in the marble-columned reception hall of the museum with what struck both Aunt Claire and her niece as a most unlikely companion, a plain young woman with long dark hair who was obviously made uncomfortable by her circumstance and surroundings. The young woman wore a long-sleeved white cotton blouse and a dark skirt that reached to midcalf, a costume so nondescript as to accentuate her general want of description.

Both Monaghan ladies were posted behind the big circular oak desk when Mr. Rafferty, after pausing to get his bearings, advanced smartly across the great foyer, with the young woman following shyly behind, and started up the broad carpeted staircase to the upper floor. He spoke all the while over his shoulder to the young woman, in undertones, while showing her an agreeable smile. She followed with a keen expression on her face.

The two Monaghans stood elbow to elbow behind the shiny oak desk, staring up in stupefaction, until the gentleman and his awkward young companion were out of view. Neither of them saw Mr. Rafferty after that until thirty minutes later, when Janice was out in the garden and happened to look up and see the two of them on the second-floor stone porch that overlooked the white rose-covered pergola that led from the Music Room doors to the glass orchid house in the garden proper. It was a decorative porch, the use of which was discouraged, if not forbidden. Mr. Rafferty was standing forward in the full sunlight with his hands raised gently in the air, as if expatiating on some subject of moment: the young woman, with her face upturned, was partly concealed in the afternoon shadow that fell along the wall.

The sight of the two of them left Miss Monaghan shaken. "I'd give the world to know what they are talking about," Janice reported back to her aunt in the reception hall.

•

As the afternoon shadows began to accumulate in the garden, Mr. Rafferty emerged from one of the tall glass doors that led from the Music Room wing outdoors onto the grass, guiding Lulu by the elbow. It was refreshing there at that hour. The sun sparkled amid the uppermost leaves of the fig trees by the orchid house, and drew soft fingers of light across the surface of the fishpond back of the trees. Lulu had visited here once before, but so long ago, in her earliest childhood days, on a tour with her grade-school classmates, that it seemed a memory of another lifetime altogether, an age when she was still capable of feeling natural and important. They had come with Mrs. Trudeau. The gardens looked different then, although she recognized at once the white-columned pergola and the glass orchid house.

Lulu obeyed the gentle pressure of her companion's fingers about her elbow as he steered her along the curving path toward the quintet of tables situated just inside the expanding shadow of the roofline. She felt desperately ill at ease.

"Of course, if someone will let me," Mr. Rafferty said, in his subdued genial way, "I'll talk a blue streak. I wouldn't blame a body for not listening."

Lulu, for whom every response was a struggle, never once replied without a pained expression. "I enjoy listening." Time and again, she searched her mind for some interesting retort, for something—anything!—to say that was not vacant or foolish-sounding; but invariably she failed. She knew that she and the man in the linen suit at her side formed a very disparate pair. People looked at them. She could feel their eyes upon them, and was sure they regarded her, or both of them, with utter bafflement. In fact, when other people were close by, she couldn't even keep her mind on what Mr. Rafferty was saying.

The day before, a Saturday, Mr. Rafferty had shown up at the candy counter at Woolworth's and had suggested that Lulu meet him today at the Wistariahurst Museum. Lulu had not possessed sufficient character to even weigh the matter; she simply agreed. Then she hadn't the power, or desire, to rescind her decision.

Lulu had turned her back long ago on even the most mundane forms of social activity. Mostly, she led a withdrawn solitary life. Today, before arriving at the museum, while walking up the hill, she had felt the anxiety growing in her at every step, and hoped against hope that the museum would be empty. Upon arriving indoors, she was all the more nonplussed, therefore, at the sight of dozens of visitors coming and going in the downstairs rooms and corridors, and by the people milling about outdoors in the garden. Lulu felt painfully exposed. Not that the museum was anything more than a dusty, small-town cultural house kept open and administered by some local Ireland Parish club ladies; but she had deviated from her own private track. Feeling naked and vulnerable, she saw herself as peculiar. It was no wonder, therefore, that Mr. Rafferty's gentlemanly manner, his effortless way of protecting her from embarrassment, flattered and encouraged her.

In a sudden and remarkable access of forthrightness, a moment after Mr. Rafferty had seated her at the outdoor table, Lulu spoke up. "I'm very much of a dunce, and don't have anything to say about anything."

"My goodness," Mr. Rafferty exclaimed, "what an extraordinary thing to say."

Lulu winced and looked away. She was clutching both elbows with her hands, and couldn't rid her face of what she imagined was a look of gaping stupidity.

"I think you have a good deal to say," he objected. "I find you very alert. Reticence can be one of the charms of youth, especially when shown by someone who is as alive to her surroundings as you are. You're very keen-minded. You ask all the right questions."

But Lulu could not reply. The attention he was showing her left her feeling more tongue-tied than ever. She avoided his eyes. When he excused himself and went indoors to buy Lulu and himself a cup of coffee, her anguish mounted steadily, until she was reduced to occupying herself with a loose thread hanging from the cuff of her blouse. She felt that everyone in the garden was staring at her, and she was still toying with the thread when her friend returned, carrying a tray with two black-lacquered teacups.

Lulu surprised herself by speaking up without prompting. "The cups are very pretty." She colored slightly, but Mr. Rafferty gave no sign of noticing as he set her cup before her with elaborate care. Within moments, he had launched into a new subject altogether, expanding on the question of whether Americans were, by training or temperament, primarily verbal, graphic, musical, or perhaps scientific in their ways and outlook. Lulu judged Mr. Rafferty to be an intellectual. While he spoke she admired the look of him in his sand-colored suit and dark shirt, and especially the rakish knot of his pink-and-salmon necktie thrust slightly forward by the pressure of the tiny gold tie bar behind it. The part in his hair was exquisite, like a fine path running straight as a rule through a silvery wood.

Time and again Lulu's eyes went to his hands. He had powerful-looking hands: but they were also beautiful. She tried following his words.

"The English," he was saying, "are decidedly verbal. Of course, the English language is a treasure, one of the true wonders of the world, if you ask me—although not one man on earth would place it, or any other language, before his own. That's human nature. Men cleave to their tongues as to their own mothers. If you want to incite a man to murder," said Mr. Rafferty, "ridicule his native tongue."

"I never thought of that," said Lulu. "My own native tongue is French."

"Isn't that wonderful!"

"My family is from Quebec. My father was born in a place called St. Hyacinthe. He died when I was six."

"I'm sorry to hear that," said Mr. Rafferty. "You speak French, then? I should introduce you to Julia Gansevoort, a Francophile of the first water. She's Jack Gansevoort's widow. Jack, whether you know it or not, was an American!" Mr. Rafferty shook his fist to emphasize Jack Gansevoort's staunch traits. "Jack ate Grape-Nuts flakes for breakfast in Paris!"

Lulu laughed. For the moment, she had forgotten all about her sheepishness. Lulu had heard of the Gansevoorts, and was impressed that her friend was acquainted with such a renowned local family.

"Jack was a wonderful fellow. He loved boats and baseball. Julia, though," he pointed out, "was mainstream. She's upper crust, no two ways about it. You know the Gansevoorts?"

Lulu shrugged helplessly. "I've read about them in the papers."

Mr. Rafferty nodded; he sipped from his teacup. "The Gansevoorts were on another plane from the social hicks around here. You hear talk of the Appletons and Wrenns and people like that, the old textile crowd, but the Gansevoorts were Gansevoorts. Julia is herself a born Gansevoort. Jack was to Julia what is called, I believe, a 'German cousin.' There was a New York family and a New England family. Jack came from one branch, Julia from the other. Their money went back to the days of the China trade. Jack, though, was in finance. He lost more money in the Thirties than just about any man alive, a king's ransom. The joke went around that Jack Gansevoort lost half his money on Wall Street, half on Fleet Street, another half at the gaming tables in Europe, and still had enough left to go down again in the next crash, in 'Thirty-seven!"

Lulu was delighted with Mr. Rafferty's talk and his vivacious humor. "I didn't think any of that family was still alive."

"They aren't," he said, "except for Julia herself, of course, and she's all but incommunicado. Jack was raised here as a boy, but he rarely came back. His only true love was Sylvia, their daughter. Sylvia was with him a lot as a child. She was about ten or so when Jack died."

"I've heard of Sylvia Gansevoort," Lulu offered. "I remember her picture in the paper. She died with her cousin in an automobile accident."

"Sylvia"—Mr. Rafferty nodded—"was the American girl incarnate—in her camel's hair coat and saddle shoes. I used to write to her during the war. She was in college. Yes," he said, "Sylvia came to an unfortunate end. She died in 1946. Sylvia was an ideal of her kind. As much as we may wish to condemn our blue-blooded gentility, in my own meager experiences of life, the three or four paragons of human excellence that I've met have all been gentle-born—and of them," he added, "Sylvia Gansevoort was the choicest."

By now, Lulu was feeling better. She had forgotten about the strangers going past in the garden, and was absorbed in Mr. Rafferty's account of the Gansevoorts. His acquaintanceship with that family, which was truly fabled locally, contained a magic appeal, and she hoped he would go on talking about them.

"Sylvia's death left Julia in a bad way," he explained, "partly because the last of the Gansevoort money—from Julia's own father—was left to the grandchildren. When Sylvia died, her share, as stipulated, reverted to her cousins, Douglas and Chloris."

Lulu waited for her friend to continue, but Mr. Rafferty paused, smiling, and looked to her for a response. She sat with her hands in her lap. Her skirt was bunched uncomfortably beneath her thighs, but she was embarrassed to move. She searched her mind for something to say.

"Is she poor?" Lulu managed to bring out at last.

"Some people are never poor. They may be broke, penniless, thrown onto their wits. But they are not poor. Truth is, I don't know," he said. "How could I? Her nephew and niece are coming of age, and one would expect that Julia will be able to stay on in her house." He smiled. "On the other hand, whenever money can come between people, it will. That is Rafferty's Law."

"By rights," said Lulu, finding her tongue, "Mrs. Gansevoort should have had Sylvia's share."

The man sitting opposite her said nothing. He was regarding Lulu thoughtfully. After a moment, he put down his teacup, and sat back. "Isn't that remarkable!" he said, and then opened his hands to signify the slow dawning of understanding. "That's why we're here, you and I. . . . That's why I spoke to you a few days back. That's what it's all been about. Of course," he amended, "if you don't mind my saying this, I *do* understand something about you, and have from the very start. I know, for example, that you're a very private person." He spoke the words softly. "I respect that very much."

Mr. Rafferty's altered attitude alarmed Lulu and caused her to turn pink. She knew what was coming. That was the odd part of it. He was going to bring her to Mrs. Gansevoort. Lulu had gripped the edges of her black skirt and was nervously rolling and folding the coarse material between her fingers.

"You do know what I am going to suggest, don't you?" He was sitting back in his chair, observing her thoughtfully, as from a great distance. Lulu looked at her hands. By now, the weight of her companion's attention actually caused her to slump a little. Her shoulders rounded, and she slouched forward to a noticeable degree. She felt as she had on that desperate afternoon in Agnes Rohan's house, when Agnes held her and kissed her. She felt powerless.

Mr. Rafferty was watching her. Something moved inside Lulu's breast, something tremulous and baleful. There was something wrong about him. She felt he was playacting. That he had rehearsed what he was going to say. He had known it all along. What was more, he knew that she knew. He was waiting for her to acknowledge their secret understanding. Lulu wanted to reply, but only managed to nod her head.

"Yes," he said, "I'm going to introduce you to her. That's why we're here."

Looking up at him, Lulu was relieved not to discover even a germ of duplicity in his face or eyes. He was looking at her with the open fondness of a new friend.

After that, Mr. Rafferty changed the subject; he told her an anecdote about his days in the South, when he was an officer in the army, in training with an engineer battalion, an amusing story about the collapse of something he called a Bailey bridge. But Lulu couldn't divorce her thoughts from that unsettling sensation of a few minutes ago, when she felt Mr. Rafferty's mind circling darkly about her. She couldn't follow his thoughts, but observed him steadily. The wind lifted his necktie. Then a shadow moved across the garden and darkened momentarily the glass edifice of the orchid house. Beyond the orchid house, a little boy was sailing a boat on the fishpond. She could make out the toy sail gleaming brightly on the dark surface of the pool. Mr. Rafferty was going to say something else private and enigmatic. She could anticipate it.

Mr. Rafferty drained his cup, and smiled genially. "I always leave a tip on the table," he said. "I'm sure no one else does. I don't know why I do it. The girl does nothing to deserve it. Do you think I should?" he asked Lulu.

"Do I?" Lulu was sitting up straight now, not in the way of correcting her posture, but preparatory to rising from her chair.

"Yes," he said. "Do you think I should?"

For an instant, Lulu was perplexed that Mr. Rafferty should even pose such a question, but sensed that the question contained the answer. He was telling her what to say. Lulu was certain she was not imagining it. As preposterous as it seemed, she felt he was testing her in some arcane way. He continued to watch her, while fishing about in his trousers for a coin. When Lulu replied, she was surprised by her own response.

"No," she said, quietly, "I don't think you should."

Mr. Rafferty stopped moving, and made a sudden show of indignation. "You're perfectly right! As many times as I've come here, that girl hasn't so much as smiled."

Lulu felt pleased as they rose to go, although her pleasure was tinged by the knowledge, or near knowledge, that her companion had initiated communication with her on a subtle, covert level. And as Mr. Rafferty guided Lulu indoors to show her the Music Room, she felt that her suspicions were confirmed by the ever-so-slight pressure of his fingertips on her waist, as she went in at the door. A wave of weakness passed over her, but only for an instant, the same instant, in fact, when the sunlessness of the spacious Music Room suddenly replaced the direct afternoon sunlight shining outdoors.

●

Janice Monaghan saw them coming into the vestibule, side by side, pacing noiselessly toward her along the dark elderberry carpet, the man, a picture of tailored elegance, curtailing his voice at every step in exact relation to the diminishing distance between the two of them and herself, and culminating in actual silence as they passed by her in the corridor. Janice took a closer look at the stranger walking at Mr. Rafferty's side: a wan-faced, slender girl, with attractive features and a noticeably delicate neck. Most remarkable was her reticent manner, an overall lassitude of movement, and the plainness of her attire. The skirt she wore was not even summery, despite the relative heat of the day, but was black and shapeless. She wore flat-heeled shoes and was bare-legged.

Janice continued on her way and went outdoors to clear the tables. Not only had the handsome gentleman failed as always to acknowledge Janice's presence in passing, but even his companion, the nondescript young woman at his side, had looked right through her! That was the thanks one got, she thought, for the trouble one went to in introducing a gracious custom. A kick in the behind.

When Miss Monaghan picked up Mr. Rafferty's empty cup, and discovered no dime beneath it, she looked up, and then gazed away into the distance in bewilderment.

At night, Lulu could hear from the windows below the soft crackle of a baseball radio broadcast. That was Henry Bisonette listening to the Red Sox in his bedroom below. Henry was a thirty-year-old who resembled a child. He had grown up and aged in the physical sense without having altered very much within. He had a boyish smile and a boy's perpetual enthusiasm. If Henry had one abiding interest in life, it was in the game of baseball. Sometimes, at night, when Lulu knelt by her bed to think and pray, she could not focus her thoughts for the constant muffled excitement of the sportscaster's voice or the roar of the spectators. Lulu knew nothing of baseball, but on Sunday evening she came upon a full-page cover photo in the weekly magazine section of the *Ireland Parish Telegram* that arrested her attention. It was a picture in vivid color of a young baseball player standing on an emerald field with nothing behind him but a line of treetops and a cloudless sky. He wore the full uniform of a catcher, with shin guards, chest protector, mitt, and mask, but the mask was up, cocked atop his head, its steel grillwork shining black in the sun. The face of the boy was unforgettable.

Lulu was sitting on her bed with the colorful picture on her lap. She thought she had never seen such an expression of human excellence upon any face, a look of youthful purity, an edifying nobleness that suggested great moral steadiness. The young man's uniform, where it could be made out, considering the quantity of protective material he wore, was offset by vertical red stripes, very fine and widely spaced. His right hand hung loosely at his side, his fingers gripping the bill of a scarlet cap. When Lulu first saw the picture, she felt an instant stab of amazement, as though she had flung open a door and found him standing there in his elaborate regalia, with the sun in his eyes, and gazing penetratingly into her face. Points of blond hair showed at the sides of his upraised mask. At the bottom of the page, let into the greenness of the grass, as it were, the legend of his name was spelled out in small white letters: Soldier McNiff.

Lulu was canny enough to realize that the powerful response invoked in her by the photograph of the Christly-looking young baseball player in the Ireland Parish newspaper was somehow related to her recent "discovery" by the man who took her to the museum. That is, she knew that her life had come to a turning. She was sure of it.

Sometimes Lulu experienced a sudden tremor that ran the length of her from head to toe, and left her lips quivering for minutes thereafter. She, who had made a lifelong art form of concealing from herself entire layers of understanding, comprehended nevertheless that a livid sexual thread ran a distinct pattern through all the weavings of these past days and weeks, as fine and delicate as the red pinstripes in Soldier McNiff's baseball uniform. But Lulu did not wish to fathom too earnestly the depths of her distress. Sometimes love feelings came welling up inside her, powerful undifferentiated feelings, a force of desire that lacked any sensible object, and left her temples smarting. At such times, she envied those women, all superior to herself, who had possessed the strength of character to enlist themselves in holy orders. To give oneself completely, heart and soul, to the Virgin Mother, seemed to Lulu, at such times, enviable beyond description. Other times, as when Mr. Rafferty came into her thoughts, she felt a mixture of bitterness and self-pity, an animus toward life, that was as mysterious in its source as the other response. Not that she disliked Mr. Rafferty. On the contrary, she saw herself as indebted to him for having invaded her private world, coming to her from out of nowhere.

One rainy evening, Lulu took her umbrella from the hall closet and let herself quietly out of the tenement. Her mother and grandmother were asleep at the back of the house. Lulu rarely walked out alone at night, but this evening she felt unusually restless. She walked along the spiked fence past the grade school, then up Jackson Street to Main. The rain pattering on her umbrella fell so steadily that it seemed a natural component of the darkness. Lulu knew where she was going. She was taking a roundabout route to the Precious Blood, the doors of which were open at all hours, but when she turned her steps into Cabot Street and saw the green flare of the neon sign sparkling in the rain above the lighted drugstore, she stopped dead in her tracks. Coming this way, she could not possibly reach the church without passing in front of Rohan's pharmacy. She stood a long minute in the rain, clutching her umbrella, her eyes wide with consternation over having perpetrated such an obvious blunder.

The massive silhouette of the venerated church rose to towering heights in the rainy darkness behind the drugstore building, the slates of the immense steeple shining moistly. Lulu's heart tightened at the thought of being accosted on the sidewalk by Agnes, and she made an instinctive move to turn back. A street railway bus, approaching in the opposite direction, shot past, throwing up a furrow of rainwater, its lighted windows forming a vacant blur. Lulu was caught. At length, frightened and out of breath, she started forward along the walk, tilting her umbrella into the rain; by the time she passed the pharmacy, with her umbrella shielding her face, she was walking as fast as she could go. In a minute's time, she was hurrying up the church steps.

Lulu was not alone indoors. An elderly woman in a black rain hat knelt in the heart of the nave with her rosary in her hands. Breathless, Lulu placed her folded umbrella beside her in the pew, and sat down to collect her wits. She had a fear of Agnes coming into the church behind her, of suddenly gripping her by the shoulder. Rising, Lulu went rapidly into the side aisle and made her way toward the side-chapel exit beyond the altar. At each stained-glass window, she could hear the rain falling against the glass. In her haste, she forgot her umbrella, but once outdoors was in no frame of mind to return for it, and went home hurriedly in the rain.

Later, alone in her room, with the lights out, she experienced a peculiar giddiness, as of someone emerging safe from a perilous passage. She had put the weekly magazine section at the bottom of a dresser drawer, concealed with the pen-and-pencil set Agnes had given her, beneath a stack of a half-dozen white blouses. Now she felt an urge to look at it. She held it up by the window, to the light from the streetlamp below. She knew the school uniform he wore, the name of which in scarlet scroll lettering was hidden behind his chest protector. He was a parochial-school youth, a high-school baseball player, a boy from the Sacred Heart. To Lulu, he seemed a model of youthful beauty. She had never seen the likes of such a picture.

●

On Sunday afternoon of the following week, Lulu went uptown, as she had planned to meet Mr. Rafferty at the museum. It was understood between them, on the surface of things, that she and Mr. Rafferty had merely crossed paths, that they had enjoyed one another's company for an hour or more, and that that was all. That was the essence of their leavetaking a week ago. Mr. Rafferty, that is, had not said one word at their parting about their meeting again. Lulu understood that. He had suggested something only once, earlier in the afternoon, and even then in a playful vein; but Lulu was certain that Mr. Rafferty's failure to repeat his invitation was intentional and conceived in the way of a test. That was how he was. He wanted her to understand him in that way, the meaning that lay between the lines, or in the omissions or silences that were most conspicuous.

As Lulu came on foot up Essex Street, approaching the museum, she was suffering from a nervous quaking in her breast, a recurring throb directly behind the medal of St. Anthony she was wearing beneath her blouse. It was a few minutes to two, the exact hour they had met last week, but on that occasion, of course, the time was specified in advance.

The Wistariahurst Museum was the centerpiece of what had once been a splendid estate, an imposing gray-and-white house, with six or eight soaring white chimneys, that occupied an entire city block; years earlier, it had been the home of one of the great Ireland Parish families, a silk manufacturer of world reputation. A brick wall surmounted by an ornate black iron fence surrounded the block, with a stand of trees at each corner that appeared connected by long rows of rhododendrons in full flower. Mr. Rafferty was not waiting for her when she arrived. The front stairway, flanked by two recumbent stone lions, was empty.

Lulu was not surprised. This week Mr. Rafferty would trust her to arrive first, and perhaps even to wait for him for several minutes. That was how it would be, she was sure of it. Knowing that, Lulu would sit down at the far edge of the stairway, under the shadow of the second lion, so that he, coming down Essex Street, would not see her till the last possible moment.

Lulu was wearing the same blouse, skirt, and shoes as she had worn last week. After seating herself, Lulu opened her black vinyl bag, extracted a handkerchief, and blew her nose. Her fingers were trembling a little. While she fumbled with the clasp of her bag, three high-school girls came past on the walk, talking gaily. They were all dressed similarly, in the style of the day, wearing jeans with boys' long white dress shirts bloused down to their thighs, and black ballerina slippers. One girl carried a scarlet-and-white school pennant that caught Lulu's eye. None of them noticed Lulu sitting in the shadows under a high bank of pink rhododendrons, as motionless as the monumental lion above her. Although several minutes elapsed, she never doubted he would come.

An instant before he appeared to view, she heard his footsteps and dropped her eyes. She studied the mottled pattern of the marble step between the toes of her shoes. Her heart pumped in agitation.

Mr. Rafferty and Lulu did not go into the museum that afternoon; to Lulu's wonderment, Mr. Rafferty assumed as a matter of course that Lulu was prepared for their appointment with Mrs. Gansevoort.

"She is not the sort of person that one keeps waiting," he said, as he turned about and led Lulu back up Essex Street. "Usually, I visit her on weekday evenings. Julia doesn't much like company, but she does like mine. That's because I'm an outsider, I believe—and I use that word with the broadest possible signification. Not, that is, as an outsider to the family, but to society as a whole!

"Mrs. Gansevoort is not social here," he went on. "She is so far removed from the Pratts and the Russells and people like that—not to mention the lawyers, the surgeons, and suchlike—that she might as well be living on a treetop. The last formal guests in that house—you and I are not formal—were a contingent of Saltonstalls and Peabodys, about fifteen years ago, before the war, and she kept them waiting," he cried, "for an hour and a half!"

Mr. Rafferty's expeditious pace and rapid-fire talk enabled Lulu to speak up at one point with unaccustomed ease, to ask

Mr. Rafferty a question, which, nevertheless, he evidently did not hear. "How do you know so much?" she asked.

"There is an inertia in social snobbery," Mr. Rafferty continued, "which can carry along certain distinctions for two or three generations, even after the wealth has dried up, but only as long as the blood can produce a Julia, or for that matter a Sylvia—who in her own way was her mother's superior. Sylvia was a nonpareil!" He looked meaningfully at Lulu. "That was what I meant last week about the advantaged ones producing the superior offspring. Advantage is advantage." He widened his eyes. "Rafferty's Thirty-second Axiom!"

Now and again, Lulu was able to glean a grain of sense from her companion's words, but she had learned already that it was the manner of his speech that bore his meanings to her; and she was sure that her ignorance, her stupidity, were nullified by these deeper understandings. He respected her intelligence. If he didn't feel she understood, he would not persist. Anyhow, by fastening her attention on his words, she hadn't time to worry about where they were going. Only when they changed streets, and started along an unpaved sidewalk, stepping here and there over the shiny exposed roots of the ancient elms standing behind a derelict iron fence, did Lulu begin to anticipate what was coming.

Mrs. Gansevoort lived in a red-brick Victorian house with steepled roofs and white gingerbread trim. The house was set back from the street. The shade trees by the fence had long ago reduced the front lawn to little more than a sandy rectangle that supported a scattering of dandelions and witchgrass. The stones of the walkway leading up to the door were granite blocks worn to a gentle concavity by decades of use. As Mr. Rafferty opened the gate for her, Lulu was assailed by doubt. Considering his eloquent description of the lady's social position, and even worse, of her obvious arrogance, her disdain for everyone and everything, Lulu felt that she was the last person on earth who should be going to her door. She could actually feel the spirit within her balking, her brain slowing down like an engine running out of fuel or oxygen, as she stepped past him and waited as he replaced the latch of the gate. It was midafternoon, and the sound of insects and songbirds emphasized the summery quietude. It was the warmest day of the year so far.

"It isn't much to look at." Mr. Rafferty indicated the house with a tilt of his eyes. "The original Gansevoort mansion went down the skids nearly twenty years ago with everything else— the brokerage, the real estate, Jack's schooner, the whole shebang. This house belonged to a poor relative, and somehow Jack and Julia got hold of it—like two drowning sailors grabbing on to something that will float."

Not laughing over his witticism, Lulu followed her friend by about a half-step as he strode up the walk. She was as speechless as the front door itself, upon which she had fixed her eye.

"Shall I tell you why we're here?" Mr. Rafferty spoke over his shoulder, smiling at her. "It will put you at ease to know. There is a purpose to things! Mrs. Gansevoort," he declared, *"needs* someone!" Mr. Rafferty expanded his eyes humorously. "I didn't want to risk telling you earlier, because your own shy nature might have balked at the prospect. The irony is that she needs someone who possesses precisely those qualities of innocence, trust, and simpleheartedness that might cause that person to shy away. So"—Mr. Rafferty gestured broadly—"to spare the poor woman having to wait an eternity or two for just such a bluebird to alight on her sill, I found one for her."

Lulu came to a halt on the walk, even though Mr. Rafferty's words, if she understood correctly, did somewhat alleviate her anxiety. "I don't understand," she said.

"Julia," he replied, incisively, "requires an amanuensis."

Lulu gaped at Mr. Rafferty with a blank expression. Her lips parted helplessly.

"For dictation," he said. "A kind of helper, a secretary, someone perfectly discreet—like yourself—a stranger to her—like yourself—and—again, like yourself!—someone of gentle disposition. You see," he turned to the house, "she is writing something, a story or memoir about herself or family. I'm not privy to everything! I'm an outsider. I told you that. For all I know, she is probably not writing anything. Maybe she's too solitary, too lonely. Although that," he qualified ironically, "I rather doubt. But the world is a bewildering place. Maybe she *is* lonely," he repeated. "Whatever the case, there is always something to be said for making a good match, however disparate the parts. Wouldn't you agree?"

"But to take dictation—" she began.

"We are not talking," said he, "about lightning-fast stenography. The technical skill is a lesser consideration, believe me—especially, as I said, as she may not even be writing a book!"

"But if she's not," said Lulu, "then why would she wish to see anyone?"

He shrugged. "I can't think of a more reasonable question. Let's find out."

●

Mrs. Gansevoort was sitting in an upholstered chair behind a round mahogany table in what Lulu guessed was the biggest room in the house. It was certainly the biggest room she could recall having been in, and was quite crowded with furniture, collections of elegant chairs and sofas that served to divide the room into separate seating areas. Mrs. Gansevoort struck Lulu immediately as being different from the impression created by Mr. Rafferty. For one thing, she was younger than Lulu had anticipated, being a woman in her fifties, perhaps. She was tallish, with an angular build and henna-colored hair. For another, although it might have been just her surface manner, something learned and rehearsed over the years, Mrs. Gansevoort impressed Lulu at once as being warm and personable by nature. Lulu hadn't been in the room sixty seconds and felt already somewhat relieved.

"So," said the lady, in a pleasant, businesslike tone, looking up from her desk-table, "this, then, is the candidate upon whose qualifications our roving minister has so tellingly enlarged."

"Roving minister!" cried he, gaily, tossing back his head.

Mrs. Gansevoort, presently on her feet, dealt the gentleman a mildly supercilious expression before reaching to take Lulu's hand. Lulu could never have anticipated that she might have spoken up at this point, but words came easily.

"I didn't know why I was coming," she said, her eyes lost in Mrs. Gansevoort's gaze.

"Just as well," Mrs. Gansevoort answered tenderly.

"That's what I told her," Mr. Rafferty put in. He was standing back from the two of them, keeping a decorous interval between.

"You *can* write?" Mrs. Gansevoort's eyes smiled with pleasure.

"Oh, yes," said Lulu. "My writing is very legible."

"Can she spell?" said Mr. Rafferty, with a laugh, obviously enjoying himself, as he saw the apparent compatibility between his hostess and protégée.

"I am not a wonder at spelling," Lulu confessed.

"Leon is teasing." Mrs. Gansevoort's slowly waving hand brushed the whole of Mr. Rafferty, not just his interpolation, toward some proximate oblivion. "If you can write neatly, with just a fair amount of speed, Lulu, and if you're of loyal character, that would suit my requirements."

Lulu was sensible at once to the occurrence in Mrs. Gansevoort's speech of the word *loyal,* which Mr. Rafferty had used earlier.

"I think I am loyal," she ventured softly, and sent Mr. Raf-

ferty an instinctive questioning glance. She had wanted to say
the word *loyal* outright, and felt now, upon saying it, that indeed
she could be loyal to this lady, for Lulu liked her very much.
Of course, she was very flattered, and everything at hand con-
spired to strengthen that feeling in her, not least of all her
surroundings. Mrs. Gansevoort's parlor was spacious and cool,
with a gentle breeze coming through from the windows at the
back. It was coolly illuminated, too, with just the reflected glow
of the daylight leaking through the tall potted ferns standing
on tables by the side windows, and casting soft rays across the
ceiling. When the breeze increased, sheets of paper moved
gently up and down on Mrs. Gansevoort's big worktable. The
woman was still holding Lulu's hand. Mr. Rafferty looked on
benignly.

"I am writing a book." Mrs. Gansevoort expressed herself
in graver tones, while slowly lifting her chin and eyes as a sign
of this more elevated subject.

"Yes, I know," Lulu breathed back.

Mrs. Gansevoort kept her gaze leveled steadily upon Lulu.
Her eyes, slightly protuberant, sparkled with hazel lights. "Would
you like to help me?" she asked, in an intimate tone.

As before, Lulu's glance went nervously to Mr. Rafferty, who,
without an instant's delay, signified with a slow closing of his
eyes that Lulu should consent at once.

She wetted her lips with her tongue. "Yes, I would," she
replied, more softly than before.

The glow of pleasure that colored Mrs. Gansevoort's handsome face gratified Lulu immensely, for it was uncommon, certainly, to be able to give joy by taking joy, and she felt her
own temples turn warm and red in consequence.

Mr. Rafferty continued to regard the two of them with an
air of satisfaction. "I should have been a broker," he said.

"I hope you're not plumping for a fee," Mrs. Gansevoort
tossed out at him, "because I am not used to paying fees."

This assertion caused Mr. Rafferty to put his head back and laugh with an abandon that made Lulu look at him. Sometimes he perplexed her. And yet, at this moment, she felt very grateful and close to him. She liked, too, the way he had secretly signaled her with his eyes, lest she should have faltered at the critical moment.

"Where are you presently employed?" Mrs. Gansevoort wished to know.

"Lulu," Mr. Rafferty was here quick to interject, as if eager once more to help Lulu over an awkward moment, "is working temporarily in the retail field, as a saleslady, but if I'm not mistaken, and I have reason to think that I am not"—he glanced at Lulu significantly—"she is certainly open to opportunity."

Mrs. Gansevoort's pretty eyes had slid around in the direction of Mr. Rafferty while he was stating Lulu's case, and returned now to Lulu. "Is that correct?" she said.

"Yes," Lulu got out, "it is."

"And where," Mrs. Gansevoort persisted in a voice so precisely modulated, so pleasant and reassuring, that Lulu felt menaced by it, "exactly, *do* you work?"

"I work at the F. W. Woolworth store," said Lulu. Glancing swiftly at Mr. Rafferty, she saw his eyes go up worriedly to the ceiling, and wondered if she had betrayed her chances by being so candid.

"At the five-and-ten-cent store?" Mrs. Gansevoort revealed neither skepticism nor disappointment.

"She's just filling in for someone." Mr. Rafferty cut in rapidly at this point.

"I see," said Mrs. Gansevoort. She appeared willing to dismiss the matter. She was still holding Lulu's hand, and could not possibly have noticed the sign of relief that Mr. Rafferty imparted to Lulu. A moment later, however, Mrs. Gansevoort returned to her table and seated herself, leaving Lulu standing awkwardly, in open space, as it were, with Mr. Rafferty now behind her as Lulu turned to face the table.

"Would you like to tell me something about yourself?" Mrs. Gansevoort smiled up at her, but at the same time sent a swift glance of appraisal up and down Lulu from head to foot. Lulu wished desperately to reply, and finally blurted out the first thought that came to mind. She was trembling.

"I went to public schools," she said.

An awkward interval ensued. Then Mr. Rafferty spoke up helpfully from behind. "Lulu is French and speaks the language. She has been trained in both English and French, and hopes in the future to continue her studies."

Mrs. Gansevoort laughed sharply, almost as though she had been trying until now to keep a straight face. Lulu wondered for an instant if the two of them were not amusing themselves at her expense. Glancing about at Mr. Rafferty, however, she noticed that he appeared offended by Mrs. Gansevoort's amused reaction. His face was a picture of wounded innocence. In her next breath, Mrs. Gansevoort dispelled the awkwardness.

"I can always tell when Leon is stretching things," she said. "Leon has been a reprobate so long that he can't even remember what it was he renounced or what it is he every day sins against."

Although puzzled by the lady's elegant remark, Lulu found herself smiling at Mrs. Gansevoort, in appreciation of the way in which she was allying herself with Lulu by teasing their mutual friend.

"Leon," Mrs. Gansevoort added, in an oily, superior tone of voice, "is a creature of another time and place, I am afraid."

"A reprobate," said he, softly, deprecating the idea.

"Are you not?" Mrs. Gansevoort followed up energetically.

"Oh, how could I not be," he exclaimed, "if, as you say, I have forgotten the very thing I have profaned?"

All three laughed pleasantly over Mr. Rafferty's comical objection. This time Lulu noticed how Mrs. Gansevoort favored her with an intimate smile. A moment later, Mrs. Gansevoort got up briskly from her chair.

"I think we shall leave Leon to avail himself of the brandy, while I show our guest around."

"I am not some fallen angel." Mr. Rafferty concluded his facetious objection on a milder note, while looking about for the brandy decanter.

In the minutes to come, Lulu followed the lady from room to room, through the spacious downstairs portion of the house. It was immediately apparent to her that Mrs. Gansevoort's expectations exceeded anything that Lulu might have anticipated beforehand, for she was showing Lulu the house in such a way as to imply that she expected Lulu to be living here soon!

"You would be able to come and go as you please, upstairs or down, at any hour of the day or night—having complete run of the place in a way that, say, Mrs. Fallon, my housekeeper, does not. Do you understand?"

Lulu did not understand, but nodded tentatively all the same. Matters were moving almost too rapidly for her now, creating a sense of oppression upon her mind. A scent of sandalwood floated back to her from Mrs. Gansevoort as they entered the dining room. The lady was talking all the while.

"In fact," she was stressing, "I shall instruct Mrs. Fallon in that particular, because, like all household help, she is extremely sensitive to her own prerogatives vis-à-vis those of others. If she knows from the start that your position here is categorically different, she will not be offended. Mrs. Fallon works for me on a day basis, from ten in the morning until six, and is pretty much restricted in her movements here. She is never upstairs, for example, after eleven o'clock in the morning." Mrs. Gansevoort showed Lulu a look over her shoulder that hinted of inflexibility in such regards. "She never goes near my desk or papers. She rarely has reason to enter the garden."

As before, Lulu was aware that Mrs. Gansevoort was allying Lulu to herself by juxtaposing the two of them against someone else. Lulu was conscious also that she was powerless to resist the flow of events, and could not even bring herself to think about whether she was imperiling her everyday life, the comfortable routine that she had settled into at the variety store.

Mrs. Gansevoort complicated the dilemma further with every utterance.

"Nothing that I say to you," she instructed, while showing Lulu a cautionary glance, "is to be repeated to anyone, such as to the housekeeper, or, even, for that matter, to Leon."

The tall dining-room windows were flooded with sunlight, the foamy white curtains ballooning gently, and the light darting about the room, amid vases and glassware, as if with a will of its own. Mrs. Gansevoort's henna-colored hair caught the little flashes of light, and her eyes glittered, as she favored Lulu with a confiding expression.

Lulu was compelled to make a reply. "I understand," she said softly. She still could not credit the idea that Mrs. Gansevoort intended her to live here, but was sure that the woman would presently clear up any mystery on that point. In the meanwhile, she had begun taking a distinct pleasure in the house. She was enchanted with the rooms. It was an old house, and was not grand or stately-seeming when seen from without, but was so roomy and elegantly furnished. She loved the feel of the soft carpets underfoot. The rooms were far prettier than the interior of the Wistariahurst Museum. There were lovely pictures in ornate frames, and elaborate white cornices gave a feeling of tremendous height and solidity on all sides. Each room was a gracious maze of velvet chairs and burnished wood, interspersed with the subdued gleam of silver and copper objects, of urns and shining jardinieres. An immense bowl of blue flowers on the dining-room table, with the petals and leaves fallen about it, stood forth like a symbol of perfection. To Lulu's mind, everything was disposed so handsomely that it might never have been otherwise.

"It isn't because I have secrets to conceal," Mrs. Gansevoort explained, "or because I am suspicious by nature; it is merely a question of discretion."

Lulu nodded compliantly. "I understand."

"That, after all, is why you're here, because I need someone both familiar and trustworthy. And it wouldn't require the offices of a mind reader to tell me that you are just that sort of person. I deduced that at once."

Lulu would have replied, but at that same moment she was mildly shocked at the sight of her own image in a looking glass. She had followed Mrs. Gansevoort through her library, a pretty sunlit room containing hundreds upon hundreds of bound volumes, and her front sitting room, and was entering the airy entrance hall. She was just about to speak when she came face-to-face with her own reflection in the mirror by the front staircase. Mrs. Gansevoort, walking in front of her, occupied the foreground in the tall, doorlike mirror. All Lulu could see of herself was her face showing above Julia Gansevoort's shoulder. Her mouth hung open; her face was pale and lusterless. The disparity between the two was alarming. They were both moving toward the glass, their figures growing larger at every step. Mrs. Gansevoort dominated the entire vertical space, as if framed that way by an artist's hand, with her reddish-brown hair and tall, angular posture, a picture of smooth self-assurance, while Lulu seemed to be peeping out at life from behind her head or shoulder. Lulu's senses reeled momentarily under the sudden disturbing impression of her own mortal inconsequence.

When Mrs. Gansevoort paused at the foot of the broad white staircase, explaining, as a point of interest, how her house had a name, Lulu was fairly gaping at her. She felt very undone inside, and actually winced at the realization that she, to Mrs. Gansevoort, was that sorry spectacle in the looking glass. She saw herself in her mind's eye, in her shapeless skirt and flimsy blouse, with her shoulders stooped and her mouth ajar.

Mrs. Gansevoort pointed up the steps to where the builders had employed someone to carve the name of the house into the woodwork above the staircase. Lulu read the name to herself: Leiden Hall.

"It's a beautiful house," she mumbled.

"It's simple," Mrs. Gansevoort stated, "but I think you'll enjoy it."

Lulu felt herself to be completely in Mrs. Gansevoort's hands, and wished to relinquish altogether the necessity to think hard on what was happening. "I didn't know that I was going to be living here," she confessed.

"You didn't?" cried Mrs. Gansevoort in her most amiable tone.

"No," said Lulu, in an apologetic effort.

"That may be just as well. After all," she smiled, "we don't any of us know we're going to live here, do we? In the larger sense, that is." Her eyes expanded to signify the metaphor intended. "But if it is a surprise, I hope it's a pleasant one. It would comfort me to have you in the house, and you," she remarked confidently, "might not find it too unpleasant to call Leiden Hall your home." She started then up the steps, and swept her arm about meaningfully. "You would have complete run of the house."

"You're very kind to me," Lulu confided, as she followed her up the stairs.

"You haven't seen the best of it."

From minute to minute, as Mrs. Gansevoort's manner grew increasingly intimate, Lulu's heart went out to her. To Lulu, Mrs. Gansevoort was becoming like a figure of the cinema, one of those grand ladies whose manners, wealth, and wit endear them to everyone on earth. Lulu pulled back her shoulders and straightened herself in an unconscious replication of Mrs. Gansevoort's own bearing.

"Let me show you where you'll be sleeping. This first room"—

she opened and closed a door—"belonged to Sylvia, my daughter. But I will not give you that room. No one uses that room anymore. Were you christened Lulu?" she asked, in an abrupt change of subject.

"No," said Lulu, "my real name is Luette, but no one calls me that."

"You are French, then?" Mrs. Gansevoort exclaimed.

"Yes. My name is Luette Peloquin."

Mrs. Gansevoort's enthusiasm was too spontaneous not to be authentic. "What a lovely name! Luette Peloquin. Has no one ever called you Luette?"

"Only two persons," Lulu replied. "Mrs. Trudeau, who was my first-grade teacher, called me Luette. And my father, when he was alive, I think called me Luette. I'm not sure, but I think so."

"Your father was in the war?" asked Mrs. Gansevoort, with concern.

"Oh, no," said Lulu. "He died of an illness in 1936, the year I began school."

Mrs. Gansevoort appeared touched. "You remember him?"

"I remember him—in the bus." Lulu grew tense, and wished to say no more. "He drove for the street railway company."

Mrs. Gansevoort turned away with a soft, understanding look, and continued along the upstairs corridor. Lulu followed. In the minutes to come, the surprises mounted. The room that Mrs. Gansevoort had chosen for her was called, she said, the North Room. Lulu stood immobile just inside the doorway; she was so impressed at once by the purity of the room, with its tall windows and filmy curtains, and the snowy woodwork, the white mantel and cornices and the tapered gunstock beams in each corner, that she lost track for the moment of what Mrs. Gansevoort was talking about. The bed itself was a dreamwork of puffy white coverlets. The windows overlooked the garden. Beyond the trees could be seen the violet summit of Mount Holyoke, lighted smokily by the afternoon sun.

"I believe it is called the North Room because someone once painted in here. Some silly, misguided devil, I'm sure." Mrs. Gansevoort's wry smile was such this time as to deprecate every-one on earth save herself and her young friend. "That was many years ago, when the Hootens lived here. Time, thankfully, covers up folly. You'll be comfortable here. May I speak freely, without insulting you?"

By now, Lulu was so thoroughly charmed by her hostess, and somewhat daunted, as well, by the lady's attractive, cynical air, that she could only nod her consent.

"I'd like to put you into something different, something fresh, and," she added, "something appropriate to my own gratifi-cations. I should tell you, you're just right for me!"

Mrs. Gansevoort expressed her pleasure in Lulu in a hearty tone of voice, as of someone who had just swallowed a tonic.

"Would you be offended?" Mrs. Gansevoort smiled in-tensely.

For an instant, Lulu had not comprehended the lady's words, and her wonderment shone in her face. Mrs. Gansevoort clar-ified her meanings at once.

"Something in the way of dressing you up. I'd like to put you into something. You have some wonderful points." Reach-ing, Mrs. Gansevoort lifted Lulu's hair back from her shoulders. "You have a fine, delicate neck and lovely profile. You should learn to keep yourself erect, with your shoulders back, because that straightens everything else, you see. It gives a lift to your head. It improves your walking. Shall we try something?"

Lulu divined what was happening, and was touched to realize that she had awakened Mrs. Gansevoort's maternal in-stincts. They stood close together, with Lulu looking up at her friend intently, and experiencing the coercive spell of Mrs. Gan-sevoort's hazel eyes upon her. Lulu couldn't be certain, but she had the distinct premonition that Mrs. Gansevoort was presently going to bring her something of Sylvia's to put on.

"You wouldn't be insulted? Because if you would find it demeaning, I wouldn't ask you."

"If it would please you," Lulu replied softly, "I would be happy to do it."

"Do you have favorite styles or colors?"

Lulu elected to confess her ignorance. "I know nothing about fashion, Mrs. Gansevoort."

"But I," Mrs. Gansevoort here proclaimed, "am beginning to know something about you. I find you to be very knowledgeable about what you don't know. It occurred to me, a very long time ago, that what we know is nothing." She smiled cannily. "It is our understanding of our ignorance that really distinguishes us—our sense of what we do not know. In that regard," she continued in this perplexing vein, "I think you know a considerable amount about yourself."

"About what I don't know?" said Lulu, sagaciously.

"Exactly. Do you think I'm right?"

There flashed upon Lulu then a sudden apparition of herself, of her face, pale and hallowed, as it stared out at her sometimes at night from the depths of her mirror, when she knelt on the floor in the dark. It was as if Mrs. Gansevoort had invaded her life at this point precisely, where her innermost soul was struggling to go back—to cross indefinable dimensions, to recover something once treasured and lost.

Lulu remained standing before her, in a brown study, as Mrs. Gansevoort turned and went silently past her and out of the room. From the corridor came the faint, musical chiming of a clock. A moment later, Mrs. Gansevoort was talking to her from a nearby room, raising her voice while opening and closing drawers.

"Other people," she called out, "never do see us as we are. They see only what we show them."

Lulu was smiling expectantly as Mrs. Gansevoort came swooping back into the room, a black dress draped carelessly over her shoulder, her hands clutching a balled-up collection of shoes, stockings, and underclothing. She threw everything in hand roughly onto the bed, then held up the dress. "This will suit you to a tee. Are you wearing stockings?"

"No," Lulu answered.

"Do you know how?" The possible rudeness of the question brought a sudden flush to Lulu's face, but Mrs. Gansevoort gave no sign of noticing. She handed Lulu the dress, seized the roll of clothing from the bed, and disentangled it. "If the shoes don't fit, I have others. These are sevens."

"I wear sevens," said Lulu, "but I could never wear a heel like that!"

"Don't be childish. I shall be back in five minutes."

With that, Mrs. Gansevoort went out and closed the door. Lulu was left to herself. Anxious lest the woman should come back and find her half naked, she began at once to undress. She had a dislike of nakedness. It was not that she disliked her body, but somehow associated the look of her bare flesh with her own deep longing for anonymity. Sometimes, though, when bathing in the tub, she was able to relax in this regard, and enjoyed soaping and sponging her body, and even felt at such times a gentle pity for it, seeing it as the soft, imperfect vessel of her mortality.

By the time Lulu had pulled on and fastened her stockings, her head was swimming. She wanted Mrs. Gansevoort to like her, but was upset by what she was doing. She glanced at the closed door, a great, white door with a carved, silver knob. She could not grasp the idea that she might live in this room. The room had a name. Her thoughts were going in circles. She looked down at herself, at her legs sheathed in the sheer stockings, and at the soft whiteness of her belly. Mrs. Gansevoort was right about the dress. The fit was so exact, as Lulu, breathing audibly, struggled into it, that it might have been tailored to her specifications that very morning. The sleeves of the black dress were silken, and transparent to the point where she could make out, through the diaphanous weave, the silhouette of her bare arms down to the tiny ruffles at her wrists.

When Mrs. Gansevoort came back, Lulu was sitting inertly on the edge of the bed, looking both transformed and exhausted. She had put on the black shoes, but was afraid to stand up in them. The sight of her legs and of her feet in the pretty shoes struck her as altogether alien, as though she were sharing her body now with a stranger. The stranger's legs were very slender and delicate, she thought, but would never respond to her own vital needs. She would not be able to stand up on them.

Mrs. Gansevoort folded Lulu's left hand over her own forearm, and led the way out of the room, with Lulu moving beside her like a creature made of glass. Of one thing Lulu was sure: Mrs. Gansevoort was pleased with her beyond anything she might openly express. Lulu could feel it. It was only through their physical contact, though, that Lulu had the strength or courage to do what she was doing. She squeezed Mrs. Gansevoort's arm with her fingers. She felt a trifle dizzy. Her soul seemed at moments to vacate her body, standing outside herself; at other times she felt it suddenly contracting, as though she were very tiny and withdrawn.

On the front stairs, Mrs. Gansevoort was even more formal and solicitous than before as Lulu moved tentatively down the steps. Her foot shook at every step in the impossible heels. Mrs. Gansevoort led the way with painstaking slowness, as if each downward step were a distinct achievement in itself. Lulu thought they were going to the parlor, to where Mr. Rafferty was doubtless still waiting. At the foot of the stairs, however, Mrs. Gansevoort ushered her back the way they had come during their circuitous inspection of the downstairs rooms, until they reached the library. She led Lulu past a wall of books to a tapestried window seat.

"Sit with me here," she said. "Here we can talk. Tell me

your impressions, Luette. What did you think of your room?"
Mrs. Gansevoort lowered herself elegantly onto the settee between the bow windows, while assisting Lulu in following suit.

Lulu's response was so obvious that she could not bring
herself to articulate it, but said instead, "My room at home is
very plain." Her eyes lingered on the toes of the shoes she was
wearing. They were somebody else's shoes, just as they were
somebody else's stockinged feet inside them.

"Would you prefer to rejoin Leon now? Or shall we talk
together for a while?"

Sitting with the sun on her lap, and the scent of Mrs. Gansevoort's sandalwood cologne in her nostrils, she felt comfortable. A bright bar of sunlight extended across the floor and
ignited the gold lettering on the bindings of a set of tall red
books.

"I'd like to talk," said Lulu.

"I'm glad you said that," replied Mrs. Gansevoort. "Because
so would I. It isn't but once in a dog's age that I find anyone
of sensibility to talk to. Do you know what I mean by sensibility?" she inquired.

Lulu cleared her throat. She had consciously corrected her
posture, but her eyes returned many times to her lap, to the
delicate silkiness of her dress drawn taut across her thighs. "Does
it mean sensitivity?"

"Yes," said Mrs. Gansevoort. "Someone with sensitive reactions to others, to everything, to one's surroundings, to life. I
am so weary of insular, petty-minded types that I have considered sometimes forswearing the human race. That may even
explain why I permit Leon to call. Not, I should say, because
of his sensibility—as I sometimes feel that he possesses none
whatsoever. Leon is rather like a cleverly conceived piece of
machinery that the gods are testing on an experimental basis.
I remember Leon in soiled tennis shoes when he was a very
young man and had arrived in town like Vulcan dropped out
of the heavens!"

Lulu regarded her with wonderment.

"Leon crossed half a continent on foot, only to discover here, of all places, that the promise of life is a mere sorcery. Leon's sensibility reveals itself in his appreciation of the blue gleam of a machine-gun barrel! Leon was something of a hero in the war. Bona fide. The truth was, he had the time of his life over there. Don't you find him a little chilling sometimes?"

Lulu had determined beforehand to say nothing critical about Mr. Rafferty, and even conjectured as to whether Mrs. Gansevoort was not testing her.

"No," Lulu answered.

"Because I do," said Mrs. Gansevoort. "I would not mention it, except as he has obviously shown interest in you. I mean to say"—Mrs. Gansevoort was quick to shift ground, as she detected the look of perplexity from Lulu—"he is a man, after all, and you are a woman, and he is—at least, after *some* fashion— admiring of you. There's nothing harmful in that. But I would hope that you would keep your own counsel."

Understanding all at once the thrust of Mrs. Gansevoort's words, Lulu straightened in her seat. "Oh, I would never tell him anything."

"Don't misunderstand. I am not paranoid. I don't see a bear in every bush. But I do feel that I can trust no one. I do trust Leon. I mean that in the strictest sense, in that I already have trusted him. Still, I am capable of worry."

"You would never have to worry about me," said Lulu.

"I have a nephew and niece who customarily stay with me summers. In fact, Chloris, my niece, is here now. She left school early this year. Chloris is high-strung. She has had one nervous collapse already, and I shudder to think she might suffer another. She's seventeen. You'll meet her. Her brother, Douglas, has just graduated from Yale, and will be coming up any day now. You shall meet him also. That was why I wanted us to talk. For whatever reason, Luette, I do not wish either of them to be privy to the workings of my private life."

Lulu had forgotten momentarily about her appearance, her dress, her stockings, her shoes, and was listening enraptured. She sat close to Mrs. Gansevoort on the tapestried settee. The older woman was so handsome; the planes of her forehead and cheekbones were chalky smooth, like the sculpted head of the Roman empress in the vestibule of the public library. "I am very loyal," Lulu offered, at last, with feeling.

Mrs. Gansevoort touched her hand. "I'm sure you are."

Only when Mrs. Gansevoort stood, and Lulu was forced to follow, did she recall her earlier awkwardness, although this time her difficulty was more mechanical than nervous. She immediately teetered on her heels; she reached instinctively and grasped Mrs. Gansevoort's forearm.

"I'm tempted to send Leon on his way without seeing you." Mrs. Gansevoort turned to Lulu as they stepped carefully through the library door into the front sitting room. "He does, perhaps, you realize, entertain some foolish ideas about you. Men who have lived alone, as Leon has, become prey to that sort of folly. Hopeless romantic attachments."

Although she was certain that Mrs. Gansevoort was wrong about Mr. Rafferty, Lulu did not wish to contradict her, and remained silent. It seemed thoroughly preposterous to Lulu that a man of the world like that could feel a romantic interest in her. The thought of such a thing muddled her senses. She was holding Mrs. Gansevoort's arm as they approached the mirror in the foyer. The afternoon light was weak in that part of the house and much attenuated in the depths of the glass, so that the slender figure in the black dress with the drawn-back hair was like the reflection of someone else. The face, isolated in the glass, was shadowy. Lulu glanced away quickly to Mrs. Gansevoort, avoiding the ghostly disturbance in the mirror.

Lulu's heels tapped clickingly across the black and white

tiles of the foyer, as Mrs. Gansevoort steered her along delicately. Lulu could feel a pulse-beat in her body, a rhythmic
throb that came up from her legs at every step. She would have
liked Mr. Rafferty to see her, if only to enjoy his initial surprise.
When she turned her eyes to Mrs. Gansevoort, she detected a
look of satisfaction, a voluptuous smugness contorting her lips.

Mr. Rafferty was not in the parlor, but had taken himself outdoors. Seen through the parlor windows, he sat on a white cast-
iron chair in the garden, with his legs crossed, facing the house.
Lulu saw him through the curtains billowing gently behind Mrs.
Gansevoort's writing table; but Mrs. Gansevoort evidently saw
more, something that escaped Lulu, because the woman's face
fell at once. Lulu was certain that it was something more than
the fact of Mr. Rafferty's removal to the garden that upset her.

Lulu was left standing there as the older woman excused
herself with a cold, polite smile. Lulu heard the report of the
back door; a moment later, Mrs. Gansevoort appeared on the
back lawn, with Mr. Rafferty at the same time getting to his
feet to meet her. Lulu could not hear the two of them, but Mrs.
Gansevoort's agitation was apparent, even at that distance, as
she stood in the sunlit space between a pair of flowering bushes
and addressed herself pointedly to Mr. Rafferty. He, perplexed,
then turned on his heel while she was speaking to him, as

though activated by her words, until they were both facing the opposite way, toward the deeper recesses of the garden. Mrs. Gansevoort slowly raised her arm and pointed.

Lulu stood in front of the black marble fireplace observing the pantomime outdoors. She would have liked to cross to the windows, but to do so, she felt, would seem a repudiation of the guarantee she had just given to respect Mrs. Gansevoort's privacy. Also, she was unsure of her ability to walk. Her high-heeled shoes frightened her. She imagined if she took one step she might pitch headlong onto the floor. She could barely see the two of them, and had, in fact, no view whatsoever of that portion of the garden toward which Mrs. Gansevoort was point-ing. Presently, however, an altogether new figure came into view from the rear, a platinum-haired girl wearing a white skirt and striped top, and moving apprehensively, as if she had been caught out at something. Lulu knew immediately she was Mrs. Gansevoort's niece, a seventeen-year-old, both girlish and adultlike, but striking in appearance; she was delicate and slim, with a spectacular tail of white-blond hair. By now, Mrs. Gan-sevoort was speaking sharply to her, chastising her in no un-certain terms. Mr. Rafferty stood by, looking about abstractedly, at the sky, or at the grass, with the disinterested air of a polite outsider. Seconds later, Chloris came running toward the house in obvious distress. Mrs. Gansevoort called after her angrily.

"When we are at home," Mrs. Gansevoort scolded in a voice meant to carry, "we are at home. When we are away, we are away."

The back screen door slammed, and Chloris's running foot-steps could be heard coming down the hall. Lulu was gazing wide-eyed at the doorway when Chloris shot into the room. The sight of Lulu, standing by the mantel in her dramatic black dress, brought a despairing cry from Chloris's throat. The girl spun about and fled the way she had come. Her footsteps re-sounded on the back stairs; Lulu was left shaken by the incident.

"I will not," Mrs. Gansevoort cried bitterly, as she reentered the house, banging the door behind her, "play nursemaid to individuals who wave the flag of daring in my face." She was talking aloud to herself. "That I should be reduced to such a part, while their mother splashes about in the Adriatic, summer after summer, is no longer thinkable."

Lulu was quick to conclude that Julia Gansevoort had been compelled by difficult circumstances to watch over her niece and nephew every summer, no doubt for years. Mrs. Gansevoort's look of anguish as she entered the room caused Lulu to transfer at once the concern she felt for the unhappy girl upstairs to the proud figure of the woman before her.

"I am so distressed to have spoiled your reception, Luette," said Mrs. Gansevoort.

"Please don't think about me," Lulu said. "I should probably go home."

"That," Mrs. Gansevoort promised, and raised her chin in a show of steeling herself against further setbacks, "is the very reverse of what will happen." She expanded her eyes. "You will stay. I will not be frustrated by a child, believe me." Mrs. Gansevoort directed a smoldering gaze toward the ceiling and the young woman upstairs.

"Twice a week," Mrs. Gansevoort explained, "she is required to go across town to her mathematics tutor, and at half past the hour of her appointment, she is discovered lurking about in the hollyhocks behind the glider swing. I believe that if corporal punishment were still in order at the Northfield School, they'd've thrashed some sense into her long before this. I hope you are an only child, Luette, so that you'll never know the humiliations that siblings are capable of visiting upon one another. It makes my blood boil. Next Sunday, at three o'clock sharp, I want you to telephone Chloris's tutor, to make sure she has arrived. I hope you will remind me of that."

"I will," Lulu replied, scarcely aware that in the space of an hour or less, her life had already begun to blend into Mrs. Gansevoort's.

"I can't tell you," Mrs. Gansevoort continued, in restored spirits, "what a happy stroke of fortune your arrival in this house has meant to me this afternoon. When you were first presented to me, I was naturally pleased to meet you—a gentle, compassionate spirit—but since that time, minute by minute, your presence at my side has given me a sense of tranquillity I haven't enjoyed in years."

Minutes later, when Mr. Rafferty caught sight of the two of them coming toward him in the garden, he appeared so thunderstruck by Lulu's transformation that she wondered if he was not exaggerating. He was not the type of man to be caught unawares in any situation. That was Lulu's appreciation of him, in any case. He was either acting or else being exceedingly polite, for he rose to his feet like something pulled up on wires.

Lulu came toward him on Mrs. Gansevoort's arm, the two of them moving with a slow rigidity that gave them a processional air. Only now, while stepping forth in the grass, her heels sinking into the spongy earth, did Lulu comprehend the oddness of it all. Indoors, she had begun to feel herself a part of Mrs. Gansevoort's private world, of her high-ceilinged rooms and tall clocks, of velvets and crystal, and the soft, distant flight of violins coming from an upstairs radio; but outdoors, in the open air, as the two of them advanced through alternating patches of sunlight and shadow to meet Mr. Rafferty, the strangeness of what was happening suddenly assailed her. She could not credit what she was doing. Or maybe it was the fact of Mr. Rafferty's presence in the garden that upset her anew. Surely he was not interested in her as a woman. That was unthinkable, even frightening.

Lulu was squeezing Mrs. Gansevoort's arm tightly for support. Mr. Rafferty stared at her with disarming frankness. She wetted her lips nervously, and avoided his eyes until the last possible moment.

"This young lady," Mrs. Gansevoort proclaimed proudly, "can wear almost anything to effect. She has fine square shoulders, a slender frame, a high waist." Mrs. Gansevoort moved a trifle to one side and made as if to present Lulu like a mannequin in a showroom.

"Pretty ankles," Mr. Rafferty put in playfully.

"Very pretty," Mrs. Gansevoort repeated, "and, for the best of it, a neck and throat that would be the envy of a swan. When I think of the fineries stuffed away in those closets, the satins and taffetas and cashmeres—the Eldorado of the moth kingdom—and no one on earth to come into them, save certain disruptive, disloyal children of my own family, well, I feel redeemed suddenly. Isn't she a picture?"

Mr. Rafferty nodded politely. "It's a lovely dress."

"I am not talking about the dress," Mrs. Gansevoort snapped, "but about the wearer." She regarded Lulu then with a level gaze. "We have had a chance to talk. Haven't we?"

Lulu nodded. "Yes," she said softly.

Before informing Mr. Rafferty of the substance of their discussion, Mrs. Gansevoort allowed for a moment of suspense. Lulu was still holding the older woman's arm in an effort to counterbalance the forward tilt of her body imparted by her uncomfortable shoes. The balls of her feet were burning; but standing in the sunlight, in the company of her two friends and the privacy of Mrs. Gansevoort's garden, she was secretly pleased and excited. Mr. Rafferty, she noticed, had leaned forward perceptibly in anticipation of Mrs. Gansevoort's announcement.

"Luette," Mrs. Gansevoort said with businesslike finality, "has agreed to come and stay with me."

While Mr. Rafferty appeared to be both gratified and relieved at hearing the news, Lulu herself was a little surprised. She glanced tentatively from one to the other. They were both smiling at her.

"Is that true?" Mr. Rafferty asked.

Lulu colored slightly. She looked to Mrs. Gansevoort, then to him.

"Yes," she said, at last, "it is."

Lulu might have imagined it, but in the very moment of her replying, she sensed a sudden look of understanding passing between her two friends. Then Mrs. Gansevoort sent a brief, surreptitious glance toward the house. A moment later, when the three of them started across the grass toward the back door, Lulu could not deny the strange sense of confidence she felt, while at the same time she resisted the impulse to look up at the second-floor window. Lulu felt sure the girl was up there.

Mrs. Gansevoort's freckled forearm was warm to the touch of Lulu's fingertips. From time to time Mr. Rafferty brushed against her as they strode slowly, three abreast, across the lawn. Their progress was quite stately, if only because of the impediment of Lulu's heels. Finally, at the last second, able to bear the suspense no longer, she looked up suddenly, her heart jumping wildly in her breast. There, framed between the curtains of the window directly above the back door, shone the glassy face of the niece.

"Your main business, in the beginning, Luette, will be to take hold here." Mrs. Gansevoort spoke sidelong as she led the way indoors to the parlor. She had not seen the shock that registered on Lulu's face at the spectacle of the girl in the upstairs window. "You are not to be discomfited in any way by Mrs. Fallon, or Chloris, or anyone."

"Mrs. Fallon is the housekeeper," Mr. Rafferty offered, helpfully, in a deliberately restrained tone.

"Neither one of them will ask anything of you. I shall see to that," said Mrs. Gansevoort, as Lulu took her arm once more in the parlor doorway. "Mrs. Fallon is just the sort of Irish domestic who will bend and twist herself every which way to ingratiate herself to you, till you respond kindly, and then despise you for your better traits. Leon, why don't you prepare us a toast."

"A singular suggestion," he said.

"As for my niece," Mrs. Gansevoort continued, "she is a

guest in this house. Nothing more than that. She is your junior, Luette. Remember that. If she steps out of line by so much as an inch, I want to hear about it."

"I'll keep to myself," Lulu consented, shyly.

Mrs. Gansevoort showed Lulu her pretty eyes. "As my companion and aide, you will enjoy a freedom in this house rivaled by no one save myself."

"Including me." Mr. Rafferty extended a glass of brandy to Lulu, but she deferred at once to Mrs. Gansevoort by not raising her hand.

Lulu's spontaneous, instinctive refusal of the proffered glass caused a pink hue of pleasure to ignite Mrs. Gansevoort's cheeks. "Leon has been too long among the Yahoos," she said, as she reached to take the glass.

Mr. Rafferty offered a toast. As Lulu lifted her own glass to her lips, she noticed how the delicate ruffle at her wrist isolated her hand. It looked like someone else's hand, fragile and delicate.

During the remainder of the afternoon, Lulu had only one opportunity to speak to Mr. Rafferty alone, and that was when he was leaving the house, about twilight. Lulu had telephoned home to explain her situation, and met Mr. Rafferty coming toward her in the front hall. He spoke up in round tones, to ask how she was getting on.

"My feet are burning," she said. "I can't get used to these shoes."

"You're doing splendidly," he assured her.

Before going, Mr. Rafferty took hold of Lulu's hand and drew her outdoors, closing the door noiselessly behind her. Lulu's heart constricted instantly, not with fright, but in finding herself abruptly face-to-face with Mr. Rafferty. A breath of air lifted his necktie. He looked different. Gone was the look of diffidence, the air of polite expectation, that he wore like a mask in Mrs. Gansevoort's presence. He was very close to Lulu in the dusk, as close to her as any man had ever been. She felt his maleness pass over her like an essence in itself, and worried that he was about to do something to her.

He spoke to her in a soft, cautious manner that Lulu found alarming. "You could score a triumph here," he said.

Lulu nodded dumbly. Mrs. Gansevoort's words came to mind, about Mr. Rafferty having an interest in her. She was sure it was not true.

"Don't be afriad to improve yourself. That woman"—he spoke in confidential tones—"will weather any trouble that comes her way. Mark my words. And when it's over, and she comes sailing out onto a calm sea," he smiled, "you'll be there. Don't forget that."

"I won't," Lulu replied softly, at length, with effort. She was certain by his manner that Mr. Rafferty was saying more to her than could be construed by his words. There was a meaning between the words. His mere closeness was a language in itself.

He was smiling privately. "Put her best interests first. And do be a little wary of that girl. Remember," he said, "she is one of *them.*"

As he reached past Lulu to open the door for her, the wintergreen scent of his cologne swam into her nostrils. He was, she thought, a very handsome man. As she turned to reenter the house, Lulu lost her balance, but Mr. Rafferty's hand came up swiftly to support her.

Inside, as the door clicked shut behind her, Lulu paused to adjust her eyes to the shadowy interior, and remained motionless, waiting for her senses to settle. Before her, the foyer materialized, the gleaming black and white floor tiles, an enormous bouquet of tiger lilies, and the broad white staircase gleaming in the last light of day.

•

She loved Leiden Hall without reservation. She liked following Mrs. Gansevoort from room to room, moving soundlessly over the plush carpets as the rooms came richly to life one behind the other like a succession of mysteries. She was enthralled also with Mrs. Gansevoort herself, with the woman's gorgeous comportment, with the way she held up her head and strode proudly with her shoulders back and spine straight, the picture of a woman of consequence. Lulu even emulated her, if only in trying to keep pace.

Once, when they were upstairs, Lulu heard a radio playing softly behind the door of the room opposite her own. That was doubtless Chloris's room. Lulu noticed, too, how Mrs. Gansevoort frowned as they passed Chloris's door. She suspected that Mrs. Gansevoort's distaste for her niece was an enduring emotion, something that went far deeper than the disappointment she expressed in the girl. Lulu could not frame the thought in conscious terms, but she took secret pleasure in the way that Mrs. Gansevoort favored her, Lulu, over her own flesh and blood.

Lulu even suspected that Chloris had probably come on tiptoe to the closed door of her room, and was listening there, as she and Mrs. Gansevoort went about the business of transferring some of Sylvia's clothing to Lulu's closet. When Mrs. Gansevoort asked her offhandedly if she favored certain colors in her dressing, Lulu sensed instantly that Mrs. Gansevoort wanted her to respond in a manner that would not be lost on their listener.

"I like violet very much," she said, speaking up in a voice neary as crisp as that of her friend, and with an ease that amazed her. "And," she added, "I like gray."

Lulu blushed to the roots of her hair, startled by her own forthrightness, as if the voice had leaped from some secret faculty that was attuned to Mrs. Gansevoort alone.

Mrs. Gansevoort had thrown Sylvia's clothing in a heap atop the bed, and thrust individual pieces on hangers into the closet, acting with great brusqueness. When they left the room, Mrs. Gansevoort scooped up Lulu's own coarse skirt and her blouse and flat shoes, the clothes she had arrived in, and carried them underneath her arm in a ball. Lulu felt certain she would never see them again.

About nine o'clock that evening, Mrs. Gansevoort and Lulu had a supper of sardine sandwiches and apple juice, which Mrs. Gansevoort prepared herself, while at the same time she showed Lulu some of her future duties, including a batch of letters that needed copying, and a collection of notes that Lulu was to transcribe onto filing cards. By this time, Julia Gansevoort was referring to Lulu as her companion, and Lulu surmised that her primary task was going to be to love and admire Mrs. Gansevoort; and that knowledge, that theory, set Lulu's heart afloat, for in all her memory no one had singled her out for affection or gratuitous kindness—save, of course, for her mother and grandmother, in their quiet, dusty world of oilclothed tables and French-language newspapers, of Parcheesi and card games, and the incessant gossip about neighbors and relatives—about Armand and Marie, and Maude and Victor, and Louis and Annette and Ti Pierre!

While Mrs. Gansevoort excused herself, and tuned her radio to a live performance of the Boston Symphony Orchestra, a door slammed upstairs. Lulu winced at the sight of Mrs. Gansevoort snapping upright, as by reflex, her face clouding over. It was not a look of displeasure, really, but of a cold, rankling hatred; and it moved Lulu to suspect that Mrs. Gansevoort must have suffered some deep torment in her past, something bearing upon Chloris—the fly in the ointment.

"Some people," said Mrs. Gansevoort, with a pained smile, "prefer strident noises to genuine music, I am sorry to say."

Lulu had not realized that the girl upstairs was slamming her door upon the swelling tones of Borodin's Second Symphony. Lulu, who had no special liking for music, other than for such popular recordings as were played over the Tel-o-wire system at the F. W. Woolworth store, had nevertheless begun by now to associate the sound of violins in concert with the look and ways of Mrs. Gansevoort, her elegant movements and rather exalted mannerisms. Without reflecting an instant on Chloris, Lulu asked Mrs. Gansevoort somewhat shyly if she might not tune the radio a little louder. When Mrs. Gansevoort expressed her own hearty approval by turning back to the radio with a dramatic flourish, and turned the volume up sharply, the music flooding into the room seemed to rush inside Lulu, and lift her up. It was exhilarating.

Minutes later, Mrs. Gansevoort spread a newspaper on the floor, seated Lulu before her on a straight-backed chair, lay a towel over her shoulders, and cut her hair with scissors. Lulu sat motionless as a doll, except when Mrs. Gansevoort applied a gentle coercive pressure with her fingertips to Lulu's head. Mrs. Gansevoort had said that Lulu's hair, long and "unnoteworthy," was a hindrance to her looks and profile, and Lulu had readily agreed. She recalled, also, the framed photo of Sylvia upstairs, with her wavy black hair cut fashionably about her ears, and experienced something like a genuine repugnance for her own hair. Nevertheless, the sound of the shears, and the occasional touch of Mrs. Gansevoort's fingers on her skull, and the sight, too, of the actual long clumps of her severed hair, left Lulu with a mixture of emotions. Mostly, however, she was affected by Mrs. Gansevoort's touching solicitude, and by the affectionate running commentary she kept up, while she worked the scissors and comb.

When Mrs. Gansevoort finished and stooped to roll up inside the gathered newspaper the impressive mass of shorn hair, Lulu did not turn to look at it. But she wished the task had taken even longer; it was so pleasant sitting like that, a child being fussed over by expert hands.

At bedtime, Lulu quietly slid the lock into place on her door before undressing, then extinguished the light, as she knew that the four tall windows, especially the two overlooking the garden, would illuminate the room in a pleasant manner. Mrs. Gansevoort, forgetting nothing, had left a white sleeping gown on the bed. Lulu held it up to her face, sensing a pale fragrance in its folds, and examined with her fingers the fine eyelet detailing of its neckline and hem. Turning, she regarded herself in the mirror. In the half-light, the figure in the glass, Lulu noticed, was possessed of a lovely neck, quite long and delicate, above which her cut hair stood out like a dark flower, like the head of an inverted tulip.

Mr. Rafferty came on the following day, but by the time he arrived Lulu felt she had been living in the house for a week. She was awake at dawn, and went about barefoot exploring every corner and detail of her room. She raised the sashes of all four windows, pausing to gaze down into the garden, where horizontal shafts of morning light trickled through a mass of wet, glittery leaves. The dewy grass below shone darkly amid flower beds and a geometric maze of shrubberies. A cinder path wound its way like a sleeping serpent among the bushes and low trees, incorporating in its aimless sprawl such luminous features as the white glider swing, a trio of sculpted stone figures by the back wall, and a white latticework gazebo, the decorative finial of which peeped forth above the dark mass of a small red maple. Often, on rising in the morning, Lulu was assailed with feelings of extreme mortality, the fragility of her person and of the timid, worried spirit within, but the garden below, silent and orderly, was so soothing to regard.

The house itself was silent. Looking about, Lulu favored a delicate upholstered chair that stood by the door, and sat herself down noiselessly. For several minutes she studied the room. She liked best of all the wide and complex cornice that ran all around the ceiling, and the way its powerful styling was re-iterated exactly in the great white mantel above the fireplace, and repeated again in miniature in the decorative chair rail above the paneling that connected all the principal features of the room, its windows, doors, and fireplace.

The andirons standing side by side in the mouth of the fireplace took the form of two black cast-iron creatures, a pair of grinning sentinels squatting shoulder to shoulder. Lulu stud-ied their faces; bulbous black cheeks shone beneath deep-set eyes and a mass of iron curls, their lips raised to reveal oversized teeth and black metallic tongues. The curious thrust of their heads put Lulu in mind of dogs eager to be fondled. She con-cluded in passing that she liked the two of them perhaps three times as much as she would have liked just one, and yet liked the two of them considerably more than had there been three. They were perfect as a pair.

While dressing, Lulu suppressed the usual recriminatory emotions that attacked her in the morning, the acute sense of having suffered a wrong, a feeling of hidden outrage that carried her forth each morning across the divide from the name-less fears that beset her at waking into the business of the day. Today she felt no anger or bitterness.

Lulu put on her stockings and underclothes, and the same dress and shoes she had worn yesterday. The soles of her feet burned, but she fairly relished the pain, just as she relished the picture of herself now in the looking glass. She stood motionless beside the chair, regarding herself sidelong in the glass. She wavered a little on her heels, and set her fingers to the chair. She was examining the line of her throat and the revolutionary shape of her head, as a cool draft of air from the open windows

moved the hem of her dress. She was someone else altogether;
like an apparition.

•

When Mrs. Gansevoort came downstairs, Lulu was sitting primly
in her slim black dress and black shoes, at the worktable in the
parlor, and had already completed eight or nine file cards. In
her round, legible hand, using violet ink, she was writing dates
and facts about someone named Zita, who was apparently an
empress who had ruled in Vienna only a few years ago. That
fact surprised Lulu, who thought that empresses existed only in
ancient times. What was more unusual, this empress appeared
to have lived in New England, having fled Europe in 1940; she
lived in the little town of Royalston, Massachusetts, and was
apparently an acquaintance, to some degree, of Mrs. Gansevoort. One of Mrs. Gansevoort's notes referred to the Empress
Zita as "the last regent of the Austro-Hungarian Empire." Lulu
was both perplexed and fascinated by her work; she hoped
that Mrs. Gansevoort had a great deal more such notes, papers,
and green-penciled texts to be copied.

Over breakfast, Mrs. Gansevoort expounded on her literary
undertaking, and in doing so naturally divulged some additional information about the Empress Zita. Up in Royalston the
empress had presided one autumn night over a reception given
in her honor in a house called the Bastille.

"There was much harmless fun made, I remember, over the
inappropriate name of that house. For the original Bastille,"
Mrs. Gansevoort explained to Lulu, "was an infamous prison.
But the empress herself said it was probably not so inappropriate, after all, as a person could just as easily be restricted of
their freedom by exile as any other way. Zita saw herself," Mrs.
Gansevoort further explained, "as a prisoner of history."

Lulu noticed how the subject of the empress excited in Mrs.
Gansevoort an energetic spirit, as if she could feel within herself

the powerful, rebellious spirit of the deposed regent stirring.

"Is she still alive?" Lulu asked.

"Indeed, she is very much alive. I have a picture postcard from her that isn't a year old—safe upstairs under lock and key."

Lulu found it hard to imagine that there was any connection between flesh-and-blood humans and the colorful figures written about in books. "Did she ever visit you here?"

"Good heavens, no!" Mrs. Gansevoort laughed. "Empresses do not go calling. They are not like that. Their dignity prohibits it. She was not a local congresswoman, but a ruler over millions. She spoke ten tongues if she spoke one, and was cultured to the nth degree. Pablo Casals played for her one Sunday afternoon on the green at Royalston—everyone in formal dress—and all of us watching for Her Highness to start the applause—like a collection of trained seals!"

Mrs. Gansevoort led Lulu outdoors after breakfast to cut some flowers for her room. Mrs. Fallon, the housekeeper, was just then reporting for work, and Mrs. Gansevoort seized the opportunity to introduce her to Lulu. Lulu noticed at once that Mrs. Gansevoort addressed her housekeeper in a stern manner, as if the royal spirit of the Empress Zita lingered within her. What was more, she introduced Mrs. Fallon to Lulu in a way that Lulu feared might be insulting to the woman. "This is Annie," she said, and then introduced Lulu. "Miss Peloquin."

Lulu colored slightly, sensing that the stout, smiling woman had taken an instant dislike to her. Before dismissing the woman, Mrs. Gansevoort had Lulu take off her high-heeled shoes, which she then thrust at Mrs. Fallon.

"Your stockinged feet will serve you nicely in the garden," Mrs. Gansevoort stated crisply.

Mrs. Fallon was left standing by the back door, holding Lulu's shoes, as Julia Gansevoort strode forth, clicking her scissors, in search of "a few bright blossoms."

Lulu was aware that her introduction to the house would

not be complete until she had surmounted a final barrier, namely Chloris, who was, after all, a Gansevoort. She, Lulu, was not only a complete stranger, but a young woman of no special distinction, either of background or of character. The niece must surely think her an unwelcome intruder. Lulu dreaded their first encounter. While Mrs. Gansevoort snipped flowers along the back wall, handing them around brusquely to Lulu, and maintaining a continuous lively discourse on a number of topics, Lulu stole surreptitious glances at the upstairs windows.

Chloris, she guessed, was still sleeping. As Lulu was going upstairs, however, in her stockinged feet, carrying an armful of flame-colored gladiolas and a crystal vase given her by Mrs. Gansevoort, the niece appeared suddenly at the stairhead. Lulu couldn't avoid her, and was gripped with fright. But in the selfsame moment, Chloris turned on her heel and withdrew hurriedly along the upstairs corridor. When Lulu reached the stairtop, the girl was nowhere to be seen. She had vanished like a wraith.

Lulu paused outside her room, her hand on the silver knob, and looked at the door across the hall. She was certain Chloris was behind the door, probably holding her breath, waiting timorously for the click of Lulu's own door.

For several long moments, Lulu did not move. She wanted to go quickly into her room and conceal herself, but at the same time she was equally tantalized by the thought that Chloris, her secret adversary, would give herself away by making a telltale move or noise. Later, after filling the vase with water and setting the flowers in a colorful spray atop the marble-top table in the heart of her own room, she made a point, upon reentering the hall, of closing the door behind her with a decisive flourish, as if imparting a signal to her neighbor.

When Mrs. Gansevoort entered the parlor, Lulu was sitting at the table, toying with her fountain pen, staring into space.

"Lost in apple dreams?" said Mrs. Gansevoort, in a sweet, singsong voice.

Lulu colored shyly, but an instant later she looked up at Mrs. Gansevoort and the apology in her face gave way to an expression of love. The response was so spontaneous that Mrs. Gansevoort lost her composure instantly. Her face fell.

"What a treasure you are to me," she said softly.

Lulu couldn't take her eyes down, but gazed up at her benefactress as Mrs. Gansevoort came to her and squeezed her shoulder.

At noontime, Mrs. Gansevoort took Lulu up to her room, and dressed her for the afternoon. She made Lulu take off everything but her brassiere and underpants, and spent an hour going back and forth to Sylvia's room, fetching dresses and sashes, tossing things about, while Lulu stood docilely before her, trying on one piece after another, and feeling wonderfully pampered and spoiled, especially in the knowledge that the older woman was enjoying herself so thoroughly. Mrs. Gansevoort looked at her this way and that, stepping back or standing to one side, her eye narrowed critically, as Lulu pulled on dress after dress. At one point, while tugging at Lulu's sash, and then turning her about with gentle, expert hands to face the mirror, Mrs. Gansevoort remarked that Mr. Rafferty might like to take Lulu to the museum that afternoon. "Not the ideal escort for you, I'm sure you'll agree, but adequate in a pinch."

"Will you come?" said Lulu.

"I don't go to such places," said Mrs. Gansevoort, standing back, dissatisfied with Lulu's appearance. "Let's take that one off and try the gray silk again."

"Yes, I liked that one," said Lulu, for she knew that Mrs. Gansevoort favored it so far over the other dresses she had tried, and wanted to please her. To Lulu, all of the dresses were magnificently wrong for her, except during those rare moments when she forgot that the young lady in the mirror was herself.

Lulu undressed again while Mrs. Gansevoort went to find additional shoes and accessories in the room nearby. Except for that one extraordinary, inexplicable incident with Agnes Rohan—

a recollection so appalling that she had relegated it to some twilit corner of her mind—Lulu had not since childhood stood naked, or half dressed, before anyone. Yet she felt comfortable enough here. Mrs. Gansevoort showed a mother's neutral, businesslike manner that diverted attention from her bare flesh. Even when Julia came skimming back into the room and handed Lulu different underclothes to put on, requiring her to undress completely, Lulu did as she was told without hesitation. Mrs. Gansevoort was talking all the while, gathering up discarded dresses from the bed, as Lulu stepped out of her underpants and sent a quick questioning look at the mirror, at the small-boned figure within, her smallish breasts, the dark patch of pubic hair, the elegant throat, and black tulip blossom of her hair.

"I hope Leon is respectful toward you," Mrs. Gansevoort said, thrusting dresses onto padded hangers. "You mustn't let him treat you like a child."

She zipped up the dress from behind, peering over Lulu's shoulder at her reflection. Lulu blushed.

"He's very respectful," she answered, embarrassedly, conscious that Mrs. Gansevoort was alluding once more to her suspicions about Mr. Rafferty's possible interest in her.

While Mr. Rafferty was a figure of mystery to Lulu, she knew better than to think of him as her admirer. She guessed he was somewhat eccentric, like Mr. Thibault, a bachelor who had lived upstairs from Lulu on South Summer Street several years ago, and used to like to dazzle the ladies of Ward Two with his spectacular good looks and expensive clothing, but who never married and had few friends. About Mr. Thibault, however, there was nothing cold or enigmatic. He smiled around the clock. Lulu's own mother was attracted to him, though she tried heroically not to show it.

Mrs. Gansevoort stretched her neck. "He's in the garden now. He arrives like a specter!" She spoke in a jocular, sepulchral voice that startled Lulu from her reflections. Without thinking, Lulu stepped instinctively to the window to see. He was sitting on the same cast-iron bench he had occupied yesterday, and was his usual resplendent self, in a dark blazer with white trousers and shirt, and a spotted tie, sitting with his leg crossed at the knee and arms folded, in an attitude resembling the eternal inanition of a store-window figure.

"Do you like Leon?"

Lulu spun about in amazement. "Mrs. Gansevoort!" she blurted out with sudden feeling, but was even further discomfited by the rather voluptuous expression on Mrs. Gansevoort's lips implying a knowledge of Lulu that exceeded her own self-understanding.

When Lulu emerged into the garden a half-hour later, she was wearing the slate-gray dress that Julia had chosen for her and a pair of matching pumps that her friend had characterized as *peau de soie*. Lulu paused at the verge of the garden path, where the shadow of the house formed a diagonal bar against the sunlit greenery ahead. She could feel Mrs. Gansevoort watching her from within the house. Before her, in the garden, Mr. Rafferty waited politely.

Mr. Rafferty did not get up, as Lulu expected he would, but uncrossed his legs and sat forward with a smile as Lulu negotiated her way carefully over the rough cinders in her delicate shoes. Even when she arrived before him, he continued to gaze at her, if not with admiration, with a playful pretense at appearing captivated by the startling figure she cut. She did not speak, but stood on display before him, feeling the silkiness of her dress moving electrically against her stockings. The lay of her dress troubled her. It seemed to be drawing attention to her belly or abdomen, to the interval between where the fluting in her bodice stopped and the pleats of the skirt began, a smooth flat expanse of gray silk pulling snugly against her stomach.

Lulu hoped that Mr. Rafferty would not insist on taking her that afternoon to Wistariahurst. The thought of going abroad in this little city, dressed as she was, filled her with alarm. Still, if she was holding on to Mr. Rafferty's arm, and could keep her attention focused scrupulously upon him, shutting out everything else, she might manage. Lulu was aware of the old failure within herself, the ancient dread of other people that had overwhelmed her long ago, far back in her earliest schooldays.

In mid-afternoon, Mr. Rafferty closed the gate behind them and he and Lulu made their way casually along the earthen path up Sycamore Street to the museum. Lulu was breathing hard, but strove to conceal it. Sensing her anxiety, Mr. Rafferty offered her a pair of sunglasses to put on, a suggestion that Lulu appreciated the instant the world around her—the street and shade trees and passing pedestrians—turned to a shadowy amber color. At the corner of Cabot Street, a woman approaching on foot, whom Lulu recognized as a regular Woolworth customer, passed them by with little more than a cursory glance. Still, Lulu could not quell the perturbations within herself, the nameless dread that something violent was about to happen to her, a vicious stroke out of the blue.

That day, for the first time, Mr. Rafferty spoke to her about Mrs. Gansevoort's sister, how both Julia and Ignatia had not only been very beautiful in their youth but had contended for the same suitors.

"As it happened," he said, amplifying on his chronicles, "Ignatia proved the wilier, or more spirited, of the two, catching her sister's own sweetheart in her nets—Willis Hull—the one and only—the Don Juan of Narrangansett Bay!—with nothing more to his name than his legendary good looks and a string of polo ponies. Julia had to settle for Jack and his millions. Jack lost it all, while Willis, the playboy of the Atlantic seaboard, managed a decent recovery at the start of the war by turning manufactured goods into scrap, and left Ignatia sitting prettily enough to go headhunting in the ruins of Europe for a coat of arms! Julia has been baby-sitting ever since."

Lulu smiled at Mr. Rafferty's way of putting things, but in truth she was not really following the thrust of his tale. The sunglasses were a godsend. When they arrived at the front steps of the museum, Mr. Rafferty cheered her further by suggesting they prolong their walk. Lulu had half a mind to confess to Mr. Rafferty how painfully exposed she felt, with her hair severely shorn, and dressed up extravagantly in somebody else's clothing, but she suspected he knew. Going down Hampshire Street, she could feel the eyes of people sitting on their porches, the eyes of strangers, following them.

Outside the Sacred Heart Church on Maple Street, a crowd had gathered on the steps. Mr. Rafferty halted. A procession of clergymen was just coming into view along the south wall of the church. Lulu detected the red skullcap of the new bishop gleaming luminously in the June sunlight. He walked among a collection of local priests, the foremost of whom was carrying a smoking thurible that swayed to and fro before him. The bishop was smiling. At one point, he directed his gaze to the rectory nearby, where a dozen nuns had gathered like birds along the porch rail to watch as he entered the church. Lulu had read about the new bishop in the newspaper. The article called him a scholar of repute and recounted something of the three years he had spent at the Vatican.

Lulu stepped forward to see and was grasping a spike of the iron fence as the procession passed directly before them on the cement walkway. The priest leading the way turned up the front steps, while the bishop, moon-faced and smiling, nodded in the direction of the passersby.

Behind the clerics came a half-dozen laymen in business suits, all austere in manner and expression, as if consciously forming an impassive backdrop. Lulu glanced up swiftly at Mr. Rafferty to catch his response to the spectacle. He was smiling, but with a wry smirk on his lips that might have puzzled Lulu if her attention had not been drawn away immediately; for her eyes flew suddenly from the face of her friend to the figure of the young man bringing up the rear of the procession.

He was carrying a tall cross in both hands. Over his dark

suit he wore a lacy white stole that was boyishly small on him. He was immediately familiar to Lulu, but like a face flashed on a motion-picture screen, he was at once recognizable and yet strange. Tallish, he looked out over the heads of the others. He was very fair. Lulu knew him from somewhere, but could not place him. Then she remembered.

He was the youth in the Sunday newspaper, the boy in the color photo. He was gazing straight at her now, as he had seemingly looked out at her through the lens of the photographer's camera on that unknown day, his catcher's mask cocked atop his head to reveal his incomparable face.

Mr. Rafferty, whistling softly to himself, made as if to detach himself from the scene before him, as the priests and laymen marched solemnly up the stone stairs of the church. He noticed that Lulu had removed her sunglasses and appeared transfixed. As the youth came by, he was still staring at her, with an astonishment equal to her own, as though she, Lulu, were both as strange and familiar to him as he was to her. At the steps of the church, the young man looked back; Lulu was still clutching the iron fence in her gloved hand.

With several onlookers closing in behind him then, the youth passed in through the church doors and vanished into the darkness. Lulu had not moved. In her mind's eye, she saw the letters of his name spelled out in white against the green grass of the ball field. He was the one they called Soldier.

Mr. Rafferty said that shyness was something splendid to be mastered. At the museum, he encouraged Lulu to go inside by herself, to go upstairs, to visit the Winslow Homer collection, to go from room to room, alone. "Make a debut of it," he said. "You look like a million dollars."

Unable to disappoint him, Lulu arose from the bench outdoors and made her way to the entrance. She stepped carefully across the marble floor of the big lobby, turning her head to avoid the curious stare of the gray-haired woman behind the desk. Upstairs, Lulu removed her sunglasses, then sat herself down on a green leather seat by the wall, and took a moment's pleasure in her solitude.

She was sitting this way, conscious of her posture and of the gentle drumming of her heart, when, through the ornate brass stiles near the stairhead, she saw Mr. Rafferty starting up the stairs. Lulu smiled to herself as she realized that he was not going to look at her. A moment later, Mr. Rafferty strode silently past, paused a few feet away to carefully examine a landscape painting, then walked on. Lulu thought him very clever and entertaining.

A quarter-hour later, after she had collected her nerve, and gone alone into the Winslow Homer Room, she discovered that Mr. Rafferty was no longer in advance of her. Somehow, he had fallen behind. As she crossed the corridor to a second room, she caught sight of him entering the room she had just vacated. His face bore the same abstracted expression as before.

Lulu was charmed. She lingered for a long while in front of an ivory and scrimshaw exhibit of South Seas carvings, aware that Mr. Rafferty would remain behind her, in the Homer Room, for just as long as she chose not to move. Minutes later, when she proceeded into the salon overlooking the garden, she was sure that Mr. Rafferty would saunter across the hall. Instead of waiting this time, however, Lulu crossed the salon at once, halted by the door just long enough to allow Mr. Rafferty to get across the corridor, then stepped forth, glancing behind her, and went quickly down the hall. He was very clever, she knew, and she hoped he would not be fooled for an instant.

She was not disappointed. She had stopped momentarily in front of a massive Victorian breakfront, and was turning sideways on her heel to peer in at the delicate jade figures as Mr. Rafferty stepped out into the corridor behind her. He was truly remarkable! From the corner of her eye, it was apparent to Lulu that he was not looking at her; he had stopped, and was showing an intense interest in a particular picture on the wall. By now, Lulu had forgotten all about her shyness, and was oblivious to everyone about her, except Mr. Rafferty. She felt her heart drumming softly as she kept her eyes detached.

Before going back downstairs, Lulu laid a second trap for her friend by leading him into an anteroom, a very small chamber with nothing on exhibit but a pair of onyx vases standing atop a sham mantelpiece. Lulu made up her mind to lead Mr. Rafferty into the little room, and then trap him in there by not

leaving the room next door. Something inside her told her that
Mr. Rafferty would stay there, in that cramped, featureless space,
even if she was to sit down in the room next door for an hour.
She sensed strongly that he would not alter the rules of their
secret game by either entering the adjacent room or retreating
into the hall.

As it happened, the room in which Lulu now found herself
was comfortable and spacious, with a series of tall windows to
her right, and three immense Spanish oil paintings on the wall
opposite. Lulu's nerves were tingling as she lowered herself
carefully onto the leather settee, with her back to the anteroom
door, and made a show of looking up at one of the oil portraits.
For the first time in thirty minutes Lulu became conscious again
of her own appearance. The game with Mr. Rafferty had diverted her from her awkward feelings. The soles of her feet
smarted, and her dress rustled softly when she moved. As the
minutes passed, she heard people coming into the room from
the antechamber behind her, and smiled to think of Mr. Rafferty
trying all this time to show a credible interest in the two black
vases.

Lulu sat with her hands folded in her lap, studying every
last facet and detail, every brushstroke, of the framed oil on
the wall before her. She waited until his discomfort would have
to be more than incidental; then, with an overt show of collecting
herself, and a telltale rustle of silk, she arose. Feeling a throb
of pleasure at the idea of their bizarre correspondence, she left
the room.

Lulu did not, however, go out by the main door, but returned
as she had come. She said nothing to Mr. Rafferty—who, as
she knew he would be, was standing before the mantel, as
elegant as ever, inspecting one of the two vases—but slipped
past him at close quarters, without looking at him, or appearing
to recognize him, and strode straight up the carpeted corridor
to the stairhead at the front of the museum.

Janice Monaghan, the curator's niece, was coming up the

stairs just as Lulu was descending, and couldn't keep her eyes off Lulu. For nearly an hour, the young lady and her aunt had talked of nothing but Mr. Rafferty and his remarkable companion. Since Miss Monaghan was going upstairs at this moment precisely for the purpose of stealing a look at Lulu, she blushed with sudden guilt as Lulu came whispering down the steps toward her. Lulu's eyes passed over Miss Monaghan's troubled face, no more conscious of the other's presence than if her face had been a window. The niece had reddened to the roots of her hay-colored hair by the time she gained the stairtop, only to have Mr. Rafferty come past. He was smiling at her with contemptuous humor.

"That," said Mr. Rafferty, later on, as he and Lulu sat outdoors over their cups of coffee, "is a grotesque." He tilted his gaze in the direction of the curator's niece as she went busily across the garden carrying a folded towel in her hand, blushing with embarrassment, as if aware that she was being talked about. "Make no bones about it."

Lulu would have liked to feel a stirring of kindness toward the young woman, who gave off such a driven, beset air, but in truth she could not help taking secret satisfaction in Mr. Rafferty's jest, as it struck Lulu as an indirect but intended compliment to herself.

"Are you going to sit there and tell me," Mr. Rafferty persisted politely, "that you didn't see her ogling you on the stairs?"

"I didn't even see her," Lulu responded. This truthful reply evidently struck Mr. Rafferty as a further effort at humor, for he put his head back and laughed heartily, while sending swift, disdainful looks at the young woman in question.

"I thought she was going to throw herself prostrate at your feet!" he cried, in a voice that carried alarmingly.

This preposterous claim struck Lulu as far-fetched to the point of comic absurdity, and despite her awareness of the obvious discomfort of the young woman nearby, she could not restrain herself; she fought it down for a moment, then suddenly released a peal of ringing laughter. Everyone turned to look as Lulu sat back and put her napkin to her lips. Mr. Rafferty glowed triumphantly. As Miss Monaghan retreated across the lawn, with a painful grimace, Mr. Rafferty completed his cruel, if amusing, attack on the curator's niece with a conclusive announcement to Lulu, intended for all in the garden to hear.

"I believe you have an admirer!" he crowed, gaily.

The thoughtlessness of Mr. Rafferty's repartee, and especially her own inability to except herself from his playful assault on the plain-faced young woman, left Lulu feeling tainted by what had transpired. Nevertheless, it was Mr. Rafferty's insistence on their communicating with one another in this subtle, indecipherable manner that absorbed Lulu's attention. Since they had come outdoors, he had not said one word about their silent correspondence upstairs in the museum. She was sure, too, that he would never mention it. This was becoming part of their friendship, a way of communicating with one another that dispensed with ordinary language.

When Mr. Rafferty escorted Lulu from the museum, she held his arm so she wouldn't slip in her heels on the glossy floor of the marble entrance hall. The two female figures were posed like gargoyles behind the circular desk, staring at her in amazement; they were as remote to Lulu as faces in a painting.

•

Lulu resigned her position at the variety story with a telephone call that Tuesday. After supper, Mrs. Gansevoort gave her money for a taxi, and she rode home to collect some of her effects. She wore a white cotton dress and white sandals and sat in the backseat of the taxi, with her amber-tinted glasses on, not uttering a word to the driver, or even looking out at the streets in passing. She was frightened. She had never felt so naked to the world, or menaced by it; she wished she had waited until dark.

She spent an hour at the kitchen table, explaining in French to her mother and grandmother about her haircut and white dress, and about her post in the Gansevoort house, then heard the horn of the returning taxi driver in the street below. Darkness was falling as she rode in silence up the hill, the tires humming as they crossed the bridges above the Second Level and Third Level canals, amid the incessant drone of nearby machine shops. The window lights glowed on the canals. Lulu was trembling slightly; she wished that life were such that she would not need to go out by herself again for a long time to come.

When she closed Mrs. Gansevoort's front door behind her, the anxiety that had built to a knot in her breast began to dissipate. What was more heartening, Mrs. Gansevoort was actually waiting for her, doubtless having heard the taxi door closing in the street. She approached Lulu through the parlor with a look of animation.

"Was your mother happy for you, Luette?"

"Yes," said Lulu, "I think she was."

Mrs. Gansevoort noted with a smile that Lulu had brought next to nothing with her from home.

"What did she say?" she inquired, politely.

"*Bon chance.*"

"Ah. I should have continued my studies in French that *I* might sometime wish you well with such a felicitous expression. *Bon chance,*" she repeated.

"I don't much like French," Lulu murmured.

"Is that true?"

"Our neighbors all speak French, and I've often wished I couldn't understand it."

Mrs. Gansevoort laughed instantly. "I know what you mean exactly!" she sang out, lifting her eyebrows in a show of shared understanding concerning "neighbors." Putting her arm about Lulu, she walked back with her into the parlor. "Leon," she imparted softly, "arrived earlier and is amusing himself in the library. You might wish to bid him good evening."

Lulu made as if to comply, but Mrs. Gansevoort arrested her with a cautionary glance.

"Perhaps first," she said, "you ought to go upstairs and put on some stockings and other shoes."

"Oh, yes," said Lulu, embarrassed at having forgotten, or not even having realized, what her friend expected of her in the matter of her appearance. She started to leave the room at once, but Mrs. Gansevoort stopped her again. "Always go up the front stairs."

As Lulu mounted the staircase, Mrs. Gansevoort continued along below into the front sitting room, which led to the library. Upstairs, Lulu went quickly about her business. By now, her closet and drawers had filled up with a quantity of dresses and accessories, brought in from the other room, some by Mrs. Gansevoort herself and some by Mrs. Fallon acting on instructions, until by now she had a wealth of choices. When she came downstairs, and paused by the gilt mirror, she was wearing the same summery white dress, but with a violet sash and violet shoes. The sash was a last-minute inspiration. Lulu guessed that Sylvia Gansevoort, Julia's tragic, exquisite daughter, might have freshened her appearance for visitors in just this fashion.

Lulu could hear the distant murmur of Mrs. Gansevoort and her visitor talking together in the library, but their voices fell at the approaching click of her heels in the sitting room. When Lulu entered, they were sitting at either side of the gleaming reading table, with the lamplight shining on their laps, and looking up at her expectantly. She paused in the doorway. She was quite sure they had been talking about her. Lulu's instincts told her that Mrs. Gansevoort had just given Leon her assurances that Lulu had come back to stay. For all her reticence, and the depth of her modesty and fears—a lifetime of hiding among shadows—Lulu couldn't help but feel flattered by their anxious concern. They sat in thrall, motionless and staring.

Mrs. Gansevoort reached up and moved her braceleted hand

laterally in the lamplight, very austerely, indicating that Lulu was to move across the open space athwart the table before them. By now Lulu was quite breathless with a nervousness that was like a thrilling stage fright. Mrs. Gansevoort interrupted with a casual remark.

"Luette looks as pretty as one of those candy gift boxes at holiday time."

Lulu laughed softly and blushed as Mrs. Gansevoort reached and turned up the light in the green-shaded table lamp. Then Mr. Rafferty got to his feet.

"Leon," Mrs. Gansevoort explained to Lulu in facetious tones, "is the last active patron of my library, but has, at least, the good taste to prefer our Morocco-bound books to those of the Ireland Parish circulating library."

"The books are very beautiful," said Lulu.

"He doesn't read them," Mrs. Gansevoort added, "so the covers and tooling alone offset all other considerations."

Here Mr. Rafferty raised to view the green-leather volume he was holding. "I have never borrowed a book from this room that I haven't read from cover to cover. I last read this Cellini book one summer week about fifteen years ago, sitting at this same table, and can recall to this day how the artist's father was said to have thought that the boy, Benvenuto, might become the foremost man in all the world. That extraordinary notion stayed with me all these years, because I felt at that time," said Mr. Rafferty, "that there lived in this house someone who had it in her to become, certainly to my thinking, the foremost woman of her time."

Mr. Rafferty's apparent allusion to Sylvia made no visible impression on Mrs. Gansevoort. "That was when you were young and presumptuous."

"I was not so young," said he.

"You were young enough to go to war with a lustful gleam in your eye."

"That was later," said he, sheepishly, and Lulu noticed once more how Mr. Rafferty adopted a self-effacing manner toward his hostess.

"Next," Mrs. Gansevoort sighed, "I suppose Douglas will be called away to his war."

"For Douglas," said Mr. Rafferty, "a month or two of armed mayhem in the mountains of Korea might just fill the bill."

Mrs. Gansevoort laughed as she got to her feet. "You go on and on," she cried, "like an element permanently out of joint with the rest of nature."

"You disagree?" he said, and raised his eyebrows.

Mrs. Gansevoort gave Lulu a confiding smile. "Douglas," she explained, "is my nephew."

"Yes." Lulu nodded, holding herself erect, conscious of her posture.

"Unlike Sylvia," Mr. Rafferty said to Lulu, "Douglas, you know, is not a Gansevoort-Gansevoort."

"Unlike ourselves, as well," Mrs. Gansevoort replied.

"Having known Sylvia," Mr. Rafferty went on, "I would argue that the concept of hybrid vigor must be the flimsiest scientific notion known to man."

Lulu didn't know what they were talking about, but could surmise nonetheless that Julia Gansevoort's own mother had also been a Gansevoort, and that her sister had been an exception to a tradition of cousins marrying within the family. She recalled, too, Mr. Rafferty's story about Mrs. Gansevoort having originally loved her sister's husband, and wondered if that was not supposed to be a secret held by Mr. Rafferty.

"My point," he insisted, "is that if Douglas were a Gansevoort-Gansevoort, instead of a half-blood, there would be no need for him to cross the Pacific to have his soul hammered to a finer consistency. It would be there."

"Your felicitations," Mrs. Gansevoort shot back, "are about as remote to reality, Leon, as a Hindu mystic explicating the mysteries of the cosmic egg. Talk English, can't you."

Laughing, Mr. Rafferty began to make his way from the room. "Douglas can't complain. At least he is half perfect. He's a man. He's well educated. He *looks* like the American ideal— in his *pinks,* as they say. His officer-training kit. I wish I were coming out of Yale in my *pinks,* with a nice tidy little war going on someplace, in some unremarkable Asiatic country, I'd know what to do."

"I expect you would!" As Mrs. Gansevoort and Lulu saw Mr. Rafferty to the front door, Lulu could barely keep pace with their playful bantering. She felt increasingly comfortable all the same, for they always included her somehow. She was totally absorbed until she heard a soft creak, from somewhere above or behind her, as of a floorboard complaining under the pressure of a foot, and knew that Chloris was upstairs in the darkness, watching the three of them. At that instant Lulu became conscious that Mrs. Gansevoort was holding her affectionately about the shoulders. Instinctively, Lulu allowed her hip to press gently against Mrs. Gansevoort, feeling the warmth of her friend's body radiating pleasantly against her own.

"One day," said Mr. Rafferty, in a playfully prognosticatory tone, "I shall be borrowing a copy of the Empress Zita book."

"It's a wonderful book!" Lulu injected with enthusiasm.

When Lulu and Mrs. Gansevoort turned back toward the parlor, after Mr. Rafferty's departure, Lulu did not glance up the stairs, but kept herself close within her friend's embrace as they strode across the black-and-white-tiled foyer. The tall ebony clock in the foyer was bonging the hour softly as the click of Lulu's heels gave way to the plushness of the Turkish carpet. Mrs. Gansevoort was frowning, and Lulu wondered if she, too, had sensed the presence of the platinum-haired Chloris lurking in the shadows upstairs.

•

It was obvious to Lulu that Chloris was intent upon avoiding her, and while Lulu wished to believe that the young woman was perhaps even more afraid than she of a possible encounter, she could not dispel the nagging suspicion that Chloris regarded her as an inferior. Sometimes, thinking about it, Lulu felt a surge of bitterness, not just toward Mrs. Gansevoort's niece, but toward herself, and her long history of cowardice and suffering among the commonplace realities of life, going about on tiptoes, full of unreasoning dread, a drab fugitive guilty of some unspecified transgression. To this day, she could not even think about Agnes Rohan, her former companion, without a sudden stab of fright in her breast, even though it was she, Lulu, who had been violated in a most horrid manner.

When Lulu encountered Chloris the next afternoon, it was under circumstances that worked happily in Lulu's favor. She was returning a handful of coat hangers from the North Room to the bedroom from which they had been taken. The closet door in the other room was half ajar, and when Lulu came briskly to it and threw it wide open, the niece was standing directly in front of her inside the closet. Both young ladies started at the sight of each other, but Chloris showed more fear than shock.

"It's you," she exclaimed. "Forgive me. I'm not supposed to be here."

Lulu was speechless. Clutching the hangers in both hands, she regarded the girl wide-eyed. She should have spoken, but no word came to mind.

"I was only looking," Chloris whispered. Quickly, she relieved Lulu of the hangers, hung them up, then departed the room without a backward glance.

Lulu closed the closet door and returned thoughtfully to her own room. Later, while sitting at Mrs. Gansevoort's worktable, she made certain to cross paths with Chloris again. As she heard the niece coming indoors from the garden, she put down her pen, and went at a businesslike pace directly out the rear of the parlor. Chloris was coming straight toward her in the back hall. She smiled faintly at Lulu, but looked away at once. Lulu felt almost brazen as she stopped and turned about to watch Chloris retreat into the kitchen. The niece was barefoot on this occasion, and appeared relatively small, even a trifle childish, with her long tail of white-gold hair, her small-boned shoulders, and slender arms.

On their third meeting that same afternoon, Lulu heard her walking above in the upstairs corridor and instantly redirected her own steps toward the front staircase. As before, Chloris was caught out. She was halfway down the flight of stairs as Lulu came through the parlor and swung into view. Lulu's heart was jumping every foot of the way, but she had contrived upon her face an immobile, flat-eyed expression. This time, catching Chloris's eye in passing, Lulu smiled at her, and continued busily up the steps.

In the end, Chloris actually came to Lulu, just as Lulu had guessed in her heart she would. Just before supper Lulu sat in the Gansevoorts' library, where Mrs. Gansevoort had instructed her to rearrange the books into a simple orderly system. With a ruled yellow writing tablet in hand, Lulu was trying to decide the best way to begin. There were nearly two thousand books in the room, running from floor to ceiling in handsome, compact tiers. First, Lulu thought, she would create several categories of books, history, poetry, and such, then tote up roughly the number of books under each head, and present for Mrs. Gansevoort's approval a brief written plan. The books were sadly out of order; that was obvious even to someone like herself, who knew nothing of books or literature, save for a despairing awareness of her own deep limitations. She was standing with her back to the door, jotting notes, when Chloris entered the room softly behind her.

Lulu didn't turn. She was sure it was Chloris, but continued studying the gold-lettered titles of the books while making neat notations on her pad. Then, after a minute or so, she turned to

Chloris with a blank expression, betraying neither pleasure nor disappointment at the sight of the girl standing across the table from her, waiting to be acknowledged. This time Chloris would not speak first.

Lulu moistened her lips, and sought something appropriate to say.

"Are you looking for a book?" she inquired, with a friendly inflection.

"No," Chloris replied. "Aunt Julia said you were working in the library. She thought I might help." Seizing the chance, Chloris was studying Lulu at close range, examining her from head to foot. As Lulu made no immediate reply, Chloris's gaze faltered, and she glanced out the window.

"I don't know what you could do," Lulu said. "I have just begun to organize the library."

"I know."

"Did your aunt send you?"

"Yes," Chloris replied, but Lulu knew at once she was lying. Without reflection, Lulu determined to keep Chloris in the room with her, even if it meant risking a betrayal of her own shameful ignorance of books.

"You could count all the histories," said Lulu. But the words were scarcely out of her mouth when she saw Chloris's face fall, for at the same moment Mrs. Gansevoort could be heard coming toward them through the sitting room.

Chloris blanched and made as if to flee, but Lulu brusquely stopped her. "Don't go."

Chloris froze on the spot, poised in fear, as Mrs. Gansevoort came sweeping in at the door, and flashed Lulu her usual warm smile. Mrs. Gansevoort's lips were actually forming to utter a kindly salutation when she detected Chloris standing to one side, her face paler than the marble bust of Oliver Goldsmith atop the pedestal behind her head. The sudden cold, white aspect of hatred that flew into Mrs. Gansevoort's face was like nothing Lulu had ever seen, a look so gripping of one's inner-most soul that Lulu could not wonder at the girl's dreadful quailing before her.

"And what, may I ask, are you doing in this room?" Mrs. Gansevoort's burning-white expression, had she turned her face and beamed it upon Lulu, would have sent her running from the house. Lulu's knees trembled with excitement as she watched Chloris struggling to respond.

"I just asked Miss Peloquin if I may help with the library."

By the cold manner in which Mrs. Gansevoort continued to stare at her abject niece, Lulu was sure that the older woman knew Chloris was lying. She stared at the girl penetratingly, as though the sheer intensity of her loathing would cause her to break down and recant. By degrees, Mrs. Gansevoort's anger gave way to a look of contempt.

"Is she telling the truth?" she demanded.

This was what Lulu had feared. It was precisely the type of dilemma she had always strived successfully to avoid. She could not dream of lying to Mrs. Gansevoort. Chloris had lied, saying that her aunt had sent her to Lulu; now she had lied again, and this time threatened to incriminate Lulu. This, Lulu realized in a flash, was how Chloris had lost all dignity in Mrs. Gansevoort's eyes, and had been reduced to a soulless alien, a creature beyond pity. Even more appalling was the revelation of the towering heights of Mrs. Gansevoort's moral expectations, not to say her capacity to revile the fallen.

Lulu stood facing the tiered books, with her yellow tablet and fountain pen in hand. The fugitive, desperate light in Chloris's eyes implored Lulu to rescue her.

"She asked if she could help." Lulu infused her words with a gentle air of reason.

But Mrs. Gansevoort had something wicked by the tail, and was evidently one of those people whose ability to smell out human perfidy and to uncover it in its hiding place was as thoroughgoing as everything else about her. She raised her voice meaningfully to Lulu. "Is she, I asked, telling the truth?"

Lulu's sympathy for the niece abandoned her at this point, or was at least replaced by a fear for her own well-being. "Not entirely," she confessed.

"I knew it!" The force of the disgust in Mrs. Gansevoort's voice sent Chloris rushing past her and out of the room.

"I'm sorry I said that," Lulu pleaded, half to herself, in view of the girl's piteous retreat.

"That's only because you're an innocent and naïve of such things as go on in this world," Mrs. Gansevoort muttered absentmindedly, while staring out the door through which her niece had fled. She proceeded on course then across the library, brooding darkly, and left the room.

Still, Chloris came down to dinner that evening for the first time, joining Lulu and Mrs. Gansevoort at the table in the dining room. Mrs. Fallon set a place for her with remarkable speed, and Chloris ate slowly and in silence, not once looking up. Mrs. Gansevoort, oblivious of her presence, entertained Lulu with several anecdotes about her childhood and college days.

Lulu concluded that the woman and her niece had thrashed out their differences, however, for she saw the two of them at dusk perched side by side on the white cast-iron bench in the garden, with Mrs. Gansevoort sitting up regally, her chin and face lifted to the twilight in a composed attitude, while Chloris, turned sideways on the bench, facing her aunt, talked on and on, busily, uninterruptedly—almost as if she were reciting something, a poem or prayer, which her auditor was pleased to listen to again and again.

Only after Lulu had lingered watching them for several long minutes did she realize that she was watching in secrecy from the same upstairs window where Chloris had stood three days ago when Lulu looked up from the garden and saw her face between the curtains. Mrs. Gansevoort had not moved until, finally, she turned her head, almost fondly, to face her niece.

The picture of Chloris sitting like a madonna on the bench beside the cool marmoreal figure of her aunt remained with Lulu as a lovely, unearthly tableau of the Gansevoorts. After that, Chloris came and went about the house with regularity. Sometimes she ate lunch in the kitchen with Mrs. Fallon, but at least once a day she came dutifully to the dining room and took her place with Lulu and Mrs. Gansevoort, sitting opposite Lulu and dining in silence. Mrs. Gansevoort ignored her so thoroughly that Lulu herself sometimes forgot that Chloris was there. Once, when she looked over at Chloris, she experienced an uncanny sensation that Chloris had become very tiny, or that she was very far away.

Once or twice that week, Lulu saw Chloris go out the front door and down the path to the street: she supposed, by the book Chloris carried, that she was going to the public library. At the same time, Mrs. Gansevoort left the house only once: Wednesday afternoon, the day the gardener came. When Mr. Brennan had finished working outdoors, he put his tools away in the garage and then backed out Mrs. Gansevoort's black Chrysler sedan, waiting for her in the street with the motor running. Mrs. Gansevoort told Lulu that she had a two o'clock appointment at the Canoe Club, in case anyone telephoned, and would return by five. Lulu was working in the library, systematizing the books. She dusted each volume carefully, and examined its cover, its toolings and engravings, as if each one were passing into her own possession and she wished to record its look and feel in a filing system in her memory.

For the first time in days, she removed her high-heeled shoes and worked in her stockinged feet. There was not a question in her mind that before too long, before even thirty minutes had elapsed on the big Seth Thomas clock standing by the windows, Mrs. Gansevoort's niece would appear quietly in the doorway. Lulu was not worried. She knew the girl now as someone who had fallen in the house, whose words and actions were tainted by her lies. Lulu supposed that Chloris had been farmed out by her mother as an incorrigible case, and that it was Mrs. Gansevoort's misfortune, because of her finances, to suffer the girl's presence.

Lulu took a break from her duties at about four o'clock. Mrs. Gansevoort had urged her to take a nap during the hottest part of the afternoon. Lulu enjoyed this time immensely, partly because she was a compulsive worker and could only pause properly under such prescribed restraint. Before going upstairs, sensing the soft summery silence of the house, Lulu decided to make a leisurely circuit of the downstairs rooms. She imagined Sylvia going about in this fashion, from room to room. Every detail, Lulu thought, was a treasure to the eye—the dark mahoganys, the crystal, the billowing curtains—each doorway a revelatory delight. Upstairs, however, upon entering her own room, Lulu discovered a spectacular bouquet of flowers in a tall vase standing on her marble-top table, a brilliant display of lilies and gladiolas. Lulu closed the door swiftly behind her, realizing instantly that Chloris had entered her room.

Standing with her back to the door, Lulu could actually feel the slow cold smoldering in her face that Mrs. Gansevoort must have experienced whenever Chloris came near. She stared at the flowers. Until now, while she was still a stranger in the house, Lulu could not have been upset or outraged in this way; but ever since she had gone home, had suffered that long, quiet ride in the taxi, and returned with her few pathetic belongings, this room had become her home. The knowledge that Chloris had secretly entered her private sanctuary was not ameliorated by the colorful gift of the flowers. Lulu was a pathologically private person: she admitted as much to herself. In her more lucid moments, she knew that half her life had been sacrificed to safeguard her secret heart, to appease that unreasonable, mortal dread she suffered of being suddenly revealed to others in a nakedness of spirit that terrified her more than the concept of God's own retribution itself.

On impulse, Lulu darted across her room and threw open

the closet door, half expecting to find Chloris hiding behind it. She was not there. Flushed with anxiety, Lulu opened the antique wardrobe in which she had foolishly hidden the colorful full-page photo of the Sacred Heart baseball player, one of the few items she had brought from home. A hasty search turned up the picture, lying as before at the bottom of a neat pile of angora sweaters, facedown in the drawer. Lulu was breathing hard. Crossing the room, she locked her door.

She imagined Chloris stationed at this minute behind her own door across the hall, sitting innocently at her desk, with her mathematics book open, pretending to be studying. Lulu was shaking visibly, but began then to recognize the distortions in her own responses. It was, after all, just a bouquet of flowers. The simple truth, Lulu was forced to consider, was that the flowers were probably put there as an overture, a pathetic effort at apology by the niece for having lied to Lulu. Exhausted, she began to undress.

Before lying down, she raised the windows and parted the curtains, then sat for a moment in her stockings and underclothes on the edge of her bed. Her senses grew quiet. She was staring blankly at the flowers when the inspiration came to her in a flash—to seize the entire bouquet, vase and all, and plant it squarely on the floor in front of Chloris's door—a solution so wonderfully suited to the situation and to the agony of her own maddening passivity that scarcely had the idea struck into the center of her mind than Lulu was up on her feet darting straight to the table.

What happened next, she could not have explained herself. She had gripped the vase with her fingers when something, an object, like a mere petal, dislodged itself in a blur of black and yellow, and struck her a distinct blow on her naked thigh. She actually saw the creature attach itself to her flesh in the very instant that the pain shot like a jolt of electricity straight up to her brain. Lulu screamed out loud, then fell back, thrashing at herself in a flurry of desperate whisking movements.

After her first outcry, Lulu lost her breath completely, but continued to retreat in horror from the table, her hands going to her mouth. The sight of the thick-bodied bumblebee, black and venomous yellow, bristling with hairs, was fixated in her mind. In the immaculate patch of milky flesh between the two vertical strands of her garters, a tiny red puncture mark was darkening ominously, about to erupt. Lulu pressed backward in shock against her closet door, gasping for air.

●

An hour later, Lulu found the empty Ball fruit jar standing on Chloris's desk, and conjectured at once that Chloris had transported to her room both the flowers and the violent insect. The jar stood as a paperweight atop a pile of Chloris's mathematics exercises, and contained a single yellow lead pencil freshly sharpened. The pencil, Lulu mused, was included in order to cast a seed of doubt as to the meaning of the jar. The jar looked out of place. Chloris, it was obvious, had translated her secretive, perverse defiance—toward Lulu, toward Mrs. Gansevoort, toward everyone—onto an altogether different plane.

Minutes earlier, Mrs. Fallon had called up the back stairs to say that Mrs. Gansevoort had telephoned and that she would be home at nine; could Lulu inform Chloris, please, as well. Lulu had gone directly into Chloris's room, not even knocking, thrusting the door in. The blue, glittering fruit jar leapt to her eye as though it and the desk it sat on occupied the space to the exclusion of everything else. Lulu examined the room and its furnishings with repugnance. The room was crowded, as it contained many personal effects: tennis racquets, books, a volleyball, toilet accessories, a black steamer trunk pasted all over with colorful school decals.

Lulu went once, gravely, about the house, reaching the main downstairs hall just in time to see the antennalike filaments of Mrs. Fallon's maroon velvet hat go wavering past the lilacs.

Lulu even wondered if the girl hadn't planned it this way, to assault her while she was alone, to deceive and violate her with a lethal gift from the garden while Mrs. Gansevoort was away. It was possible. Chloris was somewhere in the house, but Lulu would not find her, she was sure, without a thorough search. She was contesting Lulu. She had been nearby all afternoon, had doubtless even heard Lulu's stifled outcry.

Lulu stood before the full-length glass in her room and, pulling up her dress, grimaced at the evil-looking sight of the oval, blue-black bee bite swollen to the size of a plum on the soft flesh just inside her thigh. The infection was ugly, and brought tears to Lulu's eyes. It throbbed sharply with every beat of her heart.

Outdoors, the garden was aglare, the air motionless, the leaves perfectly still. Lulu listened carefully. Her eyes went to the mirror, then to her thigh, and up to the door. Chloris was nearby. Sitting at her dressing table, Lulu dried her face with a tissue. She could see the flame-colored flowers in the looking glass. Suddenly she began to make up her face, darkening her eyelashes and putting on lipstick. She rarely bothered with makeup, lest it draw attention to her needlessly, but since living with Mrs. Gansevoort, she had begun to emulate her. She never went downstairs now without some powder and lipstick.

Lulu knew what she was up to, but was powerless to desist. As she touched a pale coral tone to her cheekbones, then showed her eyes for a moment to the mascaraed eyes in the mirror, she saw the face within as a pretty approximation of a Gansevoort, a face belonging not to herself but to others, to the two of them, to Julia and Leon. She scrutinized sidelong the black, inverted tulip of her hair, the beautiful dark-shadowed eyes, the coral cheek and lips. That was what she was doing: preparing a face for Chloris, something lovely and unforgiving. Because Chloris was close by. In fact, Lulu imagined that she heard the niece's footstep just then on the front staircase, but she continued what she was doing, touching a green pencil to her eyelids. She hadn't a notion what she would say to Chloris when she overtook her somewhere in the house; but she was set in her course.

Lulu paused a moment on the front stairs to listen. It was late afternoon. The sun entered the front sitting room at a low angle from the library and splashed against a brass flowerpot. With evening approaching, the sound of birds increased, punctuated by the sharp cawing of a jay. Lulu stood stock-still, and presently discerned an alien sound from somewhere below and behind her. That, she guessed, would be Chloris stealing surreptitiously up the back stairs—and she, no doubt, also pausing momentarily to listen. Lulu's thigh throbbed as she resumed descending the stairs, her hand trailing along the hickory banister for extra balance in her precarious shoes, but going down quite noisily, wanting Chloris to hear her.

Crossing through the foyer and sitting room, Lulu entered the library. Her fountain pen lay in the fold of the big ledger. The books stood piled in neat stacks, everything disposed just as before. By now, Chloris was either in the garden or, far more likely, skulking about upstairs, watching and listening. Lulu made her way outdoors and sat down on the iron bench, settling herself just so, though pained by the ugly wound beneath her dress. She had two or three hours until Mrs. Gansevoort returned.

While sitting in the garden, Lulu scrupulously avoided looking up at the house; neither, when she returned to the back door, did she allow her eyes to flick upward to the second-story windows. She was certain beyond a doubt that Chloris was not in the garden, and latched the screen door coming in. Lulu went twice around the ground floor, two complete casual circuits, then, without a sound, situated herself in the middle of Mrs. Gansevoort's parlor on an embroidered chair and watched the late sunlight alter its pattern inch by inch on the wall behind the rose-colored sofa. She remained like that for an interminable time.

Seven o'clock had sounded when Lulu arrived steathily at the top of the back stairway, carrying her shoes in her hand. There was no possible exit now. She had Chloris trapped upstairs, as certain as the coming of darkness itself. Lulu had a peculiar sensation that she had somehow taken over in a profound personal sense the downstairs of the house, as if Chloris's forced withdrawal had ceded to Lulu everything below, the rooms, the furnishings, all of it, just as her methodical room-by-room search up here would arrogate to her, as well, this entire portion of the house. Chloris, by retreating, was yielding up, foot by foot, door by door, her rights to the house, her position, her claim by birth, as well as her right to resist, and, more importantly, the remains of her courage, her moral dignity.

Lulu did not pause to rap on Chloris's door, but entered her room casually and left the door wide behind her so as to keep the hallway constantly in view. Not hurrying, Lulu looked in the closet, under the bed, and both inside and behind the armoire.

She had forgotten she was carrying her shoes, and put them on again in the hall. The Palladian window at the head of the upstairs corridor had turned dusky with twilight. The old trees standing in a row out by the road shone with gold fingers of light in their uppermost leaves. Lulu strolled slowly, with a brazen casualness, the length of the corridor to the stairtop, and then back again, just to signal Chloris by the confident rattle of her heels a sense of her own self-assured state of mind. She had Chloris cornered, and was not eager to dissipate the suspense, either in her own heart or that of her quarry.

Returning briefly to Chloris's room, Lulu pulled open the drawers of the girl's desk, disturbed the contents within, then left the drawers ajar; before leaving, she threw wide the doors of the armoire. It was impossible for Chloris to evacuate any one of these rooms and make it without detection to the front staircase.

In each room, Lulu left the door wide open. She was in Sylvia's room when the telltale sound, a click like the dropping of a pencil, came to her with the distinctness of a gunshot. Lulu went into the hall instantly, and realized in the same second where the other had gone. She had fled Mrs. Gansevoort's own bedroom in such haste that she had left the door open by several inches, but she had made sure to close behind her the box staircase door that led to the third story, the hot gabled atticlike rooms at the top of the house. Lulu did not follow at once, for she could not be absolutely certain of Chloris's path. The girl might have entered the room opposite. That, she was reasonably sure, was not the case, but she wished to extend her slow, sedulous room-by-room seizure, as it were, of the entire second floor, even though she decided against entering Mrs. Gansevoort's master bedroom and adjoining sitting room. The last room to be searched was the white-paneled guest room that overlooked the front yard. Lulu took her time. She stooped to peer under the bed. The closets were both empty. It was, she noted, a lovely room, although she favored her own North Room, with its garden view and stately windows and woodwork.

When she felt satisfied that Chloris's wait for her upstairs was adequate to her sense of diminished rights, and sensible to the slow, further contraction to come, Lulu opened the staircase door, stepped up, and closed it firmly behind her. The sound of her own footsteps advancing mechanically up the closed stairwell, and echoing then remotely across the entire top story, gave Lulu a feeling of the inevitability of her victory. She savored the sound, neither aimless nor hurried, but as ineluctable as the movements of a clock. The two rooms situated on either side of the stairhead—one called mysteriously the Clerestory, the other nameless—were vacant as two boxes, as Lulu knew they would be. The door ahead opened into what was called the Ballroom, or Music Room, a decorative chamber with steepled ceilings and a low stage set beneath a big bull's-eye window. Chloris would be in there.

Lulu was taking her time. She walked about noisily in each of the first two rooms before returning to the hall, then strode at an even pace to the Music Room door, and paused before it. She could feel the cool, steady stroke of her heart, and was conscious, on some level of awareness, that Chloris had given in to her, had yielded Lulu her own place in the house, even the privacy of her own cluttered bedroom. Lulu pressed the old-fashioned latch with her thumb, and sent the door swinging open without a sound.

Chloris was directly before her, not twenty feet away, sitting on the edge of the low stage just a step above the floor, with the dusty, circular window shining like a lurid halo behind her. Lulu said not one word, but without turning her back to the young woman, leaned back and pressed the door shut behind her. Chloris looked petrified. She was struggling to smile, her face shining like milk glass, with tiny flickerings advancing in waves into her eyes, only to retreat each time behind a look of fear. The sight of her filled Lulu with sudden loathing. The girl seemed the embodiment of every act of cowardice which she, Lulu, had herself suffered through, going back forever.

A half-dozen steps brought Lulu across the plank floor to Chloris, whose face came up steadily by degrees, so exactly that the lift of her chin appeared to be regulated by Lulu's approaching footsteps. If Lulu believed she was herself a picture of composure, she would have been mistaken. The wound on her thigh was throbbing, and her face was nearly as bloodless as that of her quarry. She was breathing heavily, her lips parted, her fingers flexing nervously, even though there could be no doubt of the meaning in Chloris's widened eyes and upturned face. The niece was awaiting in a stupor of fear the unavoidable climax of the chase.

Lulu stood over her, trembling with anger and frustration, and waited breathlessly until Chloris should finally speak.

The girl's lips moved drily, while her eyes were imploring

Lulu to understand. When she finally spoke, the word *sorry* was lost at once in the dusty air.

Lulu stepped forward and brought the flat of her hand crashing against the girl's face. Chloris's head snapped to one side under the impact of the blow. Lulu shrieked then, and struck her a second blow on the ear.

For several days thereafter, Lulu sank more and more into a listless state of mind, lapsing into the solitude she had cultivated about herself during her long childhood years. One night, too, she awoke in bed, assailed by a sensation that she had not experienced in years, the distinct feeling, while lying in the dark, of being very tiny, frighteningly so, and lost in the corner of an immense room. It was like the experience of an infant incapable of forming a perspective of walls and ceiling.

Each morning, Lulu sequestered herself in Mrs. Gansevoort's library, and worked hard at her usual tasks, but hour by hour, her spirits languished, until, finally, she could do no more. She felt bitter now at having forsaken a world that she had built up so carefully, brick by spiritual brick, all during adolescence, trying pathetically to hide herself from the glare of a difficult public existence. Her fall had begun, she was compelled to admit, with Agnes, with sitting on the leather stool at the pharmacy, and reveling in the way Agnes looked at her.

Now it had come to an end. Lulu was sitting at the table in the library, and was holding her shoes in her hands. She guessed they were Sylvia's shoes, very pretty shoes the color of butternut. She would, it was true, like very much to become Sylvia, or even a plausible surrogate for that tragic figure, and until now had actually endeavored to do so, to renounce everything in herself that was resistant to that romantic challenge. It was Sylvia who had dealt Chloris that resounding slap, but it was Lulu who was startled to life by it. And if Lulu left the house now, she would go forever; she would take the picture of the McNiff boy, and the clothes on her back, and her medal of St. Anthony, and go quietly out the front door.

Lulu revolved the shoes in her hands. She had learned to wear them without awkwardness or pain, and saw in them now not a reflection of Sylvia, but of her own brief adventure here, of Lulu masquerading as Sylvia, of Lulu—literally—filling Sylvia's shoes for a space of some few summer days.

On the point of tears, Lulu put on her shoes and stood up, determined to leave the house. The sight of the elegant books, in their green or blue or red bindings, piled in orderly stacks on the floor and walnut table, with half the wall shelves still empty, filled her with unhappiness. But she had made up her mind. She would like to have gone now to Mrs. Gansevoort and apologized for leaving her, but she was too cowardly. Lulu headed upstairs. She had not truly come face-to-face with Chloris since the day of their encounter, but knew that Chloris was even more shamefaced than she was, for she had continued hiding all this while. Lulu knew what Sylvia would have done. Sylvia would have gone at this point to Chloris's room, and expelled her from the house. That, of course, Lulu could not even contemplate doing. It was her own fate, she realized, to be leaving.

Lulu's room affected her on this day like the room of a tourist on holiday, for as she entered it, she was immediately put in mind of her original impression, of its initial strangeness. It now seemed an alien space containing alien objects. Lulu leaned back against the closed door and covered her mouth with her hands. She couldn't restrain herself any longer, and wept shamelessly. Her unhappiness seemed to have condensed in her lungs and throat into a physical congestion. She struggled not to cry aloud, but moved along the wall, clutching her face. Stopping in the corner, she leaned her head against the cool plaster. The flesh of her arms and legs was cold. No one, she felt, had ever been so unhappy, or suffered so wrongly or needlessly, or from such a mystery of causes.

Mrs. Gansevoort must have known that Lulu was in crisis, but did not come to her door either that afternoon or evening. Lulu stayed in her room through supper, and watched throughout the evening as the daylight leaked out of the room, retreating to a pale glow in the treetops, then fading into night. Once Lulu had reached the point where she was able to leave, and had resolved to do so, she was able then to postpone her actual departure, if not for a day, certainly for an hour. That knowledge strengthened her. She had now given it all up. She had crossed the invisible line, and with nothing more to lose, felt no longer imperiled.

She lay on her back, half dressed, and dropped at last into deep, dreamless sleep, scarcely moving a limb of her body all night. Even upon waking, she lay perfectly still, eyes open, arms at her side, her senses relaxed. The dark puncture on her naked thigh had both spread and faded, with a lemon-colored hue at the edges of the wound shading imperceptibly into the natural tone of her flesh. Lulu, however, was not looking at it; her gaze moved dreamily along the snowy cornice to the corner of the room, where yesterday, leaning against the wall, she had suffered such unhappiness. Today, however, she would start over again, fortified somewhat by the knowledge that this, too, she had given away, all of it, this house and its promise, and had survived.

Her eye was attached to the fine pencil of morning sunlight just then trembling into existence high above the mantel. The crisis had passed like a fever in the night. Lulu wished neither to move nor to interrupt the placid surface of her thoughts. She felt rested and renewed, and convinced once more that God reclaimed His own, coming back, magical and instantaneous, like the light on the wall.

At breakfast, Mrs. Gansevoort must have divined something of Lulu's rejuvenated spirit, for she let fall a rather puzzling remark that caused Lulu to believe she was not only aware of the terms of Lulu's recent troubles, but of the critical need to resolve them. "Life is a contest," she sighed philosophically. "That and nothing more. It challenges all our idealisms, our pretty precepts, even faith itself. I have found it to be that way. Even the redeemed, on looking back, see a pathway littered with the fallen bodies of the gratuitous ones, the well-wishers and evildoers. The rain falls on the just and the unjust."

Lulu listened keenly, trying to comprehend what the woman was saying. Mrs. Gansevoort's eyes, focused on space, shone with a remarkable contempt, and then came round to Lulu. "It is not wise to be generous in victory until the vanquished have made offerings. An adversary in hiding can only grow bolder."

It saddened Lulu to realize that Mrs. Gansevoort still expected her to establish herself in the house by force of will. That should not have been necessary. But the empty chair at the breakfast table was eloquent testimony to an unacceptable disharmony here.

"You can appreciate my desire not to interfere," Mrs. Gansevoort said.

"Yes," Lulu murmured.

"Years ago," Mrs. Gansevoort continued, lapsing into a resigned tone, "a certain lady in this world challenged my happiness. I was to have been married in June of that year, but at Easter time, or shortly after, the challenge materialized. Someone in my own house," she said, in what Lulu took to be an allusion to her sister, Ignatia, "commited a deception so swift and nefarious, contrived to make me the unhappiest girl in

America, that when I discovered what had happened, I realized that my earlier unwillingness to compound my triumphs over that fractious young woman amounted to nothing more than a sin against my own nature. It was too late by then. He," she said, "was gone—and so was she."

Lulu's sympathies for her friend were stirred, as she descried in Mrs. Gansevoort's words something of the bleak causes of her smoldering hatred of her sister's daughter.

"I would be surprised," remarked Lulu innocently, "if you would ever have had anything to do with that person again."

"I forgave her!" Mrs. Gansevoort laughed hollowly, her eyebrows lifting. "She was flesh and blood. I counted her pathetic. Only in these recent times, while living alone, with Sylvia gone, and these other two reaching maturity, has something of the old outrage at having been swindled by mean spirits returned. Then, too," she added, "children have a way, upon growing up, of portraying inadvertently, all over again, the hopes and frustrations of another time. Extending even," she said, "to the fraudulent side of things." Widening her eyes, Mrs. Gansevoort showed Lulu an almost lustful expression of outrage longing for wrath. That was something Lulu had noticed in both Mrs. Gansevoort and Mr. Rafferty, a deep vein of cold resentment that appeared to animate them before all else, deeper even than their kind feelings toward her.

Lulu spoke up with earnest simplicity. "I know what you want me to do," she confessed.

"Yes," Mrs. Gansevoort replied, with unconcealed irony, her eyes brightening prettily, "and you *will* do it."

Not twenty minutes later, in the instant when Lulu threw open the door of Chloris's bedroom, she knew in a flash that Mrs. Gansevoort was right, that her victory, to be complete, required nothing more than a symbolic seal.

When Lulu pushed in the door, the girl leaped to her feet. The movement was so sudden that Lulu might have wondered if it was not rehearsed. The thought even crossed her mind that

Mrs. Gansevoort might have intended her niece to be here now, as part of a complex game elaborated to test Lulu's fidelity. Chloris backed up in silence to the window. In the sunlight, her face flashed like crystal. A moment later, Chloris muttered something apologetic about having missed breakfast, a lame excuse that put Lulu in mind instantly of her own feeble attempts on a thousand occasions to explain away pathetically her own failings. So that while Lulu's disdain of Chloris differed in kind and degree from Mrs. Gansevoort's loathing, the look in Lulu's eyes was not so different from the look of lustful outrage that she had seen burning out of Mrs. Gansevoort's dilated pupils at the breakfast table. She despised Chloris.

She despised her fears, her maneuverings, her fraudulence, her private-school manners—not to mention her shimmering glasslike beauty, which, for Lulu, had become like the gleaming, disinterred image of all her own defeats. Even now, Lulu was suffering. She was trembling visibly. Heroics were required just to speak.

"Go into the hall," said Lulu, perspiring, "and wait there for me."

Her face as pale as the curtains, Chloris detached herself from her post by the window. She went past Lulu like a ghost, bloodless and breathless, and crossed the threshold. Lulu closed the door between them, leaving herself in the privacy of Chloris's room. Truth was, she hadn't a notion how exactly to make obvious her ascendancy in the house, but sensed instinctively if she could compel the girl to dance attendance outside the door to her own room, while she, Lulu, rummaged through her things, that the lesson would be given dramatic form. Lulu opened and closed Chloris's drawers, handling them noisily, and messing the contents about. She snatched up the Ball fruit jar from Chloris's desk and tossed it into the wastepaper basket. She went then to the armoire and rummaged through Chloris's things, rattling the hangers. In a drawer of the armoire, she found a framed picture of Chloris's family, and was interested to discover the physical resemblance they all shared. Chloris was a child of about eight in the picture. She stood between her two brothers, Douglas and Warren. They looked about twelve and fourteen. Warren was the eldest. He was the one killed with Sylvia in the accident. Lulu squinted at the picture.

The boys were strikingly like their father, blond-haired and clean-limbed, with the same handsome, healthy glow upon their suntanned faces, and identical patented smiles. The mother, Ignatia, was darker, with handsome features and a more placid air, as she sat on the arm of a garden chair, with her bracelet and earrings shining in the sun. Lulu scrutinized at length the face of the father, as he was the target and prize evidently of Ignatia's deception, and then the younger boy. That would be Douglas, the nephew due home soon from Yale. They were all comely, like Chloris, with that rather bright, forthcoming aspect of being born to good fortune.

When Lulu emerged into the hall, Chloris was waiting for her, looking docile. Lulu was carrying the wastebasket with the fruit jar in it. Without a word, she extended the basket to Chloris, as though for emptying, and watched as the girl withdrew hurriedly down the back stairway. Not only was the issue closed, so far as Lulu could guess, but their secret appeared safe. Mrs. Gansevoort had doubtless learned nothing explicit about the assault Lulu had made upon Chloris upstairs in the Music Room. A sense of relief filled Lulu just at the thought of being able to go downstairs and resume her work in the library. The house itself once again looked wonderfully familiar to her. In five minutes' time, she was clattering down the front stairway, returning to work.

Twice that morning, Lulu intercepted Chloris in passing—and even guessed that the girl was purposely putting herself in the way of her victor—and swiftly imposed errands upon her. It was easy. She came to hand like a bird. As a function of their own understandings, Lulu dispatched the niece upon trivial, meaningless trips upstairs, once to fetch Lulu her fountain pen, a second time to adjust a window that was rattling up there. Chloris responded with an alacrity that revealed her own sense of relief. Lulu was so buoyant at heart by then that she wished Mrs. Gansevoort would depart the house again so that she could have Chloris to herself for the afternoon.

Chloris joined the others at lunch that day, and ate in silence. She didn't glance up once at her aunt, but by this time had taken to favoring Lulu with sudden looks of admiration, her eyes coming up in a kind of rapture. Lulu, who was constantly amazed by Mrs. Gansevoort's tendency to express herself with a bluntness that could be both rude and unfeeling toward others, experienced a stab of sympathy even for Chloris, when, at one point, Mrs. Gansevoort suddenly set down her teacup and let out an ear-splitting tinkle of contemptuous laughter. She was openly mocking Chloris's humiliation.

"I hope, Luette," she crowed, her temples turning pink with feeling, "you will listen to me more often in future."

The heartless remark was thrown out with great suddenness, catching both Lulu and Chloris by surprise. Mrs. Gansevoort had turned her face to Chloris, and could scarcely contain her delight in her niece's comeuppance; little ripples of amusement passed over her face like sun waves in water. It made Lulu's heart shake. The spectacle of the two of them was so flagrant that Lulu even conjectured for a second whether the two were not playing at their parts.

In the days to come, Chloris paid conscious obeisance to Lulu, at first in subtle ways, as by always leaving her bedroom door ajar, or by never coming tardily to lunch or supper. Lulu, for her part, was scarcely aware of Chloris's growing idolatry, but by the end of the week, Chloris had ingratiated herself to a remarkable degree. She was helping Lulu finish up her work in the library, spending hours with her, and never once expressed herself in a manner that was not complimentary to Lulu. When Lulu smiled, Chloris smiled. When Lulu appeared very preoccupied in thought, as when making one of her extensive series of entries in the big blue leather-bound ledger, Chloris became like a phantom in the room. She was intent upon making herself agreeable to Lulu, and succeeded, in the first stage, by making herself all but invisible. If a pencil rolled off the table, the flow of Lulu's thoughts went on unperturbedly, as though a deeper set of understandings had already assured the automatic shadowing forth of Chloris from somewhere near at hand, coming round silently behind her to pick it up. Lulu simply did not think of Chloris as other than an agreeable presence. She had ceased to be an alien element in Lulu's surroundings.

The only time Lulu was aware of her power over Chloris, or rather of Chloris's own abnegation of herself, was when the seventeen-year-old came to Lulu when she was dressing for dinner, and showed such enthusiasm for the way Lulu looked that Lulu couldn't forbear parading herself somewhat for the other's benefit. Had a third party been present, Lulu would not have dreamed of showing herself off. In this way, the niece became less a living person than a facet of Lulu's own inner being; a looking-glass personage.

Something transpired one afternoon between Lulu and Chloris which did, however, cause Lulu to question her own behavior. That was the day that Chloris's brother, Douglas, was expected home from Yale. Lulu was in the custom by then of dressing up each day for dinner. Mrs. Gansevoort insisted on that, not, she said, for Lulu's sake, or for the sake of her "education," but simply as a regular feature of her role as Julia's companion. Where duty ended, and fussing began, Lulu could not tell, but she did fuss a great deal each day in order to make herself pleasing to Mrs. Gansevoort.

It was during such a time, at a moment before dinner when Lulu had removed one dress and was readying herself to try a second, and had turned on her heel to the window light, that she realized Chloris was staring at her thigh. Lulu's eyes followed her gaze. There, in the space between her garters, could be made out the last traces of the bee sting, an oval patch of yellowish discolored flesh, at the center of which was the tiny red puncture. It was that, the infection, Lulu thought, that was their true secret! And Lulu wanted Chloris to look at the wound, and waited a very long moment without moving her leg, as Chloris continued to gaze helplessly. Although Lulu could not identify the emotion by name, she was troubled by the surge within herself of an ugly motive. The desire to torment Chloris came and went with the brevity of a passing thought.

•

At dinner, Lulu was more talkative than usual, if only because she had chosen this occasion to explain in detail to Mrs. Gansevoort the new and very orderly arrangement of the books in her library. Lulu described first the major categories into which she had divided up the many hundreds of volumes, and then several subcategories, with each division, of course, alphabetized within itself by author, but with *all* of the books entered alphabetically in the big blue ledger, by titles in the front, and authors at the rear.

Mrs. Gansevoort, while listening, could scarcely eat for all her prideful smiling. The movements of her hands with her knife and fork, and the working of her jaw, attained a robotic quality, as she beamed at Lulu during the duration of her efficient discourse. What especially seemed to please her was the fact that Lulu felt it her duty to make Mrs. Gansevoort a formal report. That was what the woman liked. Mrs, Gansevoort had not once interrupted Lulu while she was carrying out her task, and had not offered her a single suggestion. She seemed almost to have been waiting for just such a punctilious account of her companion's labors on her behalf. She was mesmerized with vanity as Lulu cited categories by name, the rationale behind each subcategory, and the overall disposition in the room itself of the specific divisions. "I'll show you, for example," Lulu said, "how I chose to place the poetry volumes in the prettiest case, which is also most convenient to the window seat and windows."

"My Browning!" Mrs.Gansevoort could not contain herself.

"But the ancient poetry I put by author in the Latin and Greek subcategory."

"You'll show me right now." Mrs. Gansevoort tossed up her napkin, and directed Lulu, even before dessert was served, to lead the way. In the library, Lulu, with characteristic thoroughness and solemn manner, delivered herself of a careful, step-by-step description of the particulars of her system, leading her friend from shelf to shelf. The room was polished everywhere and immaculate. The books gleamed as with a pride of their own at having been marshaled in flawless squads and companies.

Now and again, Mrs. Gansevoort paused elegantly to offer a discreet question, only to elicit Lulu's sober, painstaking reply.

"And these," Mrs. Gansevoort speculated as a matter of form, "would be the modern and Renaissance art books."

Lulu, who found she could not be comfortable calling her mistress by her first name, as Julia Gansevoort had several times encouraged her to do, but knowing the address "Mrs. Gansevoort" was not entirely pleasing to the lady herself, here replied, "Yes, Auntie, I put the art books separate because of their size, but they also fitted in perfectly at the end of the history section. You have a great many histories."

"Oh, indeed," Mrs. Gansevoort confirmed throatily, as though deprecating any response short of astonishment over this point. "Jack, my husband, scoured the back lanes of London for them, and showed quite an accomplished understanding of what was rare and valuable in the field."

A dark rose color had arisen in Mrs. Gansevoort's cheeks. She had not failed to notice that Lulu had called her "Auntie."

"He must have been a brilliant man," Lulu said, looking around at the rich volumes.

"Not altogether," Mrs. Gansevoort responded. "He was much

too dreamy and given to newfangled ideas and inspirations, going off half cocked every time someone broached a new idea or moneymaking proposition. He was, I suppose, a tragic example of the son or grandson who desires more than anything else to measure up to a standard that was beyond his powers to reach. Still, especially as a young man, he spent many an hour sitting outdoors with one of his books—sitting in his white pants, his leg crossed on his knee, an almost pained look of concentration on his face. Warren and Douglas," she said, "were the students that Jack would like to have been—on the male side of things, that is. Because no one was so brilliant as Sylvia. For her, it was a gift, a gift of temperament, something unexampled in all the Gansevoort family, a born brilliance, a steel-trap brain combined with such native good sense that she was just always miles in front of the pack."

"I wish I had known them, Auntie," said Lulu.

"It isn't for us to question what nature disposes." Mrs. Gansevoort raised a pedagogical finger. "But, please—show me what else you have done to put this little room of mine into such exemplary condition."

As Lulu turned about in businesslike fashion and prepared to show Mrs. Gansevoort the big blue index, which lay on display beside a vase of flowers on the reading table, she glanced up to discover Chloris in the doorway. Determined not to allow Chloris to spoil Mrs. Gansevoort's pleasure on this occasion, as her mere presence so often did, Lulu made no bones about their desire for privacy. "Don't come in, precious!" she snapped. "Auntie wants to be alone."

As Chloris vanished like a wraith from the doorway, Lulu, standing with her back to her friend, could not see Julia's reaction, but was sure she had been right to act promptly. The girl was a nuisance. Lulu lifted the cover of the big ledger and prepared to explain how she had entered in her round, neat hand, in light blue ink, the titles and authors on every third line of the page, so as to leave space for the authors and titles of possible future books; but when she glanced up, sensing the other's inattention, she found Mrs. Gansevoort standing rigidly behind her, staring coldly at the empty doorway.

"Someone," Mrs. Gansevoort spoke menacingly, "must make absolutely certain that this kind of brazen interruption is not repeated!" She gave Lulu a look of displeasure that made Lulu's heart shake. Lulu shut the ledger and hurried from the room. There were tears in Lulu's eyes. She was burning up with anger at Chloris, but at the same time was both frightened and disheartened by Mrs. Gansevoort's attitude, which implied that it was her fault, Lulu's fault, for what had happened.

A minute later, Lulu's voice could be heard ringing through the house. Having overtaken Chloris in the back corridor by the door to the garden, she berated the girl in a paroxysm of pent-up frustration. Lulu's voice soared an octave. She lost control of herself for a minute or more, and even threatened to box Chloris's ears for her. When she came back to the library, Lulu's eyes were burning wetly. It would never happen again, she promised Mrs. Gansevoort. "Because if it does," Lulu said, "I will leave."

"You have my own assurances, Luette, that it won't," said Mrs. Gansevoort.

Lulu didn't know what to believe, or, for that matter, whether Mrs. Gansevoort and Chloris didn't possess some critical piece of knowledge denied to her, for she suddenly felt foolish, and was grateful when Mrs. Gansevoort took hold of her and comforted her.

"She's only a child," Mrs. Gansevoort sang softly.

"She's not a child, Auntie." Lulu was shaking her head.

Collecting herself, Lulu prepared for the third time to explain to her mistress the manner and order of entries in the blue ledger. In no time, Mrs. Gansevoort was thoroughly absorbed in the big book, smiling as before, and simpering over Lulu's words, and even occasionally reaching out with her salmon-nailed finger to turn a page. At one point, Lulu excused herself and went briefly to Mrs. Gansevoort's parlor to get some ink, and crossed paths with Mrs. Fallon, who had witnessed Lulu shrieking at Chloris minutes earlier. Lulu noticed how the house-keeper gave her a very wide berth, just as Lulu had often seen her do whenever Mrs. Gansevoort approached.

Douglas did not come home that evening, but telephoned to say that he would be delayed two or three days; he assured his aunt that he would compensate for his tardiness by bringing her a surprise. Mrs. Gansevoort knew immediately what that meant, and instructed Mrs. Fallon to prepare a room for Douglas's guest.

"Last year," she said, "he brought home a lacrosse player, a fellow named Phipps, who claimed that his grandfather, a full-blooded Iroquois from upstate New York, was the greatest living authority on the game. He was a very charming young man, but did not utter one truthful word in all the time he was here."

"That was the year before last," said Mr. Rafferty.

Lulu had been sitting in the garden with Mrs. Gansevoort when Mr. Rafferty arrived. They were sitting under the maple. Occasional flashes of heat lightning crackled in delicate strands across the horizon.

"You are wrong, Leon," said Mrs. Gansevoort.

"Phipps was the lad two years ago," Mr. Rafferty repeated. "Last year was the Gibbon scholar, the fellow with the blue sneakers and the suntan oil, who laughed every time Douglas laughed and looked ever so earnest every time Douglas looked ever so earnest."

Mr. Rafferty set Lulu and Mrs. Gansevoort laughing as here he inclined his head and showed a very earnest expression on his face. Their appreciative reaction inspired Mr. Rafferty to further humor. "He *tolked* like this. *'Doggloss! Dew yew* lahk *Zhwahnvee?'* That's Joinville," Mr. Rafferty explained. " *'Dew yew* lahk *Zhon de Zhwahnvee?'* "

Both women laughed heartily as Mr. Rafferty turned on his heel, clapped a hand to his cheek, and widened his eyes incredibly. " *'Yew mahst* read him!' "

"Aren't you wicked!" Mrs. Gansevoort remarked upon Mr. Rafferty's cruel caricature of Douglas's friend as a figure grotesquely effeminate. "When Leon pillories someone," she explained to Lulu with a smile, "he doesn't leave them a shred of dignity, not so much as a loincloth to escape in. The boy worshiped Douglas."

"Didn't they all," said Mr. Rafferty.

"Douglas," Mrs. Gansevoort continued patiently, "is the sort of high-minded, sensitive type that attracts the artistic. He has compassion for the frailties of others and doesn't give a jot what his detractors make of it."

"Detractors?" Mr. Rafferty made a show of appearing hurt. "Not I! I couldn't agee with you more. Douglas is a Gansevoort down to the ground."

"He is everything a young man would like to be." Mrs. Gansevoort was firm on this point. "A scholar, a wit, a generous nature. What would you have him be?"

"Nothing more nor less than he is!"

Lulu had gleaned several facts by now about the Gansevoort

family situation, first from Mr. Rafferty, and later from questions she put delicately to Chloris. There was a legacy from Mrs. Gansevoort's father, but because of a "falling out" between the father and his two daughters, the old man in his closing years had chosen to name his grandchildren as beneficiaries. As Lulu understood it, the boys, Warren and Douglas, were to have inherited this house, along with a marina in Florida that had long ago fallen into dereliction. The "financial instruments," as Chloris styled it, were left to herself and Sylvia. These were by now absolutely valueless. Lulu was enchanted by the notion of wills and legatees and such, as her only comprehension of such matters derived from what she had learned of them in motion pictures. She did wonder why Mrs. Gansevoort should speak so commendably of her young nephew if in fact he was about to inherit her own house. It was all quite mysterious.

The sky crackled once more with heat lightning; the trees round the perimeter of the garden turned dark blue as the sky lighted up white behind them. An instant later, something flashed upon Lulu that left her feeling chilled. For she could not help thinking—it came to her by inspiration—that if Chloris had been beneficiary of the house, and Douglas the legatee of use- less "financial instruments," Mrs. Gansevoort would be singing praises of her lovely young niece, and that the ghostly face hidden behind the curtains of the upstairs window would be- long to him, to Douglas.

When Lulu glanced around at Mrs. Gansevoort, and at Mr. Rafferty standing close to her, she saw that both had turned their faces toward the west, toward the sky riddled with tiny veins of electricity. Lulu gazed at them in silence, at their hand- some profiles, upon which the far-off lights trembled. The mo- mentary perception of the two of them left her feeling very small and mortal by comparison. She would like to have spoken up, to have said something endearing of herself to them, not, she was aware, to upset the moment, not to have broken the illusion of their power, but rather, on the contrary, to have been able somehow to perpetuate it, from the inside, from a position of favor.

When Mrs. Gansevoort arose at last to go in, Lulu got up silently beside her. Gently, she took hold of Mrs. Gansevoort's arm. They started slowly toward the house, the three of them, and Lulu took Mr. Rafferty's elbow with her free hand. She was sure Chloris was watching them, and would have noticed how she, Lulu, had become like them, distant and austere, striding slowly between them.

When Mr. Rafferty spoke, putting a soft, casual question to Lulu, something inside her told her she was not supposed to reply. It was the way he put the question, not looking at her or calling her by name, or breaking his stride, but addressing his question vacantly to a point in space. He asked if she was afraid of lightning. Keeping her eyes before her, Lulu gave no sign of having heard, just as, after an appropriate interval, when Mrs. Gansevoort in her turn offered an idle remark about the "look of a distant storm," Lulu neither tightened nor relaxed her hold on their two arms, but maintained her delicate rhythmical stride between them. She wanted them to know she understood, not through casual speech, nor through signs or gestures or under-standing looks, but by the fluid movement of her body, the soft crush of cinders underfoot. She could feel their satisfaction.

They turned their footsteps then from the cinder walk to the lawn, and strode past the library windows at the side of the house and on in the dusk toward the front yard. Lulu felt won-derfully empowered by their formal promenade. To the eye of a stranger, they were nothing more unusual than a man and woman, with a young woman in black silks between them, taking some air at twilight, sauntering dreamily across the lawn toward the street. Lulu understood. They would walk with her to the gate, pause there briefly, perhaps to say something idle and enigmatic, then turn back, all three, and promenade up to the house. It was a way of showing Lulu the boundaries of the domain. She was right. They stopped at the gate. Mrs. Gansevoort spoke up quietly, without looking at either of them, to say how it appalled her to think that fifteen years ago she had thought this old house to be little better than worthless.

Mr. Rafferty laughed privately. Lulu turned her face very slowly to look at Mrs. Gansevoort, smiling to portray the deeper understanding that she could only feel. As they started slowly up the front walk, the sky behind them ignited with noiseless flashes.

That evening held a special meaning for Lulu. Later on, when she looked back, she recalled that some of her fears about leaving the house, or about the world in general that lay beyond the boundaries of Mrs. Gansevoort's fence and gardens, became manifest that night. She knew it while standing by the gate. She could not leave. She dreaded the street. On an evening of that week, she was supposed to have gone home to visit her mother, but when the time came, Lulu couldn't gather herself to go. Mrs. Gansevoort was understanding when Lulu begged off, and said she was just as pleased. Lulu could tell by the way Mrs. Gansevoort spoke, and the way she looked at Lulu with the color rising in her temples, that she comprehended Lulu's fears. And then, too, on the night when Chloris was late coming home from her mathematics tutor, and Mrs. Gansevoort threatened to send Lulu out to look for her, Lulu knew that Mrs. Gansevoort was probing her soul. The woman wanted to know.

"We shall wait five more minutes," Mrs. Gansevoort said, and glanced at the clock. She sat down in the parlor, put her glasses on, and made a show of reading a book. From time to time, she paused, took up a red pencil, and underlined a passage to be transposed—all the while Lulu sat at the worktable in a state of anxiety. Lulu was not fooled. While Mrs. Gansevoort did not look up once from her book, Lulu was certain her friend was watching her surreptitiously. It was a cruel test. Lulu's heart was beating agitatedly.

"Auntie!" she blurted out suddenly. "I'm not going to be able to do it! I can't do it! I can't go for her!"

In response, Mrs. Gansevoort's face registered a series of expressions, from wonderment to concern, as she slowly closed the book on her lap. The older woman appeared incredulous.

"What on earth," she demanded, "is the matter?"

Lulu was shaking visibly, and wished her friend would desist.

"You look absolutely ill," Mrs. Gansevoort said.

Lulu's face shone with a wan light as she sat forward at the table, gazing helplessly at her companion. She knew Mrs. Gansevoort was dissembling as she set down her book and came to where Lulu sat.

"How could you suddenly be so distraught? Are you afraid," said Mrs. Gansevoort tenderly, while laying her hand on Lulu's shoulder, "that if you go away, I won't take you back?"

Lulu shook her head.

"Was that why you didn't go home Thursday?"

"No," Lulu conceded truthfully, "it wasn't."

"Because I would always want you back. You are like my own flesh and blood. That is what you want, isn't it?"

Lulu couldn't reply at once. The words *flesh and blood* touched a fearful chord in her, if only because of the intonation of finality with which Mrs. Gansevoort whispered the words. They got mixed up in Lulu's mind with sacred memories, certain holy phrasings, like *flesh of my flesh and blood of my blood*. She couldn't move a muscle or detach her eyes from Mrs. Gansevoort's loving gaze. Her friend's lips moved.

"I may know what it is," she stressed.

"Tell me," Lulu implored softly.

"I think," said Mrs. Gansevoort, "that you have left something behind in your past, something despairing or frightful, and that you're happy to be here, and want to stay."

Lulu was reluctant to reply, lest Mrs. Gansevoort press her to enlarge upon her past.

"It isn't anything specific, Auntie. But here I feel safe and happy, and the longer I'm here, the less I want to leave."

Mrs. Gansevoort couldn't hide the blush of pleasure that followed these words. Lulu knew how vain Mrs. Gansevoort was at heart, and realized here that she wanted Lulu to confess her reliance upon her. Instead, on sudden heartfelt impulse, Lulu reached and kissed Mrs. Gansevoort's chalky cheek. "I love you, Auntie," she said.

Mrs. Gansevoort's eyes sparkled. "Aren't you a treasure to say it!" she exclaimed.

"Please don't make me leave the grounds," Lulu implored, in the same ardent tone. "I don't know why I'm afraid, but I am. If I went into the street alone, I wouldn't know who I was. The thought terrifies me."

Presently, Mrs. Gansevoort brought her dry, fragrant face next to Lulu, and kissed her lightly. "Here," she whispered, with melodrama, "you shall have a safe harbor. That I can promise. I have a secret for you. Chloris will be leaving us for good at the end of summer. She doesn't know. You mustn't tell her."

"I won't," Lulu whispered.

"She would be very distressed." Mrs. Gansevoort's eyes brightened at close range, as at the prospect of her niece's discomfiture. "You and I, as you may know, may not even be living here. It's possible that one day I shall have to remove to Peru Mountain, to live there year-round in my summer house."

"I understand."

"Do you?" Mrs. Gansevoort whispered, with a trace of irony.

Lulu kept her tongue, for she truly did not understand what was taking place.

"I will do whatever you want," Lulu resolved.

"I want you with me. Of course, it may not come to that, to our leaving. Sometimes, I expect it won't."

"Does Douglas want this house?" Lulu continued to whisper, the two of them talking at close range, huddled together like conspirators.

"He would never want to live here, but it does have value."

"I can't believe he would make you leave," said Lulu.

"We will do what fate requires of us when the hour comes."

"Is that, then, why Chloris is leaving?"

Mrs. Gansevoort closed her eyes slowly, and shook her head from side to side. "No," she replied fondly. "I will be sending her away. She doesn't know. She'll be going to Europe, to her mother, or off to school someplace. Anywhere but here. I won't allow her to stay with you and me. You are pleased?"

"Yes," said Lulu, truthfully.

"She dreads leaving me, and each year her demonstrations are more desperate than the last. In April, she just couldn't bear it any longer—being away."

"From you?" Lulu inquired, instinctively.

Mrs. Gansevoort showed no surprise at the sudden thrust of Lulu's question, but she straightened to full height, the lamplight passing diagonally down her face; reaching, she wiped Lulu's perspiring temples with her fingertips.

Lulu couldn't help speaking. "I didn't think she was happy here!"

"Were we born to be happy?" Mrs. Gansevoort replied.

Lulu persisted sagaciously. "I have often hoped that we weren't born to suffer."

Mrs. Gansevoort ignored the remark. "Chloris is a minx!" she said.

Outside of the yawning upward shaft of the lamplight, Mrs. Gansevoort's head appeared to float like a spectral presence. She made no effort to mask her disgust. "Nothing transpires in that pretty head, behind those pretty blue eyes, that is not an exact opposite of what is made obvious on the surface. You are too young and trusting, Luette, to believe in vipers, certainly, but the most treacherous of all are the highborn beauties. I know better than most!"

Lulu nodded. She knew that Mrs. Gansevoort was alluding to her own sister.

Later, alone in her room, Lulu thought about Mrs. Gansevoort's words, what she had said about Lulu having left something frightful behind, and she recognized the truth in those words. She was filled with revulsion at the memory of the girl at the candy counter pacing to and fro with silent tread, of kneeling on cold floors at night, walking in shadows. That was Lulu. That Lulu was dying inside her. Lulu was not unaware, either, of her reprobation, of her lapse from pious ways. Maybe there had been too much piety in the old Lulu. She remembered a wet evening two years earlier, when, sitting by herself in the great shadowy nave of the Precious Blood Church, she heard the soft, approaching footsteps of Father Charpentier coming past in the darkness behind her, his soutane swishing in the dark; he paused, and leaning to her, spoke three words she never forgot. His gray eyes twinkled behind his glasses. "God's favorite parishioner," he whispered, and moved on into the surrounding gloom.

Was she, in fact, an apostate? She knew the meaning of the word. Was her entrance into this house tantamount to a renunciation? Had she exchanged the one house for the other, the great shadowy nave for these pretty staircases and Turkish carpets? That, Lulu felt, was too rudimentary, too simple, to be true. The truth was far scarier, and more recondite. She had given herself to them. She wanted them to love her, whatever the cost, and to love them, the two of them, in return. They, after all, had rescued her, had they not, from a darkness which, however fabled or holy, was terrifying in its nature? Now, not by an action of her own will, she had renounced it all, a great darkness for a gleam of light.

While Lulu was not aware herself of how fully Mrs. Gansevoort had invaded her mind, from minute to minute, and hour to hour, she did recognize how her behavior, her mannerisms and movements and expressions, came increasingly to resemble the ways of her dear friend. Lulu walked now with her head high, as if Mrs. Gansevoort were actually inside her, or walking instructively before her at all hours. She climbed and descended the stairs with dignity, with measured footstep and a proprietary bearing. At the dinner table, Lulu sat as straight in her chair as the proud, henna-haired lady at the head of the table, and dined with the same slow, methodical poise. Her emulation of Mrs. Gansevoort was not a presumption by any means, for Mrs. Gansevoort's expectations in this regard were apparent from the first day. This was the way of the house. Mrs. Gansevoort had made her special, and expected behavior consonant with that dispensation.

Lulu was even conscious of the fact that her speech had improved in recent days and weeks. However infrequently Lulu spoke up, she always spoke clearly, with forethought, employing the most tasteful, intelligent phrasing of which she was capable. Mrs. Gansevoort often used words like *frightful* and *grotesque* and *endearing,* words which, day by day, Lulu acquired and reiterated. Sometimes she was surprised, the moment after speaking, to recall the felicity of her tongue.

A day would come, she believed, when that plain, insipid figure of the past, the silent, colorless schoolgirl, pathetic if pious, would expire altogether inside her, leaving no emotional trace, but just a factual history in her head. That she desired above all else. When that day arrived, she would not be governed by fear, but, like anyone else, by hope. In the past, Lulu felt, her prayers had failed her. She could not deny it. Her supplications had rather lighted the way, each somehow less helpful than the last, like a chain of diminishing lamps, into a nightmare. Lulu was fearful of blaspheming, but recognized the deep metaphysical implications of the path she was now to follow. Somehow, in the depths of herself, during these latter days and weeks, she had exchanged gods.

●

On Friday of that same week a coincidence took place that affected Lulu for a long time afterward. That evening, at twilight, Chloris came to Lulu to report that a young man was standing outdoors by the street. When Lulu went to look, he was gone. It was nearly dark; the iron fence under the trees was just a shadow of itself. While standing beside Lulu at the Palladian window in the upstairs front hall, Chloris described him as best she could, drawing a picture of a tallish, youthful figure, which, in its particulars, fitted roughly Lulu's memory of the young man whom she had encountered in the religious procession outside the Church of the Sacred Heart, the baseball player, the boy they called Soldier. Chloris likened the figure to an apparition: he didn't move, but just stood under the tree by the far end of the fence, looking up at the house.

Had Chloris come to Lulu with this strange account weeks earlier, she would have suspected that the niece had somehow discovered the Sunday supplement photograph of Soldier McNiff in the drawer of her armoire. But by now Chloris was the one person in the world who did not mystify Lulu. In a sense, she now belonged to her, and would not dare be deceptive. Her account of the appearance outdoors of the athletic young man was delivered in the breathless tone of the self-effacing admirer. "He was very fair," she added softly.

Lulu stood in the window, peering out through the dusk at the tree beneath which he had appeared.

"As soon as I saw him, I felt sure he was looking for you," said Chloris. "Do you know him?"

"No," Lulu lied.

The figure of the young man flashed before her eyes, not as she recalled him in the brilliant full-page photo, in his catcher's regalia, but in the moment at the church when suddenly, before entering, he looked back at her swiftly, with an innocent light shining in his eyes. She should have known that he would reappear.

"If I see him again," asked Chloris, confidentially, "shall I come tell you?"

Lulu nodded. She didn't care if Chloris suspected, or knew,

she was lying, for the girl's judgments no longer possessed moral force.

For an hour thereafter, the "apparition" of Soldier McNiff continued to work a spell on Lulu's imagination, so much so that she forgot to go upstairs at nine o'clock to join Mrs. Gansevoort in her upstairs sitting room, as it was by now her custom on certain evenings. Together they listened to a broadcast of the Boston Symphony Orchestra. It was a special hour that Mrs. Gansevoort had suggested to Lulu in the way of an honor conferred, a time when the two of them could sit opposite each other on the magnificent pink sofas in what Auntie called her Oriental Room. Far and away the prettiest room in the house, with its Chinese wallpapers and jade figures and black-lacquered furnishings, the sitting room was the older woman's private sanctuary.

Mrs. Gansevoort was sitting expressionlessly in her Oriental Room when Lulu entered on tiptoes. She didn't look up: she was visibly displeased, Lulu could see it in her face. In all the days of their acquaintance, this was the first time Mrs. Gansevoort had showed her displeasure toward Lulu so openly; and Lulu reproached herself bitterly for it. Earlier in the evening she had made up her mind to devote herself heart and soul to her new friend, however uncertain the implications. She had resolved to do everything in her power to please Auntie. She was going to ask Mrs. Gansevoort for a picture of herself to display in her room; she was going to ask if they might now, after all, despite her fears, go to the summer theater together, as she understood Mrs. Gansevoort and Sylvia used to do in years past; she was going to try to please her in new ways, a hundred ways, by asking her opinion about everything, about her clothing, her hair, her speech. Instead, what had she done but the reverse of all that?

Mrs. Gansevoort sat stonily on the big pink sofa as Lulu seated herself soundlessly, careful not to create the slightest disturbance. Lulu did not think of Mrs. Gansevoort as frightening or awesome, but in truth the sight of her at this moment, sitting in the lamplight, remote and austere, filled the young woman with trepidation.

Lulu couldn't even listen to the concert. Usually she strove to make sense of the music, especially at those moments when Mrs. Gansevoort lifted her face to the ceiling and emitted a soft, rapturous moan over some instrumental high point in the program. At the conclusion of the hour, Lulu expressed her apology at once.

"I'm terribly sorry, Auntie! I haven't any excuse for being late! I lost track of time."

Mrs. Gansevoort had turned her head around fully without appearing to have moved a muscle of her body; she gazed at Lulu unblinkingly. "You needn't explain," she said scoldingly. "Our hour together is not a duty to be performed."

Lulu's heart sank as she realized that Mrs. Gansevoort was speaking to her in the precise tones she used when dealing with the likes of Mrs. Fallon, or even Chloris.

"Tell me what to do," Lulu pleaded. "I'll make it up." She sat forward on the sofa, squeezing her fingers.

"I just told you," Mrs. Gansevoort retorted icily. "Our radio concert is not a duty."

Lulu succumbed to the pressure building inside her. "I am not asking you to understand, Mrs. Gansevoort. I'm asking you to forgive me."

Mrs. Gansevoort, intent upon leaving the room, lingered a moment at the door, her eyes on Lulu, who remained seated in a paralysis of suspense. When Mrs. Gansevoort spoke, a note of compassion was evident in her voice. "Are you telling me," she asked quietly, "that it will not happen again?"

"Never! I swear it."

"Then I believe you." She continued to regard Lulu with a steady look, as if to seal with grave eyes her young friend's solemn avowal.

Heedless of whether her timing was impolitic or not, Lulu

chose this moment to ask Mrs. Gansevoort if she could have a photograph of her for her room. Mrs. Gansevoort laughed sharply, with such spontaneity and obvious pleasure that Lulu wondered if the woman's sterner airs of a moment before had not been fabricated.

"I shall look to it," she said, "but not tonight."

From ten o'clock to midnight, Lulu conjured up a dozen different ways to make up to Mrs. Gansevoort for her lapse; but mostly she was relieved to know that her friend had forgiven her, and that tomorrow all would be well between them, just as always. The incident had served a further purpose, too; it encouraged Lulu to believe that her companionship was worth a great deal to Mrs. Gansevoort, if such a tiny failing on her part could cause such keen disappointment.

One regrettable aspect of the incident was that its cause could be traced to the appearance outdoors of Soldier McNiff. Lulu could not separate the two events in her mind. Somehow, too, she knew that the stranger standing under the trees would have been repellent to Mrs. Gansevoort. Lulu couldn't begin to understand why that should be so, except that Mrs. Gansevoort didn't exhibit a liking for most people. Lulu took the idea a step further in her mind: Mrs. Gansevoort would abhor him. By the following morning, while sitting at Mrs. Gansevoort's cherry writing table, Lulu realized that the connection between herself and the handsome Ireland Parish baseball player, with his affective innocent looks and mysterious nickname, was as tenuous or imaginary as in a child's game of make-believe. He was thoroughly unknown to her, though she perceived him to be somehow antithetical to her life in this house, and therefore menacing to it.

By three o'clock that afternoon, after napping for an hour, Lulu resumed her secretarial duties armed with the conscious conviction that nothing or no one from outside the house or grounds would upset her life there. The gardner, Mr. Brennan, had come by earlier to drive Mrs. Gansevoort downtown to the dentist. Lulu, left to herself for two or three hours, seized on the idea of writing Mrs. Gansevoort a short formal note, on pretty stationery, in which she would express her gratitude openly. The words came easily. In her round, careful penmanship, Lulu described the happiness she had found in this house, which she attributed purely to her dear friend's "loving heart," to her "generosity," her "forgiving nature."

Lulu had just set the lovely blue envelope on the mantel, tilting it against a Bohemian vase, where Auntie could not fail to see it, when a sound, a soft thud, as of a book fallen to the floor, reached her ears from a nearby room. Lulu made straight for the library to investigate, but was brought up short the instant she entered the room. Someone was sitting in the leather chair, with his back to her, the blond crown of his head peeping forth over the leather back. Lulu must have spoken aloud, or gasped, because in the next moment, the young man sprang to his feet. He was as surprised as she. He was not, of course, the stranger that Lulu instinctively feared him to be. He was Douglas, Mrs. Gansevoort's nephew, and appeared now at least as shocked as Lulu, as he took in the sight of the strange young woman gaping at him through the doorway.

"I know who you must be," he said, at last, with a dawning light. "You're Miss Peloquin."

"Are you Douglas?" Lulu asked, still shaken by her fear that the apparitional figure of yesterday evening, who appeared outside the house at sunset, had not only returned but actually entered the house.

"I knew my aunt to be resourceful," Douglas went on, in a smooth, unhurried voice, "but when she told me on the telephone that she had hired herself a companion, in the light of her living alone in this big Victorian ark, I imagined someone quite different. If you can bear my trying to sound gallant."

Smiling with effort, Lulu came into the room nervously. She had seen a photo of Douglas as an adolescent, in the family group she found among Chloris's things, but the fellow standing before her, in white duck pants and linen jacket, looked more like the older brother in the picture, Warren, and was even dressed similarly. Lulu guessed Warren to have been about Douglas's age when he was killed with Sylvia in her car five summers ago. "You are Douglas, then," she confirmed.

"If I'm not," he said, "you'd better call the police. I was surprised to find no one at home."

"Your aunt and sister have gone for the afternoon."

"I was wrong to be surprised, anyhow. You're here." Douglas offered his hand. "How did she ever tempt you to come live with her?"

"She wanted someone to help her."

Douglas came right back: "I understand her reasoning easily enough, especially after seeing you . . . this . . . this paragon of New England propriety!" He waved his hand at Lulu as though she had sprung into existence from the floor. "The embodiment of Beacon Hill! The spirit of Louisburg Square! If I didn't know better, I'd say that Julia hadn't so much hired you as *created* you."

Lulu blushed faintly; she wondered if he was not gently ridiculing her. "I'm not very astonishing," she replied drily.

"You are far more so than you think. You don't know this family. The Gansevoorts prize form. Julia," he exclaimed energetically, "grew out of the pages of a storybook! You're not so different. How does she do it? If you spend a year in this house, you will become so reverential toward everything that is past and unreal, you will think, as she does, that tonight's newspaper was written by Aldous Huxley!" Douglas laughed sharply, but Lulu sensed in his playfulness that he was being gracious in his teasing, erudite way.

"I like her very much," she said.

"How couldn't you?" Douglas was definitive. "She could only have landed you by charming you off your feet. Julia Gansevoort has an arsenal of spiritual tools, all bearing the Gansevoort stamp, most of them very sharp and pointy, with which she could hold half a universe at bay, but there have been—and I am not, as far as I know, one of them—a little handful of mortal souls whom she keeps close to her, and from time to time sprinkles with frankincense and myrrh. My aunt has lived in Ireland Parish since girlhood, and has never, to my knowledge, entered a public building here, or paid anyone a neighborly visit, or even gone walking out in the evening. But she is not a hermit!" he amended, quickly. "Julia is not one of those dusty gothic ladies living among cobwebs in the old romantic novels. She's not like that, at all. I wouldn't even call her a snob," he said, "because to do that, a person would have to disagree with her views. I could probably disagree with those views," he added, "but I don't know what they are."

Discomfited by Douglas's playfully disparaging profile of his aunt, Lulu grew uneasy. But from what he had said so far, she was able to guess that Douglas had no interest in this house whatsoever. It was only after these opening moments that Lulu began now to see him as the person Mr. Rafferty had joked about the evening he irritated Mrs. Gansevoort by questioning the manliness of some of Douglas's college friends. Lulu found Douglas manly, and would not have considered or dreamed otherwise if Mr. Rafferty had not instilled a seed of doubt. He was not manly in the way that Lulu regarded Mr. Rafferty; no one had ever struck Lulu as being so thoroughly masculine as he. Mr. Rafferty exuded masculinity like a powerful scent. Douglas was naturally more youthful and trim.

Douglas continued to tease Lulu. "I shall think of you," he said, with an imaginative air, "as a young lady who came rolling past my aunt's house in a black carriage—about a hundred years ago!—rolling down from some rural, northern outpost. An orphan from Bangor, Maine, on her way to the textile mills!" Looking her up and down from head to foot, Douglas laughed in a genial manner that nonetheless upset Lulu. "I can see you. Dressed all in black, with bonnet and gloves, a cameo brooch, high-top boots, clutching your prayer book in both hands. A

figure of signal misfortune, whom Fate"—he raised a finger—
"saw fit to redeem through the person of my own venerable
aunt."

Lulu had withdrawn her hand. She stood uncomfortably
before him, trying to appear agreeable and amused.

"Am I so old-fashioned?" she said.

"No, I don't think you're old-fashioned. All I said, really,"
Douglas stressed, "was that I feel Aunt Julia must have made
powerful medicine to get you. Is that your handwriting?" He
pointed at the library ledger lying open on the table.

"Yes," said Lulu.

"I knew it wasn't Chloris's. She writes like a Bantu. Besides,
she couldn't achieve anything so orderly as that compilation if
you set a revolver to her head. Your handwriting is clearer than
the printed word."

Lulu smiled. "It's the only thing I can do. I copy."

"We all copy," Douglas philosophized facetiously. "It's all
mimicry, from start to finish, from our days among the building
blocks clear down to the bitter end. What else do you copy?"

"I'm helping Mrs. Gansevoort with her book. About the
Empress Zita," she added.

"Jesus! Don't tell me she's resuscitated that! Oh," Douglas
cried, and put the flat of his hand to his temple, "Julia's mag-
num opus! Julia's days in Royalston among the Hapsburgs on
the run!"

Lulu's face darkened instantly. She took offense. "I'd better
go back to work," she said.

"Don't let me belittle it. We're all entitled to our illusions.
Stranger things have happened. Has Julia begun composition?
Or are we still in reading and research?"

Lulu regarded Douglas with a perplexed, twisted expression. She couldn't keep pace with his rapid-fire locutions, and
felt bad that she was unable to rally to Mrs. Gansevoort's side.
She wanted to. Also, while she didn't want to dislike Douglas,

she saw him at this moment as the son of the man who had betrayed Mrs. Gansevoort. Perhaps he, too, would betray her one day. Lulu strove meanwhile to maintain her cordial, impersonal air. "I don't think," she replied, softly, "that Mrs. Gansevoort would waste her time—or even mine—doing something that was foolish."

Douglas appeared momentarily chastened. Lulu noticed it in his eyes, the way her sober response struck home, suggesting that he was surer of his words than of his meanings. He shrugged amiably. "I hope you're right. I would like to think of the two of you driving out to the Atheneum in Boston on a winter night. Aunt Julia scheduled to read aloud certain select passages from her celebrated autohistory. I can see it. The brahmins and bluestockings of Beacon Hill sitting shoulder to shoulder in hushed assembly as the famous authoress makes her way with dignity past the frowning portraits of Holmes, Longfellow, and Whittier, up to the great podium. With Miss Peloquin trailing loyally behind, all in black, carrying Auntie's —book!"

"I would be very proud," said Lulu.

"How couldn't you be? Auntie's *particeps criminis*. Her personal librarian."

"I am not a librarian."

"You do know I'm teasing. When I don't know what to say, the words pour out. I can speak without thinking for a quarter-hour. But don't worry yourself about me. I won't be here very long. Tomorrow I'm going up to Bennington. In August or September, I go into the army. They want me."

"I hope they don't send you to Korea," Lulu exclaimed. At once, she wished she had said nothing. From what she heard, the war in Korea was not popular among young men. "Maybe it will be finished by then."

"With the Chinese pouring in by the millions? It's just begun." Douglas frowned.

Lulu wanted to leave the room, but was unable to extricate herself. He made her uneasy. She realized she was waiting for him to dismiss her in some way.

"Do you always dress up so?" he asked.

Looking down at her black dress and pumps, Lulu sought a reply. "I dress for Auntie," she said, softly.

Douglas's eyes widened. "She likes you to call her 'Auntie'?"

Lulu reddened at once. "I wasn't thinking." Douglas did not speak up to help Lulu, but waited for her to amplify her response. It was cruel of him, she thought. Her face was burning.

"Usually," she brought out, at last, with effort, "I call her Mrs. Gansevoort."

Douglas continued to scrutinize her with his searching, smiling eyes. This, she supposed, was his way of teaching her a lesson, of making her realize through a moment of torment that it was presumptuous of her, an outsider, to speak of his aunt as if she were hers. Lulu stared back at him.

When he spoke again, he dropped his voice to a playful whisper. "Where did he find you?" he asked. "Where did Leon find you?"

Lulu appeared stunned. Mrs. Gansevoort had told Douglas about Mr. Rafferty bringing her here, that was obvious.

"At a lunch counter," she said, conscious of the pathos of her reply.

"And how did he convince you that this situation was preferable to another?"

Lulu moved her head to and fro. "I don't know."

"*Are* you," Douglas asked, amusedly, "from the wilds of Maine?"

For Lulu, every word had become a torment.

"I'm from South Summer Street" was her breathless reply. This last admission seemed to Lulu a confession not only of her want of mystery, but of the general inconsequence of her life on earth. In the little space of ten minutes, she realized, he had systematically dismantled her puny defenses, ridiculing her dress and appearance, her work, her origins. When Douglas excused himself, and left the room to bring in his luggage, Lulu was still standing beside the leather chair in the library, her hands clasped at her waist, gazing dully into space.

When Lulu explained to Mrs. Gansevoort that she had met and spoken with Douglas, her friend appeared displeased. She was snipping dead leaves from the window plants behind her writing table. She stopped what she was doing, and regarded Lulu with the kind of cool, unblinking gaze that Lulu associated with Father Charpentier, her parish priest; a gaze that riveted one's attention. "Tell me what you spoke about," she said.

The note of suspicion in the woman's voice struck Lulu as a personal accusation, or at least a challenge to her loyalty.

"About me," Lulu confessed in wonderment. "I told him that I worked for you."

Lulu waited then for Mrs. Gansevoort's rejoinder, but her friend continued to examine her with an intensely expectant look. She was compelled to enlarge on her reply.

"He knew my name already. And," Lulu added, searching her mind, "he guessed that I was the person who organized your library. He asked where I came from, too. I told him." Lulu colored at the remembrance of her discomfort during his questioning. Mrs. Gansevoort stood unmoving before her, her eyes more sparkly and protuberant than usual.

Lulu felt constrained to go on. "I told him, also, that I was helping you with the Zita book." Momentarily, Lulu's thoughts failed her. Her mind was a blank. Then something stirred inside her. She was staring directly into Mrs. Gansevoort's loving, distrustful eyes, and felt a kind of swooning sensation, a moment of communion. Lulu dropped her voice conspiratorially, to a mere whisper. "He's going up to Bennington tomorrow," she said. "That's all he said, Auntie."

While Lulu was conscious of the innocuous character of this last statement, she was aware of the alteration of her manner and voice into such as she was accustomed to employ only in the confessional on Saturday evening at the Precious Blood. For the balance of the evening, Lulu felt altogether free of any embarrassment she might have endured from her encounter with Douglas that afternoon, and was vividly aware that the lightness of her conscience was a direct effect of her response to Mrs. Gansevoort's questioning her. All evening long, she felt the same buoyancy of spirit that she had known on Saturday evenings at church after unburdening herself of her doubts and failings. She would try from now on to deal with Douglas in a manner that was respectful both of him and of herself. She would not allow herself to be drawn into interrogations. If she was, she would keep her head, and even seek, in the process, to elicit information from him about himself and about his intentions that she would transmit subtly to her dear friend. It even pleased Lulu secretly to think of herself as devoted to Mrs. Gansevoort in a measure far beyond the normal expectations of a friendship.

Later that evening, Mrs. Gansevoort spoke to Lulu in an intimate manner that suggested she had divined something of the girl's reflections. "So long as you are my companion," she said, "always remember that I shall stand behind you."

Mrs. Gansevoort was replying ostensibly to the note Lulu had written to her earlier, which Lulu had forgotten about momentarily. Mrs. Gansevoort was holding it in her hand. It was growing dark outdoors, and the voices of Douglas and Mr. Rafferty carried faintly into the parlor from the garden.

"At difficult moments, think of me as being with you. Ask yourself," Mrs. Gansevoort continued, quietly, " 'What would Auntie do? What would Auntie say?' We have, remember, our pride, Luette. We are never flustered. We are never cowed."

Lulu blushed at this point, knowing that Mrs. Gansevoort was aware of her earlier awkwardness with Douglas. Not five minutes later, as Lulu was returning some of Mrs. Gansevoort's books to her library, she passed Douglas and Mr. Rafferty in the corridor. She had heard them coming in from outdoors and prepared a blank, businesslike expression beforehand. Her eyes went coolly to Douglas, then on to Mr. Rafferty, who was behind Douglas. They both said hello. Lulu smiled mechanically, without slowing her stride, and went busily on her way. Mr. Rafferty, she noticed, smiled at her in a cryptic fashion; it was as if he had actually winked at her.

When she joined the three of them in the parlor, Mr. Rafferty was chatting with Mrs. Gansevoort.

"We were shooting the breeze. Douglas here was explaining to me how this age of ours is different from all others. Weren't you?"

"No age," Douglas replied confidently, "is different from all others."

Lulu's impression of the nephew, as he stood outside the lamplight, got mixed up briefly in her mind with her recollection of the Sacred Heart athlete. There was a distinct resemblance.

"It seems quite different to me," Mrs. Gansevoort interjected, with a touch of irony that prompted a sudden laugh from Mr. Rafferty.

"But it doesn't have to be very different from another," Douglas added to his earlier view, "to make miserable people happy, or happy folk miserable."

" 'Happy folk'!" cried Mr. Rafferty. "Whatever happened to the 'happy folk'?" He turned to Lulu. "Don't miss this discussion! Douglas is going to compare the men and women of our rubber-gray age to the happy folk of yesteryear. For my money," said Mr. Rafferty, as he turned back to Douglas, "some of us could be made a good deal *happier* if they'd take some of those anguished, bawl-baby European philosophers you're so keen about and string them up."

Douglas was amused. "When murder makes people happy," he tossed off, "the darkness around them is already about complete, wouldn't you say?"

"I am talking," Mr. Rafferty raised his voice theatrically, "about justifiable homicide."

"That's what you were talking about last summer," said Douglas.

Mr. Rafferty laughed sharply. "Four years at Yale gives the mind a rapier point. Have you met Mr. Douglas Hull?"

Lulu looked up. "Yes, I have."

"Did he cut you to pieces?" said Mr. Rafferty.

Lulu smiled.

"On the contrary," said Douglas, "we spent a pleasant hour together. Isn't it so, Miss Peloquin?"

"I beg your pardon?" said Lulu, with studied aplomb.

"Luette doesn't gab," said Mrs. Gansevoort. "She's a hard-working, serious-minded young lady. *'Happy folk'! 'Justifiable homicide'!* First it was Warren and Leon, now it's you two!"

"Warren was quicker than this fellow," said Mr. Rafferty, "but both of them quicker than I. I was never that bookish." Time and again, Mr. Rafferty addressed himself, at least in part, to Lulu, as though to communicate openly his regard for her. Lulu sat at the table making notations on manila folders. "War-

ren could recite Keats from page one. He devoured the stuff.
He was a romantic."

"He was a brilliant boy," said Mrs. Gansevoort.

"I am no romantic," said Douglas.

"*Douglas is no romantic!*" Mr. Rafferty parroted loudly to
Lulu. "Except, that is, in his rather romantic portrayal of 'man
alone among the stars'! Man the poor forsaken beast! Roman-
ticism," said Mr. Rafferty, "is just classicism with its pants off."

"I didn't say man was forsaken."

"I should point out," Mr. Rafferty called to Lulu, "that Douglas has read more books and has a tougher hide than his brother.
Not that Warren was mellow or benign."

"Warren was a sweet precocious boy who was grown up
at ten," said Mrs. Gansevoort.

"You and he were quite friendly at the end," said Douglas.

"Yes, Warren wanted to know all about me," said Mr. Rafferty. "Not in the beginning, but quite steadily once he got
going. He was different from you. Warren believed man per-
fectible, Miss Peloquin, unlike this clearheaded fellow. He had
some arresting ideas. He had me all but convinced—this is
quite fascinating, when you stop to think about it—that man
travels the road of life in both directions, forward and back, at
one and the same time. Warren believed that the path to paradise was—precisely!—the reverse of the path which we take,
as physical specimens through time and space. We are coming,
you see, *from* paradise, as creatures of the flesh voyaging out—
like Cain. See it? With every waking moment, every tick of the
clock, every lost hair and new wrinkle, measuring the outward
journey from the old oneness. Tell me that's not clever!"

"Poetry." Douglas dismissed it with a murmur.

"Warren arrived at this startling point of view, he told me,
when he discovered that little tots, even the youngest of children,
will invariably weep bitter tears when told that they will never
be babies again." Mr. Rafferty was facing Douglas. "Did you
know that? It's quite true. That's the basis for their fondness of

dolls and teddy bears, not because they see them as companions or siblings or future children of their own, but as their own lost faces! He said, too, that whenever he himself contemplated the future *without* conscious deliberation, he always imagined that the future was to be the 'connecting ground' of all the broken ties and fallen lines of his past life. *If* he didn't think too hard on it. And do you know," said Mr. Rafferty, "I, at thirty-eight, find that proposition more compelling every year. If I don't *think* about the future, but just allow the prospect of future times to open out in my mind, *I* see it that way. I see it, or sense or feel it, as the very opposite of what my reasoning powers tell me that it should be."

Lulu was watching Mr. Rafferty intently, captivated by his words, but also by his revival of the memory of Warren, the dead youth who, she now believed, had once loved Sylvia.

"If Warren had lived," said Mrs. Gansevoort in her usual dispassionate voice, "he'd have done for the Gansevoorts what no other of us has done in these later generations: helped to give us back our grand name."

Douglas laughed unpleasantly. "Auntie," he said to her, "isn't that rather a modest ambition for something as earth-rattling as what Leon has just intimated? Besides, selling Leon a bill of goods would not have assured him a place among the messianic few."

"Warren didn't convert me. No," said Mr. Rafferty, "I wouldn't go that far. But I certainly listened to him with understanding and patience. He was very high-strung, you know, very in-tense." Mr. Rafferty did not attempt to conceal the mockery in his voice. "He wanted a sympathetic ear. He was not like your-self." He gave Douglas a cynical look. "Not one of the cool hearts. But what Warren might have lacked in an ice-cold nature he didn't want in courage. He had the courage to be appalled."

"And you appalled him, I suppose," said Douglas.

"More than once," Mr. Rafferty returned lightly, and again showed Lulu a smile that suggested to all that his jocular manner toward Douglas was contrived for Lulu's benefit. He winked at her. "I told the boy a tale or two."

Douglas was staring at Mr. Rafferty. "There were those," he charged, "who thought you must have told him something more than he needed to hear."

"Nothing more than what's what!" Mr. Rafferty crowed.

Douglas had fallen to looking at Mr. Rafferty with great intensity. Abruptly, Mrs. Gansevoort released a sudden peal of laughter. It was like the outburst that she had been unable to withhold at the lunch table the day she mocked Chloris. Not a second later, Mr. Rafferty also gave a gay shout, and the two of them laughed with such an infectious spirit that Lulu joined in at once. She couldn't help herself. It simply burst forth from her; she put her hands flat to her face.

"Nothing more than what's what!" Mrs. Gansevoort cried, and all three laughed anew.

Douglas looked to Lulu in the natural hope that she, the innocent stranger, might supply a clue to their outburst. But the bewildered expression on Douglas's face set Lulu laughing even more, and her two friends chimed in. This time the sudden uproar came from nothing more mysterious than their unspoken understandings. They were like one. She had crossed an invisible boundary. She felt herself bound to them by unseen filaments.

"It was nothing at all to do with you," she told Douglas, and both her friends looked at her with their eyes shining, as if to remove any last doubt in her mind of their triangular correspondence.

"Luette and I are going upstairs," Mrs. Gansevoort announced while rising from her chair. "Your metaphysical interests tire my brain. We prefer music to ontology." She directed a loving if supercilious look at Lulu that prompted the younger woman to get up at once from the table.

"I'll be going on to Bennington tomorrow," said Douglas.

"Will you?" Mrs. Gansevoort exclaimed, in her haughty

manner. "I didn't know." She showed Lulu a bewildered look, and turned back to Douglas.

"I'd like to bring my guest down then," he said, "if it won't inconvenience you. It would only be for a day or two."

"By all means! Promise you won't disappoint me," she replied with peevish auntly affection.

Mrs. Gansevoort led Lulu from the room, but drew her immediately to one side in the big entrance hall. "You will be remaining downstairs for a little while, Luette. Leon," she said, softly, "will want you with him this evening."

Mrs. Gansevoort's incisive manner discouraged Lulu from questioning her, but it was obvious that something meaningful was afoot in the house, something that she and Mr. Rafferty must have discussed already. This was the first time Lulu found herself receiving instructions concerning Mr. Rafferty. It touched off in her a sense of excitement, a tantalizing alarm, the idea of participating with the two of them, for the first time, in something she was not intended to understand.

"When Chloris returns from the movies," Mrs. Gansevoort added, "send her upstairs to me. I do not want her downstairs."

"I understand, Auntie." Lulu found herself whispering. They stood facing one another before the tall, shadowy mirror at the foot of the stairs. Lulu felt as though she were standing in the darkened wing of a theater, waiting for her cue from Mrs. Gansevoort to return on stage; she was staring at her friend in the expectation of further instruction, or at least a hint of what was transpiring. All she could deduce was that Douglas's presence in the house had brought the three of them closer together, as in a web of understanding, and that it would have been inappropriate for her to openly attempt to sound out Mrs. Gansevoort.

Before going upstairs, Mrs. Gansevoort leaned and kissed Lulu softly on the lips. "Be very attentive to Leon, if only," she whispered, "for the benefit of others."

Lulu stood at the foot of the stairs with her fingers to her lips. Mrs. Gansevoort's kiss impressed Lulu not as a good-night kiss, but as a sign that she was about to perform a role for which she had been carefully prepared. Before reentering the parlor, Lulu knew by instinct what was expected of her. Mostly, it was a certain manner. This realization came to her as she strode toward the lighted archway. She paused to collect herself, lifting her head and straightening. Mr. Rafferty, she was sure, expected her to return. But Douglas would be surprised.

The echo of Lulu's heels on the parquet caused Douglas and Mr. Rafferty to turn to her in unison. Mr. Rafferty smiled up at her knowingly. "I thought you might be coming back."

"You see, she prefers ontology to music, after all," Douglas added, politely.

Lulu seated herself opposite Mr. Rafferty in the chair vacated by Mrs. Gansevoort. She addressed Mr. Rafferty when she spoke. "Mrs. Gansevoort wanted to rest," she said without smiling.

As she sat Lulu was conscious of the calm feeling that came over her in Mr. Rafferty's presence. Had she been alone in the room with Douglas, her cool reserve might have fled. Wetting her lips, she continued to look at Mr. Rafferty even when it should have become apparent to Douglas that her attention to Mr. Rafferty was excessive. So long as Leon continued to look at her, she would return his gaze. Lulu was reminded of their afternoon at the museum, when he had somehow, cleverly, encouraged her to trap him in that little anteroom.

Mr. Rafferty's eyes dropped to Lulu's knees and to her ankles; then his gaze came back up to her face. It was intentional. Almost instantly, Douglas moved, changing his stance. He had noticed. Only then, or so it seemed to Lulu, did Mr. Rafferty break the spell, asking her if she preferred Kant to Koussevitsky; he was smiling cannily at her.

"I've come to listen," Lulu replied, and continued to show Mr. Rafferty an alert face.

"That's my only objection about music," Douglas offered, conversationally. "That one can *only* listen."

When Mr. Rafferty finally looked away from her, Lulu turned her head to Douglas, who was watching her carefully. He had seen something private going back and forth between her and Mr. Rafferty. She caught the interrogatory light in his eyes. That was what Mr. Rafferty had wanted. That was why she had been sent back into the parlor. She could only speculate, but wondered if Mr. Rafferty didn't want to irritate to life some frailty in Douglas. He was testing him.

"I wouldn't agree with that point of view." Mr. Rafferty stood up and poured a glass of brandy from a decanter. "Music is not as simple as that. We don't just listen to it."

"We certainly don't learn anything from it," Douglas tossed off.

"I would not agree with that," Mr. Rafferty objected in an airy tone. "You wouldn't deny that we react strongly to it, or that we react in a prolonged systematic way, or, for that matter, that we react in unison—sometimes passionately! Anything like that must have a bearing on our makeup."

Douglas appeared indifferent. He watched as Mr. Rafferty stoppered the crystal decanter and then crossed to where Lulu sat.

"On the other hand," Mr. Rafferty continued, "how much of the great deep iceberg of one's soul is affected by a flimsy philosophical thought? Not much, if you ask me." Without interrupting his own words, Mr. Rafferty leaned and handed Lulu her brandy. His ease of manner impressed her; it was as if he had been tending her thus for a long while. "A new thought rattling around in the top of the mind is like a little noise in the forest."

"Thank you." Lulu smiled appreciatively.

"Take the marching band," said Mr. Rafferty. "Your Plato should have witnessed one of *those* stirring ensembles marching two hundred strong through the marketplace at Athens!"

Douglas laughed. "I'd rather not think about such martial displays."

"Douglas is going to Korea," Mr. Rafferty said to Lulu.

"Is he?" Lulu affected surprise, and regarded Douglas coolly. She remarked the differences between the two men. Douglas was very collegiate and casual, with a handsome, languorous air, while Leon, although lean in appearance, was quite powerful-looking.

"Douglas is going to put an end to that nasty little war. While the rest of us are stuffing ourselves on the good things of life, here or at Julia's summer house at Peru Mountain, Douglas is going to be slinging lead at one of Mao's fabled route armies!" Mr. Rafferty laughed and looked at Douglas with disbelief.

"When is Julia going up to Peru Mountain?" Douglas turned to Lulu.

"In a few days."

"You haven't been there before, of course?"

"*I* have," Mr. Rafferty interposed. "I haven't missed too many summers up there. I shall take you walking among the cedars, Miss Peloquin, up among the owls and thrushes and other such twittering little creatures as the gods have disposed about the place." He laughed. "It's quite picturesque. Quite a bucolic retreat."

"There was a time," Douglas explained for Lulu's benefit, "when the town of Peru Mountain was all but a private preserve of the Gansevoorts. Fifty years ago, they all summered up there. Both branches of the family. They owned all eight houses on the town common. They built the church and town hall. They built the little library. It was their country seat."

Douglas wanted her to respond. He was trying to make a connection. Lulu, however, glanced away to Mr. Rafferty, as she was certain she was supposed to do. At this moment Douglas was more alien to her and to Mr. Rafferty, it seemed, and to their unspoken understandings, than Aunt Julia was upstairs. When she listened carefully, Lulu could make out the soft strains of the music overhead, and even recognized the specific musical selection. It was one of Mrs. Gansevoort's favorites, something from Beethoven's Sixth Symphony. She was playing it intentionally!—because Lulu had once said she liked it very much. Mrs. Gansevoort called it an opus. Lulu couldn't remember the number. Mr. Rafferty had just lighted a cigarette, and was staring at her again, gazing down at Lulu's abdomen, as though lost in thought: looking but not seeing. It was an intentional ploy, she felt.

Lulu stood up and crossed between the two of them. She took a porcelain ashtray from one table and set it down on the table next to Mr. Rafferty. She stood before him, lingeringly. She didn't know why. She had effectively displaced Douglas to one side, reducing the triangle of their conversation momentarily to this short, direct line between Mr. Rafferty and herself.

"I'll show you the shooting lodge." Mr. Rafferty continued to banter with Lulu in a smiling, almost provocative manner. He looked down at her waist, then up again.

Lulu couldn't detach herself. The artifice of their words was evident. "Is that a cabin?"

"You might call it that. It looks like a log house, but it's not very rustic." Mr. Rafferty sat back comfortably. "It's set back in the woods a little way. You can't see it very clearly from the house, but you can see the house from it."

"Not in summertime," Douglas put in.

Mr. Rafferty was not deflected. Lulu felt his eyes pass over her breasts. "When Sylvia was twelve, she made up her mind to spend an entire night alone in the lodge. She could be very determined. She insisted on testing her courage like that."

"I wouldn't sleep there alone," said Lulu.

"Who could blame you?" Mr. Rafferty cried. "Warren wouldn't sleep there alone when he was sixteen!"

Douglas laughed. "You didn't even know him when he was sixteen."

"I had no desire to know him when he was sixteen!'" snapped Mr. Rafferty.

"Did you know," Douglas asked Lulu in a facetious tone of voice, "that Leon was under interdiction in this house for about ten years?"

Mr. Rafferty corrected him. "Eight years."

"Leon was *persona non grata* under this roof till Jack died."

Mr. Rafferty smirked and looked at Lulu. "Douglas has just given voice to the unutterable. Tell Luette what you're talking about."

"Who other than yourself knows what I'm talking about?" Douglas's attitude was visibly nonchalant.

"There was a war going on, you know!" Mr. Rafferty retorted with sarcasm.

"Yes, but it didn't begin eight years before it ended," Douglas came back with a smile. "Jack took his secret to the grave. The last time I saw Leon in this house *before* the fabled expulsion, I was in knickers. I remember that day. Warren and I were playing croquet. The house," Douglas said languidly, "exploded with noise. Shouting! That was Jack. I think I had never heard a man shout like that before. Then the front door opened, Leon came out—smiling!—and strolled down the front walk like Lucifer in white linens."

Mr. Rafferty laughed with spontaneous humor. "Was I wearing white?" Reaching, he took hold of Lulu's hand, saying to her, "I always favored clash and tumult to the natural order of things."

"I'm not saying you didn't enjoy it," said Douglas.

"And I am not saying I did," said Mr. Rafferty.

The light pressure he exerted on Lulu's fingers told her to detach her hand from his and return to her chair. She was following their banter with interest, however. It was fascinating to discover that Mr. Rafferty had been banished from Leiden Hall for many years.

"When Warren was sixteen—was my point—you were in Europe."

"I had to be someplace, didn't I? I couldn't be here. For me, the war was just a pleasant interlude, a killing spree, nothing more and nothing less."

Douglas and Lulu laughed over Mr. Rafferty's lighthearted manner. Lulu recalled how Mr. Ranger, at the five-and-ten, also used to laugh when he described the horrors he had witnessed in the invasion of France, of nearby landing barges packed full of men disappearing forever beneath the heaving tides, amid the smoke and unearthly roar, and of his own youthful terror.

"Warren had no secrets from me." Mr. Rafferty here directed himself to Douglas.

"I would say my brother had a lot of secrets."

"I wouldn't," snapped Mr. Rafferty.

"He was like that." Douglas looked at Lulu. "He kept things to himself."

"Not from me, he didn't." Mr. Rafferty was clearly enjoying himself.

"He wasn't so fond of you," Douglas brought back.

"He wasn't fond of me one bit," Mr. Rafferty agreed. " 'Gentlemen songsters' never are." He winked at Lulu. "I don't permit them to be," he said, and widened his eyes. "I don't permit them to make free with my good nature."

Lulu liked it when Mr. Rafferty looked at her legs. She knew it was a game. Still, she felt herself growing sensitive all over, a subtle prickly sensation from head to toe, as when one has a sunburn and would like to be touched everywhere at once by something cool and delicate.

"Was Warren in the war?" Lulu asked Mr. Rafferty. She had wanted to mention Warren by name.

"*Warren?*" Mr. Rafferty cried.

"He could have been," said Douglas, "but the war ended."

Mr. Rafferty looked away in disbelief. *"He was not fit!"*

"Did he tell you that?"

"He went half insane crawling on his back under the wire in gas training. He was claustrophobic." Mr. Rafferty spat the words with contempt. "He was screaming into his mask!"

Lulu saw that the bantering between Douglas and Mr. Rafferty had quickly turned acrimonious. "Did he tell you that?" Douglas repeated angrily.

Mr. Rafferty looked him up and down. "He had no secrets from me! That was why he wasn't so *fond* of me, as you put it, because I was his confessor. He wanted to get it off his chest. He was riddled with guilt. He wanted to unburden himself."

Mr. Rafferty looked at Lulu with a triumphant gleam in his eye.

"That doesn't sound like Warren," Douglas faltered.

"Doesn't it?" said Mr. Rafferty, significantly.

"No, it doesn't."

"He confessed to me!" Mr. Rafferty fixed Douglas with a look. "It did him good. He looked up to me. He appreciated my views. . . . I showed him my ribbons and medals!" Mr. Rafferty was enjoying himself. "I showed him my souvenirs." Here, to the surprise of Lulu and Douglas, Mr. Rafferty suddenly pulled up the sleeve of his blue-cord jacket, and exhibited his left forearm, revealing an ugly, daggerlike white scar, ghastly in the lamplight.

"That was how I won the boy's confidence. He couldn't live with himself. He wanted the courage to go on. He had wanted to tell Sylvia. But he told me—instead."

"Of all the people in the world," said Douglas, "Sylvia would have understood."

"Oh, she'd've understood only too well!" Mr. Rafferty said energetically, shooting amused looks alternately at Lulu and Douglas.

Douglas appeared doubtful in the face of Mr. Rafferty's cynical recollections. "He was as cheerful and outgoing as ever when he came home. He was still in uniform, I remember, when Sylvia came back from college. They were the only two people on earth that didn't know they were born lovers. Everyone else had always known."

"I didn't know!"

Douglas gestured. "They discovered one another. I loved Sylvia myself."

"Didn't everyone." Mr. Rafferty brought the crystal decanter once more to where Lulu sat; he refilled her glass. As he poured the brandy, Lulu's eyes went to his wrist. There, beneath the retracted cuff of his white shirt, peeped the point of the white dagger-shaped scar. Lulu stared at it until Mr. Rafferty could not help but have noticed.

"It was later on," Douglas was saying, "that Warren began showing the strain."

"That was before he confessed his failings. Maybe he felt inadequate to the match."

"That's nonsense," said Douglas.

"I am speculating!" Mr. Rafferty responded in a big voice while stoppering the bottle. "Sylvia Gansevoort was the choicest, remember. I would have found her daunting, and so, my friend, would you. Sylvia was the living upshot of everything the Gansevoorts had ever been or done. From the day three hundred years ago when they put up their stockades at Bowling Green and flayed a couple of Indians alive, down to the latest hour, in all their luminous undertakings, the shenanigans at Broad and Wall, the tailored marriages, the love, the corruption, the real estate, the bonds and stocks, and Ivy League schools—and then, all of it gone, just like that, like the detritus of a butterfly— bits and pieces of dry scale—with Sylvia shimmering like pure gold amid the ashes.

"That's how I see it," said Mr. Rafferty. "This old-fashioned house was her temple." He gestured about him. "Warren came to the temple door, fell head over heels in love, bought her a vanilla Coke down at Caesar Equi's, played her some badminton, talked a Hegelian streak, and had a severe case of the heebie-jeebies. It was the gas mask all over again."

While Douglas appeared somewhat detached by now, as if Mr. Rafferty's theories were too farfetched, Lulu was listening keenly. She enjoyed the story. She saw something of herself in

Sylvia, and to her Warren was a gentle, bespectacled version of Douglas. She knew, too, that something of an evil nature had happened to someone.

"There was, of course, another dimension. There always is." Mr. Rafferty was sitting back comfortably on the sofa, facing Lulu, but sharing his attention between her and Douglas. "Sylvia was more than just a Gansevoort. She was a gorgeous physical specimen—what some might call 'a hell of a woman'—and everything that that might mean to a man. What it might have meant to a certain gentleman scholar from New Haven, a fellow with a congenital dread of confinement and dark places, who was about as vigorous on a ball field as anyone's mother, is too dismaying to think about. To put it crudely, at some point along the way, the boy was going to have to come through." Mr. Rafferty was eyeing Douglas. "The boy was going to have to deliver!"

"From Leon's lips," Douglas replied, "the most ordinary aspects of life take on extra dimensions."

Minutes later Mr. Rafferty asked Lulu to see him out. "Miss Peloquin," he said to Douglas, "has become a dear friend of mine."

"I can see that." Douglas smiled at Lulu warmly. She studied him for an instant, and found him handsome. She liked his smile. Mr. Rafferty, she assumed, must have completed his business by now with Douglas, whatever its nature; she suspected it was nothing more important than to see her own installation in the house—or even, in a sense, in the family. To Lulu's mind, Mr. Rafferty had stood her up in a flattering light, compelling the nephew's respect.

As Lulu preceded Mr. Rafferty across the room, she had the odd sensation that he was looking at her hips and legs in a manner intended to excite Douglas's attention. She couldn't see them, but she could feel the chain of attention developing behind her as she walked. She kept her head and back very straight, and was amused to think what a trickster Leon was, and how smoothly attuned to one another they had become. At the door, he smiled intimately, widened his eyes, then fashioned with his lips the word *Yale*.

"We haven't been out together lately, you and I," he said, with a roguish light in his eye. He was prompting her to reply softly, in kind, under her breath.

"Maybe," Lulu said, "we'll go to the museum again."

"I'd like that!" he exclaimed in a loud voice. "Would you?"

Despite the humor of the moment, of their shared understanding, Lulu felt a shiver at the thought of leaving the house. "I wouldn't go myself," she said. "I couldn't."

"I wouldn't let you. Perhaps," he teased, "I shall take you in disguise."

Lulu couldn't probe the meaning in his eyes, but she felt once more the hot tingling sensation coursing across the surface of her flesh. She laughed nervously, but held her voice to a whisper. "Yes," she said, "I would like that."

●

After Mr. Rafferty left, Lulu went directly up the big staircase, determined to avoid Douglas. She didn't want to see him alone, fearful that he might try to undo Mr. Rafferty's work by intimidating her anew. Lulu never forgot that, compared to the likes of herself, a brilliant Yale scholar was as remote from her as the nobleman of another age from an illiterate peasant girl. Mr. Rafferty had striven to ameliorate that. Hereafter, Lulu would show Douglas an icy demeanor, both polite and distant, like that of Mrs. Gansevoort herself. She had sensed in Douglas a secret weakness, a tiny, pulsing frailty that sometimes showed itself, if only surreptitiously, and which he quickly concealed when the will of another challenged his own. He was not, for instance, at all sure anymore about his brother's manhood. That doubt was a novelty in his soul. That was why Mr. Rafferty had wanted her there. It was clear to her now. She sat between them in Sylvia's clothes, and Mr. Rafferty showed Douglas, by his own manly interest in Lulu, how Warren might have failed.

As Lulu went past Mrs. Gansevoort's door in the upstairs hall, she heard Chloris's voice resounding within. The light showed in a crack beneath the door. Chloris's voice droned softly, as from a different part of the room, rising and falling with a regular rhythm, like a child in school reciting a poem. Reluctantly, Lulu continued on her way to her room. While undressing, she felt a stab of jealousy at the thought of Mrs. Gansevoort permitting anyone other than herself into her private sanctuary, even for a special purpose.

Usually Lulu wore a plain white nightgown to bed, similar to the nightclothes she knew Chloris wore. But tonight after undressing, she shut off the light and took from the drawer of her armoire a violet nightdress and matching negligee which were so delicate and costly, with lavender lace trimmings, that it seemed preposterous as nightwear. Lulu knew for a fact that the nightdress and negligee were not Sylvia's. Chloris had told her that they belonged years ago to Ignatia, her own mother.

Lulu put on the sheer nightgown and the slippers and modeled them before the mirror in her darkened room, while holding the negligee—what Mrs. Gansevoort called a "peignoir"—in her hand. She had never looked so tall and slender. The nightgown clung to her frame like a violet skin. The heels were tall. In all her past days, even in early adolescence when children enjoy masquerading, Lulu had never had the capacity to prance in front of a mirror. She had never felt private enough. That was the irony of Lulu's days; that she who lived in a torment of concealment had never known a moment when she did not feel the eyes of conscience upon her. Only now, in these past few weeks, as though it were a recompense for her abrogation of that other life, was she free to revel a little in herself. She turned this way and that before the shadowy mirror. Her head was beautiful. Her hands appeared pale and delicate. Above the gown's fine embroidery, her breasts swelled attractively. She pirouetted slowly.

Lulu was not unaware of what she was doing. She had put on something very precious that belonged not to Sylvia, but to Ignatia. Lulu would not have had an inkling of the strangeness of her behavior were it not for the sensation at the back of her legs, the same sudden electric impulses running down the back of her body that she felt when Mr. Rafferty and Douglas watched her walk across the parlor to the front hall. Mr. Rafferty had tormented Douglas with something frightening he knew about Warren. And it had been Douglas's helplessness, and Warren inside of Douglas, staring at her in Sylvia's clothes, in Sylvia's house, with Mr. Rafferty displaying a blatant interest in the movements of her body, that excited Lulu.

Mr. Rafferty, she suspected, had loved Sylvia. Why not? He had come home from the war, in his captain's uniform, with blood in his eye, and found Sylvia and Warren together. In the months to follow, something happened. Mr. Rafferty conquered Warren; he destroyed him. Lulu shivered as she stepped forward to the glass, and turned her torso to catch the pale light from the garden. She put her hands flat to her belly and moved them downward slowly along the silken surface to her hips. Ignatia was swimming in the Adriatic, while her children struggled across the gluey strands and filaments of the past, with Mrs. Gansevoort at the center of it all, wanting justice for her sufferings.

When Lulu returned to the hall, hairbrush in hand, and made her way to the bathroom, she was brought up short. The light was out now in Auntie's room, but she could still hear Chloris's voice inside! Lulu listened at the door, but couldn't make out the words. Shamed by her curiosity, and with a throb of apprehension in her heart at the thought of Mrs. Gansevoort suddenly opening the door, Lulu continued on her way in the dark, her thoughts in disarray. When she later returned to the corridor, the silence behind Mrs. Gansevoort's door was dramatic.

Lulu draped the negligee over a chair in her room and

climbed into the cool bed in her violet gown. The house and its occupants, it struck her, were like a flower that opened in mystery, day by day, petal by petal. She lay awake for an hour, her mind running to lurid extremes. Try as she might, she could not avoid thinking the obvious, no matter how monstrous and unlikely the possibility, that Chloris, all previous signs and evidence to the contrary, not to mention the weight of unarguable common sense, was lying in Auntie's bed; that the platinum-haired girl was devoted to her aunt in ways too awful and alarming to think about. It couldn't be possible, and wouldn't even be thinkable, she realized, but for her own failing weeks ago, at Agnes Rohan's house on Dartmouth Street. That was the key. What had happened once, to herself, had corrupted her, given her the power to see what was not: smoke without fire, snakes among satin ribbons.

At dawn, nevertheless, Chloris was sleeping peacefully in her bed, her white-gold hair spread upon the bedcovers like a silken web, as Lulu, very softy, pulled the door shut, and tiptoed back to her room. A sheeting rain blew against the windows. In the yard below, Douglas's yellow convertible glistened. Lulu lay down on her back in bed, taking in the details of her room. She was ensconced here now. She felt important here. And if a time came when Douglas, for whatever reason, either practical or perverse, should contrive to steal away Mrs. Gansevoort's house, Lulu would relish the chance to show her mettle. She would take hold of her dear friend by the hand, and bear stoically with her whatever trials fate held in store. The reason that Mrs. Gansevoort had so far postponed going up to her summer house in Peru Mountain, Lulu divined, was that Auntie feared inwardly the approaching day when she might need to remove herself there for good.

Mrs. Gansevoort and Lulu took breakfast together. Chloris

and Douglas were still sleeping. Outdoors, the wind blew the rain past the windows, and shook the leaves of the chokecherry tree on the side lawn. Lulu found herself staring at the older woman as she seated herself. She wondered if Mrs. Gansevoort would betray signs of anything unusual in her behavior. As always, though, Mrs. Gansevoort came to the breakfast table looking both genial and austere.

"Well, this was a morning when we got out ahead of the robins," she said. "I hope you enjoyed your evening. Did you charm them both? I'm sure you did."

"Leon was very entertaining."

"I'm sure he was."

Lulu reached for her coffee cup, but as she took it in hand, she felt Mrs. Gansevoort's gaze lingering heavily upon her, a brooding look that Lulu understood. Mrs. Gansevoort expected her to enlarge upon the evening without explicit prompting.

Without detaching her eyes from Lulu, Auntie questioned her.

"Was he pleased?"

Lulu replied in a small voice. "Yes, Auntie, I think he was. They . . . spoke about Warren mostly." Lulu's eyes here went to the door, as though to confirm the fact of their privacy. "Leon seemed to know a lot about him." Lulu struggled to express herself indirectly. That, she felt, was her charge. She would communicate by not specifying who was who. "He seemed unsure of himself," she said, shifting the subject subtly, ungrammatically, from Leon to Douglas. "He listened very carefully but pretended not to. I thought he was fascinated by him."

"By whom?" Aunt Julia's question struck Lulu as a test.

"By *him*," she said, under her breath.

Mrs. Gansevoort smiled and then turned to her breakfast.

Lulu's fingertips were still touching her coffee cup, her arm extended on the table, as she leaned gently toward Mrs. Gansevoort, her face lifted in confidence. "He was watching him watch me. I'm sure of it," Lulu whispered. "Yes, I think he was fascinated by him."

"Just so long as you enjoyed yourself," Mrs. Gansevoort remarked idly.

"I did, Auntie. Of course, I was not able to keep up with the two of them."

Mrs. Gansevoort put her head back and laughed merrily, as if Lulu's admission were, by their understandings, conceived as the very reverse of what her words denoted. "I can imagine!"

At this point Lulu wanted very much to say something about Chloris, or to just utter the girl's name aloud, in order to evoke a response, a word or sign from her friend that would disperse the mystery of the night before. A moment ago, when Auntie put her head back and laughed, Lulu, to her own disbelief, had stolen a look at Auntie's breasts—her eyes flying away at once in alarm.

Mrs. Gansevoort spoke matter-of-factly. "Leon always favored Gansevoort women. Now that you're here, Luette, I am afraid you shall have to contend with the ambitions of men like Leon. Would you enjoy being a Gansevoort?"

"I wouldn't know how."

"These others"—Mrs. Gansevoort's eyes went up contemptuously to the ceiling—"are not true Gansevoorts. It seemed to me, thirty years ago, when I was desperately unhappy, that Ignatia, my sister, had made a match that assured the family its integrity for at least another generation. It turned out quite differently! Fate plays a hand, I suppose. I, after all, as I had always expected, was the one marked to propagate the line. Ignatia's children have all but withered on the vine. One of the two remaining is altogether a lost soul." Mrs. Gansevoort glanced at Lulu. As she alluded to her niece, Lulu was all ears. "We needn't worry about that one ever making her mark upon the world, or performing in any way other than as a mechanical toy to be moved about at will."

Mrs. Gansevoort was no longer speaking to Lulu in their private cipher, but quite openly, as if the time had come for Lulu to consider certain ostensible enormities as mere trifles. Lulu was mesmerized. She felt as though her heart had stopped beating altogether.

"Some mortals are past praying for," Mrs. Gansevoort added with offhanded ease. "Do you understand what I'm telling you?"

Lulu, dropping her gaze to her plate, was speechless. She dearly hoped that she misunderstood Mrs. Gansevoort's words, and that her dear friend would express something in her next breath that would set all the rest of it at naught. But in her heart, Lulu feared the worst.

"Don't think I'm not appreciative," Mrs. Gansevoort continued, "for what you've done. I am not insensible to the way you took the child in hand some while ago! I was at my wits' end."

"*I* did?" said Lulu, faintly.

"Until you came, I don't think she realized how general my displeasure was, or how another might be similarly outraged."

Though Lulu could not comprehend the exact meaning in Mrs. Gansevoort's speech, she felt the power that chained the words together, the malevolence, the vengeful triumph, as surely as if Mrs. Gansevoort had thrown open a door onto the very picture of her thoughts.

"Are you going to tell me you didn't know? For the love of heaven," Mrs. Gansevoort cried, "take credit where it is due. The child is in awe of you! Of course you know. What is even more important is that *I* know!"

Mrs. Gansevoort spoke with great vigor. Her face was radiant. She was so magniloquent this morning that Lulu could only construe her high spirits as the flush of victory, as if she had just vanquished an adversary hours before, and couldn't forbear gloating.

"I don't mind your being timid with me, or modest, or, for that matter," Mrs. Gansevoort added, "even ignorant of the meaning and value of your works, so long as you don't find me thankless. If I am anything, I am appreciative. I shall think of an appropriate reward."

Lulu responded with effort. "I don't deserve a reward."

"Isn't that for me to say?" Mrs. Gansevoort looked at her with facetious sternness. "Would you deny me the pleasure of giving you something? Would you?" She smiled. "What pleasure *would* you deny me?"

Lulu shook her head. "None."

"And didn't I know that before I asked?"

Lulu nodded. "It's just," she said, "that I would be ashamed to accept anything from you for something I might have done . . . in ignorance. Whatever it may have been."

Mrs. Gansevoort laughed in disbelief over Lulu's words. "Very well," she said. "I shall not consult you in future about how I might wish to reckon my accounts with you. Is it enough for me to tell you I am pleased?"

"Yes, Auntie."

"And if you choose to be ignorant of your loyalty and good works, so long as I am beneficiary, perhaps, truly, I should not cavil. I give you my blessings!" she cried. "My blessings and benedictions. And if something small comes your way, a little trinket or memento from my own past, you may look upon it as pure largesse."

Lulu worked all the morning in the parlor while Mrs. Gansevoort came and went busily in the downstairs rooms; she and Mrs. Fallon were packing some things for Peru Mountain. Upstairs, the niece and nephew slept on. Douglas's car stood outside the windows, shining in the rain. In the shrubs beyond, the big violet hydrangea blossoms drooped like bowed heads under the peppering drops. Lulu couldn't concentrate on the papers before her. Time and again, Chloris's face came between her and her work. She saw Chloris sitting on the lip of the low stage in the Music Room, her eyes imploring Lulu to do something for her. It was that light of hope that Mrs. Gansevoort was talking about, and that Lulu had struck from her eyes.

That's what it was all about. As surely as if she had picked Chloris up, and carried her in her arms, she had delivered the girl body and soul to her aunt.

Later that morning, still feeling vaguely sick over the matter, Lulu went to her room—only to discover on her marble-top table a package loosely wrapped in bright gift foil. It contained three photographs of Mrs. Gansevoort. They were not recent photos, nor were they portraits from Auntie's early years. Lulu guessed them to be about fifteen years old; they were pictures of Mrs. Gansevoort in her prime. Lulu sat with the package on her lap, studying the pictures one by one. She did love Mrs. Gansevoort, and couldn't help but respond in her heart to her friend's thoughtfulness. The prodigality, too, of the gesture—the conscious excess—was somehow both irregular and appropriate.

The biggest of the three portraits was the prettiest. In it, Mrs. Gansevoort's head was turned to the camera. Her eyes sparkled softly, and a gentle, benign attitude radiated from her lips and pale flesh. It was the sort of expression Lulu had noticed from time to time when her friend dwelt on the past, especially her days at college.

Taking pains with it, Lulu placed the picture on her night table beside her bed, positioning it so that it faced both the bed and the room at large. She stood the second picture on the marble table, and the third atop the mantel, making a triangle of them. In fact, when Lulu stood before the tall mirror and looked at herself in the glass, she was aware that it was here, exactly, that the eyes of the three pictures converged.

Later, when Chloris came to her door, Lulu wanted to feel something new for her, something kind and generous; but as the girl materialized in the corner of her eye, appearing so facile and cowardly, even coy, coming silently into the room, Lulu couldn't stifle her contempt. She now doubted sincerely that anything vicious had taken place the night before; but the fact that she could have entertained such an idea only made her despise the niece that much more, since her doubts did not derive from any assumption of innocence in Chloris. That the girl was capable of any depravity was reason enough to deplore her existence.

Chloris was speaking in a murmur:

"Douglas is going up to Peru Mountain in a day or two. I hope he doesn't bring a friend. I've never liked his friends." Suddenly, she fell silent.

Lulu could sense Chloris's astonishment as she discovered the photographs of Aunt Julia disposed about the room. She stepped past her to shut the door. An impulse had seized Lulu, an urge to do something to Chloris. Not something harmful, but proper in the circumstances. Even as she clicked shut the door, she did not know what she was going to do. It was only when she turned back, and Chloris pivoted to face her, that the impulse took thought. "I'm going to fix your hair," Lulu said.

Chloris sat on Lulu's little embroidered chair, both of them facing the mirror, while Lulu plaited her hair. She was making Chloris two long pigtails. While clearly pleased by the attention, Chloris kept up a running discourse on the subject of her aunt's summer retreat in the mountains, about the woodland paths and the fresh mountain air. Lulu worked the strands of hair expertly, pulling each tightly into place, crossing the next, weaving them, her fingers moving deftly. To Lulu's eyes, the docile figure in the mirror was regressing in age. She looked about twelve. After completing the second pigtail, securing it with a rubber band, Lulu was inspired to add two white bows, one atop each plait. The sight of the ribbons set Chloris giggling.

The desire to be mothered shone in Chloris's face and eyes. As Lulu stepped back, examining the girl's pretty doll-like face and platinum plaits, just as Ignatia might have done, she recalled her sensations of the night before, the sensual feel of Ignatia's violet nightdress stretched tautly across her abdomen. That was how she felt now. Chloris was completely in her hands.

"Why are you paying attention to me today?" Chloris asked.

"I always pay attention to you," Lulu replied, conscious of the motherly tone in her voice.

Lulu left her sitting before the mirror, and went across the hall to Chloris's room to find her a dress. She returned with a short white tennis dress, and handed it to Chloris.

"Auntie won't like that."

"Try it on."

As Chloris pulled the sleeveless white dress over her head, Lulu stepped forward and tugged at the side seams, gauging the fit. The transformation was remarkable. Chloris didn't look at all like herself, but like a schoolgirl at summer camp. The white bows were the crowning touch. Lulu regarded the two of them in the tall glass, conscious at once of the dramatic discrepancy between them, of Chloris barefooted in white, and of her own comparatively tallish figure. Chloris looked up at her ardently.

"I want to ask you a question." Her voice was a whisper. "Does Auntie have a secret plan to send me back to school?"

Lulu avoided the issue. "Aren't you supposed to go back to school?"

"Aunt Julia told me in April that I could stay here forever. But I can't tell what she's thinking. It frightens me. If she sends me away, it will be like the end of my life!"

Lulu had no desire to see Chloris in torment, but could not help smiling. "Do you think Auntie was lying?"

Chloris shook her head. "I just dread that she's changed her mind. That would be the end of everything." Chloris gazed up at Lulu helplessly. "I used to be her favorite! More than Warren or Douglas or anyone. When they called me to the telephone at school, they would say it was my mother calling. I asked Auntie to be my mother. Sometimes, in private, she let me call her that. She hates Ignatia."

"Does she?" Lulu was growing impatient with Chloris's passions. She distrusted the girl, and felt a wave of apprehension when she glanced up and saw Mrs. Gansevoort staring at her from a photograph.

"Not openly! But I have always known. Auntie detests my mother."

As Lulu descended the front staircase afterward, she censured herself for having permitted Chloris to speak to her of Auntie, and to have shed her crocodile tears for a past that doubtless never existed in the first place. Auntie had probably detested Ignatia and her children always, and with good cause, as they had brought her much unhappiness, and even today threatened her well-being.

Mrs. Gansevoort was sitting at her worktable with a book and a red pencil. Lulu looked at her deadpan.

"I just put Chloris up in pigtails!" she said.

"*Pigtails?*" cried Mrs. Gansevoort, in excellent humor. "What a lovely surprise that must have been for her."

As Lulu sat and settled into her work, she was conscious that Mrs. Gansevoort continued to stare at her with affection. At length, Lulu looked up, and felt the light of love pass over her like a warm ray of sunshine.

"Thank you, Auntie, for the pictures," she said.

"I thought that you might like to select one for yourself."

"I displayed all three," Lulu assured her.

Mrs. Gansevoort's eyes closed dreamily in affirmation, then opened brilliantly.

Lulu glanced out the window. Mrs. Gansevoort watched her cannily.

"Will Leon be coming to lunch today?" asked Lulu.

"Oh," Mrs. Gansevoort deprecated that possibility with a deliberate throatiness of voice, "I don't see a need for Leon today. I'm saving Leon for the country. Are you pleased Leon will be with us in the country?"

Lulu pondered before replying. "I'm pleased everyone will be there."

Mrs. Gansevoort got up from her place and came past Lulu

with an air of such conscious elegance that it struck Lulu as a pictorial statement of Mrs. Gansevoort's confidence in their mutual undertakings. "Carry on for now, darling," she said.

•

Lulu was not unaffected by the sight of the handsome, blond-haired Douglas, sitting across the table from her at lunch. He was very at ease, very attractive, very much the sort of young, educated man of the world who would find his way eventually into important posts. That was how Lulu saw him, and was never confused about the impassable gulf between herself and him. She pictured him walking with his books under his arm on beautiful imaginary walkways at Yale. Twice during lunch, she detected his eyes lingering on her. He was looking at her dress. Lulu wondered if the dress might not have been Ignatia's, for she was beginning to suspect that many items in her wardrobe had never belonged to Sylvia. She could feel her breasts thrusting against the black silk as she sat absolutely straight in her chair, like a replica of Aunt Julia. However much Lulu acknowledged Douglas's brilliance of mind, his scholarship, his social standing, nevertheless, in this room, in Mrs. Gansevoort's presence, Lulu felt herself under the influence of an even more powerful medicine. She could almost tell when he was going to look up. He couldn't help himself. That was because of the way that both of them, Auntie and Mr. Rafferty, had made her important in Douglas's eyes, and the way Auntie had cleverly encouraged Lulu to emulate herself.

Douglas talked all through lunch about his military training. He told amusing anecdotes about a young man in the officer-training corps at Yale who was inept at every facet of their training. "One morning, we had to reassemble the M-1 rifle blindfolded, and had to stay at that table for as long as it required. He was still standing there at sundown!" Douglas exclaimed. Closing his eyes and extending his hands over the table, he gave a comical approximation of the inept trainee trying to fit together the little components.

The burlesque set Lulu, Chloris, and Mrs. Gansevoort laughing. Chloris appeared happiest of all. Everyone had teased her about her pigtails when she came to the table, but she took it in good part. Like Douglas, she often stole looks at Lulu over lunch. To Lulu, Chloris's standing in the house had plummeted to nothing. Presently, Douglas's eyes returned, as if by compulsion, to the pretty shelf of Lulu's breasts, and, as before, Lulu felt inside herself the dark stirring of buried emotions, a little pocket of darkness opening and closing around her heart.

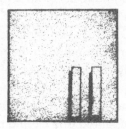

Lulu might have imagined it, but from that time forward her place in the house, her status as Mrs. Gansevoort's companion, took on more the aspect of a peer, or sister. She recognized the source of the change; it was a consequence of Douglas's return. Later that afternoon, she encountered Douglas as she was going up to her room from the library. She was sure he had been waiting for her. He had come exploring; he wanted to confirm something.

He asked Lulu when precisely Mrs. Gansevoort was going to the country. "Usually," he said, "I help Aunt Julia with her move."

They were at the stairhead. Lulu could see past him into his room, to the tennis trophy standing atop the bookcase by the window, and the old Deerfield school pennant attached to the wall. That Lulu inhabited the North Room, second in size and beauty only to Mrs. Gansevoort's own bedroom, was not, she realized, an accident, but something planned by Aunt Julia to make an effect.

"I was supposed to spend two days up in Bennington," he said, "but I wouldn't want my aunt sitting here, twiddling her thumbs, waiting for me."

"Why don't you ask her?" Lulu felt uncomfortable.

"I thought you might know." He spoke to her in a quiet, confiding way. "My original plans have been upset by the army. I was supposed to go to law school this autumn, and was going to spend the entire summer in Peru Mountain, with my studies. Now I'm not sure what to do."

Twice his eyes dropped to her bosom, but he was not looking at her in the way of a young man regarding an attractive stranger. Lulu was now convinced that the dress she was wearing must have been Ignatia's. She sensed a mystification in Douglas, as though he were trying to decipher the meaning of her presence in the Gansevoort house.

Truth was, she was drawn to Douglas. He had a poetic, dreamy look that touched her. While it shouldn't have mattered, Lulu was also affected by the fact of his being a Gansevoort. She was still thinking about him at four o'clock that afternoon when she joined Mrs. Gansevoort in her upstairs sanctuary. Her friend was sitting amid her Oriental surroundings. She was in a playful mood.

"One night in the mountains," she said, "I am going to take you to a dance program at Jacob's Pillow, darling. We shall dress you up very mysteriously."

"That would be fun. I've never been to a theater."

"All the more reason. You shall make your debut in public. We'll take Leon as our bodyguard."

Lulu was charmed. "Leon would be a wonderful bodyguard!"

"He isn't everything a man might be, but is the match of ten if it's a show of controlled savagery you want." Mrs. Gansevoort's eyes sparkled.

Lulu laughed aloud. She saw the truth in Mrs. Gansevoort's witticism. They were facing one another across the low, black-lacquered Chinese table. Lulu was sitting in the same posture as her friend, with her knees together, her legs slanted to one side like a pair of sticks, her saucer and cup in either hand. She consciously replicated Auntie's bearing. They understood one another at such times, Lulu felt. A moment later, when Aunt Julia passed Lulu the silver creamer, Lulu felt a soft, voluptuous pleasure, something secret and illicit moving inside her, because she knew that Auntie was going to say something of an intimate nature.

"Does he show interest in you?" Auntie asked.

Lulu recognized the shift in subject instantly. The question pertained to Douglas, not Leon!

"I don't believe so," Lulu replied.

Up came Mrs. Gansevoort's eyes. "It isn't unthinkable."

Lulu regarded her friend steadily. She was blushing. "I don't think it would be possible."

"Oh, it would be!" Mrs. Gansevoort was incisive. "After all, you have me."

Lulu reveled momentarily in her companion's flash of egoism, feeling her soul grow small in Auntie's presence. Mrs. Gansevoort's vanity was palpable.

"I am not talking about the heart of an Arabian prince."

"No one has ever been interested in me." Lulu colored with embarrassment.

"You know that is false. Are you speaking just for effect?"

Lulu guessed at Mrs. Gansevoort's objection. "Before you took me in, Auntie, is what I meant to say."

"He is, I take it, coming to the country with us?"

Lulu's face was a blank. Mrs. Gansevoort was testing her. She wanted Lulu to say something intimate. While Lulu had no valuable intelligence to impart, she lowered her voice conspiratorially nonetheless.

"He seemed unsure of himself, of his summer plans, and wonders, Auntie, when you intend to leave."

"I see." Mrs. Gansevoort reached a braceleted hand and adjusted a jade figure of a horse on a tiled chessboard. "Some people, did you know, are given to dissembling. You, Luette, do not lie. Do you?"

"No." Lulu avoided Auntie's eyes. The rainy daylight fell in a pale bar across the colorful carpet. She could feel a revelation trembling in the air. Auntie was watching her avidly.

"Thirty years ago," Mrs. Gansevoort said, "I was lied to, desperately."

"I understand." Lulu's voice was soft and dry.

A light of hatred flickered to life in the hazel depths of Mrs. Gansevoort's eyes. "After which, *I* was left to feed and raise the foul brood. Those are the deserts of innocence. I was once an amateur botanist!" Mrs. Gansevoort said bitterly. "I collected leaves. Can you imagine? I wrote sonnets and villanelles to spring."

Mrs. Gansevoort's pain came toward Lulu in the afternoon air like a living substance flowing unseen across the interval of the two sofas.

"She was wearing pink," Mrs. Gansevoort went on in a hollow voice. "I was to have met him—Willis—here in the city, but the two of them were already gone. They were in the mountains, precisely where we're going, for twenty-four hours. All the livelong day, and all night together. In our own father's summer house. By arriving on time, I"—Mrs. Gansevoort whispered the irony—"arrived late. I *loathe* a lie. I detest a lie. She was waiting for me by the road. She saw our father's car coming, and came out to the road. She was, of course, weeping!"

Lulu wished to say something, if only to express her sympathy. "She was wearing pink?"

"Yes. A pink dress, pink hat, pink shoes. She had him in pink—not indoors, she was too cowardly for that, but in the woodlots! Willis and I were to have been married in a matter of days or weeks. We had a storybook courtship. We met on a tennis court at Mount Holyoke. Willis had an automobile, which was quite a novelty at that time. A green roadster." Mrs. Gansevoort paused. Her lips shook. "Those were summer days that God gives only to twenty-year-olds—with one's books and combs and perfumes—and a young man in white trousers waiting for you by the campus pond."

Lulu followed Mrs. Gansevoort's touching reminiscences with close attention, but her mind returned several times to the lurid picture of Ignatia, in pink, lying beneath Julia Gansevoort's fiancé in the grass, to the two of them—not with faces of their own, but the faces of the children. Lulu knew the meaning of betrayal, but Mrs. Gansevoort's knowledge formed an indelible picture of it in her mind, of the glassy-faced lover hunched atop a confusion of pink silks.

"The devil only knows the lies she told him on that day. Something about me. He asked me, later, when I married, was it true, did I love Jack. I said I did. But I smelled the presence of a lie behind his questioning. He might have been asking did I always love Jack. That question, that lie, you see, was going round and round in his mind all that while, for two years or more. I even know where she said it. I found the place." Mrs. Gansevoort was sitting up, motionless as the furniture behind her. "There is a path up to the mountain from the house and lodge. I walked up that path—not that day, but on the day following—to destroy myself. I had decided to do so, and climbed up the path between the cedars the way someone desperate might climb the steps of a tall building. There was an immense gray boulder at a level spot, with moss growing on the sides, and I stopped and leaned against the rock. How unhappy I was!"

Lulu was riveted. "You found something," she said.

"Yes. I found my sister's scarf. It was in a clearing not bigger than this rug, covered all over with brown needles, and the sun falling into it in a perfectly circular pattern, like a spotlight in a theater. Not a yard from my foot lay her scarf. It could only have fallen there on that day. That was simple to deduce. Other articles lay nearby in the shade. Horrid!" Mrs. Gansevoort's face contorted. "Sordid!"

Mrs. Gansevoort trembled with disgust. A look of revulsion swept over her face.

"Oh, Auntie!" Lulu sat forward. She wanted to get up and go lovingly to her, but was kept back by Mrs. Gansevoort's cold aspect.

"I, naturally, picked it up," said Mrs. Gansevoort. "It was pink chiffon. I kept it among my things. I had such a mind for vengeance. . . . For days thereafter, everyone treated me with great tenderness—and none of them was sweeter than she. She smiled with gentle pity!"

Mrs. Gansevoort stood up and went to a lacquered cabinet by the windows. The curtains were billowing as she opened a drawer and removed something wrapped in plain white tissue. "If someone had told me when I was a little girl, and was the pride of my father's and mother's house, that I might become the target one day of such hateful resentment, or that I might be reduced in times to come to the status of my little sister's summer drudge, I would have thought that the earth would have burned up to a cinder before that was possible. I was as virtuous as a child in a fairy tale. I was simple! I collected leaves and seeds and catkins in a book." She handed Lulu the parcel wrapped in tissue without comment, and Lulu received it without taking her eyes from Mrs. Gansevoort.

Lulu was not intended to open the parcel, but could feel between her fingers the weight and shape of the silk chiffon neckpiece inside. Auntie meant her to have it. Lulu saw the act as full of curious significations. It was frightening.

In her room, Lulu placed the parcel underneath her sweaters, atop the Sunday newspaper photo of the youth they called Soldier. She didn't look at the pink scarf, but stored the package away with the studied, tentative movements of a lay person entrusted with the handling of a holy relic. Her own room, she later realized, had become like a shrine.

That evening, Mrs. Gansevoort insisted on opening a bottle of wine to mark their last night of the summer in Leiden Hall. They would leave for Peru Mountain in the morning, she said. The wine made Lulu glow inside, and left her feeling very warm and charitable toward everyone, especially Douglas. He was clearly too much of a man, she thought, to be distressed by his aunt's obscure stratagems. Once or twice, Lulu even had the odd notion that the wine inside her head had somehow sobered her, for she saw the three of them, Mrs. Gansevoort and her niece and nephew, in an altogether harmless light, as if they were, in fact, just three very ordinary people.

"What about you, Miss Peloquin?" Douglas asked, at one point. "Will you be going home for a visit before going up to Peru?"

Lulu felt too mellow to be agitated by Douglas's question. All she knew was that a great chasm had opened between her and her former life. She could not express even to herself the gathering unreality of those days and years, of her mother and grandmother chattering away in French at the kitchen table, with their beano and their horoscopes and card games, and of her own pathetic box of a room, with the dried palms sticking up from her dresser mirror. Three times in these past weeks Lulu's mother had telephoned the Gansevoort house to say hello, but only once, the first time, had Lulu taken the call. She had crossed the line, and could not go back. And when Mrs. Gansevoort reached across the table now, and closed her hand over Lulu's, and showed Lulu her proud, shining eyes, Lulu felt her friend's spirit close down over her own like something silent and winged, and she looked back at her in simple rapture.

Mrs. Gansevoort was unequivocal. "Luette is at home," she said.

"Well, I think you're both very fortunate," Douglas exclaimed, in a spirited tone, "to have found one another. Your compatibility reads like an open book. I envy you."

"What would you know about such things?" Mrs. Gansevoort retaliated with disdain.

When Mrs. Gansevoort was affronting to Douglas, Lulu worried that Auntie might be imperiling her future in Leiden Hall. Douglas, however, seemed to be taking Mrs. Gansevoort's cuts with open amusement.

Before supper was concluded, however, Douglas was called away to the telephone by Mrs. Fallon, and something transpired at the table that astonished Lulu more than anything she had witnessed so far. Auntie turned to her niece.

"When he returns," Mrs. Gansevoort instructed Chloris, "we shall talk only about Peru Mountain. Ask him how long he intends to be with us this summer."

Chloris nodded secretively. "Yes, Auntie."

The wine had created such a webby feeling in Lulu's brain that she had to strive consciously to make sense of what she had heard. She was staring at the two of them in disbelief. Chloris was in league with Auntie. Nor was Aunt Julia making any effort to conceal the fact from Lulu. On the contrary, she was demonstrating it. It was an open truth among them: Chloris was aligned with Auntie against her own brother.

"Tell him," Mrs. Gansevoort continued thoughtfully, "also, that Leon will not be joining us this year. Tell him that first." Having thus instructed her niece, Mrs. Gansevoort prepared to leave the table. Before doing so, she turned her attention to Lulu; she stared at her long enough to impress upon Lulu the meaning of what had just occurred. "You may stay and finish your cake."

Lulu nodded dumbly, but said nothing as Mrs. Gansevoort rose and departed. When Douglas returned to the table, Lulu listened in fascination as Chloris carried out her commission with the aplomb of an actress. She informed Douglas that Mr. Rafferty was not going to join the family at Peru Mountain.

Douglas confessed then that life in the country might be pleasanter if Mr. Rafferty was not. there. Lulu sensed in his rumi-
nations an element of fear concerning Mr. Rafferty. She felt a
trifle shamefaced, too, that Auntie had called upon Chloris to
act as her conspirator. Lulu felt a compulsion to take the upper
hand. Scarcely aware of what she was doing, Lulu carried matters a step further.

"Leon and Auntie," she said, at length, "are not so friendly
as they were."

The fabrication was inspired. Lulu detected instantly the
change in Douglas's expression, the pleasure that he sought to
conceal behind his words.

"You're not going to tell me," he cried, "that Julia and Leon
have had a falling out?"

His glance went swiftly from Lulu to Chloris, then back
again. Chloris, it was obvious, was compelled to silence by the
audacity of Lulu's remark.

Lulu replied evenly. "About that, you would have to ask
Auntie. It isn't my place to say."

"But you do know." Douglas was delighted. "Neither of
you," he said, "can appreciate the irony in that, if it's true. The
hero of Omaha Blue! The scourge of the Normandy beachhead!
Of the Atlantic Wall! Come back to town after the war, with his
medals and campaign ribbons, and the same old impossible
dream—year after year—coming to her door—sedulous as a
little squirrel. Like a monk in love with the prioress of the abbey."
Douglas threw himself back happily in his chair. "Warren's
demigod!"

He waved his hand expansively toward Chloris. "Tell Aunt
Julia I shall spend the summer at Peru. You can count on me!
Tell her I'll spend my time doing nothing more selfish than
applauding her good sense."

As Chloris went hurriedly from the room, Douglas launched
into an account of Mr. Rafferty's "inauspicious advent" into the
lives of the Gansevoorts years back.

"I'm one of just two or three persons on earth," he said, "who have seen Leon in both his manifestations. The ancient and the modern. You," he said, "have seen only the latter-day Leon, the man of stiff bearing and cold intelligence, who fusses for an hour with his collar and tie clip. But there was another Leon," Douglas explained, "a Leon from which this silver-tongued miracle sprang. I saw him with my own two eyes, when I was a boy of six or seven—when he first came. He wore dirty white sneakers and white coveralls."

Alone now with Douglas, Lulu wondered if she had not perhaps lied about Mr. Rafferty and Aunt Julia in order to suit her own interests. The sight of Douglas sprawled attractively in his chair before her, and holding forth with great charm, was exciting to her. She wanted him to come to the mountains.

"It's impossible to imagine Mr. Rafferty in such a state," she said.

"They were hard times," Douglas said, "but for Mr. Rafferty, as you call him, they were really bitter. I can't tell you everything about his past, because I don't know a lot about it. The only one he may ever have confided in was Warren, my brother. Warren knew something! It's my guess that Warren knew more about Leon than he ever needed to know about anybody! Leon came to town as a youth with a WPA fine-arts team that was sent in to paint murals in public buildings. Leon was in charge of the turpentine!" he cried. "He spread drop cloths for the painters. He cleaned their brushes. They must have despised him. Leon was a loner—even then. The classic outsider. The fifth wheel! That winter, when he came to Jack's and Julia's house to borrow books, he was like a creature out of the books, the shy, reticent, humble-mouthed pauper's son! He first met Julia and Sylvia at the dedicatory ceremony for the War Memorial Building on Appleton Street. Sylvia was still a child then. Did I say he 'met' them? He fixed Sylvia's bicycle. He replaced her chain. Julia gave him a dollar. A *dollar!*" Douglas cried. "Do you know what a dollar meant in the winter of 'Thirty-five?

It was half a day's pay. But to Leon, I'm sure it was more than that." Douglas was enjoying himself. "It was something more in the nature of an historic discovery." He raised his hands to the ceiling. "A revelation hypostatized in the vision of a jeweled hand holding out to him a pretty piece of paper."

Douglas's amusement over the hardships suffered by Mr. Rafferty in his early manhood would ordinarily have troubled Lulu, as her mere interest in the story would have seemed a betrayal of her principles and of her admiration for Leon; but she guessed that Douglas was more motivated by a desire to entertain her than to mock the older man's misfortunes. Still, she was prompted to contribute a saving remark.

"Many people have suffered poverty," she said.

But Douglas, shaking his head, had anticipated her sympathetic view. "That's not the point. Of course people have suffered. The Gansevoorts suffered a fall from the heights. Who suffered more? There is something worse than being poor, and that is being made poor. For Leon," he said, "it was more than just an awareness that some people still wore mink and bought their children new bicycles." Douglas paused as Mrs. Fallon appeared and began clearing the table. Lulu stared at him, and waited for him to resume. "For Leon, I believe, it was an honest-to-God revelation. It was like an immense door that opened in the middle of the afternoon, as if the scene before him—the living scene, the grass and trees and people in the street, the automobiles going by, all of it—the afternoon itself!—had been a mural! It just opened up! He saw in! There was a life behind the traffic lights and the smoky air and the people trooping past."

Douglas opened his arms wide once again to illustrate the mystical revelation.

"Leon," he said, "found himself. He found a purpose in his existence. Not a full purpose." Douglas smiled at Lulu. "Leon is not like that. He doesn't lead a full life or have a full purpose. He found about half a purpose. The other half of him is still back there, in his soiled white paint clothes, sitting on the edge of things, contemplating the abyss. He gave himself to the Gansevoorts! People do that," Douglas exclaimed. "You may do it yourself one day. I may, myself. They just give themselves away—to an idea, or a habit, or to other people. Jack liked him, too. To Jack Gansevoort, Leon was probably everything poor and footloose that he might have wished to be himself. The bum in paradise! The American vagabond. That's very romantic to some people. And he liked Leon's mind, he said. Jack found Leon a place to live. He gave him some clothes, maybe even some money. Jack was like that. The soul of generosity."

"Yes, I heard he was," Lulu said.

"It's true. He was also credulous and kindhearted. He might as well have succored a dragon. Not because Leon fell in love with anyone, as some people might suppose. He isn't like that. He's not a complete person. He's not interested in the happiness of the good-hearted! The part of him that might have been was probably the price of his revelation. Leon found life on the other side of things."

Lulu was taking pleasure in Douglas's allusive, obscure way of talking, as much for his tutorial pose as for his strange assumptions and theories. The pictures he drew of Mr. Rafferty as a kind of half man worked an odd spell upon her, however, and she could not tell whether it derived from the genius of Douglas's imagination or from her own latent fascination with Mr. Rafferty himself.

"Warren," Douglas went on, "tried to explain to me once how happiness begets its opposite. The feast, he said, is anything but a feast for the lamb on the spit, or the roasted hen. Happiness can just as easily be produced by its opposite, by the willful making of unhappiness. It was one of those harebrained ideas that freshmen dream up when they display their rhetorical gifts over a bottle of beer. Warren, who knew more about Greek philosophy than Plato himself, should have known better, but by then he was already far gone. He wasn't making conversation. He believed." Douglas whispered the words to Lulu in a low, frightening voice. "*He believed!* The words weren't his words, at all. They were Leon's. That was how Leon got to say what he would not otherwise say. Those words were the fruits of Leon's great solitude, and, of course, of the time they spent together. That was how it came out. Through Warren's lips!"

Lulu felt a shiver of fright at the thought that Warren had gone mad at the end.

"But by then," said Douglas, "as I said, Warren was already far gone. He worshiped Leon."

"I saw his picture once," said Lulu, sensing that Douglas's spirits were ebbing. "It was a family picture. You resemble him. He was very handsome."

Lulu blushed at once, aware of the unintended compliment in her remarks.

But Douglas was not listening. He was still thinking about his brother.

"He had already lost Sylvia and didn't even know it."

"If a day comes," said Mrs. Gansevoort, "when you and I are left to fend for ourselves in a little mountain house, it will not be because we shamed ourselves!"

"I would live with you anywhere," said Lulu.

"They had everything of mine. Love, money, all of it." Mrs. Gansevoort spoke abstractedly, while leading Lulu from the car to the back door of her summer house. "Finally, I struck back! Just when they thought me vanquished—dethroned!—I caught them unawares. And I shall continue to strike. Up here"—she gestured toward the fields and nearby mountain—"where I was once violated without pity, a helpless girl attacked by serpents, I am quite safe. In the mountains, I'm indestructible." She uttered the word with relish. "And you, Luette, have given me added strength."

Mrs. Gansevoort's summer place was more imposing than Lulu had expected. It was a pretty, white frame house set back from the gravel road, about a mile from the village of Peru Mountain. Mrs. Gansevoort was sole owner of the house and acreage. Lulu was aware of the irony that Auntie's portion of the earth was at the same time the site of her spiritual mutilation thirty years earlier.

Within minutes, Lulu had removed her rain cape and was busy with the unpacking. She admired the house very much, recognizing Auntie's hand everywhere, her unique touch. The vacation house seemed an extension of Leiden Hall. The scenery without, however, was wild, with trees massed shinily on all sides, the rain falling steadily. The air was rather cold, and the atmosphere desolate, but only in the sense of the quiet, lonely uplands imposing a timeless indifference upon the consciousness of a stranger.

Lulu was touched by Mrs. Gansevoort, not so much by her declarations of affection or appreciation, as by Lulu's comprehension of Auntie's suffering: behind Mrs. Gansevoort's haughty façade and fine words were the unhealing wounds. Lulu prided herself on being able to see through to the genuine unhappiness, the anguish and disgust throbbing behind the cold, aristocratic exterior. For Lulu knew, more than most, what it meant to be cheated. Only since she had come under Mrs. Gansevoort's protection could she see, with painful clarity, the pathos of her own previous existence, the bleakness, the lonely streets and mean room, the unreasoning dread of others. She understood, also—with a little stab of fright—exactly how her friend had struck back. It was as plain as the rain on the window. Aunt Julia had struck back at Chloris, the child, as it were, of her betrayal. She had knocked her to earth. Nothing was clearer to Lulu. Chloris adored her aunt to an unnatural degree, and Auntie openly deplored her. All that was left of Chloris was that little part of her heart that Aunt Julia had chosen to spare.

"Last year," Mrs. Gansevoort explained, while later showing Lulu into her bedroom, "this room was unoccupied. Before that, it was a guest room for weekend visitors, and before *that*, it belonged to Sylvia. No one has called it their own since that time." As she spoke, Mrs. Gansevoort indicated a photograph of Sylvia standing atop a white chest. Lulu stared at it, a casual facial shot of Mrs. Gansevoort's daughter, with just her necklace and the collar of her coat showing beneath her throat, her eyes turned to the camera. She was a beautiful young woman, with delicate cheekbones and spiritual eyes.

"Except for the master bedroom, which I long ago adopted for my own use," Mrs. Gansevoort confided, "this is the choicest room, darling."

Lulu expressed her thanks in a soft voice. She stood in the doorway, holding some of Mrs. Gansevoort's clothes on hangers over her arm.

"My daughter loved white!" Mrs. Gansevoort exclaimed, as the two of them surveyed Lulu's summer quarters, the startling whiteness of it all, the room and its furnishings. Even the cast-iron firedogs were white, standing in the border between the tiled hearth and a luxurious white shag carpet. "It was a kind of fetish, which I approved," Mrs. Gansevoort added, quietly. "Everything was white. Even the pencils she took to school. But this room, Luette, is not a mausoleum. I'm not like that."

When Mrs. Gansevoort turned her eyes to her, Lulu felt a sudden urge to confess her gratitude. Her voice quavered as she spoke. "You saved me, Auntie," she said, passionately. "When I came to you, I was lost."

A blush of pleasure swept across Mrs. Gansevoort's forehead, betraying her powerful vanity. For a long moment she continued to scrutinize Lulu with her bright, protuberant eyes, as though sealing Lulu's gratitude. "You do know," Mrs. Gansevoort added at length, her eyes widening with love, "that you belong here? To me?"

"Yes," Lulu replied tremulously.

"No matter who opposes us. No matter what I want. No

matter why." Mrs. Gansevoort gave her categorical pronounce-
ment the ring of a binding vow.

Lulu swallowed nervously. She knew what Mrs. Gansevoort
implied. She was telling Lulu what to expect. It was about
something that would come to pass, something as yet formless
and obscure. It concerned her nephew, Douglas. He was like a
figure, looked down upon from a great height, drawing slowly
closer and closer. As Lulu gazed up in wonderment at Mrs.
Gansevoort, she felt certain that Douglas would soon come among
them, pass into their common world, and be susceptible then
to Auntie's heart in ways he could not imagine.

That afternoon, after the rain had stopped, and a watery
sun struggled to penetrate the clouds dissipating above the
mountain, Douglas offered to show Lulu about. Before going
with him, Lulu went to Mrs. Gansevoort.

"I hope you're not asking my permission," Mrs. Gansevoort
replied, with a perplexed expression. "If you're not showing
initiative on the first day, what am I to expect tomorrow, or next
week?"

Surprised at being upbraided, Lulu gazed at her friend in
silence. Mrs. Gansevoort never spoke sharply to her.

"I wasn't sure whether to go," Lulu managed to reply.

"Then I'll tell you! You are to do anything that your heart
dictates up here, so long as it suits our needs. You needn't come
running to me every fifteen minutes." Mrs. Gansevoort spoke
with startling candor. "I want him to know that his presence is
essential. If tomorrow he takes it into his head to go flitting off
to New York State or up to Vermont, I will not be happy. I'm
putting the matter into your hands."

When Lulu arrived outdoors, Douglas was standing in the
wet grass, pulling up a rotted garden hose that had been left
outside the previous summer. It clung tenaciously to the earth,
coming up bit by bit with clumps of soil and dead grass stuck
to it.

In the sunlight, the grounds looked different. Beyond the gravel drive was a derelict orchard, the wild trees standing in knee-tall grass. Farther back was the forest, and beyond that, over the line of the treetops, like a great spiny animal sitting back on its haunches, arose the mountain against the sky. The air was fresh, the atmosphere buoyant. Lulu liked the feeling of solitude, the imposing silence, the resonance of the air at this altitude. She stood watching Douglas as he wrestled energetically with the serpentlike hose. In his dark blue Yale athletic jersey and white trousers, he looked his usual trim, immaculate self, a picture, to Lulu's mind, of the handsome Ivy Leaguer depicted in magazines.

Within minutes of joining him, however, it was obvious that Douglas's request to go walking with her was conceived to provide him an opportunity to question her. Lulu guessed that he sensed some mystery afoot in the house. He regarded her quizzically from time to time.

"I've never known anyone to change her clothes so often," he said, remarking on Lulu's dress and sandals. "Do you do that to please Aunt Julia? Are you Aunt Julia's *poupée?*"

Lulu laughed over the word.

"Chloris says that you speak French," he added.

"I do," Lulu replied, "but I don't like it." She smiled at him. She was more conscious than ever that her place in Mrs. Gansevoort's life mystified him. A lifetime of keeping silent and maintaining a shadowy presence, she was aware, served her well now, making a mystery of what was a colorless abstraction.

"You didn't answer my question," he said.

"I'm just Mrs. Gansevoort's helper," Lulu responded, genially.

"I don't doubt your word," Douglas conceded, "but sometimes I get the impression that you're more like a professional agent of hers. Or maybe," he theorized, "she's taken you aboard just to add luster to herself. That is a possibility. A clever one, too. By appointing an aide-de-camp, one arrogates to oneself, out of thin air, an aura of power that is not entirely distinguishable from power itself. Others *are* impressed."

"I don't think that Mrs. Gansevoort is trying to impress other people like that."

"Shall I show you the lodge?" Douglas asked. "That's where Leon stays when he comes to visit. You and he, if my sources are correct, have become something of an item these days."

"Your sister is not a reliable source," Lulu said, and was immediately pleased with her reply, as it avoided the heart of the matter while at the same time thrusting Chloris into an inferior light.

"I thought you might like to see his quarters." Douglas persisted in calling Mr. Rafferty to mind, while watching Lulu with an amiable expression.

At once, Lulu felt a compulsion to reiterate the falsehood she had endorsed the night before. "Leon won't be coming this year," she said.

"Usually," Douglas said, "he does."

As the two of them walked out to the gravel road, Lulu enjoyed the feeling aroused in her by the recognition that she would actually perjure herself for her friend. It was her way of giving Mrs. Gansevoort some part of herself; a willingness to violate herself, if necessary. The color or scope of the lie was immaterial; all that mattered was that Aunt Julia should approve of the deceit and profit by it. Lulu could not recall ever having lied, but knew she would do it again if she had to. She felt a dark, twirling sensation inside as they started along the gravel road.

The only sign of life from the outside world was the drone of a distant airplane. Lulu had just two thoughts in mind. One was to strengthen Douglas's resolve to stay with Aunt Julia and herself all summer. The other was to demystify nothing. Sometimes, as at this moment, Lulu was amazed to realize how secretive her thinking had always been. She could recall pacing silently to and fro, hour after hour, behind the candy counter at the variety store, mulling over the several different ways she might respond to a personal question that someone might ask, and distilling each possible response into a single utterance, five or six words that would reveal nothing about herself not already known, while at the same time discouraging a further probe. If Lulu had an art, that was it: the art of concealment.

Douglas, she was sure, was quite fascinated and perplexed about something concerning all three of them—his aunt, Leon, and herself—and had chosen her as the key to open the door. She believed, also, that her ascendancy over Chloris bewildered him. But Lulu thought she understood. It had to do, somehow, with Ignatia. That was the path to take to safeguard the mystery, to be loving and superior now toward Chloris, while saying absolutely nothing about anyone else. Beyond that, she couldn't guess what was going on. Aunt Julia, of course, understood everything. Auntie had a genius for such things. That was why Chloris could both dread and worship her aunt. Not because Chloris wished to be ensnared in anything so complicated, but because Mrs. Gansevoort wanted it that way. To Julia Gansevoort, Chloris was just a perverted reflection of Julia's own sister, a mere twinkling of lights upon the surface of the pool in whose depths the real deceiver lurked.

Douglas spoke speculatively. "Leon is just at that point in life where he could redeem everything by one brilliant stroke. The youthful poverty and pessimism, the wandering, the hopeless ambition in the face of the Gansevoorts, his years in the war, and this later phase—that of the dapper hermit. With his needle and thread, his tie bars and shoe trees. That's why I credit Aunt Julia."

"What does Aunt Julia say?"

"Well, she doesn't say anything outright. People never do in such circumstances. But you would have to admit that she believes him attracted to you and may even be encouraging him, or encouraging both of you, in that way."

"If that were true," Lulu answered, "she would not have hired me."

"Is that what you call it?" Douglas expressed delight. "Are you, then, an employee? You know better than that."

Lulu was enjoying the secret bantering with Douglas. She was flattered by his interest in her, even though she realized that it was nothing more vital than a curiosity over the fact of his aunt having taken a stranger into her house.

A brook sparkled beneath the overhanging bushes beside the road. The sun grew brighter as they walked. The road lay dry and white before them.

"Unless"—Douglas lowered his voice facetiously—"she truly wants you for herself."

"I don't think that Mr. Rafferty or his desires are too important to her." Lulu deflected his remark, but winced inwardly at its implications. He was trying to unsettle her. Lulu glanced back at the house, which had dwindled by now to a little patch of white glowing between trees. Douglas brushed against her as they walked. He was peeling a green branch.

"My intuitions aren't as keen as they ought to be," he said, "especially when dealing with people who have a taste for secrecy, but on the surface of things an outsider might suppose that Aunt Julia was preparing you for something out of the ordinary, Miss Peloquin. Something of moment! Something even, perhaps, romantic," he added.

"You don't see me as she does," said Lulu.

"I wouldn't deny that! But even if I did, that wouldn't rule out her conceiving some very original plans for you."

"Mostly," Lulu continued, touching lightly on the sensitive matter of Mrs. Gansevoort's house in the city, "I think she fears the day when she will be alone, living in the mountains, with everyone gone." Here Lulu avoided looking at Douglas, and worried for an instant about whether she had said too much.

"That's plausible on the surface," he replied, ignoring Lulu's allusion to the menace hanging over Mrs. Gansevoort's house in Ireland Parish, "but it raises as many questions as it answers. My aunt could not expect to hold a youthful companion forever at her side in the wilds purely through the powers of her personal charm."

"Are you saying," Lulu came right back, with a blush of color in her cheeks, "that I would abandon my friend?"

Instantly, Lulu wished she could have retrieved her words. He had tricked her into revealing the depth of her feelings.

"Not at all," he said. "I was putting myself in Julia's place, and concluded that that was not, in fact, her plan, as it would leave her at the mercy of her own protégée. She would be *your* ward."

"I am not your aunt's ward!" Lulu cried, but regretted her emotional words even in the moment that she spoke them.

"Anyhow," Douglas continued, "since it was Leon who unearthed you, and Aunt Julia who favors you so, a stranger like myself can be forgiven for supposing that someone sees Leon as an appropriate suitor, some one of the three of you, or even two of the three of you, or, for that matter, who knows, all three of you!"

By this time, Lulu had determined to steer their talk to Mrs. Gansevoort's concern about Douglas staying in the mountains with them all summer, and to discourage other subjects. She felt a stab of shame at the thought of Mrs. Gansevoort overhearing the words transpiring between them. The idea of Mrs. Gansevoort becoming Lulu's ward! Or that she, Julia Gansevoort, should be preparing her for a romantic attachment with Mr. Rafferty. Or, most vicious of all, the suggestion that Auntie wanted Lulu for herself, for reasons too hideous to articulate.

With each step, however, Lulu's resolve faltered. The house was lost to view now in the trees behind them, while the road ahead, ascending gently, formed a glistening green tunnel under the overarching trees. Lulu felt increasingly queasy as they paced quietly along, and wished that she were walking with Mrs. Gansevoort, or even Mr. Rafferty, in either of whose company she always derived a certain dark comfort.

At the top of the incline, Lulu stopped walking. "I don't want to go any further." Turning, she peered back into the welter of shining, dripping trees. A bird flew wildly across the road, its black wings shimmering, but throwing a sudden dart of crimson light.

"I hope you weren't offended by my remark suggesting you were my aunt's ward. You don't know me very well. I'm one of those people who is apt to say anything."

They stood facing one another. It might have been her imagination, but Lulu sensed in Douglas's attention something soft and perplexed. She stood motionless, with the sun falling in pale spangles about her feet. The woods were fragrant. Then, abruptly, Lulu felt the same extraordinary sensation she had experienced before; it materialized in her breast, solid and vertical, and descended inside her. It went down slowly, then came up again, like a plunger. At the same time, she had posed Douglas a question, and was not even conscious, she realized, of having given thought to it before the words passed her lips. "Do you know why he is not coming this summer?"

Douglas's eyes met her own. He had beautiful hazel eyes, Lulu reflected, just like Auntie, but with sandy lashes. She thought him immobilized by the question. He was also, Lulu was convinced, very frightened of Mr. Rafferty. She did not know why.

"I wondered about that," he replied, in a voice that struck Lulu as forcedly casual. "He used to come regularly to Peru Mountain. Not every year, but more often than not."

"Auntie didn't want him to come," Lulu explained significantly. "She wanted you to come."

Lulu spoke the words almost gravely, as if Mr. Rafferty had been sent to the far ends of the earth in order to make room at Peru Mountain for Douglas. If Lulu was wrong about Douglas,

LULU INCOGNITO

he would treat her assertion as idle. Something inside herself revolved slowly about her heart. She was lying for Auntie.

"I think," said Lulu, "that she told Leon a tall story to convince him not to come." As before, her tone was quite solemn; she could feel the power her words worked upon his attention. "She wanted you."

A smile flashed to his lips. "I used to be a necessary evil," Douglas said, referring to the many summers he spent with his aunt, as a paying guest.

"She's not afraid to be alone." Lulu began to embroider on her lie, but was careful not to suggest that Mrs. Gansevoort could not someday manage by herself in her country house. "I believe she wants her family to be with her this year. I think she's too proud to say so herself."

Douglas laughed appreciatively. "I know what you mean. Monarchs," he said, "do not petition peasants or parties of inferior degree!"

"Even," Lulu agreed, "if they are her flesh and blood." Lulu was pleased with the felicity of her reply, as more and more she found herself capable of conversing with Douglas on his own level. "I can't read her thoughts—" Lulu commenced to add in a smart tone, but Douglas cut in spiritedly.

"I thought you, of all people, could!" he cried. "The gift of the alter ego! The divination of angels!"

"But I feel this is a special summer for Mrs. Gansevoort," Lulu persisted in the same serious-minded vein, "although I'm not sure why. Maybe she sees it as the end of something important. Whatever the reason, I hope she won't be disappointed."

"By me?" Douglas had recovered his spirits entirely, with the troubling allusions to Mr. Rafferty apparently receding in his thoughts.

"Yes." Lulu stood perfectly still in the center of the road, determined to fulfill her commission, to elicit from Douglas his word that he would stay with them all summer. His good spirits encouraged her to expect success. She was wearing one of Ignatia's pink dresses, a cotton sheath that fitted her to perfection. Earlier, while dressing, she had wondered if Douglas's mother—in Italy, or Trieste, or wherever she was—was the same size today as she had been on that day a few years ago when she was fitted for this dress. She wondered, also, if Douglas recognized it.

"You can't imagine how bizarre it is," said Douglas, "to be accosted by someone—anyone!—whose concerns appear to coincide exactly with hers."

"Why is that odd?"

"You don't understand. This is not how it's done. Aunt Julia doesn't need allies. At least, she never has. I hope this doesn't mean the old system is losing current. Aunt Julia," Douglas explained, patiently, "was raised to a stricter code, to know her own mind, to follow no one, to trust no one not to fail. She has a hard core."

"Everyone requires a friend," Lulu suggested innocently. "Your aunt is no different. Maybe when she was younger, she *was* different. That's not important to me."

Douglas laughed, shaking his head incredulously. "I can't doubt that it's happened."

"That what has happened?"

"You're here." He gestured vaguely toward the house. "You're with her. You're fond of her. You care about precisely the things she wants you to care about."

"I care about her needs!"

"Tell me something." Douglas was evidently enjoying himself. "What does she pay you?"

"Do you mean money?" Lulu had not touched a coin or bill since the day she came to live at Leiden Hall, and was conscious all along of the pleasant relief she felt at never needing to do so.

"In what currency," he repeated himself, smiling, "does she pay you?"

Although a trifle insulted by the nephew's manner, Lulu decided to respond sincerely to his question.

"With respect," Lulu replied, and kept her gaze fixed upon his face.

Douglas nodded thoughtfully. "Okay." He conceded that. "We're all needful. Aunt Julia needs her lawn mowed. She needs her eggs to be boiled. She needs doing for, but she doesn't need, or, at least, never has needed, looking after!"

"I don't look after her," Lulu stated calmly.

"You look to do what she tells you needs doing. That's why you're here today. I just can't believe that you've deduced out of thin air that *Auntie,* as you sometimes call her, has certain needs touching on me which you've decided to represent to me on your own." Douglas let a moment elapse. "She sent you," he said, "didn't she?"

For the first time, Lulu felt a little rush of panic in her heart, as she realized that his intellectual toying with her portended a menace to her plans. She hoped her fear didn't show in her face.

"No! She didn't tell me to do anything."

"Then she's had a stroke of luck in you that she didn't deserve."

Lulu watched Douglas anxiously. "You'll stay, then?" she put in softly.

"Of course," he replied. "It was never in question. I had already agreed."

Lulu felt a surge of affection for Douglas, and at the same time a return of her confidence, of her powers, although later she would castigate herself for having shown weakness at the critical point. He had led her about by the nose, probing her life and motives, while knowing all along that he had no intention of leaving Mrs. Gansevoort in the lurch. It was only later that Lulu suspected he might have been flirting with her. This possibility struck Lulu with far greater force than it could have upon nearly any other young woman, for Lulu was not accustomed to receiving overtures from anyone.

Troubled by this line of thought, she went a step further. She wondered if her own very complex intrigues that afternoon, her anxiety and subtle schemings, might not have been themselves two-sided. She had to ask herself if she had not been spinning a web of her own. While sitting later that afternoon on a wicker chair in the sun room, her legs crossed and a writing tablet poised on her knee, Lulu considered consciously for the first time whether such a fine person as he, so wonderfully educated and so handsome to look at, so remote to everything she knew, could possibly—by any stretch of the imagination— find her attractive.

●

"Do you have it all down?" Mrs. Gansevoort paused in her pacing. She was dictating a letter to Lulu. In recent days, the hour of three o'clock to four in the afternoon was often taken up with letter writing. Lulu realized—and knew that Mrs. Gansevoort did, also—that the dictation of letters was developing day by day into a little ritual that was as important to Auntie for its value as an activity between them as for any practical ends. It had started one day by chance, when Mrs. Gansevoort, knowing that Lulu could type somewhat, had her type up a letter that she had composed to her lawyer. After that, Mrs. Gansevoort had begun inventing reasons for the composition of additional letters. By now, the hour had evolved a format. Lulu sat primly in her chair, with pad and pencil, while Aunt Julia paced the room, lips pursed, her handsome face lifted thoughtfully, dictating her words with great exactitude. Lulu enjoyed the hour as much as did her friend. The truth was, Lulu liked those times when Mrs. Gansevoort gave off that special air of consequence. She liked to participate in her friend's self-indulgent moods by lending herself actively to Mrs. Gansevoort's natural egoism.

"I haven't missed a word," Lulu replied with eagerness, as she thrust the thought of Douglas from her mind.

"Read me back, please, the last paragraph," Mrs. Gansevoort instructed importantly. She was in the midst of a letter to a Mrs. Gilbertine Cross, an old family friend. "With punctuation."

As Mrs. Gansevoort in dictating struck a definite authorial air, Lulu, in reading back, fell naturally into the manner of the conscientious secretary. Clearing her throat, Lulu recited distinctly from the pad on her knee:

" 'Of late—comma—a good deal of my thinking has centered upon those past years—comma—specifically—comma—when you and I and the Morgans enjoyed such a welcome—comma—if undeserved—comma—favoritism among the summer cognoscenti out here. Period. It's a crying evil that life stole you and Hubbard away from me—comma—although we should truly thank fortune for granting us such gratuitous favors as our original meeting at school. Period. Here I am compelled to stay—comma—with my newly adopted niece—comma—or daughter—dash—whom I call "Zita"—in quotes—dash—at least—comma—until I—comma—or we—comma—contrive a more auspicious manner of life. Period.' "

"I don't like 'manner of life,' " Mrs. Gansevoort remarked with nice thoughtfulness, while staring away into vacancy with a narrow expression. "Change 'manner of life,' please, to 'life circumstance.' "

As Lulu hastily scratched in the correction, Mrs. Gansevoort folded her arms and resumed pacing and dictating. Lulu marveled at Mrs. Gansevoort's ability to express herself so exquisitely, sometimes salting her sentences with words and phrases taken from Latin or French, incorporating quotations from poetry, and generally maintaining an exalted tone. She never stooped to communicating banalities. Lulu took the words down onto paper with the relish of the true acolyte, and, by developing from day to day her own personal form of shorthand, prided herself on the fact that only once or twice had she asked Mrs. Gansevoort to repeat herself. Lulu's devotion to her friend's words, to her elegant phrasings and sentiments, was intensified, too, by the fact that Mrs. Gansevoort regularly made reference to Lulu in her letters, sometimes calling her "Zita," or even "Zita G.," with the "G." standing for "Gansevoort," as well as the fact that several of Auntie's letters contained obvious distortions of the truth, while others expressed open dispraise for her own family. More than once in her letters, Mrs. Gansevoort had referred to Chloris and her brother with sudden vicious sarcasms. One remark in particular seared itself into Lulu's memory, when, in a letter to a bookstore lady in Boston, Mrs. Gansevoort characterized her niece and nephew as "Ignatia's progeny, the serpents of her womb."

Only a few hours had passed since Lulu's arrival at the old summer estate, but she was already feeling wonderfully acclimated. The cool air, the resonant silence outdoors, and the big sunlit solarium with its wicker furnishings and pretty Navajo rugs, worked as a balm on her nerves. She loved the feel of the house and grounds, and of the great mountain massed against the sky beyond the ruinous orchards and distant wood. Lulu worked at one end of the sun room, while Mrs. Gansevoort settled in behind the big glass-surfaced wicker desk by the far windows. Equipped with a fat blue dictionary, Lulu checked her spellings scrupulously before she began typing her friend's letters. Mrs. Gansevoort had special stationery for use in the country. The paper was dove gray with the letterhead "Holland House—Peru Mountain" printed in the upper right-hand corner in small black letters. As she set to work, Lulu felt in her heart a customary surge of affection for the lady in the gray jacket and gold turtleneck seated at the other side of the room. She was touched by Aunt Julia's lonely circumstance in life, with her husband and daughter gone forever, and she resolved for the hundredth time to devote herself to Auntie; not just in the larger sense, but in detail, exquisitely, in every tiny application of her energies, as in the way she fussed now to get the margins exactly right on the page, or in the way that she would present the letters to Auntie for her signature, placing one sheet before her at a time, withdrawing it, and presenting the next, so that Auntie could feel very spoiled and important.

Three or four hours had elapsed since Lulu had gone walking with Douglas, and elicited his intention to remain in Peru Mountain for the balance of the summer, but Lulu had not yet reported this fact to her friend. The reason was that Auntie always cued Lulu in some discreet way when she wished Lulu to deliver herself of a report, just as, by the same token, she had encouraged Lulu to express herself at such times according to the vague, imprecise terms of their private language.

"I hope," Mrs. Gansevoort spoke up in an oily, businesslike tone of voice when Lulu came to her with the typed letters to be signed, "that you didn't go traipsing about in the wet grass earlier today."

Lulu saw her opening to apprise Mrs. Gansevoort of what had transpired with Douglas, but the older woman was in no rush. She smiled at Lulu.

"I have reserved for myself the task of showing you about. Not," Mrs. Gansevoort explained, "because there is anything to be proud of out there." Her hazel eyes signified the grounds toward the rear of the house. "In fact, it's quite shameful. So much so that I am reluctant to show you." Mrs. Gansevoort adopted here the point of view she often used when wishing to please and flatter Lulu, treating her like a princess used to only the most delicate refinements. "You will be shocked," she protested. "I am not exaggerating. When I was a child, the grounds up here were fussed over by none other than my father himself, a man who could make flowers bloom from a rock.

But year by year, it has all steadily decomposed. You would have to have a taste for things derelict not to see these outdoors as a sin. It's all gone—the dam, the lily pond, the footpaths, the acres of carefully pruned hardwood groves, the old belvedere," she added, "the great lawn, all of it."

Lulu came to the point. "Since Douglas *is* going to be with you all summer, couldn't he help you with the outdoors?"

Mrs. Gansevoort withheld her reply, but continued to stare at Lulu for a long interval. The room was exceedingly bright. The breeze blowing the curtains abated, and the sunlight winked in the crystal inkwell on Auntie's desk top. Outdoors, from afar, came the soft toiling sound of an engine, as of a farm machine perhaps at work in a distant field. Mrs. Gansevoort's eyes twinkled with a golden light. Lulu was holding the letters in her hand, and felt a twinge of excitement, of fear, stirring inside herself, as the silence lengthened between them. Sometimes Mrs. Gansevoort's eyes frightened her. She couldn't imagine what her friend would say next.

"Does he realize," Mrs. Gansevoort commented in a soft, throaty voice, "that you are perhaps not altogether free? . . . Does he suspect such a possibility?"

Lulu's mind raced to comprehend Mrs. Gansevoort's meanings. She would not dare to confess her perplexity. That would go against the unwritten rules of their understandings.

Mrs. Gansevoort was smiling faintly. "Isn't he curious?"

"About me, Auntie?" Lulu endeavored to match her friend's smile, which was both lustful and cryptic, at least to Lulu's mind.

"About both of you," Mrs. Gansevoort came back. "Doesn't he wonder? Doesn't he wonder, I mean to say, about all of us?"

"I'm not sure," she said.

"But, really"—Mrs. Gansevoort persisted in the same pensive, businesslike vein—"shouldn't he? Wouldn't it be improper to delude him? To appear altogether available? I'm sure he suspects the existence of something, however uncommon or unlikely, between the two of you."

After a moment, Lulu nodded tentatively, acknowledging at least the possibility.

"Of course he does," Mrs. Gansevoort agreed in an easy manner, as if granting her nephew benefit of intelligence. "How could he not?"

Lulu was perspiring. She stood beside Mrs. Gansevoort's chair like a schoolgirl, clutching the letters before her. Mrs. Gansevoort's assumption that Douglas might entertain a romantic interest in her amazed and upset Lulu.

Aunt Julia continued. "You would not want to appear altogether available, then—at least not openly so—would you?"

Despite her qualms, Lulu was following the direction of her friend's thought. She wanted Lulu to do something to invoke Mr. Rafferty's name in suggestive ways. She wanted Douglas to be mystified about the two of them.

"The idea of a pristine flower, such as yourself, Luette, passing by degrees into the grasp of such a seemingly steel-hearted figure as Leon can be quite provocative, particularly if the flower herself were consciously apprehensive—for the most old-fashioned reasons!—of this developing entanglement."

"I will be," Lulu consented, softly. (Lulu had only to think about Mr. Rafferty in reality, about the wintergreen scent of his cologne, the scar on his wrist, to be—in that way—truly afraid. That would be easy.)

"The means and method I entrust to you," said Mrs. Gansevoort.

Lulu wished to say something that would show that she understood Auntie's desires. Auntie was waiting for her to speak. "When," Lulu asked, at length, significantly, "*will* Leon be coming?"

"Naturally," Mrs. Gansevoort replied, "when I shall summon him."

Something here in Mrs. Gansevoort's resolute, sinister air caused Lulu to reflect that a similar season must have come and gone for Chloris, one such as her brother was now entering, a time when she, the girl, like a mere bit of dandelion fluff afloat in the summer air, dropped soundlessly into Auntie's hands. Douglas, she believed, was about to have his turn.

Lulu looked out the open window to the wooded mountainside, green and primeval, massed above the tops of the fruit trees. Here Aunt Julia dwelt like a regent in exile, among her broken fortunes. This was her natural domain.

●

As promised, Mrs. Gansevoort showed Lulu about the grounds the next afternoon, and Lulu was quite amazed by the extent of the place. She should have known, of course, that the old summer quarters of a family like the Gansevoorts, people who once possessed wealth and power, even if this was one of the lesser houses, would be imposing to her eye. She listened religiously as Mrs. Gansevoort, walking before her under a row of pines, described the garden parties and *fêtes champêtres* held on the great lawn in the old days. The lawn consisted now of nothing more than an army of saplings surrounded on all sides by a decayed stuccoed wall. Mrs. Gansevoort painted a picture of tall, gaily striped tents and pavilions, a brass orchestra, and crowds of luxuriously dressed men and women. At the far end of the overgrown field stood the remains of a main gate, two tall pillars still surmounted by a forlorn cast-iron decoration, a kind of iron pediment etched in filigree against the sky.

Lulu was enthralled. Beyond the great lawn, the hill sloped down to a broad, shallow depression, choked with thick-leaved plants crowded among isolated pools of dead water gleaming in the sun; at the heart of the swamp, inaccessible by foot, stood what was left of a large gazebo. The roof was still on it, but the narrow wooden bridge that led out to it had vanished years since in the slime. The pond itself, which once had twinkled all about it, was a thing of the past, just a thick growth of horsetails and purple-leaved wild cabbage. Through the trees to the right the guest lodge was visible. It was quite big and looked in good repair.

Mrs. Gansevoort strode through the tall grass; from amid the milkweed and blue thistles about her feet arose the steady crackling of insects. She spoke of the worlds of trailing arbutus that once decked the mountainside, as she signified with her eyes the nearby mass of Peru Mountain swelling against the sky. Lulu turned on her heel to look at it. The looming mountain was a powerful presence. In all, the estate seemed vast to Lulu's eye, and sadly decomposed.

"It's very desolate," Lulu said, "but I love it all, Auntie." Lulu searched her mind then for a superior way to express the emotion she felt. "I am only sorry," she said, selecting her words with care, "to see so much of it disappearing in ruins."

Mrs. Gansevoort had paused, and was staring importantly at the mountain, with an attitude suggesting that she and it were worthy of one another. Lulu liked that quality in her friend. Auntie seemed to be posing, holding her face up proudly in the sunlight.

"It's we who make ruins," Mrs. Gansevoort declared. "No one asked us to clutter the earth!"

In order to strengthen her positive reaction to Mrs. Gansevoort's summer house and its sprawling grounds, Lulu decided to touch here upon a possibility they rarely raised. "I could be happy to live with you here, Auntie," she said. "I would be honored."

Mrs. Gansevoort didn't look at Lulu, and gave no reply, but stood motionless in the hot grass, her sunlit face turned impressively to the mountain.

Lulu had just formed the idea that Mrs. Gansevoort had allowed her summer estate to go to ruin simply because she did not want to admit to herself that she might ultimately lose everything else and be compelled into exile here. Lulu was moved by this realization. Suddenly, she spoke up with ardor, stepping closer to her friend. "Promise you won't be angry, Auntie, for what I am going to say."

"I won't," came the distant, ironic reply.

"I would cook for you, and keep house for you, anything," she said, "if you required me to. I would work indoors and out." Lulu's sincerity shone through her words.

A brief, pitying smile distorted Mrs. Gansevoort's lips. "And the snow?" she inquired facetiously. "When the storms come, you will bundle yourself up and shovel me a broad path to the road?"

The woman's scathing cynicism could not deflect Lulu now. Her passion prohibited her from being discouraged. "Yes," she responded firmly, "I would."

"Am I to understand," Mrs. Gansevoort showed Lulu her glittering eyes, "that you would be as happy living up here, in this rustic ruin, as in our own house—at home?"

Lulu altered her attitude at once, as she perceived the vein of smoldering anger coming to the surface in Mrs. Gansevoort.

"No," Lulu admitted, chastened, "the other would be better, of course."

"An idiot," Mrs. Gansevoort snapped unpleasantly, "with no brain whatsoever, exchanges something dear, something valuable, for nothing!" She was incensed; her voice trembled with anger. Lulu made no reply to this remark, as she noted how Mrs. Gansevoort's face shook with a cold rage.

With a sudden imperious gesture, her bracelets shaking out flashes of sunlight, Mrs. Gansevoort pointed a finger at the earth before her feet, and condemned her niece and nephew. "I shall see them on their knees!" she said.

In the days to come, Lulu was pleased to discover that Mrs. Gansevoort was more active socially in Peru Mountain than she had known her to be at home. Doubtless, Auntie was more comfortable with the summer people on holiday than with her neighbors in Ireland Parish.

Mrs. Gansevoort smiled at Lulu over breakfast one morning. "I tell them all now that you're my niece," she said, "my cousin's niece, really. Zita Gansevoort!"

"She might as well be a Gansevoort," said Douglas. "No one has ever got closer."

Mrs. Gansevoort questioned him sharply. "What is that supposed to mean?"

"Oh, I'm not knocking it!" Douglas cried gaily.

Chloris cut in. "I love the name! It's very exotic. Zita Gansevoort!"

Mrs. Gansevoort reached and squeezed Lulu's hand. To Lulu,

the occasion seemed opportune to obey one of Mrs. Gansevoort's secret injunctions. "I hope Leon likes it," she said.

Instantly, Mrs. Gansevoort seized upon Lulu's gambit. "If he doesn't," she exclaimed vivaciously, "we shall change it back in a twinkling. You never know about men. While Leon certainly has a taste for the exotic, he just might object to it. Especially as it was he who discovered you."

Lulu could feel Douglas watching her from his place at the table, and knew in her heart that Auntie was right about her nephew's weakness—his fascination at any hint of her having an affiliation with Mr. Rafferty. It was uncanny. When she looked up, the concern in his eyes was unmistakable. Lulu realized for the first time that she could not rule out the possibility that he was beginning to care for her. She was so affected by this notion that her brain began to swim; and reaching carefully, she set her fork down on her plate, very tidily, as though that simple act might somehow restore the balance of her senses. She wanted him to care.

●

By this time, Lulu's compact with Aunt Julia, her pledge, that is, to work a subtle influence upon Douglas, preparatory to the arrival of Mr. Rafferty, was an open fact to Chloris. In the course of a day, Chloris would come several times to Lulu, bringing word of Douglas's whereabouts or activities, usually delivering herself of her news with the soft, breathless whispering of a little woodland sprite bearing messages to a real-life princess. Sometimes a lustful light appeared in Chloris's eyes, which, when she noticed it, filled Lulu with contempt for the girl, for she knew Chloris's ambitions were vicious at heart. How anyone so pretty, so delicate and innocent in appearance, could play the part of the wicked little demiurge intent upon—her own brother's moral undoing?—upon God knows what—mystified and repelled Lulu.

"I think he wants to stay up here because of you," Chloris

reported to Lulu one afternoon, at a time when Mrs. Gansevoort
had gone with friends to attend a dance program at Jacob's
Pillow. "I heard him talking on the telephone," she said. "He
called you Zita. He said, 'If it wasn't for Zita, my cousin, I would
be bored out of my wits up here.' "

Lulu was sitting at Auntie's wicker desk in the sun room.
She was wearing a garnet ring that had once belonged to
Chloris's mother, Ignatia. It was obvious the girl recognized it.
She stood motionless in the sun, staring at it. Lulu didn't move
a muscle. She found herself so disdainful of Douglas's sister, of
her depravity, that she could not resist tormenting her as she
sat back in Julia Gansevoort's chair and regarded Chloris with
a look of perplexity.

Chloris hovered before her, looking both frightened and
adoring. The girl's face shone prettily in the sunlight, the bones
delicate, the eyes like those of a doll. Lulu's response could have
been Auntie's own; she could hear Auntie speaking through
her. "You interrupted me," she said, "to tell me that?"

"I think it means something! He's going outdoors now to
scythe the grass in the orchard." While Chloris whispered on
conspiratorially, a slow, cold shudder passed through Lulu's legs
and knees as she considered the destruction that must have
taken place inside the girl recently. The thought was frightening. "You do believe me," Chloris added with growing discomfort.

"I know you wouldn't lie." Lulu found herself smiling ironically at the young woman, in a manner that Mrs. Gansevoort
often used. "You do realize," Lulu persisted, badgering her,
"that what you're doing is sinful."

Chloris's face altered swiftly. "I would never do anything
sinful!" she protested. "I revere Aunt Julia."

"I wasn't talking about Auntie," said Lulu. "I was talking
about your brother."

"My brother?" Chloris's puzzlement appeared genuine. "I
only want for him what Auntie wants for him."

"And what is that?" Lulu asked, gravely, while studying the niece with a thoughtful air.

"I want him to be happy. I want him to have what Aunt Julia wants."

Lulu repeated herself. "And what do you suppose that is?" She glanced outdoors at the distant wall of pines hiding the derelict pond, then up at Chloris once more. "What do you suppose Auntie wants for your brother?" The idea came slowly to Lulu that some of the repugnance she felt for the girl was associated with her own growing affection for Douglas, her appreciation of his basic decency, his confiding nature.

Tiny beads of moisture glistened along Chloris's hairline. She couldn't hold Lulu's gaze. Her eyes turned abstractedly to one side, and stayed like that, fixed on vacant space. "I don't know," she confessed softly. "I wouldn't dare ask."

Abruptly, Lulu gave voice to an outrageous impulse. "You do know," she said, "that I'm wearing your mother's things."

"Yes."

Lulu watched Chloris acutely. "How long have you known?"

"Since the beginning," Chloris replied. "When I helped you put on her gray dress, the one with the fluted top. Before that, some of the things were Sylvia's, except for your shoes. All your shoes were Mother's. When you first came, Aunt Julia told me to put all of Mother's shoes in that same closet."

Lulu surmised that the niece was probably forgetting herself and confessing more than she should have. She was violating Auntie's trust. Lulu said nothing, but sat back in the sunlight.

Chloris looked up. "Auntie favors you above everybody else. As for Douglas"—her eyes went to the window—"I think she would like him to be closer to us. And that she would like him to see you as she sees you."

"You don't really believe that your aunt wants Douglas to come up here this summer for such a foolish reason as that, do you?" This question struck Lulu as the most incisive of all, and she was very curious as to how Chloris would respond.

"I don't honestly know," Chloris answered. "But it doesn't matter to me. Auntie," she said, "doesn't reveal herself. She will only reveal herself after it's over."

"It?" said Lulu, startled.

"Yes," said Chloris. "That's how Auntie is. She works more or less in secret. I trust her more than anyone. I believe in her. That's why I came home from school. I couldn't bear being away. I telephoned her every night from Northfield. I used to cry on the telephone, until, finally, she let me come back."

While the girl was speaking, Lulu's mind was circling round and round something the girl had said a moment earlier. She wanted Chloris to elucidate it. "Was that," Lulu asked, "when Auntie . . . revealed herself?"

"Yes." Here Chloris smiled so pathetically that Lulu felt her heart suddenly jump in her breast. She was staring intensely at Mrs. Gansevoort's niece.

"Tell me about that." Lulu commanded her softly, her own mind come to a standstill in the meanwhile.

Chloris appeared perplexed. "But it was the same for me," she said, "as it was for you." She was regarding Lulu with incredulity. "She revealed herself!"

Chloris remained puzzled that Lulu should make such an inquiry of her. Lulu's heart was shaking. She didn't know what Chloris was talking about.

"But where," said Lulu, "did it happen?"

"Oh, that," Chloris answered, relieved at the specificity of Lulu's wonderment. "We were in Auntie's sitting room, the Oriental Room, listening to music."

While desperately eager to hear more, Lulu struggled to keep her composure. She searched her mind for a tangential question that would veil her own ignorance while inducing Chloris to say more.

"Were you crying?" Lulu asked.

"I had been," Chloris said, "because Auntie was only going to keep me for the weekend."

Lulu pressed carefully. "And what did you say to her that caused Auntie to . . . reveal herself?"

Chloris made a face. "I don't remember exactly. I didn't need to say anything. She knew." When Chloris's eyes came up to meet Lulu's, Lulu imagined that she could see in their depths that same twisted blue light, the little corruptive blue flame that invariably shone out of the girl's irises whenever she came to Lulu with secret intelligences about her brother.

"You see," Chloris explained, as in an allusion to Douglas's ignorance, "I didn't know, all that past year—all last summer and during the long fall and winter at school—I didn't know that she was thinking about me. She wanted me." Chloris smiled weakly. "She knew."

"That you were ready," Lulu whispered in awe.

"Yes," came Chloris's soft reply.

Lulu couldn't resist repeating the dreadful words. "And then Auntie," she said, ". . . revealed herself?"

"Yes," said Chloris.

●

Lulu waved Chloris out of the room with a slow, grand gesture that reflected her stupefied state. She put her head back on the chair and closed her eyes. She couldn't get Auntie out of her mind. When she shut her eyes, her senses swam. She was perspiring freely, not because the air was hot, but in the distinct consciousness of the power of Mrs. Gansevoort's influence upon her, the force of her moral character. It exhausted her. She could not think straight, but felt something toxic swimming about inside her heart.

A short while afterward, Lulu went outdoors in search of Douglas. Chloris, she was certain, was right about that: Douglas welcomed her company—not because he was attracted to her, but because he couldn't fathom what was going on. He was sitting by the brook, sharpening the long blade of the scythe with a whetstone. He wore a faded baseball cap and a Yale athletic jersey with the sleeves cut off. His neck and arms were sweated. Now and again, he reached and extended the great blade of the scythe into the stream, allowing the current to wash away the lather.

"I'm surprised," said Lulu at one point, as she strove to make conversation, "that you and Mr. Rafferty and others haven't helped Aunt Julia fix up this place. I don't mean the house, of course. But the gazebo and the lawn and everything out back."

"I hope," Douglas said, "Julia hasn't been poisoning your mind with such ideas."

"No, she hasn't."

"My brother, being the eldest, set the example for the rest of us. He was not," Douglas emphasized, "a jack-of-all-trades! Warren was the sort of fellow who could open and close a rusted door from May to September and never once consider the benefits a squirt of oil might produce. Besides, you will learn that my aunt does not reward initiative. If she had wanted work done, she'd have had it done! Leon himself would have done it. We don't see the place as you do." He smiled up at her. "To me, it looks remarkably the way it did last year. Just as Aunt Julia herself seems, since then, not to have changed a particle. That's life!" Douglas smiled. "You went to Sunday school. It wasn't only man that fell—but the whole grand scheme of nature and time." Douglas gestured extravagantly toward the estate on all sides. "It falls and falls."

"If you think like that," said Lulu, "the grass will never get cut."

Lulu's reply tickled Douglas. "Oh, you're too quick for me," he said. "They ought to give you a chair in philosophy at Yale. Aunt Julia could endow it. The Zita Gansevoort chair! The chair of terse rebuttals!" Douglas was enjoying himself. He was up on his feet, mopping his forehead with the top of his cap. "Men of learning would come to you from all over the world, logicians, metaphysicians, logical positivists, expounding their nicest theories, just so that you, Zita G., in the flesh, may rebut them with something as pithy as that! 'If you think like that, Mr. Ayer, the grass will never get cut!'

"Oh, yes," Douglas continued, "I'm beginning to appreciate Julia's wisdom more and more. Julia is the one human being who always impressed but never surprised me. Now, this year, she's done even that. She has you! I hope this is not the beginning of a new dispensation, like a war of the titans to be followed by a new pantheon of gods. Julia was once the brilliant hope of the Gansevoorts, you know."

"I can believe that," Lulu affirmed.

"She was the apple of her father's eye. It was she, Julia, who was to lead the holy host to Orléans! Instead," said Douglas, "she got trapped in a quiet domestic life, and watched the last of the family legacy leak away. The sword of St. Michael was passed to Sylvia. We know what happened to her."

Douglas had begun to lead Lulu along the earthen path toward the lodge. When he spoke again, his words, despite his playful air, took Lulu by surprise. He glanced over his shoulder at her. "Tell me, is something peculiar going on around here?"

"Do you mean," said Lulu, grasping instantly his meaning, "has Auntie some new special plans?"

The bill of Douglas's cap shaded his eyes. "Exactly."

"Do you mean, also," Lulu elaborated, choosing her words carefully, "am I somehow a part of her new plans?"

She enjoyed walking behind Douglas in this fashion, addressing his back. Her confidence waxed. She recognized the spontaneity in his friendliness, the pleasure he couldn't conceal over her having come outdoors to him.

"Are you?" he asked softly, at close range, while holding branches aside, allowing her to pass before him.

"No," Lulu lied, "I'm not. I'm Mrs. Gansevoort's assistant. She's writing a book."

"She's not writing a book, and you know it," he replied. "That book is a part of—what would you call it?—of her myth."

Lulu halted, and turned to him. "You shouldn't say that," she objected, in a hurt tone. "Not to me."

Facing one another on the path, they shared an intimate moment. Lulu saw in his eyes a look of concern, of something personal.

Douglas sought embarrassedly to dispel the sudden intimacy. "Well, I wasn't attacking her everlasting soul."

"You might as well have been."

Douglas showed his amazement again. "You can't know how extraordinary it is to discover someone defending Julia Gansevoort."

"I'm not defending her," said Lulu. "She doesn't need that. But I am loyal."

Douglas touched Lulu's bare elbow as he guided her. "I understand," he said. "I marvel over it. When I see you together, you seem so natural, beyond anything, beyond even herself and Sylvia. You're more like her peer—or even her sister—than an employee or companion."

His words had barely touched Lulu's consciousness when she stopped and studied him intently. It was he, not she, who had woven into their words the sudden mention of his mother. Lulu was wearing two of his mother's rings today, as well as her dress and shoes. Lulu was so absorbed in her thoughts of Douglas's mother, Ignatia, that she took very little notice of the interior of the lodge when Douglas showed her indoors. It was obvious to Lulu that he was still fishing for information.

"I know you don't like me to speak critically of Aunt Julia," he said, "and that if I do, you will leave and go back to the house; but she has a contemptuous streak in her, something high and mighty, so I'm naturally intrigued to discover suddenly someone whom she admires."

"She doesn't admire me." Lulu argued the point. "She has shown me love and respect."

"Is there a difference?"

"Yes, there is. I love Auntie, and I look up to her. She does not look up to me. How could she?"

"So, you are her companion, then, and nothing more."

"Of course. What else could I be?"

"If Aunt Julia values you, she won't let you go without a struggle. You ought to know that about her."

Lulu was standing in the heart of the room with her back to the fireplace. "Go where?" she asked, innocently.

She couldn't help herself, but was experiencing feelings of physical excitement, a fluttering in her stomach and a tightness along the backs of her legs, as she regarded him steadily.

In the next instant, Douglas surprised her with his reply. "With Leon," he said. "Where else?"

Lulu marveled at the way Mrs. Gansevoort had contrived matters to a point—contrived it out of nothing—where by now her nephew was thoroughly puzzled. He sensed something dark and licentious going on around him, and couldn't dismiss it from his mind. She saw herself as the prettily dressed bait that Auntie had cunningly set forth—not in the belief that it would excite his romantic appetites, but in order to perplex and challenge his intellect. Lulu measured her reply. "I don't think Auntie is concerned about Leon."

"She seems to be throwing the two of you together. . . . And the constant innuendoes!"

While gazing at Douglas, Lulu felt a lie developing inside her. "Auntie knows," she said, quietly, "that I'm afraid of him."

Douglas appeared relieved. "I'd be surprised if you weren't."

"Do you ever feel afraid of him?" Lulu asked, quietly, wanting him to admit it to her.

But Douglas balked. "Some people have been."

"I've noticed," said Lulu, "that Chloris always goes off by herself whenever Leon comes to visit."

"I'm surprised you don't!" Douglas cracked.

"I'm not afraid of him like that," said Lulu. "I like his company as much as anyone's."

"That's the bind," said Douglas. "He makes you feel both flattered and unworthy." A shadow appeared and subsided in his face.

"No." Lulu excepted herself from that idea, even as she glimpsed the truth in it. "He makes me feel attractive and important."

Douglas couldn't resist the opportunity her reply afforded. "You are attractive and important."

"I'm afraid of him," Lulu continued, conscious of her obeying Mrs. Gansevoort's instructions, "in the other way." Instinctively, she took the issue a step further. "I would be afraid of any man in that way."

Douglas had not moved a muscle, but was staring at her with total absorption. He had taken off his cap; his eyes shone with the same hazel hue as Aunt Julia's eyes. In a moment, he might reach out to touch her.

"Then it isn't Leon you're afraid of," he concluded quietly.

"Yes," said Lulu, "it is. I would be afraid to be alone with him. I've thought about it."

"He has a crazy power." Douglas fairly whispered the thought. "He was always remote from all of us until Warren, one June, took Sylvia to a dance at the Canoe Club. After that, Leon favored Warren. He involved himself all that summer with Warren and his studies. They spent long hours together in this room." Douglas signified their pine-paneled surroundings. "Talking philosophy and mysticism. Leon reads philosophy for fun."

"I know," Lulu lied.

"That was after Warren had come home from the army. He wouldn't tell anyone why he was discharged, but he must have told Leon. He and Leon spent the summer out here, while the rest of us, including Sylvia, were quartered in the house. Warren and Sylvia played tennis together, and Warren took Sylvia sometimes to concerts at Tanglewood, but I noticed," Douglas said, "that whenever Sylvia went off with Warren, Leon would disappear. He used to go up on the hill with his books. With his Meister Eckhart! But all that while, Warren was getting worse. His nerves were gone. A time came," Douglas added, "when he and Leon were inseparable. He followed Leon wherever he went. Leon can be abusive, too, if he's given a chance."

"He was probably jealous over Sylvia," Lulu suggested.

Nodding, Douglas turned his attention to a photograph on the wall, which, even at that distance, Lulu could make out quite clearly. It was taken at twilight at the once beautiful white gazebo, with a dark ring of water shining about it on all sides, and a little girl dressed in white standing inside it. Lulu was sure the child was Sylvia.

"I think what happened," said Douglas, "was that Warren couldn't bear it anymore, and went for a drive with Sylvia, and told her something about himself, something so horrid and unnatural that Sylvia turned the wheel and drove them straight into a tree."

Lulu winced in disbelief. "Even if it were true—about Leon, do you mean?—Warren wouldn't have told her."

"No one in his right mind would have," Douglas agreed, "unless he was compelled to. Unless he had no moral strength left."

Lulu was numbed by the sinister turn in their talk, for, despite herself, she felt powerfully induced to believe Douglas. She likened Warren, the eldest of Ignatia's children, to Chloris. Warren had come home from the military shamed by something frail in his nature, had fallen in love with Sylvia, and she with him, and Mr. Rafferty had risen up before him like a specter out of the ground, and destroyed him. Lulu's mind was racing. "Wasn't Warren driving?" she asked.

"In the wreckage, they couldn't tell for certain, but they said he was. I always thought otherwise. Warren had his own keys. The keys in the ignition were Sylvia's. They were traveling about forty-five miles an hour on a deserted road. There were no smudge marks on the asphalt from the tires. I'd say she drove them straight into the tree. Of course, no one expected anything like that! Even the gods abhor accidents. It was over in a second. Warren was gone, and Sylvia was gone. But you needn't think about the two of them. I only mention it as a caution against naïveté. You're a new leaf in the Gansevoort chronicles! You are!" Douglas exclaimed. "Zita Gansevoort! Sprung full-formed from Auntie's head! One thing is obvious." He smiled at Lulu. "My Aunt Julia has begun looking forward to a new day."

Beyond the open windows, the sunlight shimmered on the weeds and tall grasses. Lulu was trembling slightly, as she anticipated Douglas touching her.

"You look pretty in pink," he said.

Lulu made no movement. She was reminded by his words of the pink silk scarf lying at the bottom of her dresser drawer, the scarf Ignatia had worn on that afternoon years ago when she had violated her sister's trust. When Douglas leaned and set his lips to Lulu's mouth, she started instinctively. She felt his lips quiver.

"We all have our fears," he said. "I have mine, too."

All that evening and into the night, Lulu was absorbed with thoughts of Douglas. Time and again, she went over in her mind the words they had spoken. She had never been infatuated before. Sitting before her mirror, she felt quite stupid, for, while enjoying the distraction of her senses, she knew she was encouraging it. She stared at her reflection in the glass, her black hair cut short and sleek, her face glowing, her slender throat, and knew that the feelings coursing through her body were a woman's experience of love. Later, after locking her door, Lulu opened one of her drawers and took out the big colorful newspaper photo of the Sacred Heart baseball player. The resemblance between the two young men, Soldier McNiff and Douglas, was remarkable, if only to Lulu's own eye or imagination. She had begun confusing the two of them in her thoughts. She saw the innocence of the one in the other, and the other's brilliance of intellect in the former, and was moved by the beauty of both.

The following day, Lulu went about her tasks of dealing with Mrs. Gansevoort's notes and correspondence in a loving, hazy state of mind. She felt generous toward everyone, including Chloris, whom she now looked down upon as a pathetic child. That evening, to intensify matters, Douglas made Lulu the gift of a book; it was a Thomas Hardy novel, on the flyleaf of which Douglas had composed a poem. By then, Lulu could restrain herself no longer, and made up her mind to apprise Mrs. Gansevoort of Douglas's behavior. Aunt Julia was in high spirits when Lulu came to her in the front sitting room. The older woman had been out for the evening and had obviously consumed more wine than she should have. She sent Lulu upstairs straight off to fetch the book. When Lulu returned with it, carrying the volume in both hands, and trying to conceal in her expression any sign of her happiness, Mrs. Gansevoort was standing in the middle of the room waiting for her. Her eyes sparkled triumphantly.

She seized the book from Lulu with a brisk gesture, and thumbed back the cover.

"This inscription!" she cried. " 'Thoughts like *bees*?' This from a dean's list scholar?" A peal of disdainful laughter followed as Mrs. Gansevoort suddenly dealt the book back to Lulu. "You must show Leon! You're quite the little thespian! Did you bat your pretty eyes at him? Did you catch at your breath?" Mrs. Gansevoort's face appeared to heat up with embarrassment over her nephew's pathetic scribblings.

"No," Lulu replied. She had never seen her dear friend appear so full of herself. But Lulu could not deny, either, that Auntie's jubilant outburst did seriously depreciate the value of the book she was holding.

Suddenly, Aunt Julia turned on her heel, and to Lulu's amazement, began parading herself to and fro across the Persian carpet. She marched back and forth, like a primitive chieftain, so full of her conviction of victory and of her contempt for her adversaries that nothing could express it as well as strutting.

While recognizing Auntie's sudden display of barbaric vanity for what it was, Lulu could not help being impressed. The sight of Mrs. Gansevoort actually flaunting herself like that, as she paced back and forth, with the lamplight flickering in the liquid folds of her moving skirts, only served to increase Lulu's awe for the woman. Lulu realized at this moment that Auntie was not the sort of person who would be large-spirited in victory. She had only to think of Chloris in that regard, and of how easy it would have been for Auntie to soften her heart now and show her adoring niece a little compassion from time to time. But Auntie was not like that. She was vain, and doubtless vindictive, too, by nature, even beyond anything Lulu had observed in any other person.

"Tell him"—Mrs. Gansevoort spoke as if dictating a letter, as she stepped proudly past Lulu—"that poetry seems to you the fullest, most refined form of sentiment—of contact!—there could possibly be between man and woman. Long-headed fellow that he is, he will understand your meanings." Mrs. Gansevoort's voice dripped with sarcasm. "Convice him of your sincerity. Dissemble at will. Tell him *anything!* Anything your art instructs. Make use of our friend, Leon, in that regard. Explain to him, darling, how a young lady can be both attracted and repelled by that *other* sort of male, the physical type, the man of action. The man of nature!"

"I don't believe," Lulu protested, softly, "that he meant much by giving me this book." The volume in Lulu's hands had taken on more the aspect of a piece of evidence now than of a loving gift.

"Oh, trust me!" Mrs. Gansevoort sang back confidently. Suddenly, without warning, she turned and faced Lulu. "Do as you're told!" she commanded. "Would you doubt me?"

"No," Lulu replied, shakily.

"How you choose to effect your deceptions is your own business." Mrs. Gansevoort eyed her steadily. "Do what is expected of you."

Frightened and enthralled by her friend's angry outburst, Lulu stood stock-still, clasping the book in her hands. She was shaking inside; she had rarely been scolded by Mrs. Gansevoort, and even wondered if Auntie hadn't somehow looked into her heart and discovered her secret infatuation. As Mrs. Gansevoort continued her admonitions, enjoining Lulu to "concoct fictions" for her, and making strange, abstruse references to "pointless falsehoods" and "the lie that benefits no one," Lulu felt the shadow of their secret iniquity fall softly over her mind.

"If it spreads ruin in some alien, far-off place"—Mrs. Gansevoort gestured vaguely toward the darkness beyond her windows, her eyes shining with a winy glow—"even that would not be displeasing to me."

●

From that moment, Lulu had a mind to warn Douglas of the dangers she sensed brewing about him, although she could not begin to identify them. Late the next evening, after Julia had driven off in the rain to a dinner party with some of her summer friends, Lulu, carrying Auntie's big black postman's umbrella, let herself out the back way, and started for the lodge. In all her weeks with Mrs. Gansevoort, she had never felt so fragile or transitory as she did tonight. She was conscious that her previous existence, as the devout, hardworking individual in the High Street store, had by now grown fantastic in her mind, while, at the same time, the vision of the delicate young beauty framed in her upstairs looking glass remained disquietingly insubstantial, as well. Lulu no longer saw herself as the frightened, once solid girl who had inhabited the dreary room overlooking the little park on South Summer Street, but as a mere extension of Mrs. Gansevoort, of her colorful, impulsive nature.

Before Lulu had gotten ten feet from the back door of the house, she spotted Douglas. He was sitting in his car with the windows rolled up, his face showing pale behind the streaming window glass. He had come outdoors to listen to a baseball game on the car radio, he said, as he folded up Lulu's umbrella, and helped her into the car. She was certain already that he wanted to take her driving.

"I've been here an hour. The radio in the lodge is on the blink. Also," he added, "I like the sound of the rain on the canvas top."

"Yes, it's lovely," Lulu agreed, and was immediately glad that she had come outdoors. She sat forward on the leather seat. The car radio was playing softly, with the distant-sounding voice of a baseball announcer rising and falling amid static. The air in the car was cool, but the windows were steamed up.

"I'm surprised," Douglas said, "that Julia didn't take you with her."

"Oh, I don't want to meet people. You don't know what I'm like. I've never wanted to meet people."

"Would you like to go for a ride?" he asked.

"No," said Lulu, "I wouldn't."

Douglas had turned and was watching Lulu with a concerned expression. "We could just drive down the road and through town to the lake and back. We needn't stop. I'll drive slowly. Sometimes movement itself can be very relaxing."

Lulu wanted to consent, and struggled to overcome her fears; the drive, she felt, would somehow change things between them in a way she desired.

"If I didn't have to get out of the car," she said, at last.

The truth was, the interior of Douglas's convertible, with the rain falling on all sides, was oddly reassuring. In the minutes to come, as Douglas backed the car out of the drive, and started slowly along the gravel road toward the town of Peru Mountain, Lulu mastered her emotions. She was sitting up straight, with her hands in her lap, her gaze fixed on the blur of the headlights shining on the road ahead. To ease her anxiety, Douglas had resumed teasing her about her devotion to his aunt.

"Does she swear you to silence?" he inquired, playfully.

Lulu laughed. "There's nothing to swear or be silent about."

"She used to invoke the Book!" Douglas exclaimed. "One summer, one of us kids trampled a bed of marigolds, and Julia brought out the Holy Testament and made us swear our innocence on it. It was a very solemn affair. Warren, as the eldest, swore first; then Sylvia, then I."

"Someone lied?" Lulu said. She had turned sideways, and was facing him at close range.

"God knows, I didn't. I was only about eight. The sight of that big fat Bible sitting on the tablecloth in the dining room, with Aunt Julia standing over it, scared the daylights out of me."

Lulu laughed once more at the comical expression of terror on Douglas's face.

"I was so frightened," he said, "I came within a breath of confessing it! I was going to confess to it just to spare the guilty one from having to tell a lie. I would have, too, but of course when my turn came, I was sure that the culprit had already lied."

"I doubt Sylvia would have lied."

"Oh, she would have, believe me. She probably did. They both probably lied. So would anyone else have lied."

When Douglas reached to change the radio station, his elbow rested momentarily on Lulu's knee. Lulu pretended not to notice, as she gazed at the road unfolding before them in the rain; the love feelings of the past two days were reviving in her. As they drove slowly through the village of Peru Mountain, Douglas pointed out the principal houses, explaining how each had been built by one of the Gansevoort families decades ago, and the church and town hall, and the Civil War monument half hidden behind the tall trees on the common. Lulu followed his descriptions with interest. She had leaned closer to him while peering out the driver's window toward the stone figure gleaming in the rain. At the foot of the common, Douglas brought the car to a halt before a flashing red traffic light, and in a moment was kissing Lulu. She touched his chin with her fingertips in a reflex of surprise, but without having moved her head an inch.

"I think we both have some secrets," he said.

"Yes," Lulu whispered back. Instantly, she felt a dark surge of emotion within herself, in the knowledge that Auntie wanted her to encourage his trust. She felt infected by it; she wanted to tell him.

"I know that you're not just her secretary. You *are* more like family." He was whispering.

"That's true," said Lulu, softly. She was looking into his eyes. The dim light in the car illuminated his cheekbones and temples. By now, she was conscious of the gentle rise and fall of her breasts. He wanted to be provoked, she was sure.

"You belong to her, don't you?" he said.

"Yes," she said, in a quiet voice. She wanted to appall him. She could feel Auntie working a spell inside her. "I love her more than anyone."

A mile outside of town, Douglas pulled the car over. Through a screen of pine trees the glow of a red-and-blue neon sign atop a roadhouse could be seen. Lulu was leaning close to Douglas in the darkness. He wanted to take her indoors, but seemed to understand her fears.

"There'll be almost no one in there. It's dark and private."

Lulu was honest. "I have a fear of going places."

They were conversing at point-blank range.

"That's because of your new life," he said.

Lulu wanted to respond to that, to enlarge on her fears of other people, but no words came. She wanted to go in with him, but only if he realized somehow that it was his knowledge of her frailty that made the difference. Incapable of affecting feminine helplessness, Lulu spoke the plain truth to him. "You would have to take care of me."

"We'll just look in. If you want to leave, we'll go at once. If we decide to stay, I won't leave you for a second."

Douglas parked under the pines on the hill, and helped Lulu out her door. He was holding up her umbrella. While getting out of the car, Lulu had the queer idea that she, of all people, was being treated with a tenderness and solicitude that she would have thought appropriate to the historical figures in Mrs. Gansevoort's book. Her legs quavered slightly as, clutching Douglas's arm tightly, she started forward over the wet, lumpy earth.

Indoors, Douglas and Lulu sat in a wooden booth at the back of the tavern, with Lulu situated comfortably between Douglas and the wall. The nephew was talking all the while in a diverting manner.

"If they knew you were a Gansevoort," he teased her, "they'd line up to pay their respects."

Lulu responded with an effort at making a joke of her own. "I feel if they knew who I was, they'd beat me with sticks."

When the waitress brought their order, Douglas set Lulu's cocktail before her. He sensed her needs, she thought, with an uncanny insight into her nature. For all of her fears, though, Lulu was conscious nonetheless of her beauty at this moment. She could feel it as she allowed her eyes to go from the backs of her hands and her manicured nails to the eyelet border of her dress. She was aware of the breath of perfume about her throat and hair.

"Did Sylvia come here?" she asked.

"I'm sure she did. She and Warren, especially. This is just the sort of ramshackle, rustic nightspot the summer people up here see fit to patronize, if only to show their liberality of outlook."

"I think it's pleasant," said Lulu, feeling more cheered with every passing minute. She sipped from her stemmed glass. The beverage was both sweet and strong-tasting. "Was Sylvia a snob?" she asked.

"Do you mean, like Aunt Julia?" he exclaimed.

"Yes!" cried Lulu, laughing.

"Is anyone?"

"I suppose not." It pleased Lulu when they spoke of Mrs. Gansevoort in a playful manner that was at the same time commendatory.

"Sylvia was too dignified, too grand, to be snobbish. Anyhow, I idealized her. I loved Sylvia. Did you know that?"

"No." Lulu was surprised.

"I was also somewhat afraid of her. No one knew about my feelings for her, except, probably, for herself. Sylvia would have known. If she did, she pretended not to. I'll never know."

"It doesn't matter now."

"Her feelings for Warren puzzled me. I couldn't imagine anyone so beautiful and brilliant being attainable by someone who resembled me as much as a brother must. So I was sometimes suspicious of her motives."

By now, Lulu was glad she had come riding with Douglas, and was trying not to reveal, in the way she was looking at him, the feelings of love pulsing inside her. "Maybe she didn't love Warren."

Douglas answered thoughtfully. "I think she did."

"What frightened you about her?" Lulu asked, softly. She felt the intimacy growing between them as the minutes passed. Her emotions left her forehead feeling warm. Despite the near emptiness of the roadhouse, they continued to speak in soft, confidential tones.

"That nothing was as it seemed," Douglas replied to her query. "When she was with Warren, or with Warren and others, she was girlish and talkative. With others, she was not like that."

"With her mother."

"Yes. She was different."

Lulu was sitting erectly, almost primly, but tilted toward
Douglas. "It isn't likely, is it," she said, "that Warren would
have ever married Sylvia?"

"Do you have reason to know?" said Douglas.

"I?" said Lulu.

"If Aunt Julia speaks her heart, it would be to you."

Not wishing to deny what she took for a compliment, or to
undermine her own implied importance here in the Gansevoort
family, Lulu gazed back at him insignificantly. Douglas awaited
her reply; his eyes expanded a little. Lulu's instincts told her to
make an ambivalent observation. "I would guess," she said, at
length, "that Auntie was not happy with Warren."

Douglas nodded. "Yes. Sylvia was her best hope. But she
did encourage them. She wanted Warren with them. But even
if you knew something about those days which has been kept
from me, you wouldn't reveal it, anyhow—because Auntie, as
you call her, has you in her charms."

Lulu watched Douglas intently. He seemed obsessed by her
life with Mrs. Gansevoort. She remained silent.

"I never knew what happened," he said. "When Warren
came home from the service, Leon called him the 'sunshine
warrior' to his face. Warren was finished. I know only one thing.
Warren's death was ordained, but Sylvia's was not. Sylvia,"
Douglas specified, "died of an accident. Julia's grief was in-
describable. It was literally beyond description. She didn't wail
or carry on. It just turned her to stone. I felt very bad for her."
Douglas's sincerity touched Lulu. "More even than for myself,
my own loss. That's the truth."

"I believe you."

"Warren's death was like a death, but Sylvia's removal—
even for me—was something of another magnitude. After she
was gone, you wouldn't have thought she had ever lived. You

wouldn't have thought, later on, that the world was poorer by another person, but changed at its foundations, changed," he said, "into something ignoble, perhaps into what, really, it is, a world that can't retain the treasures it creates. And, of course, you hadn't thought about that before."

Lulu was moved by his words. They expressed a delicate nature. She guessed that he dwelt a great deal on these thoughts. She sensed once again something vulnerable in him, and wondered if he was on the verge of revealing himself to her.

"That was the year before I went to Yale. I was at Deerfield Academy. My mother flew over from Italy that Christmas, and we spent the holiday at a hotel in New York, she and Chloris and I."

The window close to Lulu stood open a few inches. The rain spattered on the sill. The light of a wall lamp fell over Lulu's shoulder onto her lap. She felt she had never communed so comfortably with anyone, and wished that Douglas might talk on indefinitely.

"My mother had a friend in the city," he said, "named Maureen McKeon, a jewelry designer, who was an aficionado of opera and the ballet. She took me one afternoon to the Met. I was sixteen or seventeen. She was my mother's age, but very stylish and warm-natured. I began writing to her that winter."

"Did you write to your mother?"

"Oh, yes, her, too, but I had nothing to say. To Maureen, I could have filled books, and did. I wrote to her twice a week. And every Saturday, like clockwork, came a letter back to me." Douglas laughed over the memory. "I fell in love with her. I wasn't so stupid as to say it, but I was thinking about her from morning to night. It was wonderful. I made up my mind to learn everything about jewelry design and classical music. Why," he exclaimed, "I read Prescott's *Conquest of Mexico* in the space of about ten days just so I could spout out something smart and esoteric about Aztec jewelry. And every Saturday," Douglas repeated himself, "as predictable as the moon and tides, I found a pretty little blue envelope in the mail, addressed to me in her lovely blue hand—two or three small pages filled top to bottom with her neat, delicate scrawl, expressing always the most interesting thoughts."

"It must have been exciting," said Lulu.

"She sent me a picture of herself, but not until I had pestered her to death about it for weeks. I told her—which was not true—that I had a gallery of photographs of family and friends on the wall of my room at Deerfield, and how pleased I would be to install her own picture among them. In fact," Douglas laughed, "the walls were covered from floor to ceiling with magazine shots of high-fashion jewelry, everything from emeralds to clay beads, and with hundreds of newspaper clippings bearing on the world of music and dance. I was obsessed with her!" he cried.

Lulu laughed as Douglas affected the look of a moonstruck adolescent.

"She sent the picture," he said. "It came parcel post, carefully wrapped. I don't think she wanted to send it, but having decided to, did so with her usual flair. The picture was taken by someone who knew his business. I mean to say," Douglas cried, "it was glamorous! It was a big black-and-white profile shot of her, with her hand cocked underneath her chin, a bulging jade bracelet on her wrist, and a sleepy, haughty look on her face that took my breath away. The power that that picture worked in me!"

Lulu was smiling dreamily as her mind drifted along on the current of Douglas's words.

"And, believe me," he said, "although I'm not eager to admit it, I didn't entertain one concupiscent thought about her during all those weeks."

"You were in love," Lulu said, as she felt the first effect of the alcohol in her system.

"I was chumming around at that time with three or four other senior boys who fancied themselves the literati of the school. Two of the boys were homosexuals, one of them a very spoiled, effete type, named Welson, who liked to shock people. Well, I think it troubled me that he, Welson, was the only person I knew who made a great fuss over my priceless photograph of Maureen McKeon. Sometimes, he would stop in just to look at the picture—duck in, look at it, duck out—as if it were a sacred relic. You see, I didn't want to think"—Douglas paused to collect his thoughts—"that Welson and I, out of all the circle of my schoolmates, were somehow unique in this way, in the ability to appreciate this exquisite artifact, this beautiful, soulful face, because if that were so, it might have been necessary to postulate other similarities. Do you understand?"

Lulu shook her head, but was gazing at Douglas now with a look of affection that she had stopped trying to conceal. She sipped from her cocktail.

"Neither did I," he said, "nor did it once occur to me that Welson might have guessed instinctively at my own weakness concerning the portrait, and even unwittingly simulated his own infatuation with it. Maybe he was infatuated with me. He was such a brilliant boy, I was flattered. He used to say of Maureen's picture that *that* was a woman; that the girls from places likes Miss Porter's, or even those Mount Holyoke College choir women who came to chapel one Sunday, were, by comparison, he said, like 'little beasts of burden.' " Douglas smiled over the memory. "I never disagreed. Truth was, I was rather afraid of those little beasts of burden. But for some reason, I associate all of that with Sylvia, and her death. And to the way I used to see something almost ominous in her, something of the fateful infinite, whenever she went past me." Douglas smiled once more. "I am telling you all."

"It's very interesting," Lulu said.

"That Easter," Douglas added., "I spent my spring vacation with cousins of mine in New Jersey. I didn't come home to Julia, as I usually did. I wanted to be near to New York. Oh, the excitement! Just hearing her voice on the phone! And, of course, because she knew, I'm sure, what I was thinking and feeling, Maureen sometimes made allusions to it. To us. To her and me. She treated my crush on her as something deliciously forbidden. She found it amusing. I was relieved that my feelings were out in the open. I wanted her to know. I went to her apartment twice for dinner. She lived on Park Avenue. I could describe to you tonight, in detail, every cushion and vase, every plant, picture, and wine bottle in the place. The carpets, the china, the silver jewelry she wore. She knew my every thought, I'm sure. I wouldn't have reached a hand to touch her if my life depended on it. It was a passing phase, and she was making the most of it. Who knows," he said, "maybe, like Julia, she resented Ignatia—for whom she used to make up jewelry. I wouldn't be surprised. Or maybe she wanted a son."

"Maybe she wanted more," said Lulu, absorbed in the enjoyable picture that Douglas painted of the sensitive schoolboy and his chic substitute mother, but conscious all the while that her own physical presence was creating a spell that enabled and encouraged him to talk on and on in this vein. She was very conscious of her body and breathing; her nipples tingled now and again, and her legs trembled slightly. Outdoors, the rain had increased in intensity, and kept up a continuous roar in the trees.

"Did you write her poetry?" Lulu said.

"Yes, all that spring and summer, and into the fall. By then, Welson and I had gone on to Yale together."

Lulu's voice was as soft as the rain splashing on the sill. "Was it love poetry?"

"Oh, sure," he said, "but it was veiled behind other words, just as her own letters to me sometimes took on double meanings."

"Was she in love with you?" Lulu asked outright.

"I don't suppose so, but by then we *had* stopped mentioning Ignatia. Mother's name never came up. I'm not saying Maureen had a romantic interest in me. She was probably just charmed by it, just as I, in some comparable way, was enthralled by her. Whatever the case, my mother ceased being my mother in the process, and has never recovered value for me. Something in me was altered in the process. Somehow," he added, "I never got back to myself."

"I know how that can happen," said Lulu. "It has been happening to me. When did you see her last?"

"My mother?"

"No," Lulu replied, "the woman."

"I never saw her again. The letters continued coming till about Christmas, or a little beyond, and then just stopped."

Lulu could feel the liquor warming her insides. "I think she was in love with you," she said.

Later, as he was escorting Lulu from the tavern, Douglas set his hand lightly against her waist. "Are you as happy as you say?" he asked.

"I'm very happy," Lulu replied. "But I have a good reason to be happy. I used to hate myself. Now I want to please Auntie. That's more important to me than my own comfort or happiness."

"You don't know what you're saying. Aunt Julia is not a figure in a storybook. What would happen," he suggested, "if suddenly she sent you away?"

They had paused on the porch of the roadhouse, and were watching the rain splashing and dancing on the gravel lot.

"She won't," Lulu said. "She expects to be living up here, in Peru Mountain, someday soon, and will want me more than ever." Lulu realized she was provoking him intentionally. She wanted him to object.

"That's rot," said Douglas. "She'll never live up here. In the *winter?*"

Lulu said nothing, but colored and looked away in the rain.

"Is that what she told you? That her house was in danger? That she might give it up? Could you believe such a thing? She was ribbing you."

"I don't think Auntie would lie."

"And if it were true," Douglas went on, "which it is not, you would come up here, the two of you, like a pair of Carmelite nuns, Mother Superior and her faithful postulant, and lock yourself away in the snow and ice?"

"I would be flattered." Lulu could feel the warm tumult of her body pulsing against the flat of his hand upon her waist.

"Doesn't it unnerve you," the nephew insisted, "that she should exercise such power over you?"

"It makes me feel safe."

Douglas, however, was shaking his head dubiously. "I would resist that. I'm not a religious sort, but I do believe that a human being can be infected in that way. It happened to a fellow I knew at Yale. I saw it happen. It happened, too, to Warren, I'm quite sure. If what you're telling me is true," Douglas said, "then you're at her mercy."

"I am," she said.

"Aunt Julia is a woman of superhuman vanity. What would happen to you if her own selfish desires came between you and your happiness?"

Lulu did not reply, however, for in the same moment Douglas was kissing her, as though that act were the logical sequel to his last utterance.

During the slow ride home, Lulu sat as she had earlier, turned sidelong toward him, her head and back erect, her hands on her lap. She knew why he had told her the story about the chic New York woman; he was unsure of himself. He wanted her to know that. The knowledge of his secret fears, and the fact that he had wanted to share them with her, touched Lulu. She had not loved anyone before.

Lulu kept to herself the following day, but could not deny that the intimate hour or two that she had spent with Douglas had awakened feelings in her that she was surprised to discover. Her thoughts were full of him. At the breakfast table that morning, when Mrs. Gansevoort made no reference whatever to Douglas, or to Leon, or to any aspect of her secret plans, Lulu even wondered if her own sinister interpretation of the events going on about her was not just the product of an overworked imagination. She couldn't believe that any human being as grand in nature as Mrs. Gansevoort could contemplate doing harm to someone as sensitive and innocent as Douglas. It was true that Auntie felt very bitter toward life, and doubtless saw in Douglas a living reminder of the cause of her own past unhappiness—of the way in which her precious girlhood came to ruin when Douglas's mother and father fell in love with one another. She may, too, have seen in Douglas reflections of Warren, upon whom she might have cast blame for the tragic death of Sylvia. Lulu understood all of that, and as a victim of life, she herself could sympathize heartily with her dear friend. She could see how Julia might look upon her sister's children with a lingering, corrosive anger. But she knew, too, that Douglas was Aunt Julia's flesh, and that Auntie, in her wisdom, could only admit that the young Yale scholar was as guiltless of complicity, intended or accidental, as any person on earth.

In the late afternoon, when Auntie was sunning herself in a canvas chair by the trellis, Lulu brought her a tall lime drink. Douglas was scything grass under the apple trees by the brook. Lulu avoided looking in his direction.

Mrs. Gansevoort spoke up to Lulu in a hearty tone as she reached for her iced drink. "I understand you went driving last night."

Lulu's cheeks brightened, but she said nothing. She could feel Douglas's eyes upon her from somewhere back among the little squad of stunted fruit trees. He had stopped scything. Mrs. Gansevoort was smiling extravagantly, while scrutinizing Lulu with brilliant eyes. "The Green Knight has begun his quest?" she said, with sarcasm.

Lulu was unsure how to respond. "I think so," she mumbled, at last.

"I hope you're not surprised."

"A little," Lulu confessed.

"Ah, the attractions of youth, and the disingenuousness of age!"

"We drove a couple of miles," Lulu muttered, embarrassedly, "and came back. . . . I was nervous about going."

"It was well for you to go." Mrs. Gansevoort was unequivocal. She spoke up so clearly that Lulu flashed a look of alarm, for Douglas might have been in earshot. Mrs. Gansevoort swiveled her head around and looked back toward her nephew. "He is trying to show us, with his exertions, that he has a robust side to him. Why don't you turn round, darling, and look at him." Mrs. Gansevoort's sudden exclamation caught Lulu off guard, and she colored even more vividly than before. "On second thought," Mrs. Gansevoort turned back in her chair, and rattled the ice in her drink, "follow your own lights, sweetheart. I have a sneaking suspicion that your own instincts, your own wiles, are far, far superior to any suggestions I might make."

Lulu was left until suppertime to digest Auntie's provocative remarks. Sometimes she could not tell whether Auntie was praising or belittling her. The fact was that Mrs. Gansevoort mystified Lulu much of the time. That evening at the dinner table, for instance, Auntie adopted a sharply baiting attitude toward Douglas which both amazed and intimidated Lulu. At one point, while sitting up with a characteristically superior smirk on her lips, Aunt Julia asked Douglas if he was still writing poetry.

Instantly, Douglas shot Lulu an inquiring glance. "I wouldn't call it poetry," he replied, surprised by the question.

Lulu flushed in the sudden fear that Auntie might openly ridicule the poem that Douglas had inscribed in the book he had given her. She kept her eyes fixed on her plate.

"If you ask me," Douglas added, evasively, "the human race has already perpetrated enough bad poetry. I prefer writing letters."

"Now I feel especially neglected," Auntie sang back at once. "Or do you only compose your deathless epistles for the young ladies and gentlemen of your social set?" Mrs. Gansevoort was clearly on her high horse. With a simpering, supercilious expression she turned then to Lulu and Chloris. *"Are* any of your friends prominent, may I ask, Douglas? . . . Have you established some useful connections for your future? Does the name Gansevoort still elicit a response in that world? Or have you dropped it altogether?"

"I use Hull," said Douglas.

"Naturally!" Mrs. Gansevoort snapped with instant scorn. "Douglas Hull!"

Chloris spoke up, wishing to please her aunt. "I hyphenate my name. Several girls asked me about my name."

"You!" Mrs. Gansevoort showed disgust. "You be quiet!"

"It's just another dead name," said Douglas.

"You had four years at Yale to resuscitate it. Four years to distinguish it anew. But you," she ridiculed him, "chose to call yourself Hull, and to mix in with a collection of silly-minded aesthetes who would like nothing more of life than to design their own wallpapers."

Douglas laughed at once at Mrs. Gansevoort's sarcasm. "Aunt Julia," he concluded, "you're the bitter end."

"I *am* the bitter end! It sickens me to realize that. The sad, bitter end of a magnificent family line, not to say a cultural tradition as old as this nation. Our people produced things! We made things happen. We didn't just float along on the tide of time like so much sewage. We didn't substitute a thin veil of erudition for the solid rewards of success."

Douglas was taking his aunt's harsh teasing well, but Lulu saw his head come up swiftly when Mrs. Gansevoort suddenly turned to her and involved Mr. Rafferty's name.

"Did I tell you, Zita," she said, "that Leon called yesterday evening while you were out?"

For an instant, Lulu was incredulous. "Leon telephoned?"

"He gave you his best." Mrs. Gansevoort was glowing happily, her eyes going about the table. Her manner and tone struck Lulu as brazenly provocative. "He asked were you enjoying yourself. Wishes it were September, he says. He misses you!"

Lulu's eyes fluttered wildly as she realized how Auntie was directly challenging Douglas.

"I told him I'd permit you to call him," Mrs. Gansevoort added regally.

"I will," Lulu muttered. "Thank you."

"We spoke for about twenty minutes. Leon was in one of his rare nostalgic moods. Of course, he knows I'll pay for the call! Leon"—here Mrs. Gansevoort addressed herself to Douglas

in particular—"can sense when I am susceptible to blandishments. He has a sixth sense for that. If I hadn't cut him off when
I did, he would soon have been reciting me passages verbatim
from the little handful of letters I wrote him while he was with
his unit in Europe. He keeps them under lock and key. Knows
them by heart."

"He probably does," Douglas observed wryly.

"He does!" said Mrs. Gansevoort. "How else do you think
he might have recommended himself to my affection, if not
through something as appropriately grotesque as committing
to memory every casual word I have ever written or spoken to
him!" Mrs. Gansevoort laughed over her own humorous utterance. "Leon is adept, you see, at anticipating my likes and
dislikes to the letter. That is his genius."

All the while Mrs. Gansevoort continued to taunt Douglas
with Mr. Rafferty, and with remarks betraying an uncontrolled
egoism, Lulu marveled at the way Douglas seemed to have
drawn himself into a shell. The aunt's gratuitous cruelty, and
Douglas's mysterious reticence in the face of it, competed for
primacy in Lulu's mind. Then Auntie suddenly shifted the focus
of her monologue directly onto Douglas.

"He likes you," she said, "very much."

"Not only does he despise me," Douglas stirred in his seat,
"but he despises everyone like me."

"You are wrong. He admires you. He admires intellect, he
admires beauty, and he admires everything the Gansevoorts
have ever been about."

Lulu realized by the movement of Mrs. Gansevoort's eyes
that she was prompting her to speak up about Leon.

"He certainly admires Zita." Chloris laughed nervously, and
turned a shade of pink.

"That goes without saying." Mrs. Gansevoort was smug on
that point.

By then Lulu and Douglas were looking at one another, and
Lulu divined in the nephew's eyes at that moment a fascination

for Mr. Rafferty that left her feeling very shaken. She was sure it was not the emotion of jealousy that aroused Douglas's hypnotic attention, but a pathological dread of the older man, and that she, Lulu, had become the intermediary, the prism through which the dark lights of Mr. Rafferty's violent nature were refracted for Douglas. It was not Leon the dapper recluse that fascinated Douglas, nor Leon the wartime killer, but Leon the indomitable suitor after Lulu's own innocence; that, she was certain, was what galvanized the nephew's soul. The realization coursed through her like something physical. It was thrilling to be looked at in such a way!

Lulu daubed at her temples with her folded napkin. She could feel their eyes upon her, but was unable to look up. Sometimes Lulu had the oddest feeling that everyone else in the world was performing according to a secret script, while she alone was cursed with the freedom to act and the capacity to suffer; that life was an insidious game, a piece of stagecraft, an elaborate deception and perpetual test.

"What is more," Mrs. Gansevoort suddenly announced, as she reached out and seized Chloris by one hand and Lulu by the other, "I have my little accomplices!" She squeezed both their hands while glaring with satisfaction at Douglas, and then making him a startling proclamation. "I have a plan and method to survive. I am not finished yet. Sometimes"—she lifted her voice to a musical pitch—"I even have an expectation of victory!"

Douglas appeared ignorant of Julia's sarcasm, but his rejoinder was halfhearted. "What victory was that?"

"Something only the vanquished have the good fortune to understand."

Lulu stole a look at Chloris, who was gazing up in raptures at her aunt, her glassy face and blue eyes as flawless as something stamped in plastic. Lulu was impressed with Auntie's outburst, but what happened next left her breathless. Aunt Julia had turned her attention to Chloris, and was staring at her niece with a look of burning intensity. The conversation at the table ceased. Douglas stopped smiling. Lulu could feel her own heart pounding softly as she anticipated something egregious about to take place. The expression on Mrs. Gansevoort's lighted face was so absorbing that Chloris appeared unable to look away. She stared up adoringly at Mrs. Gansevoort. It was not the girl, though, but the woman at the table who inspired awe. Aunt Julia's face was pink with triumph; her breathing was audible; her shoulders and bosom rose and fell in time with her exaggerated breathing. Finally Chloris stirred; and the instant she did so, Lulu anticipated what was about to happen, and glanced swiftly at Douglas. He appeared momentarily enthralled. Mrs. Gansevoort had released Lulu's hand, but was still clasping Chloris by the fingers as the girl got up from her chair and stepped close to where Aunt Julia was sitting. For several seconds, the niece stood motionless beside her aunt, her face and eyes alive with a special radiance; then, slowly, she lowered her head, and kissed Mrs. Gansevoort softly on the lips.

Lulu's heart was pounding. She could feel the tiny hammerblows of her pulse throbbing at the back of her neck. It was not the spectacle of Chloris's sickening devotion to her aunt that upset Lulu, or even the pathetic and garish method by which she had dramatized her unquestioning love of the older woman, but the appalling way Aunt Julia herself had chosen to reveal to Douglas that it was she, Auntie, who had virtually destroyed the girl.

●

When Lulu encountered Douglas outdoors later that evening, she had no doubt that she had gone outside expressly to put herself in his way. In her heart, she still sensed that all would be well, in time. She couldn't believe that Mrs. Gansevoort, even in cooperation with the strange, formidable Mr. Rafferty, could offer more than a passing threat to Douglas's moral well-being. It was nonsensical to compare Douglas to Chloris, or, for that matter, to Warren, the older brother. Still, the strange, wildly disparate looks on the faces of Auntie and of Douglas when Chloris had kissed Auntie at the supper table had imprinted themselves unforgettably in Lulu's mind, and prognosticated something frightening to come.

Douglas mentioned the episode immediately. "My sister," he said, "enjoys playing the part of the damned. She knows it's unnatural and shocking."

"You don't believe it, then?" Lulu asked, hopefully, as she and Douglas stepped noiselessly along an earthen path in the old garden east of the house. In the darkness ahead, the silhouette of Peru Mountain rose blackly under a scattering of stars.

"Oh, I believe Aunt Julia has Chloris in her toils," he said, "but I don't believe it's come about without Chloris's active willingness to be had. She enjoys Julia's selfish, tyrannical ways. It makes her feel notorious!"

After less than a minute or so in his presence, walking beside him in the dark, Lulu felt something like a purifying air blowing through her. When he touched her arm, Lulu brushed against him.

"Does it shock you?" he exclaimed.

"Yes," Lulu responded. "It does."

"But don't you also revere her? . . . Haven't you been trying for days to convince me of that very thing?"

"It's possible to love someone without smashing yourself to pieces." Lulu looked up at him. She was holding his arm. Her thoughts were racing. She found it hard to believe that she and Douglas were establishing a romantic link. When Auntie was not nearby, Lulu was more sharply aware of the great admiration she felt for him. His was another world from hers. Last night, though, he had opened his heart to her in a way which, Lulu's feminine instincts told her, only a lover would do. "I can't imagine that your sister is happy," she said.

"I'm the outsider here," said Douglas. "You *all* seem happy to me. Julia, Chloris, yourself—even," he said, "perhaps Leon."

Lulu winced at the mention of Mr. Rafferty's name, recalling how Mrs. Gansevoort seemed to have sensed a frailty in Douglas concerning Leon, and sought to torment him with it.

"I thought I was the outsider," Lulu suggested.

"You?" he said, fondly. "You seem like the beating heart of it all. You've brought some life back to this place. When Aunt Julia calls you a Gansevoort, she knows what she's talking about. I was watching you at the table tonight."

Lulu said nothing, but was moved by the affectionate feeling in his words. They had reached the road, and started walking east along the shoulder in the dark.

"I understand, too, why Auntie wants you to dress up like a flower every minute of the day. She sees you as, somehow, the incarnation of the great Gansevoort line!"

"Oh, no," Lulu protested earnestly, resisting Douglas's far-fetched interpretation of her place in her friend's life.

"You're her personal creation. She did make you, didn't she? For Julia, you're the living, breathing—and," he added, "innocent—memory of it all. It's true. I'm sure that's how she sees you. The wild blossom of an ancient stem."

"Oh, my!" Lulu's thoughts were swimming. She had never been complimented in such rhapsodic terms. She forgot all about Mr. Rafferty and Auntie's recondite scheming.

"That's how I see you, too," he said. "And so do the others. Chloris and Leon. But you could become lost in all of that. It's only as rich and enduring as Julia Gansevoort desires to make it so."

Lulu saw the truth in his words, but was much more impressed by the irony of the fact that Douglas had been worried about *her* at supper.

"It's one thing," Douglas explained, "to be the pretty little dauphine sitting on her satin tuffet, but it's another thing altogether—and a lamentable one—to sit at the feet of vain creatures who have fallen from the heights, as she has, or who, like Leon, actually revel in their sycophancy and live just in the hopes of pleasing their embittered patrons by demolishing something, or somebody, however blameless, just for the thrill of doing it."

Instinctively, in the instant to follow, Lulu uttered what she knew was a blasphemy. The words sprang to her tongue. "You should leave here!"

Lulu felt the blood drain out of her face at once, as though realizing she had just been tricked into betraying Auntie. Instantly she regretted what she had said. She realized, too, that Auntie's desire to keep Douglas close to her coincided with her own secret ambition to keep him close to herself.

"Do you believe that?" He appeared amazed.

"No," said Lulu, reversing herself.

He had stopped walking, and Lulu, pausing beside him, turned and looked back through the dark to the sight of Auntie's house lit through the trees. In the developing silence, Lulu could actually feel his next question materializing, and knew, even before he posed it, the reply she would make.

"Is it true about Leon," he said, "not coming to Peru Mountain this summer?"

"Yes," Lulu lied, "it is."

●

Lately Lulu had gotten so bound up in trying to guess what Mrs. Gansevoort was up to, and whether she had a timetable for what she was doing, and how Leon, or even herself, figured in those plans, that she had begun to lose sight of her own good fortune. So it was natural that she should have retreated into herself at about this time. She closed her door behind her and gave some thought to the great changes her friends had brought about in her life. It was far pleasanter to sit at her mirror and marvel over the way in which the wan, pasty-faced candy-counter girl, with her long hair and thick woolen skirts and vinyl handbag, had magically vanished from sight, than to attempt to peer into the heart of anyone as formidable, as proud and complex, as the lady of this house. It was enough for Lulu to perform her secretarial work conscientiously, to pander pleasantly to Mrs. Gansevoort's vanity (as Lulu was always pleased to do), and to enjoy the summer in her mountain surroundings.

Lulu focused her thoughts on the wonderful notion of what it meant to be a Gansevoort. It was lovely to let her imagination run free; to sit up elegantly by the foot of her bed, with a book in her lap and her feet positioned just so, staring at her mirror, imagining herself inheritor of Sylvia's place in the house. Only her modesty and innate fears argued against her reaching out and taking what was offered to her. Lulu likened the role to an empty chair, something tall and grand, which only required her coming and sitting in it in order to complete her investment in the Gansevoort house. It was exciting to daydream about such things.

The air in the mountains was thin and resonant. Sometimes, from the east, came the soft, toiling whine of a distant farm machine. Lulu imagined the machine cutting a wide swath of hay in a sun-filled meadow on some hillside she had never seen. Day by day, the summer grew somnolent. Mrs. Gansevoort, for her part, was quieter than usual, and spent two or three hours outdoors every afternoon, sunning herself in a canvas chair at the side of the house. Her aloof, preoccupied air discouraged familiarity. At the table, she was quite remote, smiling mechanically, obviously absorbed in her own thoughts. It was on just such a quiet, uneventful afternoon, an hour or two before dinner, when Auntie came smiling past Lulu in the little corridor leading to the dining room, that Lulu comprehended all at once what was happening. It flashed upon her. She realized Leon was coming. Auntie had summoned him, and was waiting. Everything was in place for it; nothing remained to be improved. Lulu saw straight through Auntie's triumphant calm. It was as though Auntie were an actress, collecting herself in the last moments before the curtain went up on the final act of a performance, about which, so far, she felt wonderfully proud.

●

Exactly twenty-four hours later, while sitting at her glass-topped desk in the sun room, Lulu glanced out the window toward the row of quince trees and saw them walking side by side in the dry, matted grass about a hundred feet in back of the old garden. Lulu gaped at Mr. Rafferty walking next to Auntie, his head inclined in a listening attitude, while she spoke to him. The sun, stationed high above the mountain in a flawless blue sky, flashed and shimmered. Lulu put down her fountain pen. She had the peculiar sensation that Mr. Rafferty had just materialized, fashioned out of thin air. The stately, mechanical movement of his arms and legs as he paced through the grass riveted Lulu's attention. He looked perfect. He wore a crisp blue-cord suit, white shoes, and a white necktie. Her fingertips poised suspensefully on the edge of the glass desk surface, her mouth open, Lulu sat deathly still, watching the two of them.

More than once Lulu had a compulsion to hurry outdoors and notify Douglas of Mr. Rafferty's arrival on the mountain. She was sure in her heart that Leon's appearance among them foretokened something vicious for the young man. But on each occasion, she checked herself, worrying that Douglas would interpret her nervous state as a sign of guilt, and see her, not as his lover, but as one of those whom he had already characterized as vain and unfeeling. Lulu couldn't act. Only later, after going upstairs to her room, when she looked out her window and saw Mr. Rafferty walking out through the orchard by himself, was she able to do something. She went downstairs at once to locate Mrs. Gansevoort.

Lulu found her friend outdoors. Mrs. Gansevoort was snipping small pink roses from a trellis. She smiled at Lulu.

"You will never guess, darling, who's come to join us."

Lulu was visibly flustered as she halted before Auntie. "I saw him," she said.

With a casual gesture, Mrs. Gansevoort dealt Lulu the wicker basket that she had brought outdoors with her to contain the cut blossoms. Auntie liked to float the rose blossoms in a crystal bowl as a table decoration. As Lulu took the basket, she detected a flush of color in her friend's cheeks, and felt a stab of fear in realizing that something diabolic was underway, and that the prospect was much more exciting, or even tantalizing, to Auntie than she would ever reveal. Auntie was smiling to herself as she reached with her snippers to cut another rose.

"Comes the hour of truth?" she said.

Lulu started, as if to reply, but could frame no response to Mrs. Gansevoort's enigmatic remark. The older woman turned and regarded Lulu with a simpering, sidelong expression. Lulu wanted to say something appropriate and agreeable, but the instant she spoke, she regretted her words. "I'm glad he's come," she said.

"Well, I should think you would be," Mrs. Gansevoort sang back vivaciously. "Even if it means your having to negotiate a rock and a whirlpool. Someone up here, I needn't tell you, is going to be less than overjoyed to learn that your court of admirers has suddenly doubled." She smiled, while staring at Lulu. "Douglas, I have discovered, has an ingenuous side. . . . I was like that!" Mrs. Gansevoort's eyes flashed devilishly.

"Yes, I know." Lulu's reply was inhibited by her friend's facetiousness.

"The trouble with innocence," Mrs. Gansevoort went on, endeavoring to make a fine point, while reaching with her fingertips to touch a prospective blossom, "is that it provides its own sole protection against the depredations of nature; and nature—God, for that matter, the grand texts notwithstanding—has never shown much liking for it. Nature favors the bright eye! the sharp tooth! the cunning few! Nature is a tyrant queen. Make a mistake with her, and she cuts off your head."

Mrs. Gansevoort tossed her cutting tool into the basket, and slapped the flats of her hands together as she started toward the house. "I love midsummer. I love the longness of the day, the foliage, the deep woods. I expect that everything that ever lived, or ever shall live, must flourish in midsummer."

Lulu was scarcely listening, for she had spotted the distant figure of Mr. Rafferty. He was striding at a smart pace along the rim of the hill leading toward a stand of walnut trees on the knoll to the east. Beyond him, the mountain loomed darkly. Lulu felt a sudden rush of sympathy for Douglas. It was childish of her, she knew, but as the only man who had ever kissed her, or shown desire for her, she felt bound to honor and protect him. At the back door of the house, she glanced round swiftly toward the lodge among the trees. The nephew was nowhere to be seen.

In the quarter-hour that followed, Lulu kept close to Mrs. Gansevoort in the hope that she would apprise Lulu of what was going on. The picture in Lulu's mind of Mr. Rafferty striding mechanically across the top of the fields left her unnerved. She couldn't put her finger on it, but he looked unnatural out there, so brisk and businesslike against the soft lines and colors of the trees and hills. Lulu's alarm mounted by the minute. She dreaded being confronted by the two men at dinnertime—not only by Douglas, whose disappointment in her would certainly come out at once and trouble her sincerely, but by Mr. Rafferty, as well, whose purpose in coming to Peru Mountain was mystifying and scary. Lulu was conscious, also, of how odd it was that she, a person so insignificant among those about her, should find herself caught in such a dilemma. She could not even remember what actions, either her own or others', had brought her to this pass.

When Lulu went upstairs to change clothes for dinner, she couldn't quell the shaking of her fingers. Her mind was muddled. She could not think consecutively. In the end, she made up her mind to attempt nothing more demanding at the dinner table than to maintain a polite, pleasant-mannered silence. Later, when descending the front stairway, and praying just to brave it through, she found reassurance in the realization that all three of them had shown her nothing but kindness so far.

"I know now how the wandering heroes of ancient times must have felt at landfall," said Mr. Rafferty, greeting Lulu as she entered Mrs. Gansevoort's parlor.

Auntie was sitting in her high-backed walnut armchair in the middle of the room, with Mr. Rafferty standing formally behind her. He was clasping in either hand the walnut finials atop the chair. At first glance, he looked almost artificial in his elegance.

"Isn't she a picture!" Mrs. Gansevoort chimed in promptly, her eyes sparkling with pleasure.

As Lulu came forward to greet Mr. Rafferty, she sensed the importance of the moment—of what was in effect a carefully planned reunion. The late afternoon sunlight lay in a series of pale parallelograms on the rose-and-blue Persian carpet. Lulu felt the bars of sunlight pass alternately over her face as she came forward. Mr. Rafferty was very suntanned, and looked hard as nails. His hand was rocklike to the touch. Lulu was reminded instantly, though, of the congenial effect that the two of them always had upon her spirits, reinforcing her sense of herself, as in the way they looked upon her now. They filled her with pride. She felt a surge of confidence as Mr. Rafferty, holding her fingertips, guided her politely past him to a nearby chair. Before seating himself, he waited conspicuously until Lulu appeared comfortable. They were both beaming at her, examining with approval her salmon-and-white dress and shoes.

Mr. Rafferty inquired after Douglas, while feigning wonderment. "Where is our little world beater this afternoon? Where is Lord Randall?"

"Douglas," Mrs. Gansevoort responded sarcastically, "has taken to writing poetry lately. He's quite pastoral."

"I'm surprised he's still up here," said Mr. Rafferty.

Hearing that, Lulu questioned, just for an instant, whether Mr. Rafferty was not speaking in earnest. More than once, it had occurred to her that what was real concerning her two friends and herself was perhaps closer to simple appearances than to her own subtler constructions. She had considered this possibility before, and had gone so far as to question her sanity; but in the next instant, Mrs. Gansevoort nullified any doubts on that score, when, with a slow, rather magical movement of her hand, she gestured elegantly toward Lulu, signifying that the girl was to stand once more, and display herself before them. Obediently, Lulu rose slowly to her feet, as smoothly as though drawn upward on strings. As she did, she felt the full force of their hidden confederacy.

While posing for the two of them, Lulu felt noticeably calmer inside. She turned slowly on the pivot of her heel, took three measured steps toward the sunlit windows, stopped, pivoted, and came back. Both Mrs. Gansevoort and Leon were regarding her with clear, expressionless eyes, but their approval was like something physical in the air. A shudder of excitement ran the length of Lulu's body; the three of them were so inexplicably attuned to one another.

●

At supper, Lulu avoided looking at Douglas when he came into the room; she fumbled guiltily with her napkin. Mr. Rafferty was already at the table, and greeted both Douglas and Chloris with characteristic levity, remarking on how he had made up his mind tardily to join the others on the mountain. Feeling painfully uncomfortable, Lulu sent inquisitive looks several times toward the front stairs, for Aunt Julia had not yet appeared.

"I needed the intellectual stimulation," Mr. Rafferty was explaining. "I spent two entire afternoons this week in the public library with my papers, and two more afternoons at the art museum, and there wasn't one living soul in sight at either place."

Douglas spoke up then in reply, saying something idle about Mr. Rafferty's "papers," but Lulu kept her eyes averted. She couldn't look at him. She had violated his trust. The sound of Mrs. Gansevoort coming through the front foyer offered Lulu a respite from her discomfort, however, especially as Mr. Rafferty made a sudden show of politeness by getting to his feet as Auntie entered the room. Mr. Rafferty's manner offered a courtly illustration of the way in which a man of parts could appear alert, relaxed, and deferential at one and the same time. He stood at the foot of the table and regarded Mrs. Gansevoort with the dignified air of a cabinet minister waiting upon the head of state. What was far more remarkable to Lulu at that moment, though, was the overall appearance of Mrs. Gansevoort.

Lulu couldn't guess what impression Auntie intended to effect upon her guests, but she looked so beautifully prepared that her appearance became for everyone the center of interest for the next several minutes. She was wearing a dramatic black-and-apricot dress that Lulu had never seen before, and she glittered with jewelry. To heighten the effect, she entered the room with a distinct air of consequence, a look of impatience or displeasure distorting her lips, and dealt peremptory glances at Lulu and Mr. Rafferty, while conspicuously ignoring her niece and nephew sitting on her left. However, just as Mrs. Gansevoort was seating herself importantly, with a contemptuous look that darkened her features, and as Mr. Rafferty sat down again and took up his napkin, Lulu thought she divined the meaning behind it all. Auntie's enchanting appearance and august airs were signaling the onset of a new phase in the drama. Lulu was quite sure of it. She even guessed—correctly—that Mrs. Gansevoort would maintain her regal manner throughout dinner, and have little to say to anyone. She was merely presiding over the rest of them. Unable to restrain herself, Lulu shot Douglas a look, and was immediately moved by the expression of open, youthful innocence on his face. She felt a stab of love for him. He was very handsome, with a gentle, trusting nature. Auntie, on the contrary, looked at that moment like a figure

LULU INCOGNITO

who had been lifted up from below, chair and all, and placed profoundly among them.

Mr. Rafferty talked all through dinner in such a way as to spare his elegant hostess having to make conversation with anyone. Lulu doubted that the two of them had planned matters as such, but Mr. Rafferty's behavior at the dinner table was flattering of Mrs. Gansevoort to a degree Lulu had not seen before, while Mrs. Gansevoort remained all the while icily remote. At one point, Mr. Rafferty intimated that Douglas's elder brother, Warren, had secretly loved and revered Aunt Julia to an unnatural extent during his teen-age years. When Douglas deprecated that idea, and turned laughingly to Aunt Julia for her views on the matter, Lulu noticed how Auntie made no pretense at replying, or even looking up. Lulu sensed the dark lie embedded in Leon's implication; but Auntie's cold, indifferent aspect convinced her that Leon and Julia were, in fact, clutching at something weak and susceptible in Douglas's nature, a little hem or corner of his soul, and had begun, mortally, to toy with him. The thought gave Lulu gooseflesh. She noticed, too, that whenever she isolated her attention on Douglas alone, he seemed distinct from whatever was going on about him. Somehow he looked safe. Only when she returned her attention to the others, to the sight of Aunt Julia sitting grimly, if beautifully, at the head of the table, or when allowing Mr. Rafferty's insidious words to reassert themselves, was Lulu invaded once again by the knowledge that something diabolical was operating among them.

Lulu made no attempt to find Douglas that evening, but late the following morning when she looked out the sun-room windows and saw him walking up the drive, returning from the mailbox, she went directly out to meet him. The fact that she had lied to him about Mr. Rafferty's not coming to Peru Mountain had preyed on her conscience since dawn. She could remember no occasion in her life when she had deliberately deceived someone. She was sure she hadn't the moral courage to confess to having dissembled, but felt confident that whatever would naturally transpire between them would reduce the anguish she felt inside, and at the same time alert him, in some way, to a realization that something inimical was collecting forces behind him.

As Lulu emerged from the front door, however, Douglas stopped walking, and stared with visible consternation at an open letter in his hands. He glanced up at her with a troubled look as she crossed through the grass to him.

"It's from the army," he said. "My commission has been turned down."

As he lowered the sheet of paper, Lulu caught sight of its official look, the seal of an eagle at the top of the page. She didn't know what Douglas was talking about.

"Somehow," he added, fatefully, "I expected this to happen."

The look of worry in his face was mirrored at once in Lulu's own concerned expression; the softness of her reply bespoke the intimacy she had come to feel for him. "What does it mean?" she asked.

Douglas looked at Lulu blankly, not answering; he lifted the letter again, and scanned it. She thought his fingers shook. In the same moment, Lulu's thoughts darted back to something vicious Leon had said weeks ago about Warren, the older brother, being sent home by the Army. Leon's voice echoed in her mind: "He was not fit!"

While wanting desperately to say just the right thing to Douglas, she didn't understand the dilemma. She had an impulse to reach and touch him.

"Can anything be done?" she asked.

"Not about this." Douglas folded up the letter. He explained that the army had rejected him as an officer, and notified him he would be eligible to be drafted as an enlisted man. Lulu sensed a feeling of shame in his words and attitude. She was standing very close to him. Nearby, the wind passed audibly through the treetops. Across the road, the sunlight on the hillside meadow appeared broken with dark blotches.

Without saying anything, Douglas withdrew and walked away toward the lodge. Lulu watched him go. She had already made up her mind not to tell anyone about Douglas's unhappy news, even though she felt—guiltily—unreasonably—that the timing of the nephew's blow was somehow connected to Mr. Rafferty's arrival on the mountain, and to her own recent moral failing.

As Lulu let herself into the front hall, and closed the door, she could hear Aunt Julia raising her voice emotionally to someone in the parlor. To Lulu, in her anxious state of mind, the sudden sharp echo of Auntie's recriminatory speech seemed the voice of misfortune itself.

"Patience has its place!" Auntie scolded. Lulu stopped in the cool, shadowy foyer to listen. Mrs. Gansevoort was speaking to someone, doubtless either Chloris or Mrs. Fallon, in a manner she rarely affected; it was the same throaty, overweening tone of voice that Auntie had used the day she ridiculed Lulu for having come late to her Oriental Room. "I was never patient," Mrs. Gansevoort continued, gravely, "when conditions are conducive to success. Why should I be?"

Motionless in the front hall, Lulu was certain that Mrs. Gansevoort's dictatorial words were not intended for her own ears. She retreated instinctively. As she grasped the doorknob, and started to step outdoors once again, the aunt's voice resounded anew, sending a slow, cold shock running through her. Lulu had a horror of ever again being spoken to like that. "That is my way!" Aunt Julia's voice gathered power. "That is my method!"

As Lulu hurried nervously across the grass of the front yard, she could no longer ignore the pathological cast to her own thinking and reactions. She tried to picture in her mind Mr. Rafferty sitting before Mrs. Gansevoort in the parlor, looking for all the world as cool and flawless as a store-window mannequin, while absorbing the violent thrust of Auntie's complaints. Lulu was sure Auntie was talking to him, after all. She was voicing the law to Leon!

Lulu had stopped under the first quince tree; she stood in the shade with folded arms, rubbing her bare elbows with her fingers, and gaping helplessly into space. She felt that her thinking was disconnected from what was going on about her. Nothing extraordinary had transpired in recent days to inspire such feelings of dread, but the fact was that she was deeply worried that something truly corrupt had shown its head. She wished she could go comfortably to Douglas, not just to help him over his own difficulties about the army, but because in Douglas's presence she felt free of malignant influences.

Twice before the noon hour, while going about her duties in the house, Lulu crossed paths with Mrs. Gansevoort. On the first occasion, the older woman strode right past her in the parlor, and neither spoke nor looked at her. She appeared displeased. Lulu would have thought that Leon's recent arrival in Peru Mountain would have cheered Aunt Julia; in fact, from the time he came, she had looked unhappy to the point of appearing harsh and vindictive, detaching herself from all the others. Mrs. Gansevoort spoke to Lulu only once, a few minutes before noon, when the telephone rang and Lulu hurried to answer it. Mrs. Gansevoort had picked up the telephone, but before greeting her caller, she placed her hand flat over the mouthpiece and admonished Lulu.

"Have you become a wraith?" she demanded. "Make yourself apparent. Ask Leon to show you the village."

By midafternoon, the time had already come and gone, Lulu feared, when she might have reported to Auntie, or even to Mr. Rafferty, what she had learned that morning about Douglas's disappointing news. She felt powerless to do anything that might further imperil Douglas. Lulu was sitting at her wicker desk, an hour after Aunt Julia had driven off with friends, when she saw Douglas emerge from the dark wall of pine trees out back, and go pacing off by himself in the direction of the mountain. His dejection was apparent. Lulu was tempted to follow him. When she got outdoors, however, she came upon Mr. Rafferty sitting at Mrs. Gansevoort's white table under a tree. He was facing east, toward the dark silhouette of the mountain. He gave no sign of having seen Douglas moving along through the tall grass on the hill, but Lulu was sure he had noticed. She thought she saw a subtle change flash through his face as he turned round at the sound of her footstep, a long and pensive look being replaced from behind, as it were, by an amiable smile at the sight of her.

"I was just thinking about you," said Mr. Rafferty, as he got to his feet beside the table. "I was thinking what a model of tact you are, in the way you handle . . . herself."

As Mr. Rafferty reached out to greet her, Lulu offered her hand to be clasped. *"Herself?"* she inquired, aware of the way Mr. Rafferty had widened his eyes as he spoke the word.

She was conscious, also, at that moment, of the lonely, airy look of the fields and woodlots at that hour, and of how the cool, radiant uplands, not to mention the silent mountain, had probably exacerbated her tremulous spirits day by day since leaving the house on Sycamore Street in Ireland Parish. The elevated countryside was surprisingly unearthly.

Even before she sat down, she knew that Mr. Rafferty was going to ask her to walk with him to the village. This was just the sort of sudden divination, too, which time and again reinforced Lulu's worries that something vicious was stirring to life, and argued against her blaming her suspicions on her own shakiness of mind.

"You've succeeded beyond anything I could have anticipated—way back then!" Mr. Rafferty's compliment seemed sincere. He was speaking of their original meeting.

"That does seem a long while ago," said Lulu.

"Was there a time"—Mr. Rafferty showed here an almost scientific curiosity in Lulu, as he raised his hands as if to frame the question—"when you felt you had crossed the line from the one to the other, from your previous existence, that is, to this one?" He gestured in the air with his fingers.

Lulu understood him at once, and responded candidly. "Yes," she said. "It was the night I went home for my things."

"That long ago?"

"I think so." She felt comforted by Mr. Rafferty's line of thought at this moment; it was as though her friend saw through to the source of her shakiness, to the perils of having abrogated one's past forever. "But since then," she added, "my attachment to Mrs. Gansevoort and to my life in her house has grown and grown." As she spoke, Lulu's nerves quieted. Many weeks had passed since the afternoon in late spring when she and Mr. Raffferty had shared an outdoor table in the garden of the Wistariahurst Museum, but the sense of his protectiveness toward her, as she had first experienced it at that time, was being revived inside her. For a long while now, Lulu had suppressed any memory of her life on South Summer Street; those days now seemed so squalid and humiliating that she could scarcely acknowledge their reality, though some part of her trembled at the idea of having become a rootless flower. She was staring fixedly at Mr. Rafferty. When she spoke, she could not hide the look of pathos in her face. "Auntie has favored me in every way."

Mr. Rafferty lit up a black cigarillo, which looked tiny between his fingers. He blew up a blue net of smoke. "She's transformed you," he declared.

"I feel she has created me," Lulu responded instantly, surprising herself by the speed and nature of her reply.

Mr. Rafferty commented at once, as if perhaps to demystify their exchange. "And a magnificent piece of work, too!"

Lulu sat up straight, her hands folded on the edge of the table. She was admiring Mr. Rafferty's polished manner, and that quality of masculine power forced down and kept in check, like a handsome, but very violent jack-in-the-box. It was at this moment, while watching him, that Lulu anticipated what was coming.

He had turned his head and was gazing away to the east, to where the afternoon sun was falling perpendicularly on the mountain, when she noticed in his face the same cool, poker-faced expression that he had shown her in the upstairs room of the museum. She knew what he was going to say.

"I hope," he said, "no one has shown you the town of Peru Mountain yet. Because if they haven't, I shall."

"I'd like that," Lulu replied without reflection, but pleased by her astuteness.

"You can't be a really proper Gansevoort," Mr. Rafferty teased Lulu, as they started along the cinder path toward the road, "without at least once paying the locals a visit from on high!"

"Oh, my!" Lulu colored pleasurably, unable to conceal the delight that she usually suppressed at the realization of her surrogate position in the Gansevoort house.

"I hope I haven't disappointed Auntie," Lulu said.

"It would be a mistake to condemn yourself for her every unhappiness. Or what you perceive as an unhappiness. Her own understandings of these affairs are of another magnitude altogether."

Sensing an intentionally reverential note in Mr. Rafferty's observation, Lulu encouraged her friend to say more, but decided to advertise her awareness that Mr. Rafferty might have been speaking for effect. "Was it true," she asked, "what you said last night about Douglas's brother adoring his aunt?"

"Oh, that goes without saying!" Mr. Rafferty's tone remained perplexing, however, as he responded in a broad voice that might have been intended as ironic.

Lulu's mind went back instinctively to the story Douglas had told about his infatuation with the chic Park Avenue jewelry designer; it emboldened her to bring out something even more provocative. "Was Warren in love with Aunt Julia?" she said.

"I would say so." Mr. Rafferty turned to Lulu with a blank but mirthful expression that rendered such an outrageous idea plausible.

Lulu felt her knees weaken; the notion that the dead boy had indeed fallen in love with Julia Gansevoort left her momentarily distressed. Mr. Rafferty continued smiling at her with a pranksterish light in his eyes that intimated certain tantalizing but obscure understandings—at least one of which was that Douglas, who was by now somewhere in front of them, perhaps on the knoll to the right, was watching her coming closer and closer to himself. Lulu had put on Leon's sunglasses. The sun was in her face. From behind her cheeks she could feel the glow of embarrassment at what she was doing. She had stopped thinking about Douglas's predicament, however, and she imagined that she could feel his eyes focused on the steady, rhythmical movement of her body. Her glasses muted the sky and the powdery whiteness of the gravel road ahead. As she walked, she glanced up at the row of walnut trees atop the knoll, the upper branches of which were lighted up gold. The trees looked like titans with bright helms marching in single file toward the mountain. She was sure the nephew was up there. Mr. Rafferty knew it, too. He would have to have known.

Lulu straightened her posture and stepped along as erectly as possible. She was wearing one of Ignatia's cotton dresses, a sleeveless blue dress with a white sash, and was struck by the fact that an hour ago, without realizing it, while thinking compassionately about Douglas's troubles concerning the army, she had chosen white accessories that harmonized with Mr. Rafferty's necktie and shoes! Now and again she stole looks at him from behind her amber shades. He was not like other men. He was always costumed to perfection. Lulu liked that, and interpreted it now as a consistent form of respect toward the house of Mrs. Gansevoort. He looked very pleased, stepping along smartly in the sunlight. She was sure that he was parading her.

A thrill of excitement ran through Lulu as she realized what he was doing; she couldn't help wondering if Mrs. Gansevoort herself wasn't behind it all, orchestrating everything. It was this last suspicion that convinced Lulu, more than any knowledge of her own about the nephew, that Douglas was, in fact, nearby; that her two friends were privy to something spectacularly defenseless inside him, an infirmity of the will, and had now got hold of him.

"After all, she's a beautiful woman," said Mr. Rafferty, and by now he was smiling openly.

"Yes, she is," Lulu remarked.

"He was in love with Sylvia"—Mr. Rafferty minimized the point—"in the way boys fall for girls, but he would not have gone the limit for her. He would not have given himself to the girl as he would have to the woman. He puzzled the life out of the girl, if you ask me. Toward the end, he was spouting a line of pure philosophical gibberish—talking about 'monads' and 'nexuses' and 'cosmic synapses'—stuff like that. What he really wanted, you would have to have suspected, was nothing more earth-rattling than a few honeyed words from the lips of the only person who really mattered. I mean to say—from herself!"

Mr. Rafferty talked on in this fashion as he and Lulu strode quietly along the shoulder of the road toward the village. They walked in step. Lulu felt that Mr. Rafferty was talking just to create a casual impression. She was positive they were being watched. The knoll was behind them now.

The first house in the town of Peru Mountain appeared as a patch of white through the trees ahead. From this point, the road was paved; the asphalt unfurled like a black ribbon before them. Presently, Mr. Rafferty stopped talking; a moment later, Lulu felt his hand come gently about her waist. Her senses swam. She could smell his cologne, and felt the impression of his arm against her back, and of his fingertips riding upon her moving hip. They were promenading now. The slow, mechanical rhythm of their walking left Lulu feeling both anxious and excited. She had lied to Douglas about Leon. She had consciously deceived him. Her legs trembled slightly at each step. This was the first time, she realized, that she had had to grapple with the consequences of her devotion to Auntie.

Lulu wanted desperately to look back, but kept herself in check. As much as she might have deplored it, she could not deny the fact that she wanted Mrs. Gansevoort's nephew to be aroused, even frightened, by what he saw; and the steady, clocklike rhythm of her legs somehow assured her that that was the case. He was connected to the two of them, to herself and Leon, just as surely as had all three of them been bound up with invisible cords. For a fleeting second, though, Lulu considered once again that her suspicions about her two friends, their motives and words, was nothing more than a will-o'-the-wisp facet of her own most cherished desire—that Douglas should want her.

As they approached the town common, Mr. Rafferty pointed out the sights, describing to Lulu how the finest of the Colonial-style houses that surrounded the green were all built, years ago, by various Gansevoorts. He was holding Lulu more firmly about the waist as they walked onto the green. Ahead of them, in the spaces between the great oaks, the sunlight blazed with a scintillating, almost metallic, brightness. She felt secure in Mr. Rafferty's company. Not once since they had left Mrs. Gansevoort's house and grounds had Lulu experienced feelings of discomfort from being abroad. The heel of Mr. Rafferty's hand rode reassuringly on her hip and left her acutely conscious of the steady, mechanical movement of her legs. Her body seemed synchronized to his as they strode side by side over the dreamy grass, walking through patches of shade and brilliant sunlight.

Lulu admired the look of the little town, with its pristine steepled church and town hall, its shrubberies and ivies, and scattering of white fences. Douglas had called Peru Mountain the "country seat" of the Gansevoorts. To Lulu's eyes, it was a

260

lovely, if forlorn, New England mountain town. Mr. Rafferty halted at the heart of the green to say a word or two about the bronze Civil War horseman that formed the centerpiece of Peru Mountain. He was smiling as he spoke, citing the battle names engraved about the granite pedestal—Wilderness, Antietam, Richmond—giving Lulu to realize that he was treating her with a deference that would be visible to others. He was not holding her any longer, but was playing the part of the courteous tour guide. Lulu saw through it, and was secretly charmed: not because he was playacting in an amusing or agreeable way, but because she, by extension, had become the Gansevoort heiress. She knew what he was doing. That was his aim. Lulu stood politely at attention, listening as Leon talked about the sculptor of the equestrian statue.

When they resumed walking, Mr. Rafferty pointed illustratively with one hand, while touching Lulu's back delicately with the other, guiding her past stone benches and flower beds. Now and again, she noticed people watching them, from a porch or front yard, and was alive to the flawlessness of the picture that she and Leon formed.

"The library," he was saying, "was built and endowed by Julia's grandfather, in the 1880s, and functions to this day on those same revenues. I'm sure the town administers the endowment. He planted those maples with his own hands." Mr. Rafferty signified a pair of lush red maples that flanked the polished granite steps and doorway of the library standing opposite the head of the common. "I'll show you the cornerstone," he said.

"It's a very pretty building."

"That it is." Mr. Rafferty offered Lulu his arm as they crossed the street next to the blinking traffic light where Douglas had kissed Lulu the night he took her driving. Lulu blanched at the thought that the nephew was following surreptitiously. Presently, as she gazed down at the chiseled building block, she felt herself filling with pride. The little library was built of gran-

ite and red limestone, and was very pleasing to look at. A series
of small, circular stained-glass windows extending high across
the front wall glittered iridescently in the sun. Mr. Rafferty kept
up his running commentary as the two of them mounted the
steps; but as he opened the door for her, Lulu forgot for an
instant the unspoken restraints of their charade; she snapped
her head around, and glanced out across the town common.
Her heart leaped! There, about fifty feet back of the Civil War
monument, was Douglas. He was standing motionless, in a
white shirt, his hands at his sides, He was watching them.

Mr. Rafferty, for his part, did not turn around, but was
smiling openly at her now, as Lulu, breathless, stepped past
him into the cool interior of the library. Her heart was thudding.
Whatever her agitation, though, the sudden profundity, the
richness, of the interior of the library, with its marble floors and
soaring white dome, the cool geometry of the green reading
lamps and gilt columns, competed aggressively for dominance
over her senses and attention. The building was breathtakingly
beautiful inside. To Lulu, it resembled a sacred temple. She
looked round instantly, in awe, at her companion. She couldn't
mask the look of shock, the effect of one powerful impression
following another with startling rapidity. She wavered on her
feet. Mr. Rafferty clasped her bare elbow, and, lowering his
voice respectfully, resumed his descriptions.

"It's a copy in miniature, point for point, of a centuries-old
library in Amsterdam." His hushed voice lent an additional
sacerdotal feeling to the moment, as he explained himself to
her in the manner of a courtier addressing with dignity a royal
personage, no nuance of which was lost upon a little bald-
headed man peering directly out at them from behind his desk
back of an oaken doorway. There was a stirring in the little
office, then a gray-haired lady peeped out. Since Mr. Rafferty
scrupulously avoided looking at the two of them, Lulu followed
suit. She was fascinated, besides, by the spectacle of a tremendous oil portrait, a massive gold-framed painting, depicting

the founder of the library, Jacob Lewes Gansevoort. She had recovered her senses, and was absorbed by the kindly expression on the face of the Gansevoort patriarch. He was depicted sitting in a glimmering high-backed chair, his eyes aflare with a benevolent blue light. Lulu felt momentarily arrested and favored by his gaze.

She touched the sleeve of Mr. Rafferty's suit jacket as he guided her along into the reading room, and pointed out to her the name Gansevoort engraved in elegant lettering above the windows. This time Lulu did not look outdoors toward the common, but was conscious of the teasing play of Leon's eyes as he glanced once or twice over her shoulder at the outdoors. The thought of Douglas lingering about among the oak trees left Lulu feeling pleasantly faint. More than anything else that she had learned so far, the fact that he had followed the two of them this afternoon bespoke a fascination in him—not for herself, she was quite sure, but for him, Leon.

By the time Mr. Rafferty and Lulu emerged from the reading room, the librarian and his assistant had posted themselves in an open space on the marble floor athwart the great circular desk. They stood side by side. The little man's head shone like an onion. They were both smiling officially. Their eyes went from Mr. Rafferty to Lulu again and again as they anticipated an exchange of words.

Mr. Rafferty did not hesitate. He gestured about with a wave of his fingertips. "I've been showing Miss Zita Gansevoort your wonderful library."

The effect of Mr. Rafferty's words upon the man and woman was instantaneous. Both colored, smiled, and started forward instinctively.

"We were correct, then," blurted out the tweedy little man, pleasantly. "You can't fault us in that regard!" He was speaking then directly to Lulu, who, in her blue-and-white summer costume, stood straight as a pipe before the two of them. She was smiling. The librarian couldn't disguise his flattered feelings. "I suspected you were a Gansevoort the moment you came in! It must be something sympathetic in the building." With that, he stepped forward ceremoniously and reached out his hand to her. "I'm Phillip Laughlin, the librarian. This," he said, "is Theresa Lively, my assistant."

"How do you do," Lulu replied, with a handshake. When she reached her hand toward the woman, Miss Lively showed herself a trifle flustered. She passed a book she was holding from her right hand to her left, lost control of it, and dropped it as she reached out to clasp Lulu's proffered hand. The book landed on the marble floor with an echoing boom. While Mr. Laughlin stooped to retrieve the volume, the woman managed to touch and squeeze Lulu's hand. She was blushing.

"We haven't seen Mrs. Gansevoort in aeons," she said, rushing her words in a noticeably thin voice, her eyes darting this way and that with birdlike nervousness.

Mr. Rafferty stood to one side, beaming.

While rubbing his pallid forehead with the palm of his hand, Mr. Laughlin asked if they would not like a cup of coffee. Mr. Rafferty deferred courteously to Lulu, who shook her head. "Thank you, no," she said.

"If I'm not mistaken," Mr. Laughlin continued smoothly, with studied composure, "you've been enjoying what you see of our facility?"

"Oh, very much!" Lulu exclaimed. "It's very pretty—and wonderfully kept up!"

"Miss Gansevoort is an aficionado of older buildings." Mr. Rafferty was enjoying himself. He was smiling like a cat. "She loves 'em!"

"Oh, I do," Lulu put in, earnestly. "I love the stained-glass windows, and the columns, and the skylight. It's really so beautiful!"

"Well," the librarian replied, flattered by the little barrage of compliments, "we can only hope to safeguard what we found when we came to it, and pass that along in good order to, hopefully, another generation."

"I'm sure you will," said Lulu.

She reached up and removed her sunglasses. While she felt an urge from within to resist acknowledging what her senses dictated, the surprise of the man and woman before her was an instant reaction, she knew, to the beauty of her face. They were both staring at her. An interval of silence ensued.

This, Lulu felt sure, was what Mrs. Gansevoort had wanted to happen, and she felt herself to be, at this instant, the living result of Auntie's magic. She stood in the heart of the cool, oaken-and-marble templelike structure, with Mr. Laughlin and his elderly lady assistant spellbound before her, convinced that Auntie had extinguished the frightened, colorless Lulu that once dwelt within her. That was the lesson of this afternoon's pilgrimage into Peru Mountain. The sufferings she had undergone and endured were here dissipated. She felt herself to be standing in the light of Auntie's glory, under the skylighted dome of this mountain sanctuary.

Before she and Mr. Rafferty left the building by a side door, which led outdoors to a collection of bronze animal sculptures, Lulu stopped and looked back. The light from the high ceiling ignited the heart of the library, and the man and woman stood side by side in the pale glare, like effigies, with two rows of green-shaded reading lamps twinkling behind them.

As she pulled the big door shut and turned, Mr. Rafferty was standing directly before her, very close. "You are," he said, "a wonderwork, of course."

The cool wintergreen scent of his cologne invaded her senses.

●

During the long walk back, she did not see Douglas, nor did Mr. Rafferty once mention his name or give any outward sign of their having been followed. All Lulu remembered later was a return of that pulsing sensation she often experienced when walking with Leon or Aunt Julia; it commenced in her abdomen, and coursed downward into her leg with every step, ending with a throb that set her thigh vibrating, again and again, with clocklike regularity. Mr. Rafferty paced silently at her side, his face up, his arms swinging. The episode in the library had produced a mystical effect on Lulu. By some power or agency, she felt herself truly to have been made over, body and spirit, into a Gansevoort, a creature of Auntie's own flesh—more so, even, than Chloris or Douglas. There were moments, also, as she and Leon stepped noiselessly along under the great pines at the edge of the town, when Douglas receded in her mind into an abstraction. She recalled how his conversation some-times took on the quality of a recording, with a thread of awe, or horror, running through his words. She recalled the look of him a few minutes ago, standing under the distant trees on the common, looking boyishly remote, helpless, impalpable. Lulu could not imagine, in truth, into what labyrinth Douglas had descended, or what Aunt Julia and Leon intended he should endure there, but was quite certain that she, Lulu, was his only ally.

Later on, Lulu and Mr. Rafferty were standing under one of the quince trees by the side of the house when she saw Douglas coming back across the fields, in his shirtsleeves, returning the way he had gone. Overhead, a breeze passed with a dry rattling sound through the leaves of the fruit trees. Mr. Rafferty did not turn to look at Douglas, but by now Lulu knew beyond doubt that he was thoroughly aware of the nephew's whereabouts. His knowledge was like an intrinsic facet of his perfectly tailored appearance and fine manners, or of that special air he portrayed of a controlled, coiled-up violence.

Sometimes Lulu had the sense that the five of them were inhabiting a deep, sunlit underworld, a thin-aired, upside-down realm, with the mountain inverted above, and the sky a re-flectionless, cloud-flecked sea, a country without access points or egress, which, some few years ago, had swallowed up Warren and Sylvia. It must have been the silence of the place, the unchanging aspect of the violet mountain. Sometimes, strangely enough, only Douglas seemed alive. That was because the others were a part of the embroidery, she supposed. If so, Lulu might have stayed on forever, among the colorful, stitched-on birds, and the fixed stars in the black sea at night. Auntie, for her part, was very aloof lately, almost frighteningly so, keeping to herself, as if waiting to pull, with her fingers, the last loose threads of the composition violently into place.

Lulu was sure, also, that Chloris sometimes went to Auntie at night; twice, she had heard the girl's voice in there, the recitative voice, and conjectured she was reading to Mrs. Gansevoort from the slender, leather-bound Dante Gabriel Rossetti book on the night table, Beyond that, Lulu refused to speculate.

While gazing off at the small, white-shirted figure of Douglas in the distance, and toying with a quince leaf between her fingers, Lulu alluded overtly to the nephew, inspiring Mr. Rafferty to say something shocking.

"I'm surprised, now that you're here," Lulu stated, leaving Douglas nameless, "that he hasn't left yet."

Mr. Rafferty responded instantly. "Surprised?" He flashed her an amusing look of feigned wickedness. *Where on earth would he go?*"

The question sent a thrill through her. It was scary. This time the lights actually danced in the depths of Mr. Rafferty's eyes. And for the first time, as if by paradox, Lulu felt a sudden impulse to move closer to him. It was all so intimate. She imagined a curtain coming down secretly over the sun, and in the resultant shadow Mr. Rafferty would be holding her in his arms. It would be cool and dark in the sudden midday eclipse. She would touch the scar on his wrist with the delicate point of her fingernail. He would speak softly to her. Lulu shivered as the realization of what Aunt Julia and Leon were doing passed icily through her mind: they were going to kill Douglas! They were going to kill him just as surely as they had destroyed Chloris and Warren.

17

The next time Lulu was with Mrs. Gansevoort she could barely quell the shaking of her fingers. Auntie was preparing to go out for the evening, and was sitting in evening dress at her vanity, rummaging through a jewelry box in search of her coral earrings, while Lulu stood beside her, admiring the smooth, creamy surface of her neck and bare shoulders. Auntie had exquisite flesh. In fact, Lulu thought she had never looked upon any human being in quite the way that she had fallen to studying Aunt Julia at this moment. She was holding Aunt Julia's shoes in both hands, and focused her gaze dreamily upon Auntie's naked shoulder. Whenever in the past Lulu had conjured up an idea of the opposing worlds of time and the everlasting, of flesh and the spirit, never had the first of these worlds been so powerfully disclosed to her imagination as at this instant, in the smooth ivory expanse of Aunt Julia's scented flesh.

When Auntie spoke up, Lulu's heart was pumping apprehensively. Without mentioning his name, Mrs. Gansevoort spoke of Douglas; she glanced at Lulu's reflection in the mirror. "You *have* seen how weak he is?" she inquired.

Lulu's response was tiny and breathless. "Yes."

"You know, also, I suppose," Mrs. Gansevoort continued, "that he has no longer any desire to leave us. Did you know?"

Lulu struggled here to make an apt reply, as she sensed the deep vein of cynicism, even menace, in Auntie's question. "I believe he appreciates your wanting him to be here—and would like to stay."

"I think so, too!" Auntie responded in a vigorous, husky voice, as if to deprecate by her confident manner any contrary possibility. "I've told Leon to help him in any way he can. After all, if the child lacks strength of character at twenty-one, he'll be forever dependent on others. Mind you," said Mrs. Gansevoort, "I thought twice before loosing Leon, who, as you know, darling, is not enamored of 'talkative little cadets,' as he once phrased it. But the boy listens to Leon."

By now, the venom that seemed fairly to drip from Auntie's words set Lulu quavering from head to toe.

"We'll just leave them be for now." Mrs. Gansevoort took her shoes from Lulu's hands. "Only pray," she added, "that Leon's need to do good outweighs his dislike of the boy!" This last remark brought Auntie's eyes swimming upward to meet Lulu's, and divulged in their hazel lights a look of cold, voluptuous desire that appalled Lulu. She even imagined that Auntie's breathing had quickened, and she found her eyes going helplessly, in this same moment, to the sight of Auntie's pretty breasts swelling attractively above the bodice of her strapless silk dress. This was the moment, exactly, Lulu knew, as she felt herself to be virtually afloat in Auntie's loving spirit, when she might have confessed to her dear friend the shattering news that Douglas had received from the army. But the moment came and went. Minutes later, she was following her elegant friend down the front staircase, carrying her handbag and gloves, and was compelled to realize that her loyalty to Auntie was no longer intact.

In the next two or three days, Lulu was beset with guilt. She wanted desperately to see Douglas alone, to talk to him, to plumb his feelings, even to warn him away. Other times, she had a sudden urge to drop everything and go rushing to Auntie, and unburden herself of her secrets. Sometimes, at night, lying sleepless in the dark, Lulu's dread of Mrs. Gansevoort reached unholy proportions; nothing under the heavens appalled her more than the prospect of an angry Aunt Julia. In all Lulu's days as a young religious adept of the Catholic Church, from girlhood to young womanhood, never once had the idea of divine retribution terrified her so much as the possibility of Auntie one day rising up in fury against her.

Lulu, for all her simplicity of thought, realized by now that she had, in fact, suffered a fall. She couldn't even think straight any longer without the person of Aunt Julia invading her mind. Wherever she went in the house, somehow Auntie was there. Her world, it seemed, had shrunk to the limits of Auntie's personal domain, to the climate of the older woman's needs, to the morality of her likes and dislikes. More than once, Lulu questioned her own sanity. Her memories of her past life were like the glimmerings of another existence altogether. Sometimes, to recover her balance, Lulu locked the door of her room and fished out the picture of the young Sacred Heart baseball player. She held the youth's photo on her lap, and sat for a long time, allowing the innocent calm of his gaze to stabilize her heart. One afternoon, she even tried praying. Lulu knelt on the floor by her bed, but in less than a minute's time was gripped with an unreasonable dread that Auntie would find her out.

By this time Mr. Rafferty had moved his things into the lodge, and was evidently spending a great deal of time with Douglas. Lulu rarely saw them, though, except at meals. Mrs. Gansevoort kept to herself, by and large, but continued to present a cold, sublime aspect. She almost never spoke. Lulu did realize, however, that the behavior of her friends would not have appeared distressful to anyone who was not acutely suspicious of what was transpiring. The days of August were peaceful; the grass of the neglected lawn grew parched and yellow; a midsummer quietude had fallen over the house.

Late one afternoon, while Lulu was sitting in a chair by her bedroom window, and enjoying the sensation of the sunlight baking her lap and legs, she saw Mrs. Gansevoort and Chloris coming across the fields together. Chloris was carrying a little galvanized blueberry pail, and walked with her free arm wrapped around Mrs. Gansevoort's waist. Their air of intimacy struck Lulu as strangely inappropriate. As the two of them approached the house, striding in silently through the derelict orchard, Lulu, as always, found herself staring in fascination at Mrs. Gansevoort, at her regal bearing and the proud lift of her head. Lulu had just sat up in her chair, the better to see her friend, when Mr. Rafferty and Douglas appeared in view. They were walking away from the house, crossing the drive toward Douglas's automobile as Mrs. Gansevoort and Chloris emerged from the orchard. To Lulu, the window of her room formed a perfect picture frame for the chilling enactment that took place below; for a moment later, Mrs. Gansevoort stopped walking, and turned her head to face the two men. The sun lit up her face. Chloris was still clutching her about the waist, and had halted at her side. Mrs. Gansevoort had caught Douglas's eye, it was obvious, and was glaring at him. Douglas, too, came to a standstill, and was regarding his aunt with an expectant air, as though waiting for her to give voice to the expression with which she had fixed him. Mr. Rafferty had strolled on by himself in the meanwhile, but had stopped at a discreet distance, and appeared to be waiting.

In the silence that followed, while the four figures stood immobile in the low, slanting sun, Lulu recognized what was happening. The nephew's terror was like something palpable in the air. He couldn't move, but stood before her, inert. The worst of it was that Lulu could actually see the expression on Aunt Julia's face, a look of frozen, cobralike malevolence that set her own heart fluttering. The silence persisted excruciatingly, during which time Lulu saw through the motionless configuration of the four figures in the driveway below to the soul of what was happening. Mr. Rafferty had got Douglas entangled in his toils, and hour by hour the nephew's vision of his aunt had assumed the character of a fixation. The sight of Douglas staring back helplessly at Auntie, like a creature of a lesser world stricken with awe, left Lulu feeling sick. She sat back dizzily in her chair, and closed her eyes.

All that evening and the day following Lulu sought to shut her mind to the vicious activities that she sensed transpiring among the four of them, but she could not ignore the testimony of her senses. Julia and Leon had taken hold of the nephew, and were literally shaking the life out of him. Time and again, Douglas's face appeared before her thoughts. She was reminded of what she had heard about Mr. Rafferty and the elder brother, Warren, of how the elder boy had fallen into Mr. Rafferty's power, and been reduced to a state of helplessness where he had actually desired to "confess" to Leon. Being one of those religiously indoctrinated individuals for whom the idea of confession summoned up images of cramped, darkened enclosures in which lisping penitent souls sought to invoke God's mercy, Lulu shuddered physically at the thought of Mr. Rafferty, in his own special, rather frightening splendor, cast in the role of confessor. But the fact was that she could conceive it. She could actually picture Warren, the corn-haired, bespectacled boy in the family photographs, humbling himself before Mr. Rafferty in a way no rational human being could ever do; for Lulu saw now in Mr. Rafferty a vanity so overpowering of the humane qualities that make up a human being that she guessed he must have reveled in the role of Auntie's ruthless agent. Lulu could not recall at what point exactly she had come to believe in Leon's obsessive attachment to Mrs. Gansevoort, but was convinced now that it was extreme even to a profane degree; that Leon had probably even discovered something sublime in the way he had given himself to her all these years, having transformed the original awe that he must have felt for the beautiful aristocratic woman years back into something fierce and unnatural.

While working at her desk in the sun room, Lulu avoided looking outdoors. Although the paperwork she dealt with was pointless, for Auntie had shown no interest recently in her book, as time passed Lulu regained her presence of mind, and even began to anticipate that Douglas might soon come to her of his own, and that he would appear relaxed and confident, every inch himself, and thus prove the irrational character of her fears. She made up her mind to abstract herself from her nightmarish worries by avoiding everyone. The only time that day when Lulu's becalmed spirits were upset was when Chloris came clicking into the sun room, wearing white heels and a white summer dress, looking quite tall and self-possessed. She seized a piece of paper from Mrs. Gansevoort's desk and marched out again without a word or glance.

About twenty minutes later it struck Lulu that Chloris's white dress closely resembled one of her own, a sleeveless summer dress containing an impressive amount of hand-sewn embroidery, which had once belonged to Ignatia. Dropping everything, Lulu went directly upstairs to her room to see if the girl had invaded her closet. On the way up, Lulu realized that she was more fearful than angry at such a possibility, and was astute enough to attribute her fears at once to the fact that Auntie's contempt for her niece was not so apparent anymore. Lulu breathed easily the instant she opened her closet door and found her own dress hanging where it belonged. Sighing, Lulu reached her hand and touched the dress, as though to dispel her silly anxieties with a physical gesture.

Chloris was constantly in Auntie's company lately; she followed the older woman everywhere. That was nettlesome to Lulu, partly, she was sure, because the niece's constant presence prohibited Lulu from having a private encounter with her dear friend. Auntie almost never spoke to Chloris, or showed any sort of affection or tenderness toward her, but evidently enjoyed trailing the pretty girl along behind her everywhere she went. Invariably, if Auntie went striding past the solarium door, Chloris came following quietly along behind her. Twice, when Lulu saw Auntie sitting in her parlor, reading a letter or magazine, Chloris was there; she sat on the gilt, wooden music chair close by, her face and hair shining with doll-like luster, and was as silent as the sunlight itself. At all hours of the day, she shadowed Aunt Julia. Lulu might have imagined it, but she sensed that Auntie's vanity and recent taste for showiness somehow required the slavish devotion of her adoring niece. A more sinister interpretation, which Lulu resisted, was that Auntie's demonstration of the young girl's mindless devotion to her was intended for the brother's benefit, as a provocative display of the power of Auntie's "love." What Lulu also resisted admitting was that she felt pangs of jealousy over it, as she would gladly herself have kept constant company with Mrs. Gansevoort, had Auntie only wished it. Quite naturally, too, Lulu sometimes feared that by now Auntie had learned something damaging about herself from Chloris, either about the young man named Soldier who had appeared by the fence on Sycamore Street, or, worse, that Auntie now was apprised of Lulu's unfaithfulness to her in not having reported at once the stunning disappointment Douglas had received from the army.

Much as Lulu tried to dispel these worries, her fears of Mrs. Gansevoort assailed her again and again. She felt very alone. At suppertime, neither Mr. Rafferty nor Douglas came indoors.

Mrs. Gansevoort sat importantly at the head of the table, and ignored both Chloris and Lulu to such a degree that barely a word was uttered throughout dinner. As always lately, Auntie was dressed handsomely, and wore jewelry; and on this occasion the scent of her perfume was strong on the air. By this time, Lulu couldn't help but associate Julia Gansevoort's air of elegant detachment with something frightening.

Mostly, Lulu kept her eyes fixed on her plate during supper, but now and again she stole glances at Chloris. The girl had never looked so intriguingly beautiful; she sat with perfect poise, the room lights twinkling like starfire on her clear plasticine face; her platinum hair, beautifully brushed, dropped down dreamily beneath her shoulders. Lulu was still sitting at the table after Mrs. Gansevoort coolly excused herself, arose, and left the room; the girl followed suit. High-heeled sandals made Chloris look different, and something in her stride, a newfound pride, betrayed a subtle emulation of the way Aunt Julia walked. Staring at the empty doorway, Lulu listened to the echo of their heels, as Julia and her niece mounted the front staircase. When Mrs. Fallon came in to clear the table, she removed Lulu's teacup without a query as to whether Lulu had finished. A little later, as she switched off the dining-room lights, Lulu heard male voices from outside. It was almost as though the extinguished lights were a signal in a secret script for the voices to sound.

It was completely dark outdoors, but she saw them go past the windows, the two of them walking in the grass.

Douglas was speaking. Lulu winced at the strangeness of his words.

"Protocol sentences," Douglas was saying, "are intersubjective. They're testable, but remain logically tentative."

After several days of not being close to him, the sudden sound of Douglas's voice touched a sensitive chord in Lulu. Her heart filled up for him. She felt a burning sensation behind her eyes. She stepped close to the bay windows just in time to see the two of them, two pale silhouettes in their white shirts, going side by side around the front corner of the house. If nothing else had impressed Lulu of Douglas's evil plight, the echo in her mind of his bloodless, enigmatic words was enough to excite dread; for she was sure that he was talking on and on like this, cryptically, meaninglessly, all but insanely, from morning to night, with Mr. Rafferty walking calmly beside him, like a sentry.

That was not the worst of it, either. At ten o'clock, while Lulu was sitting in the sun room, trying to formulate a plan— any plan—by which she might ameliorate the painful tension within her, she heard Auntie lash out from upstairs in a scolding voice. There had been radio music before that, but the music was suddenly turned down, and Auntie raised her voice powerfully. The harsh, almost hoarse quality of her voice left Lulu shaking. As though seeking personal safety in darkness, Lulu switched off her desk lamp. For a full minute, Auntie railed away upstairs in a thick-toned voice from behind the closed door of her sitting room. Only when the door opened, followed by footsteps overhead, did Lulu realize that Auntie was not castigating Chloris, as she had supposed. It was something else altogether. A second later, Lulu saw the two of them coming down the front stairs. Douglas came down first, with Mr. Rafferty behind him.

The bright lights over the staircase in the foyer ignited Douglas's face. Even at that distance, across the darkened room, Lulu could see the desperate, haggard look on his face. A growth of golden whiskers covered his cheeks; he had not shaved for three or four days. He looked distraught and sleepless. Mr. Rafferty, descending the steps behind him, appeared very much his usual self; his obvious unconcern with what was happening reflected the attitude of a formal escort. When Aunt Julia suddenly lashed out again, in the same powerful, rasping voice—a parting shot about a "creature who would offer me title to my own house!"— Mr. Rafferty barely smirked.

When Douglas went past the sun-room door, Lulu saw his

face clearly, pale and feverish behind the gold whiskers, a picture of perdition, of suffering, like the pictures she recalled from her schooldays, of a dolorous Saviour at Golgotha. That, or worse, she thought; like an animated vision of death. His hair and eyes flashed in the foyer light; his cheeks lit up golden. Mr. Rafferty spoke up then, in a playful, lilting singsong voice. "Back to barracks," he told Douglas.

●

Lulu had made up her mind that she was going to seek out Douglas at her earliest opportunity, whatever the difficulty, but in her secret heart she despaired of such a chance arising. She even wondered if Douglas had not perhaps descended willingly into whatever savage regions he now found himself. The next morning she saw the two of them walking on the knoll, one behind the other, with Mr. Rafferty leading the way. They were walking quite rapidly across the rim of the sunlit hill, with an air of urgency that Lulu sensed was more theatrical than real. Leon was wearing his blue seersucker suit; his white shantung necktie blew in the wind. Douglas, in white shirtsleeves, followed behind, striving to keep pace. They put Lulu in mind of a man and boy going quickly to investigate a report of something amiss beyond the hill. They looked small on the horizon. Somehow the meaninglessness of their urgency was contained in the massive black formation of the mountain rising behind them.

That afternoon, Mrs. Gansevoort had a second tempestuous outburst. Lulu was outdoors at the time. She had taken a canvas folding chair, and walked out past the quince trees and old garden, and was sitting in the shade of a maple, facing the house, when it began. Only this time, to Lulu's dismay, Auntie was evidently alone. That is, the sudden loosing of her fury was directed at no one in particular, but seemed simply to burst gratuitously out of the open windows into the sunlight.

Lulu sat up straight, as the crack of Mrs. Gansevoort's voice shot across the sunlight toward the fields and wall of pines out back. Lulu was staring at the house in disbelief. The house shimmered in the sun, as if trembling to its foundations. After a moment Chloris appeared—she was running—returning hurriedly along the path from the lodge; but she halted instantly when Auntie released a second violent outcry. Lulu had perceived all at once the grotesqueness of what was happening; Auntie, all by herself in the house, had loosed a scream of wild, unchained egoism. The outcry echoed for a long minute in Lulu's ears; a cry that might have originated in the depths of the earth itself. A picture formed in Lulu's brain of Aunt Julia sitting all alone in her high-backed chair, clutching the chair arms tightly with both hands, and simply expelling the fury within her, a paroxysm of inhuman hatred, as upon the spirit of life itself.

Even Mr. Rafferty, later on, when he joined Lulu, appeared a trifle shaken. He was coming through the fields from the knoll, he said, when he heard the distant shout. By now, though, Lulu could not tell whether Mr. Rafferty was being earnest or cunning. The surprise in his face was probably artful.

"Has anyone gone indoors to help?" he said.

Lulu was standing in the tree shade by her canvas chair looking nervously back and forth, from Leon to the house. "Chloris," she answered.

"You should have seen the boy!" Mr. Rafferty tossed out, and his eyes twinkled suggestively at the mention of Douglas's reaction. "He was petrified!"

"It was very frightening." Lulu was distracted. "I don't understand any of it."

"It's happened once or twice before," Mr. Rafferty explained, "but never quite like this. Never in broad daylight."

Mr. Rafferty excused himself and went across the dry grass toward the house. Lulu could not divine what he was thinking. When he returned, she was still standing under the tree. Douglas, she realized, was nowhere in sight, but she was certain as could be that Mr. Rafferty was cognizant (and doubtless in control) of the nephew's movements and whereabouts.

Mr. Rafferty looked relieved as he came across the grass to her. This time, Lulu anticipated him. She knew what he was going to say.

"She's sleeping?" Lulu guessed.

Mr. Rafferty nodded. "Like a corpse," he said.

Lulu didn't wish to be alone again, but could not think of anything appropriate to say to Mr. Rafferty. After a moment's hesitation, she reached and took hold of his elbow. She wanted him to stay, even if she distrusted him. He was Auntie's confederate, she was sure of it.

"I suppose you know," said Mr. Rafferty, "that the brother is in the throes of a mad schoolgirl crush." He gave a shout of laughter. "I can't mention your name but he turns white as a lily, and begins to sputter and stammer!"

Lulu saw through the facetiousness of Mr. Rafferty's assertion, but couldn't help protesting. "Not me," she said.

"Oh, believe me," he raised his voice, "it's only too true. This morning he was lying on his belly up in the woods, reading Keats and Shelley, and mooning over the first love of his life, and came back to the lodge at noontime with a case of poison ivy that would kill a skunk! He must have been eating the stuff! I spent a half-hour painting his face and hands with baking-soda paste." Mr. Rafferty had moved closer to Lulu, and as he spoke he urged her into motion, with his fingertips at her waist.

Lulu was walking then at his side. "Where *is* Douglas?" she asked.

"Ivy Leaguer!" Mr. Rafferty added. "Thought he was immune to the stuff! Do you have any conception of what he's talking about out there?" He gestured vaguely toward the woods. "Can you imagine a steady diet of Ludwig Wittgenstein? Meister Eckhart? Duns Scotus? If it isn't that, it's something called Boolean logic and machines that are being taught to think! I," he said, "have trouble just reading. I'm not one of those armchair litterateurs who can read an account of the Battle of Poltawa, and actually smell the smoke. Reading gives me a headache. After an hour under a reading lamp, I'm ready to kill!"

Mr. Rafferty was enjoying himself. While walking at his side, Lulu could feel the warmth of the earth underfoot. She was trying to picture Auntie lying in bed, sleeping like a god, with the reverential girl seated motionless nearby.

"It's a joy to talk to a human being for a change." Mr. Rafferty smiled, and winked at Lulu.

"Yes, it is," she said. Lulu had been conscious in recent days of her own growing loneliness. The feeling of her friend's fingers on her waist recalled their visit to the hallowed little library in Peru Mountain. She was sure that Mr. Rafferty was steering her along now in an ordained direction. Douglas was doubtless nearby. The thought of Mr. Rafferty having treated the young man's inflamed face with a mask of white baking soda struck Lulu as painfully grotesque.

He spoke as though he were reading Lulu's mind. "I wouldn't fret about them," he confided, softly. "Those two youngsters have been riding a little trolley through sunny fields for years, without the faintest expectation of things ever changing."

When Leon dropped his voice intimately and addressed her

in this sinister, allusive way, Lulu felt once more the dark current of his power coursing through her. A feeling of corruption invaded her. She wanted to be held. She wanted him to speak unconscionably, in private, to her secret, innermost yearnings.

"They both seem innocent to me," she replied quietly, hoping Mr. Rafferty would say more.

The sun was getting low, but the sky was very bright. The mountain trembled darkly in the sun, like the upended hull of a sunken vessel.

"Being ignorant of what is going on," Mr. Rafferty insisted, "is not the same, though, as being exempt from consequences, is it?"

Lulu shuddered momentarily. Mr. Rafferty's manner both frightened and excited her. Douglas, she felt certain, was at his mercy.

"It's the oldest game there is," he said. "The innocent pay. They can argue, holler, cite Scriptures, do anything they please— they can kick and squeal from sunup to dark—but when the time comes, they pay."

Lulu made a feeble effort to penetrate the obliquity of Mr. Rafferty's words. "Won't you tell me," she said, "what is happening to him?"

"You have to keep in mind," he said, "that Julia Gansevoort has been the soul of kindness to you and me. We're living arguments to her benevolence."

Certain that Mr. Rafferty was aware of her perfidy to Mrs. Gansevoort, Lulu nodded helplessly. "Yes," she said.

"And that"—he raised his voice gently, and lifted an instructive finger—"from an egoist of mythical dimensions!"

"I understand," Lulu confessed. She, too, expressed herself in whispers. His hand on her hip was warm and reassuring; but his words were strange.

"They could blow me into a hundred pieces tomorrow, and all of the pieces would point toward herself. That's how it is."

Lulu would like to have impressed upon Leon her sympathy for his words, but stepped along noiselessly at his side. He was alluding, she feared, to her own breach of faith.

"We have no past, you and I," he said. "There is absolutely nothing there. There is no past."

"I know," said Lulu, acknowledging breathlessly the profundity of what he was saying.

She knew that what she was about to ask had a portentous ring. "You are in love with Mrs. Gansevoort?"

Mr. Rafferty's eyes brightened to a shine. "That's a way of putting it." He was smiling. He had drawn Lulu closer to him by an inch. They were approaching the grove of pin oaks adjacent to the lodge. The late sun ignited the crowns of the trees; beneath the sunlit canopy, the straight slender trunks rose up in the gloom, like columns supporting a glowing roof. "Of course," he added, "she has no practical need of a person like me. She prizes faith, devotion, intangibles. In that way, I suppose, she is an idealist."

Time and again, the vision of Auntie lying asleep, pale and magnificent, intruded on Lulu's thinking.

"I could sit in my rented room, across from the public library on Chestnut Street, for months and years on end, with nothing better to do than await being summoned to her house, and she would be more pleased with me than any tradesman, employee, or public servant that ever came to her door."

Lulu whispered again, in awe. "And you would do that."

As before, Mr. Rafferty's eyes brightened attractively. "Naturally."

Lulu looked up at him. "And if she never called—"

"Exactly. I would wait. . . . Of course," he admitted, with a hint of humility, "as I suspect you may have gleaned by now, she defrays my modest living expenses." He smiled oddly. "As she says herself, I wasn't born to spin or toil."

If Lulu had not herself tried so hard all these weeks to

establish a selfless relation to Mrs. Gansevoort, she could not have appreciated Mr. Rafferty's extraordinary remarks.

"I'm not saying," he added, "there aren't joys to be had— or that loyalty is its own reward!" He laughed over that. "She pays in appropriate coin. The telephone does ring. The call does come. And if a body is sensible to that quality of moral approbation, then her smallest desires become like adventures in the wilderness. Holy undertakings."

Lulu winced at the realization that her own longing for Auntie's approval—whether dressing up for her with almost ritual care, or, worse, delivering pain to someone as defenseless as Chloris—had caused her to violate something spiritual in herself.

The two of them were entering the oak grove now, stepping soundlessly among the gray, templelike trees, the leafmold, decayed mushrooms and twigs crushing softly underfoot. Lulu's senses tingled with the knowledge that Douglas was present; he was not in the lodge, but somewhere just beyond the twilit grove, his ghastly, gold-whiskered face concealed among the shadowy leaves. Her legs quaked perceptibly with every step she took. She wanted Mr. Rafferty to hold her.

At length, Lulu formulated a question that she might easily have posed to Mr. Rafferty weeks ago. "Was *I*," she asked, quietly, "sent for? Did she send you to find me?"

"I cannot tell a lie," he quipped. "I spent two hours one afternoon, describing the virtues of a real-life Cinderella whom I had chanced upon at a coffee bar in a five-and-ten-cent store, a creature of sweetness and innocence such as our Divine Maker produces only once in a hundred years, and two days later the call came from on high."

A swooning sensation caused Lulu to sway and bump gently against Mr. Rafferty. He was holding her more proprietarily about the waist. Then they had stopped walking. High above them, pencils of sunlight sparkled dustily in the roof of leaves.

Leon was facing Lulu, with his hands around her, and she knew, by the way he had positioned her, that the nephew was behind her.

Lulu couldn't keep silent any longer. "I'm very afraid of Mrs. Gansevoort," she said, "but I do love her. I've loved her from the beginning. From the very first day, when you brought me to her house, my heart went out to her."

Mr. Rafferty smiled.

"I wanted to be hers. I would have done anything! She taught me how to sit, how to walk. She cut my hair. She dressed and praised me. I would have followed her anywhere. And if she was vain and selfish," Lulu allowed, "I was glad!"

"She is that."

"It pleased me to see her puff herself up. I could feel her pride. It was all like a miracle to me. A miracle. But I knew it was different from anything like that. I never believed for a second that Auntie was a gift of God."

"She's not," said Mr. Rafferty.

"Still"—Lulu had pressed softly against Mr. Rafferty, looking up at him—"I think Douglas is innocent. I know that he and Chloris and Warren are the children of something very vicious that happened to Auntie. I know that she was terribly— horribly!—cheated. I know that. But no one can be blamed for being born! That's the awful part. No one can blame us for that. No one," Lulu repeated, with feeling. Her past unhappiness welled up inside her. "I've lived in terror all my life. I prayed over and over, a thousand times, for God to save me."

Mr. Rafferty nodded uncomfortably. He glanced over her shoulder. She was sure the nephew was there. She could see Douglas's beautiful, whiskered face in her mind's eye, glowing pallid and deathlike among the leaves. He was watching and listening.

"I knew from the very first," Lulu admitted, "when I saw my room, the size and prettiness of it, that someday I was going to have to do something dreadful. How did I know?" Tears stung her eyes as she recalled the beauty of her white room, with its magnificent bed and cornices and the tall windows over the garden. "I knew also"—Lulu hesitated—"I knew the first time I saw *him,* that it involved him. At first," Lulu continued, staring up at Leon, "I thought that he was somebody else altogether. When I saw the top of his head over the chair in Auntie's library, I thought he was somebody else. I thought he was the other one! The real one! The . . . Christly one!"

"You speak," said Mr. Rafferty, "in the accents of apostasy."

"Whatever has happened," Lulu concluded, "I did want to give myself to her. I *was* willing."

Mr. Rafferty responded with practiced disinterest. "Well, I," he said, "am not an ambassador at her court, after all."

"What are you, then?" Lulu stood helplessly, staring up at him with wet eyes.

"You do know," he said, quietly, "that someone is nearby?"

Lulu nodded. Her mouth was dry. She knew what was expected of her. She didn't wait to be prompted by Mr. Rafferty, but raised up slowly onto her toes, and fixed her mouth to his. She closed her eyes.

Lulu pressed firmly against Mr. Rafferty, as tightly as she could, kissing him. The ground grew meaningless under her feet. She could hear Douglas moving across the clearing behind her. She could hear his footfall on the soft earth but did not dare look round. Mr. Rafferty held Lulu to him. Her eyes remained closed. She moaned instinctively; Mr. Rafferty was rubbing her back. She could feel the corruption passing in waves through her, like a fluid, like vapors closing in about her heart. They had destroyed Douglas. She, too, had willed it to happen.

"He's going to her," said Mr. Rafferty, cannily. "He'll be safe."

Lulu was shaking her head. She could not look at Mr. Rafferty; she couldn't bear witnessing the expression on his face.

Minutes later, Lulu returned alone to the house. By then, darkness was approaching. The great shadow from the house spread out past the quinces, mingled with the darkness of the bushes and shrubberies of the old garden, and sprawled beyond into a broadening band of blackness that lay like a river of dark flowing down from the mountain.

●

Auntie remained upstairs all night and half the following day, with the door to her room closed tight, and Chloris and Douglas sequestered inside with her. The house was silent, hour after hour, except for two or three occasions when Lulu heard a strange, soft grumbling coming from the direction of Auntie's quarters, like the sound of a bird of prey grumbling contentedly. Or was she dreaming?

Lulu slept fully clothed that night, tossing restively. When the sun came into her room at dawn, she lay motionless, staring at the ceiling, watching milky spangles of daylight streaming pointlessly overhead. The morning was windless, the sky devoid of clouds. Somehow she knew that Mr. Rafferty would not appear. She would see no one. They had finished with her. Outdoors, in the late morning, Lulu walked by herself in the dry grass all the way to the wall of pines. The world appeared static, lifeless. The windows of the house glittered abstractedly. She was wearing a black silk dress, but could not remember if she had worn it yesterday, or had changed; it was her favorite, the one with the delicate hem and diaphanous sleeves that Aunt Julia had once fitted onto her with her own hands. Sometime today, Lulu knew, she must encounter Auntie; she had a premonition, too, of great personal danger. Her sense of time was failing her.

She was standing east of the house, under the walnuts, hours later, when she saw Aunt Julia come outdoors, followed close at heels by her niece. They did not raise their eyes toward Lulu, but went, one behind the other, to the lawn chair at the edge of the derelict garden, where presently, in a decorous fashion, Auntie slowly seated herself. The girl was behind her.

Auntie was bare-shouldered. Lulu watched in fascination as Chloris began to apply a lotion to Auntie's skin. Within twenty minutes, Lulu had made her way back to the pine grove, and started round toward the back door of the house, out of sight of Auntie and the platinum-haired girl. Her heart was thudding softly. The sunlight sparkled in the glasslike pebbles embedded in the old carriage stone by the back door. After pausing a moment, Lulu mounted the steps. Indoors, the vestibule reaching past the dining room to the front hall lay in gloom; the house was quiet. Lulu crossed the hall to the dining-room door to ascertain Auntie's whereabouts, and spotted her at once through the bay window, sitting as before, in her lawn chair, with Chloris stationed behind her. Lulu stared at them, at the unchanged picture of the magnificent woman, her temples and auburn hair glimmering in the sun; she was sitting by the maple tree like a figure carved from stone—gorgeous and indestructible—the wraithlike, slender-boned girl posted motionlessly behind her, her fingertips resting on Auntie's gleaming shoulders.

Lulu turned to ascend the back stairs, thought better of it, and went the length of the central hall to the front of the house; it was as though the only protection left to her in a moribund world was the little formality of climbing the front staircase. Until now, she had never thought of ruin as being anything but a falling to pieces, a crumbling asunder, but the perfect stillness of Mrs. Gansevoort's house and grounds this afternoon seemed to Lulu the ultimate expression of chaos. Upstairs, she opened Auntie's bedroom door, let herself in, and closed the door soundlessly behind her. Douglas, she was positive, was ensconced in Auntie's adjoining sitting room, the tall white door to which, in the right-hand wall, gleamed significantly. As always, Auntie's bedroom was flawless; the little bottles and enameled boxes upon her vanity were disposed with geometric care; her smooth satin bedcovers gave off a silver-lavender sheen; even the folds of the voluminous velvet draperies framing her two windows seemed a mirror image of one another.

Lulu crossed the room. Hesitating momentarily, she grasped the silver knob of the sitting-room door. It was locked.

For one second, Lulu felt a rush of relief. Maybe she had been mistaken, after all; maybe he was not there; maybe he and Leon were walking the hills; but she knew better. She was not wrong. Every part of her was alive to Douglas's presence in the room behind the door. She could see him in her mind's eye: he lay asleep on Auntie's satin love seat, stretched out full-length in his white flannels and dress shirt, his face ghastly.

Lulu rapped softly on the door panel, and waited a long moment. He would not reply, she was sure. He was as much a part of Auntie's house and possessions, of her cold, static estate, as the little gold music chair standing by her bed.

Impulsively, Lulu seized the knob and shook the door; but it wouldn't budge. As she turned to go, the mirrors of Auntie's vanity caught a beam of sunlight and the looking glass turned suddenly aglare, as though the sun itself had contrived to obliterate Lulu's reflection. As she emerged into the upstairs corridor, her impulse to escape the house and hide outdoors was overpowering. In a matter of two or three minutes, she had gone on a beeline across the driveway and out through the stunted apple trees toward the woods west of the house, where she collapsed in the grass. She could go no farther because the dark tangle of the trees before her was no less frightening than the spectacle of Auntie's house looming behind her in the sunlight. After a while she leaned forward and rested her head on the ground; the idea of her equilibrium leaving her seemed almost bliss to contemplate. The earth beneath her temples was warm and comforting. Lulu closed her eyes.

By sundown, though, she had made up her mind to brave her dear friend in person. The knowledge that such a desperate step was her only chance to save herself galvanized her will. She hadn't a thought in mind but to put herself in front of Auntie, and leave the rest to chance and fate. If Auntie failed her, it wouldn't be because Lulu had not gathered her courage and offered herself into the teeth of something she had never really understood. If she was to believe Mr. Rafferty, or construe his frightening allusions as she knew he wished her to do, then her dear friend was something far more awful than just a vain, embittered, vengeful woman who saw her sister's children as the living issue of an old pain. To believe Leon would be to suppose that Auntie was something more like the flesh-and-blood epitome of a great destructive principle loosed upon the earth.

Lulu stopped to catch her breath on the landing of the front staircase; she sat down a moment on the steps. Music was playing upstairs: Auntie was there, and Lulu could hear Chloris's voice, as well. For the first time, Lulu acknowledged that Chloris had grown formidable in her eyes. The vision of the girl following Auntie about, day in and day out, a creature of fairy-tale beauty, in her filmy white dress and delicate sandals, had driven Lulu deeper into herself. Truth was, she found the girl daunting. Chloris frightened her now. And if the niece's cool, pacific exterior betrayed nothing of the loathing she must have felt for Lulu, it was only because her obsessive adoration of Auntie had eclipsed everything else.

As usual, Mrs. Gansevoort surprised Lulu in the way she greeted her. When Lulu knocked on Auntie's bedroom door, and heard the click of Chloris's heels approaching from within, she prepared herself for the worst. Auntie could have been stretched out like a stone effigy on her immense lavender bed, or she might have been glaring up in anger at her from behind her little spinet desk, or doing just about anything imaginable. In reality, at that moment, Aunt Julia and Chloris were playing a game of checkers. Just as Chloris pulled open the door, Lulu saw Auntie—sitting all the way across the room at a maple piecrust table by the windows—raise her elegant arm and move a piece on the board.

"Well," said the older woman, quite airily, as Chloris seated herself anew, "that should contain your skills." She reached and removed a red checker from the board. "I rarely lose."

"I rarely win," Chloris returned, in her usual soft-voiced manner, with a germ of a smile on her lips.

"You were walking in the woodlots?" Mrs. Gansevoort addressed Lulu matter-of-factly, turning her face only partially.

Lulu stood in place just inside the door. The nephew, Douglas, was nowhere to be seen. Lulu's eyes went at once, surreptitiously, to the closed door of Auntie's sitting room. She felt panicky, and strove to maintain her composure. "Yes, earlier," she said.

"You do know," Mrs. Gansevoort continued, "that our little miracle play has about run its course?" Turning now to Lulu, Auntie raised her braceleted hand histrionically. "Revelations tremble in the offing!" she declared. "The gods stir! Where do you suppose," she asked, with sudden harshness in her voice, "our nephew is at this hour?"

"I don't know." Lulu's eyes went nervously from Auntie to Chloris, and then unavoidably to the locked white door of Auntie's sitting room. The niece, Lulu noticed, never once looked up, but sat in her chair like a porcelain figurine.

"You don't know!" Mrs. Gansevoort parroted her unpleasantly. She got up then, and left the table for the tall violet chair by the fireplace opposite her bed, where she seated herself importantly. From the point where Lulu was standing, the chair was on a direct line to the sitting-room door. Auntie had seated herself thus, intentionally, it seemed, with her back to the door. Carefully, she arranged the folds of her skirt, then looked up, and took hold of the chair arms in either hand. Lulu actually quailed inside as she recalled her earlier intuition of Auntie, two days ago, sitting thus—in this very chair!—when she had suddenly raged out in a terrifying voice that seemed to inveigh against the whole of God's creation.

Lulu stood before her, tongue-tied, struggling to make sense of Auntie's words.

"I came," Lulu managed to bring out at last, "to ask your help."

"You did?" Mrs. Gansevoort appeared the soul of ingenuousness. Her hazel eyes dilated prettily. "I am surprised. It astonishes me to be petitioned by you, especially at this late hour. Was it for *ourself*," she asked, "or for the boy? Because if it isn't self-concern that brings you here, let me put your worries to rest. We have the boy's best interests at heart."

Lulu was encouraged to draw a step nearer to Auntie. She stopped directly before her. Auntie reached then and touched Lulu's hand; the iciness of her fingers caused Lulu a momentary shock. The vision of Douglas lying asleep in the closed room flashed across Lulu's brain.

Lulu was regarding her friend with a stunned expression. "Where *is* Douglas?" she asked.

"Where is he, indeed!" Auntie was supreme. "Wasn't I just asking the same!"

Time and again, Mrs. Gansevoort's triumphant spirits bubbled to the surface, and brought to her eyes a sudden lustful shimmer.

"Please, Auntie." Lulu begged to be understood, as she strove to quell her nerves. She was panicking. "Trust me! I don't know what is happening."

"Does anyone?" Auntie was empyrean.

A grimace distorted Lulu's face. "Only you can help!" she persisted.

"I promised you everything," Mrs. Gansevoort cut in swiftly. She sat forward in her chair then, and lashed out hotly at Lulu. "I promised you *life!*"

"You gave me life!" Lulu cried. Her fears mounted. "You did! I loved you every day, every minute!"

Lulu lost control. Although appearing rooted to the floor,

she sent wild glances all about the room. Chloris had risen from her place at the table by the dusky windows, and come dreamily across the room, oblivious of Lulu's desperate pleading, and lowered herself silently, with the delicate movements of a ballerina, into a sitting position on the floor beside Auntie's chair.

Auntie's eyes blazed. "You would worship two gods."

"I wouldn't!" said Lulu. "I didn't! I swear it. I've tried to do right, Auntie! Always! All my life!"

"Your life!" Mrs. Gansevoort expelled the word with disgust. "Do you call that trifling, wretched existence which you endured a *life?*"

The depth and extent of the older woman's revulsion carried a deathly pallor into her face. In the dusk, her chair now appeared quite immense, with the glowing white door of the sitting room rising up behind it like an integral feature of the great chair itself.

"You knew what I expected. You knew who I was! You— of all people—knew who I was. Would you deny it?"

"No!" Lulu was distraught.

"And I favored you! Out of all the great lackluster mob! You," she said, "dwelt at my side. Dined at my table. You had the freedom of my house and gardens."

"I do want it," said Lulu. "It's true, Auntie. I would do anything. I would say anything. I would renounce anything!"

"Did you ever, truly, doubt my victory?"

"Never." Lulu couldn't stop the tears, for Auntie's adamant nature was evident everywhere in her appearance. She was obdurate. Chloris sat on the floor, close by Auntie's violet chair, abstracted.

"Please, help me." Lulu finally broke down. A sob escaped her. "Save me, Auntie."

At this moment the sight of Auntie allowing her hand to drop languidly over the chair arm until her fingers came to rest atop Chloris's blond head fixated Lulu. The beautiful globe of the girl's pale silken skull seemed molded by the powers of creation to fit to perfection the spanned fingers of Auntie's jeweled hand.

A diamond shimmered in the dusk; Auntie's head and throat glowed. After a moment, Auntie dismissed Lulu in a soft, peremptory voice.

"Go now to Leon."

Lulu hid outdoors in the garden behind the quince trees as the light in the west faded by degrees, forming, at last, a black glassy hemisphere overhead, crowded with stars—the brilliant dome of Auntie's own personal estate, to Lulu's eyes. The night was flawless, she thought, except for herself, of course, who had no place in Auntie's dispensation. She listened to the rattling of the dry, yellow quince leaves. Once or twice, she experienced lurid premonitions of being pressed facedown against the earth, of Mr. Rafferty pinning her from behind; or imagined casting herself full-length onto the floor in front of Auntie's prodigious chair. She could not be certain later whether Aunt Julia and Chloris had dined that evening, or if she had imagined seeing the two of them, across the darkness, sitting at either end of the dining-room table, like the last living beings. Only much later, when Lulu changed position, stepping quietly along behind the row of trees—and noting the dim light that illuminated the windows of Auntie's sanctuary, where Douglas, she guessed, was by now awaiting the onset of a fate he could not even reckon—only then, did Lulu feel the presence of Leon. She divined a movement corresponding to her own taking place in the darkness beyond the garden, as if he, too, had been standing motionless all this while. Immediately Lulu remembered the afternoon months ago in the museum gallery when the two of them had moved silently about, from room to room, in secret conjunction with one another; only this time, it was he, Mr. Rafferty, who exercised the superior freedom. Not looking back, Lulu made straight for the house.

Groping up the back staircase, she had only one thought in mind. She would lock herself in her room. It appalled her to realize that she believed in Auntie's malignant dominion just as surely as she had ever believed in anything. As she glanced along the corridor to Auntie's door, Lulu acknowledged the extent of the corruption within her; for there was nothing under the sun that she would not exchange to be redeemed at this moment by Aunt Julia. She even envied Chloris, and would have been happy to feel Auntie's hand resting upon her own skull. At the door to her room, the idea flashed upon her that the knowledge of her undoing constituted her undoing; that her ruin lay in her willingness to repudiate everything she had ever believed and treasured.

Still, when Lulu opened her bedroom door, and saw her belongings strewn about in the dark, her heart jumped wildly. Her dresses and blouses were scattered across the floor. The doors of the armoire were thrown wide. Lulu gave a cry and threw on the light switch. Shoes from her closet were tossed in a heap on her bed; her powders and perfumes were overturned. To Lulu, the violation of her room was the cruelest stroke. It awoke her most primitive fears. Chloris, she was sure, had retaliated. More than anything done to her so far, this assault left her physically unnerved. She trembled from head to foot. Instinctively, she seized her clothing from the floor, spilling everything onto her bed. Auntie's pictures, she noticed, were gone. The three framed photographs of Mrs. Gansevoort had been taken out altogether. Noting that, Lulu turned at once to the armoire; immediately, her eye lit on the colorful newspaper photo that she had hidden among her things. It lay in plain sight at the foot of the big wardrobe. In a second, Lulu had the picture in hand and was scrutinizing the figure of the blond-haired youth. Her senses were swimming, but the peaceful, everyday look of the young man in the photo was like a summons to common sense. For an instant, Lulu recognized in her torment signs of hysteria.

Standing under the light, clutching the picture of the Sacred Heart baseball player in her fingers, she had a magnificent urge to reject as lunacy the entire mad construction that she had imposed upon the things going on around her. It was the production of a distraught mind. The truth was, she lived at the mercy of others. The bed she slept in, her place at the table, her clothing, her work, her leisure—all of it—derived from others. Time and again, as Lulu strove to regulate her breathing, her attention returned to the face of the youth in the picture, and she even felt a wave of momentary relief. Her thinking grew more lucid. For the first time in weeks, it seemed, she was able to posit the existence of an actual world going about its business somewhere; he, Soldier McNiff, was probably sleeping in his bed right now; she tried to imagine it, the sight of him fast asleep, his head on his pillow. . . .

Lulu's sense of relief lasted only a second or two longer. She was staring down with a preoccupied expression at the boy in the photo, with his catcher's mask poised atop his head, when a sense of something developing behind her caused Lulu to turn suddenly on her heel to the window. In the pale oblong of light that shone down from her room onto the grass below, a man stood staring up at her. It was Mr. Rafferty. He had been watching her all the time. The weak light that framed his figure gave his cord suit a gaseous hue; his white shirt collar and cuffs gleamed statically. Lulu's first impulse was to go to him. Folding up the picture she held, she started from the room. She wanted to tell Mr. Rafferty how foolish she had been; how the eerie aspect of everything taking place around her was more the result than the cause of her lonely torment. She had created her own demoniacal state. Leon, better than others, would understand her meanings. He was a sympathetic spirit in that way. Like herself, he had once known great deprivation; he had suffered.

Lulu left her door ajar and hurried to the back staircase. Before descending, she noted that Auntie's door was open a trifle, giving out a wan band of light that touched the opposite wall. It must have been the glow from Auntie's room that arrested Lulu, for all at once she was overwhelmed once more by the frightening unnaturalness of it all. Auntie had abandoned her forever. Only Mr. Rafferty remained. She couldn't ignore any longer the glaring portents, and knew in that same instant that Mr. Rafferty was coming indoors, pulling the door behind him, shutting up the house. As she started down the steps, she actually heard the metallic click of the back door. He was in the vestibule.

Lulu darted forth in a panic into the dining room. There was no place else to go. By now, the darkness of the night outdoors could not have been more forbidding to Lulu had it been a solid wall. She was standing by her own place at the table, with her hands to her face. Her thoughts were spinning. She didn't know what to do, but was certain that something dreadful was coming. She could see nothing before her but the glowing tablecloth and the motionless curtains of the bay windows. It was then— in the depths of the hallway mirror toward the front of the house—that she caught sight of Mr. Rafferty. His reflection was reduced by the distance to boyish dimensions. He was standing sideways in the back vestibule. In the looking glass, he was far away; in reality, he was near at hand. Clutching the back of her dining-room chair, Lulu watched in hypnotic fascination as the man in the glass turned slowly and removed his suit jacket.

Lulu was mesmerized. One moment, she was all but welded to the floor; in the next, at just the moment when Mr. Rafferty's head came up, and his face in the distant mirror shone with a soft light, she was in flight.

On a line, Lulu dashed out of the dining room into the front hall, and up the stairway. As she fled up the steps, she saw Mr. Rafferty standing in the back corridor in his shirtsleeves. He was not looking at her, nor did her sudden conspicuous rush across the foyer appear to catch his notice. Upstairs, the door to Auntie's bedroom was still open. A night light on a marble table cast an even glow across the smooth silvery field of Auntie's bed. This time, though, the door within that led to Auntie's sitting room was ajar. Gaping at the open inner door, Lulu swayed nervously back and forth.

After a pause she stepped forward into Auntie's bedroom. The meager light spilling from the doorway that led to Auntie's private sanctuary incited dread in Lulu. At the same time, she imagined Mr. Rafferty advancing quietly through the downstairs hall, closing the distance between them. Lulu had a powerful urge to rush headlong into Auntie's sitting room and suffer whatever fate awaited her. Instead, slowly, dreamily, Lulu stepped forward into the open doorway.

The sitting room was dim. Auntie was there, as were Douglas and Chloris, on the opposite side of the room from Lulu. All three were sitting on the satin love seat, with Auntie in the middle, the others disposed on either side of her. In the feeble light—the source of which Lulu never detected, for it seemed either to emanate from, or to be drawn to, Auntie's glowing temples—the sitting-room sanctuary was suffused with an unearthly stillness. Only as Lulu's eyes adjusted to the three shadowy figures sitting opposite her did the spectacle make sense. Dropping back a step, she gaped at the three of them in terror.

Auntie's bare shoulders gleamed softly. She was clutching Douglas and Chloris to herself. She was holding their heads with either hand. The golden crowns of their heads shone faintly above her breasts. Above it all loomed Auntie's magnificent head; she was expressionless as stone. Lulu heard herself gasp for breath, and an instant later came the sudden piercing echo of her own scream, a cry of such intensity that she could hear it coming back to her from the rooms below as she fled into the hall. The staircase, foyer, and front door were but barely noted points along the course of her headlong flight from the house.

Lulu shot into the darkness, with the front door of the house thrown wide behind her. She was running with abandon. The fields and road were black; overhead, the sky was alive with wind.

She started in one direction, toward the mountain, then reversed and came back the other way. Her mind was in pieces. She ran in the deep grass underneath the row of quinces toward the house, then turned suddenly, and darted out across the driveway into the night-lit fields. In less than a minute, she was gone. She had entered the forest.

It was naturally assumed that Lulu would have fled the opposite way, along the road—that is, eastward, in the direction of the mountain. Not that any extensive search was conducted, for it was supposed that the vanished young woman, whatever direction she took, had satisfied her desire to put behind her an unhappy situation.

Mrs. Gansevoort returned from the country that same week, to her house in Ireland Parish, on Sycamore Street, and her friend, Mr. Rafferty, returned to his room downtown. Nevertheless, the story got out that the young woman, Lulu, had absconded mysteriously three or four days back from the Gansevoort summer house in Peru Mountain. On Saturday, a local detective came to Julia Gansevoort's door and made some polite inquiries, from which, among other things, he deduced that the figure in question was a rather "strange-ish" girl. Sadly enough, Lulu's own mother confirmed that opinion. Her daughter was a "loner," she said, a girl who lived in dreams, and was excessively religious. The plainclothesman found his way, as well, to the pharmacy nearby on Cabot Street, where he spoke to Lulu's friend, Agnes Rohan, the druggist's daughter. Agnes called Lulu "a frightened little bird" (adding privately that Lulu Peloquin had never had one original thought). Mr. Rafferty was the only person interviewed who admitted to having seen Lulu in the late hours on the night of her departure. He said he saw her hurrying through the dark along the side of the house, under a row of quince trees—he had stepped outdoors in his shirtsleeves to smoke a cigarette and contemplate the night—and only realized the next day that she had gone.

On that same Saturday, though, a second visitor made very much the same rounds as the policeman. He climbed the stairs of Lulu's tenement on South Summer Street, and spoke to her mother, and then later appeared at Mrs. Gansevoort's front door. At the Gansevoort house, however, this second caller, a young man wearing white duck pants and a white sweater and tennis shoes, was not admitted. He spoke on the doorstep to Mrs. Gansevoort's nephew. Few words were exchanged, however, as the nephew gave signs of impatience. The athletic youth at the door was the baseball player whose picture Lulu had concealed among her belongings. He was later observed, that same day, standing under a yellowing elm in the garden of the Wistariahurst Museum, talking to an elegant man seated at an outdoor table drinking a cup of coffee. Janice, an employee of the museum, saw the two of them. She could not remark ever having seen the youth before, although he created a vivid impression. As she went past them, bearing a tray of empty cups, Janice Monaghan overheard a fragment of their exchange.

"You would say," said the young man in white, "that she was not on the mountain still."

"That," Mr. Rafferty replied, in an earnest tone, "would be my guess."

Janice heard no more, but watched with her aunt as the young man came silently past the desk in the great lobby of the museum, and departed by the front doors into the bright glare of the afternoon.

By Monday evening, when a tiny news item appeared on an inside page of the local newspaper, citing the mysterious disappearance, and implying that a search was contemplated, the drama was already concluded. On the previous day, in the late afternoon, the youth in white had already been on the grounds of the Gansevoort summer estate, forty miles away, in Peru Mountain.

The countryside on that Sunday was as silent and empty of human influence as if an entire geologic age had intervened. Because of the hour, the mountain nearby imparted a brooding, monumental presence. For about ten minutes the young man strode to and fro beneath the quince trees, walking with a concentrated air. Then he turned on his heel abruptly, and stepped out across the fields. The trees ahead obscured the western horizon. At the edge of the forest, he stopped, walked lengthwise along the black, primitive wall of cedars, and halted.

Reaching down, he recovered a black suede pump with a rhinestone clip. As though the shoe had been deposited there as part of a game, he started instantly into the woods at that point. Before penetrating the trees a hundred feet, he found a torn strip of black silk, the texture of which, with its fine eyelet working, appeared almost transparent on the palm of his hand. As he resumed walking, he continued to scrutinize the scrap of silk, as though the direction he was taking no longer required his full concentration. He did not pause again—and then only for an instant—until his footsteps brought him out of the trees once more, onto the sun-dappled gravel road a few hundred yards west of the house. Almost instantly, he crossed the road, following an oblique course consistent with the line of his emergence from the cedars behind him, and reentered the cedars, on a similar tangent, on the opposite side. A short distance into the trees on the northern flank, he found nearly half of Lulu's dress.

It was torn into an incredible shape—a four-foot-long strip of black fabric, the ragged configuration of which might have been thought of as a lurid representation of the state of mind of the young woman at that moment, when, while rushing through the trees in the dark, she snagged it on the burnt, dead branch from which it dangled. He found, also, a silver bracelet, and farther along, a porcelain lipstick tube.

The atmosphere under the cedars was cool and sunless. At a clearing in the forest, the young man waded out into knee-deep ferns, the sun igniting the alien whiteness of his clothing and shoes; a moment later, another curtain of evergreens closed behind him.

The subdued roar of a brook echoed among the trees a few yards ahead, its voice as timeless and perpetual as the massive gray boulders strewn up and down the steep banks of the brook, like the heads of decapitated gods. Lulu was lying face-down on the far side. Except for signs of dry blood on her head, she looked like a doll thrown down helter-skelter by someone else in a state of flight. Her arms stretched out straight above her head; the long trailing remnant of her dress fluttered repeatedly in the stream. Close to her head, a vortex of foaming water whispered and gurgled, spinning round and round endlessly.

How it was that the boy in white was led to this precise point in the forest, where he was able to retrieve her, was perhaps no more mysterious than the blind processes that had brought Lulu to it. Perhaps, after all, that was the mystery of him, the one they called Soldier—the boy on the emerald field.

About the Author

Raymond Kennedy is the author of five novels. In 1986, he was awarded a fellowship in fiction by the New York State Foundation of the Arts. Mr. Kennedy served for several years as the Anthropology Editor for the *Encyclopedia Americana,* and currently teaches fiction writing in the English Department at Columbia University. A native of Massachusetts, he has lived in New York City in recent years with his daughter Branwynne.

V I N T A G E
CONTEMPORARIES

"Today's novels for the readers of today." — VANITY FAIR

"Real literature—originals and important reprints—in attractive, inexpensive paperbacks." — THE LOS ANGELES TIMES

"Prestigious." — THE CHICAGO TRIBUNE

"A very fine collection." — THE CHRISTIAN SCIENCE MONITOR

"Adventurous and worthy." — SATURDAY REVIEW

"If you want to know what's on the cutting edge of American fiction, then these are the books you should be reading."
                              — UNITED PRESS INTERNATIONAL

On sale at bookstores everywhere, but if otherwise unavailable, may be ordered from us. You can use this coupon, or phone (800) 638-6460.

Please send me the Vintage Contemporaries books I have checked on the reverse. I am enclosing $ _____ (add $1.00 per copy to cover postage and handling). Send check or money order—no cash or CODs, please. Prices are subject to change without notice.

NAME _____

ADDRESS _____

CITY _____ STATE _____ ZIP _____

Send coupons to:
RANDOM HOUSE, INC., 400 Hahn Road, Westminster, MD 21157
ATTN: ORDER ENTRY DEPARTMENT
Allow at least 4 weeks for delivery.

005   38

VINTAGE
CONTEMPORARIES